ALSO BY ANNE BISHOP

THE
QUEEN'S
BARGAIN

A BLACK JEWELS NOVEL

Anne Bishop

ACE
New York

ACE
Published by Berkley
An imprint of Penguin Random House LLC
penguinrandomhouse.com

ISBN: 9781984806635

Ace hardcover edition / March 2020
Ace mass-market edition / January 2021

Printed in the United States of America

Cover image of woman © Ashvini Sihra / EyeEm / Getty Images
Cover design by Adam Auerbach
Book design by Alison Cnockaert

For all the readers who asked for another story.
Welcome back to the Realms.

JEWELS

WHITE
YELLOW
TIGER EYE
ROSE
SUMMER-SKY
PURPLE DUSK
OPAL*
GREEN
SAPPHIRE
RED
GRAY
EBON-GRAY
BLACK

*Opal is the dividing line between lighter and darker
Jewels because it can be either.

When making the Offering to the Darkness,
a person can descend a maximum of three ranks
from his/her Birthright Jewel.

Example: Birthright White could descend to Rose.

Note: The "Sc" in the names Scelt and
Sceltie is pronounced "Sh."

BLOOD HIERARCHY / CASTES

—————◈—————

MALES

landen—non-Blood of any race

Blood male—a general term for all males of the Blood; also refers to any Blood male who doesn't wear Jewels

Warlord—a Jeweled male equal in status to a witch

Prince—a Jeweled male equal in status to a Priestess or a Healer

Warlord Prince—a dangerous, extremely aggressive Jeweled male; in status, slightly lower than a Queen

FEMALES

landen—non-Blood of any race

Blood female—a general term for all females of the Blood; mostly refers to any Blood female who doesn't wear Jewels

witch—a Blood female who wears Jewels but isn't of one of the other hierarchical levels; also refers to any Jeweled female

Healer—a witch who heals physical wounds and illnesses; equal in status to a Priestess and a Prince

Priestess—a witch who cares for altars, Sanctuaries, and Dark Altars; witnesses handfasts and marriages; performs offerings; equal in status to a Healer and a Prince

Black Widow—a witch who heals the mind and weaves the tangled webs of dreams and visions; is trained in illusions and poisons

Queen—a witch who rules the Blood; is considered to be the land's heart and the Blood's moral center; as such, she is the focal point of their society

THE
QUEEN'S
BARGAIN

PART ONE

ONE

Facing the freestanding mirror in her bedroom, Jillian used Craft to secure the pendant that held her Purple Dusk Jewel to her green tunic so that it wouldn't swing when she moved or flew. Then she spread her dark, membranous wings to their full length before closing them in a relaxed position.

Was she plain? Was she pretty? Until that brief touch of Tamnar's lips against hers, Jillian hadn't considered the question at all, let alone wondered whether such a thing was important. She was Eyrien, one of the long-lived races, and she was strong. *That* had been important to her for a very long time. Now being strong didn't give her the same satisfaction, and she wasn't sure why.

She turned to the side and studied her shape in the mirror. Her breasts had been developing for the past few years, and she had noticeable breasts now and had to wear undergarments that kept the bounce to a minimum, especially when she was training with Eyrien weapons. But . . . Did this tunic make her look fat? Was it the wrong color green for someone who had brown skin and gold eyes? Nurian had said that shade of green was a good color on her, but her elder sister, who was an excellent Healer, wasn't necessarily the best judge of clothing. There had been too many years before they had come to live in Ebon Rih when any clothing that covered the body and wasn't worn to rags was good, regardless of color or style.

Then again, there weren't that many styles that suited a winged race.

Combing out her long, straight black hair, Jillian swiftly worked the hair into a multistranded braid that began high on the back of her head and ended at the base of her neck, leaving the rest of the hair to flow down her back in a loose tail. After securing the braided hair with a decorative clasp, she studied herself in the mirror again and wondered whether a man would find the hairstyle attractive.

Since there was a man spending time in their home again, maybe she didn't want to look attractive. Not that Lord Rothvar had said or done anything inappropriate, but Prince Falonar had seemed like a good man until he became Nurian's lover. It wasn't long after that the Eyriens who were loyal to Prince Yaslana found out Falonar wasn't a good man at all.

She needed to stop fretting. She didn't have time for it, not if she wanted to do a morning warm-up with her sparring stick before flying over to the Yaslana eyrie and helping Marian with some of the early chores before escorting Yaslana's two elder children to the Eyrien school.

She crept out of her bedroom, listening for any sound that would tell her whether Rothvar was still in her sister's bedroom. Once she passed Nurian's door, she fled to the kitchen and started the coffee for Nurian and the . . . guest.

There were a vegetable casserole and some muffins left over from yesterday. Enough for two people.

A glance at the kitchen clock told her there wasn't time to cook anything else.

Looks like I'm skipping breakfast.

"You're up early."

Jillian gasped and almost dropped the casserole dish. Seeing only Nurian standing in the kitchen archway, she offered a wobbly smile. "The day starts early in Prince Yaslana's household." She put the casserole in the oven.

"There's plenty here, and there are some muffins. Coffee will be ready in a few minutes. Yours always tastes like rubbish, so I—"

"Rothvar didn't stay over." Nurian studied her. "He's not here, Jillian."

But his psychic scent and physical scent still lingered in their home, reminding her that he'd been spending enough time there for wood and stone to absorb his presence.

Jillian rubbed sweaty hands on her tunic. "I have to get going. Don't forget to take the casserole out of the oven once it's warmed up."

"Jillian . . ."

"I have to go."

Sadness filled Nurian's eyes, but she sounded brisk when she said, "I made more tonic for Marian. Can you take it to her?"

"Of course." Jillian walked over to the archway, then hesitated. "She had the baby months ago. Shouldn't she be well by now?"

"It was a hard birthing." Nurian sounded like each word could start a fatal avalanche. "Sometimes it takes an Eyrien woman a long time to recover."

And some never recover. That was the thing no one said and everyone who lived in and around the valley feared— that Marian Yaslana, wife of the Warlord Prince of Ebon Rih, would be one of those women robbed of vitality by childbirth and would fade away, despite Nurian's best efforts to heal her.

"Do you know what's wrong?" Jillian asked.

Nurian shook her head. "I'll get the tonic." She went to her workroom and returned a minute later, handing the shielded bottle to Jillian.

Using Craft, Jillian vanished the bottle, then hugged her sister. "It will be all right."

"Will it?"

Were they talking about Marian's health or Rothvar's presence in Nurian's—and Jillian's—life?

"Don't forget to take the casserole out of the oven," Jillian said again as she stepped back. Nurian's focus and attention when it came to the precise timing required to make tonics and healing brews didn't extend to the kitchen.

Stepping out of their eyrie, Jillian studied the Eyrien men who were already flying over the valley. Was one of them Rothvar? Was he watching her? Or was he at the communal eyrie, sparring to keep his fighting skills sharp?

She would do a brief warm-up when she reached Yaslana's home. There should be enough time for that.

She spread her wings and launched herself skyward. As she flew, she wished she'd put on the belted cape that Eyriens used in colder weather. Autumn mornings were crisp, but today the air held a sharp reminder that winter would be there soon.

Landing on the flagstone courtyard in front of the eyrie, she walked up to the front door and put her left hand on a stone inset next to the door. Eyries were built from the stone of the mountains or were built into the mountains themselves, but this stone didn't come from this particular mountain and had a specific purpose. The Yaslana eyrie was shielded inside and out—inside so that frisky children couldn't scamper off before their parents were awake, and outside so that no one who wasn't keyed into the spells placed in that stone could enter when the doors were locked and the shields were up.

There had been enemies. They were gone now, destroyed years ago, but Lucivar Yaslana didn't take chances with his family's safety.

Jillian set her hand on the stone and waited until she felt the shields part around the door. She opened the door and slipped inside. Moments later, the shields were back in place.

Using Craft, she called in the bottle of tonic and left it on the kitchen counter where Marian would see it. Since no one seemed to be up yet—was she really that early?—she left the kitchen, crossed the large front room that held nothing but a coat-tree near the door, and opened the glass doors that led to the yard where the children played. Fortunately the shields that protected the eyrie extended around the yard, so she wouldn't be stuck out there if she finished her warm-up before the household woke up.

She called in her sparring stick. It wasn't as thick or as long as the sticks used by the adult males, which meant the wood might snap in a real fight against one of them, but it fit her hands.

She went through the slow, precise movements, warming up muscles in her arms, shoulders, back, and legs. Her body had been going through changes for years, but lately she felt like a stranger in her own skin, and she didn't know—

A finger ran down her back between her wings, right where Prince Falonar had . . .

She spun around and struck out, her stick hitting another already in position to counter her attack.

Mother Night! Had she been so lost in thought that she hadn't heard him approach?

Lucivar Yaslana gave her a long look before taking a step back. "Let's talk."

She didn't want to talk, didn't want to be told she was being selfish and unreasonable because she wasn't comfortable with Rothvar staying overnight. She didn't want to be told she was spoiling Nurian's first relationship in decades because of the memory of a man who had been gone for just as many decades. She knew that already, but she couldn't explain why it wasn't easy to accept Lord Rothvar into their lives.

Daemonar and Titian, Yaslana's two elder children, rushed out of the eyrie, their own sparring sticks in hand, and headed toward them.

"You two stay near the house and go through the sparring warm-up." Yaslana's mild tone didn't make the words any less a command.

"But, Papa . . . ," Daemonar began. The expression on

his father's face silenced him. "Yes, sir." He looked at Jillian with concern and asked on a psychic communication thread, *Are you in trouble?*

No. At least, she didn't think so.

"Let's talk," Yaslana said again, tipping his head to indicate the far end of the yard, where a mountain stream filled a small pool before spilling over and continuing its journey to the valley below.

She led the way with him a step behind her. She stiffened and jerked to a stop when his hand closed over her tail of hair, turning it into a tether.

He leaned over her shoulder. She tightened her wings.

"Listen to me, witchling," he said softly. "Are you listening?"

"Yes, sir."

"If Rothvar ever raises a hand to you in anger, if he ever does anything that isn't appropriate, I will skin him alive."

His words thrilled her—and scared her. Lucivar Yaslana didn't say anything he didn't mean.

"But he's your second-in-command," she protested. Rothvar, wearing the Green Jewel, was the most powerful Eyrien Warlord and the second most powerful Eyrien male living in Ebon Rih.

"Doesn't matter."

Jillian's heart pounded. Prince Falonar had been Yaslana's second-in-command before he tried to take control of the valley and become the ruling Warlord Prince. When his followers were defeated, he was sent away to a Rihlander Queen's court and disappeared shortly after that.

"I'm thinking that Rothvar spending time with your sister, spending time in your home, has stirred up memories that are causing you some trouble," Yaslana said.

"Lord Rothvar hasn't done anything wrong," she whispered. "He's not Prince Falonar."

"Your head knows the difference, but your skin and your back remember the strapping Falonar gave you, and your heart remembers the pain. It's going to take time for you to trust Rothvar because things turned sour for you after Falonar became Nurian's lover and thought he had the right to control you. There's nothing wrong with you feeling cautious. I just want you to know that if Rothvar hurts you in any way, he'll deal with me." Yaslana released her hair and stepped back. "Of course, if you think that gives you leave to act like a bitchy brat in order to make him miserable, you should also know I won't hesitate to put you over my knee and whack some sense into your ass."

He meant it. All of it.

"I don't think that's where sense is stored," she said, trying for a lighter tone.

"You'd be surprised how much sense can be acquired when it hurts to sit down," he replied dryly. Then he gave her a lazy, arrogant smile that had her nerves humming. "Let's review the rules."

She would have rolled her eyes if it had been anyone else saying that, but he was the Warlord Prince of Ebon Rih and he wore Ebon-gray Jewels, which made him *the* most powerful male in the Territory of Askavi—and the second most powerful male in the entire Realm of Kaeleer. No one rolled their eyes at *him*.

"I know the rules," she said.

"Then you won't have any trouble repeating them." His smile had an edge now, warning her that he would ignore all his duties and they would stand out there all day if that was what it took for her to answer him.

She sighed. "Look equals tell. Touch equals tell. Permission before action." That last rule made her very uneasy, because she'd broken it—but just a little. And not intentionally. Not really.

If she said anything now, after the fact, Tamnar would get into trouble, and he didn't deserve Yaslana's anger. Not for something that had barely broken the rule.

She eyed him and wondered if he already knew about the barely broken rule.

"Something else you want to tell me?" Yaslana asked.

"No, sir," she said quickly. Too quickly?

He studied her until she wanted to squirm, then said, "If someone tries to hurt you, what are you going to do?"

He'd asked that same question decades ago when he found out Falonar had strapped her, so she gave him the same answer. "Kick him in the balls."

Yaslana huffed out a breath that might have been a laugh. "Before that."

She pretended to ponder the question. "Put a defensive shield around myself and holler for you?"

"That is correct. And then, witchling, you fight with everything in you until I can get to you. You understand me?"

"Yes, sir."

Yaslana looked toward the eyrie. "Did you get any breakfast?"

"No, sir."

"Then go eat." He lifted his chin to indicate Daemonar and Titian, who were heading into the eyrie. "You can do some sparring after school."

Jillian turned toward the eyrie, then hesitated. "I brought another bottle of tonic for Lady Marian."

"It's appreciated."

She took a step away from him and felt something wash over her—a heat that made her nipples tighten, that made her feel warm and tingly between her legs. That heat was almost a scent in the air. Sheer intoxication, like catnip for human females.

She knew what it was—not because she'd felt it before, but because Nurian had told her about it when she had wondered why some women acted . . . odd . . . when Yaslana and Marian attended a play or some other public event.

"Jillian?" Yaslana sounded puzzled and—maybe?—wary.

She gave him a distracted smile and bolted for the eyrie.

Sexual heat. It was part of a Warlord Prince's nature, something he could keep leashed to some degree, but it was always there, a lure designed to attract females, because Warlord Princes were dangerous, volatile, extremely aggressive men who were born to stand on killing fields. A Queen's living weapon. A man like that was feared, but a man like that also needed a way to keep a woman with him in order to sire children and continue his bloodline.

Nurian said Warlord Princes usually kept the heat leashed as much as possible when they weren't with their chosen lovers, but it still pumped out of them, washing over everyone, producing a kind of scent that made women feel womanly—and desirable. But that leashed heat was no more an invitation to sex or an indication of carnal interest than the scent of moon's blood was an invitation to attack a woman during the days when she was vulnerable and couldn't use the reservoir of power in her Jewels to defend herself.

When she reached the eyrie, Jillian looked back. Yaslana was going through the movements of the warm-up—and he looked wonderful. He looked like a *man*.

She blinked, felt her face burn with shame for thinking such a thing. He was *Yaslana*, the Warlord Prince of Ebon Rih. She worked for his wife. And until today, she had *never* thought such a thing about him.

Until today, when she felt the sexual heat for the first time. *He* wasn't any different than he'd been yesterday. *She* was the one who had changed. Warlord Princes didn't pick up the scent of moon's blood until they reached a level of maturity during adolescence, so it stood to reason that a level of physical maturity was also required before a girl—a *woman*—reacted to a Warlord Prince's sexual heat.

Woman.

Jillian smiled.

Swelling breasts and moon's blood were signposts that a girl was becoming a woman. She had a feeling that today she had just reached another significant signpost.

Then she was in the kitchen and in the middle of the noise and chaos that made up mornings in the Yaslana household and didn't give the man another thought for the rest of the day.

Lucivar went through the warm-up a second time, increasing the speed of the moves. Normally he'd be in the kitchen helping Marian feed the children and get them ready for school. But he'd seen something in Jillian a few minutes ago that kept him outside.

The girl had been running tame in his house ever since Nurian signed a service contract with him decades ago and came to Ebon Rih, claiming her younger sister, Jillian, as her dependent. He'd been busy getting the Eyrien adults settled and couldn't say exactly when Jillian became Marian's "helper" in looking after Daemonar. His boy had been a toddler then—an ever-moving bundle of arrogance and energy—and having Jillian around to keep hold of the little beast had allowed Marian to get some of her own work done.

Didn't take long for him to stop seeing the girl as someone else's dependent. Sure, she'd gone home most nights, but she was in his home so much she became his to protect—an honorary daughter in the same way his father had been an honorary uncle to most of the Territory Queens in Kaeleer.

Now he wondered if that was going to be a problem.

The potency of sexual heat was linked to the power that flowed in the veins and made the Blood who and what they were. The darker a Warlord Prince's power, the more potent the heat. It made a kind of sense for preserving the darker bloodlines and keeping a woman in thrall long enough to make a baby and carry through all the years after until paternal rights to that child were formally granted. But it could be damned inconvenient the rest of the time, since a man let the heat slip the leash in order to seduce a lover and give her a very good ride, but even leashed, it could create too much unwanted interest from other women.

Unlike his brother, Daemon, who could seduce anyone and everyone just by walking through a room, he hadn't had to deal with much unwanted interest for one very simple reason: he had a reputation for being violent and vicious in bed—a reputation he had earned when he'd been a slave in so many courts in Terreille. The stories of how he'd savaged the Queens who had tried to use him had found their way to Kaeleer with the people who had emigrated to the Shadow Realm. Because of that, he was feared more than other Warlord Princes. Women might enjoy the feel of the heat as he passed by, but they were also grateful that he had a wife and wouldn't look in their direction.

Jillian wasn't afraid of him, and that could be a problem. He hoped she would be able to accept the sexual heat as something that had always been there but was only now being noticed, and shrug it off the same way all the Queens who had been part of Jaenelle Angelline's coven had shrugged it off. If the girl couldn't ignore it, he'd have to bar her from his home to keep her from making a lethal mistake.

He watched Jillian, Daemonar, and Titian fly toward the eyrie where Lord Endar taught the Eyrien children.

Vanishing the sparring stick, Lucivar crossed the yard and went inside.

Marian—his wife, friend, and partner, and the love of his life—smiled when he walked into the kitchen. She poured a cup of coffee and handed it to him. "You missed breakfast. And you missed the chaos."

"Did you notice how much quieter it was last week when Daemonar was visiting his uncle?" Lucivar asked.

"Oh, I think everyone in Riada noticed how much quieter it was," Marian replied. "But he is your son, after all."

"You had something to do with him being here," Lucivar protested.

"Not that part of him. That all came from you."

Hard to argue the truth of it. His son was growing into

a formidable—meaning a pain-in-the-ass—Warlord Prince whose Birthright Green Jewel almost matched Rothvar's Green Jewel of rank in strength.

"I saved you a plate of food," Marian said. Then she frowned. "Lucivar?"

She insisted she was fine, but she hadn't regained her strength or energy since baby Andulvar's birth. He knew she wasn't happy about his lack of enthusiasm for sex and had started wondering if he no longer found her attractive, which was so far from the truth it was laughable. He wanted her desperately some nights, but even when he was gentle and careful, their lovemaking seemed to devour her strength.

He'd insisted that she go to the Healer who served the Queen of Amdarh, Dhemlan's capital city. Lady Zhara's Healer couldn't find a cause for the slower-than-normal recovery from the birthing. Like Nurian, Zhara's Healer tacitly agreed that something wasn't right, but neither of them could find anything wrong. And Marian insisted she was getting better, so there wasn't much he could do—and the only person whose opinion could have made a difference had died years ago.

Still, with Marian feeling sensitive about their restrained lovemaking, he needed to tell her about Jillian.

"Jillian felt the sexual heat when we were outside talking." The words felt like splinters of glass ripping up his throat.

Marian set the plate of food on the table and gave him a puzzled look. "She's growing up, Lucivar. It was going to happen sooner or later." She paused. "Is that why she was here so early?"

Lucivar shook his head. "That was because of Rothvar. His being in Nurian's bed has stirred up memories of Falonar."

"*Him.*"

His darling hearth witch didn't usually put that much venom in her voice. Then again, Falonar had arranged for

him to stand on a killing field alone against all the Warlords who had wanted Falonar to rule Ebon Rih. He hadn't
thought about what he'd looked like after that fight, hadn't
considered how a wife would react to seeing her husband
drenched in his enemies' blood.

Just as well the man had disappeared after being sent to
Lady Perzha's court.

"Yeah, well, Falonar didn't hurt Jillian until he became
Nurian's lover, so it's going to take her some time to accept
that Rothvar filling that spot isn't going to mean he'll
change and try to control either of them," he said.

"Rothvar will just have to be patient with her—and so
will you."

The words were a small slap, but still a slap that shouldn't
go unanswered.

Lucivar gave his wife a lazy, arrogant smile. "I'll remind you of the need for patience the first time Daemonar
catches the scent of moon's blood and gets bossy."

She looked like a bunny that had run straight into a
pack of wolves.

"Well, you'll just have to explain things."

She sounded so flustered—and appalled at the thought
of *two* Warlord Princes fussing over her—he set the coffee
on the table in order to take her in his arms and give her a
long, sweet kiss.

"Don't worry," he said, grinning at her. "I promise to
explain *everything.*"

TWO

Sitting on the side of his daughter's bed, Daemon Sadi, the Black-Jeweled Warlord Prince of Dhemlan, turned the last page of the book and said, "And they all lived happily ever after."

Because they had steak, Khary said.

Daemon eyed the furry companions who had joined his girl for storytime—the young Sceltie Warlord who had spoken and the younger Sceltie witch, who just wagged her tail at him. "Yes," he replied dryly. "They all lived happily ever after because they had steak."

"And cake."

Now he eyed his daughter, who entertained his mind and delighted his heart. Jaenelle Saetien had the black hair and gold eyes typical of the long-lived races, but her skin was closer to her mother's light sun-kissed brown than his own golden brown tone, and she had the delicately pointed ears of the Dea al Mon race. In fact, except for the eyes—Surreal's eyes were gold-green and slightly oversized—Jaenelle Saetien strongly resembled Surreal at the same age.

"And cake," he agreed. Recognizing her intent, he vanished the book and pounced first, tickling Jaenelle Saetien, causing her to squeal in delight as the Scelties barked and bounced on the bed. "They had cake with buttercream icing that was decorated with mounds of pink and blue flowers." Which was his girl's favorite kind of cake.

He eased up to let her catch her breath—and she jumped him, as he'd known she would. Being an obliging father, he fell back so that she could have her turn to tickle. Of course, him being prone also seemed to be an invitation for the Scelties to pile on. Thankfully it was Morghann, the smaller of the two dogs, who planted a paw on his balls before he thought to put a shield over that part of himself.

"I give up," he said, laughing. "I give up."

Jaenelle Saetien sprawled over him so they were almost nose to nose. Morghann had a piece of his jacket sleeve between her teeth as her small claim to him, and Khary, who had recently had his Birthright Ceremony and now wore a dark Opal Jewel, stood behind his head staring down at him.

"Papa?"

"Witch-child?"

"Wouldn't you like to have cake?"

Ah. So that was where they were going with this. "Decorated cakes are made for special occasions."

"But I have a special Jewel now."

And she did. A Jewel that was like no other. A Jewel that had been created especially for her by the Queen who had been, and always would be, the love of his life. But there were responsibilities that came with guiding a young witch who wore a Jewel like Twilight's Dawn—responsibilities not just as a father but as a Warlord Prince. Lines could be gently drawn, but they had to be drawn.

"You do have a special Jewel, and we celebrated when you received it. As I recall, there was a very big cake with mounds of buttercream frosting that Mrs. Beale made for that celebration." Just thinking about that frosting made his teeth hurt.

Of course, that cake might have been partially responsible for him and Lucivar having to deal with overexcited children during that party. Not that he would ever say that to the large Yellow-Jeweled witch who was his cook here at the Hall.

"But that was forever ago," Jaenelle Saetien protested.

A few weeks. But even a child from the long-lived races measured time differently from the adults.

"I take it you asked Mrs. Beale to make a cake."

"She said she'd already made out the menus for the next fortnight and cake wasn't one of the sweets."

"Well, then . . ."

"But she'd make a cake if *you* told her to make one."

Every time Mrs. Beale felt she had something to discuss with him, she brought her well-sharpened meat cleaver to the meeting—and even though she wore Yellow and he wore Black, he would admit to himself, if to no one else, that he felt a tiny kernel of fear when he had to deal with her directly. He much preferred going through Beale, the Red-Jeweled Warlord who was the Hall's butler as well as Mrs. Beale's husband, whenever he requested a particular dish or special treat.

"She might," he agreed, "but as I just pointed out and as you already knew, those cakes are made for special occasions."

"But, Papa . . ."

"No." Daemon kissed her cheek to take the sting out of the word, then sat up, bringing her up with him—and dragging Morghann as well, since the Sceltie didn't let go of his sleeve.

After convincing the dogs to settle into their baskets and tucking in his girl for the night, Daemon walked down the corridor to his bedroom to get undressed before he tapped on the door that connected his suite of rooms to Surreal's. Whether they had sex, made love, or just cuddled a bit before going to sleep, he spent most of his nights in her bed. Her bed, her rules—and he the lover who had the privilege of pleasing her.

As a Warlord Prince, he needed his own room, his own bed for sleep, for rest, for solitude. He slept in this room when Surreal stayed at their town house in Amdarh or visited one of the family's other estates as his second-in-command. He didn't feel the need or the desire to stay away from her when she was in residence. Besides, withholding his body from her would have been a breach of the promise he'd made to be her husband in every way.

Her pregnancy had been unplanned and unexpected—the result of them comforting each other on the night his father died. Their marriage had had more to do with him not allowing her to leave with his child than with heated passion. But they had loved each other in their own way for decades, as friends and family, and Surreal had understood—and accepted—that he never could love anyone else with the depth and passion that he had loved, and still loved, Jaenelle Angelline, the living myth, dreams made flesh. Witch. His Queen.

Surreal had known Jaenelle, had been friend and sister to the woman and a sword and shield to the Queen. She had been there throughout his first marriage, taking the position of second-in-command to give him as much time as possible with Jaenelle since Witch's life span had been measured in decades, not centuries. And she'd been there during the year of mourning and the years after.

But even after he and Surreal had married, there had been a distance between them, a wariness. They had been friends, lovers, partners, parents. But until the Birthright Ceremony, until she had formally acknowledged paternity and given him irrevocable rights to his daughter, there had been that distance, that wariness. Now . . .

The door opened. Surreal walked into the room. *His* room.

"Did you get them settled for the night?" she asked.

As he turned to face her, something inside him relaxed, swelled. Bloomed into a heady, dark desire.

Mine. He looked at her, standing there in *his* room, wearing a long green nightgown shot with gold threads—a gown that was every kind of invitation—and felt that one word fill him until there was nothing else. *Mine.*

"Sadi?"

He wanted to play. Oh, how he wanted to play. And so did she. Why else was she in this room? *His* room, where he wasn't a guest. Where there were no boundaries to what he could or couldn't do.

But there had to be choice. Always a choice.

"Daemon?"

Using Craft, he closed the door behind her. But not all the way. Not yet.

"Do you want to play?" he purred, approaching her slowly. Stalking her.

"Well, you're in a mood."

She couldn't hold on to the sassy smile as his sexual heat, freed of all restraint, wrapped around her, as he leaned toward her, his mouth so close to the corner of hers she probably believed he was touching her. But he wasn't touching, wouldn't touch until she made her choice.

"Do you want to stay here tonight and play? Or do you want to go to your own room and sleep alone?"

If she didn't stay with him here tonight, he couldn't be with her, couldn't be the considerate guest in her bed. Not tonight. Not when he wasn't holding anything back. Not when he felt—truly felt—that the woman, like the child, was his, and with the woman he wasn't interested in lovemaking or even sex. Not tonight. Tonight was about possession, about making her body sing in a way that told her there were no barriers between them anymore, that he would finally give her everything he was.

But only if she made that choice.

"Do you want to play?" he purred again.

Nerves. Excitement. Arousal spiced with a little fear of what he intended to do.

Delicious.

"Stay or go?" he whispered.

Her hard nipples strained against the delicate gown. He smelled the wet heat of need between her legs.

"S-stay."

The door closed. The lock clicked. She trembled when his fingertips lightly brushed her skin.

His mouth touched hers in a kiss so delightfully, viciously gentle, he had to lick the tears from her face before doing anything more.

When he finally laid her on his bed, she whimpered with the need for his touch—and he focused everything he was on pleasuring her body before pleasing his own.

Mine.

Surreal's eyes snapped open. Her heart pounded so hard she feared the sound would wake the man sleeping beside her.

She did not want to rouse—or arouse—the man sleeping beside her.

What she wanted right now, more than anything, was to get out of that room.

She rolled on her side, bringing herself closer to the edge of the bed, and waited. No hand suddenly anchoring her hip. No arm reaching out to pull her close again. No head lifting off the pillow to look at her. No deep, sleepy voice asking where she was going.

She eased her feet out from under the covers, then her lower legs to the knees. She rolled a little more and slid out of the bed, crouched beside it, waiting.

Daemon still slept.

Staying crouched because she was sure an upright figure in his bedroom would bring him instantly awake and riding the killing edge, she made her way to the door.

Please. Sweet Darkness, please let this door open. Let whatever locks he put on the door and around the room be released now.

She turned the handle. The door opened, bringing a whiff of fresher air compared with the sex-saturated smell of his room.

She slipped into her bedroom and closed the door. It was tempting to put a Gray lock on the door, tempting to put shields around the room. But a Gray lock wouldn't stop him. It might make him curious or concerned—or enraged—but it wouldn't stop him.

She hurried into her bathroom, put an aural shield around the room to cover the sound of water, then took a long hot shower. She shook as she washed her hair, as she thoroughly washed her body, as she stood and let the hot water ease tight, sore muscles.

A Warlord Prince's bedroom is his private place, and he tends to be more possessive when he's there.

Jaenelle Angelline's words, spoken decades ago as both instruction and warning.

Surreal knew about possession. The first night she'd had sex with him, the night they made Jaenelle Saetien, they had ended up in his room, in his bed, and he'd been . . . more than Daemon but not quite the Sadist. He'd been riding a side of his nature that had been somewhere between the two—and the way he'd ridden her that night had been breathlessly exciting.

The sex since that night was staggering and wonderful and better than anything else she'd experienced, but it didn't always have the edge that made it breathlessly exciting.

But last night . . .

What had she done to provoke him into doing what he'd done last night? Into being what he'd been last night? She'd recognized the glazed look in his gold eyes. She knew who had controlled her body and played with her until she was drowning in terrible pleasure that made a woman deliciously satisfied one moment and craving the next touch, the next permitted climax with a sharp, desperate need.

She had been in bed with the Sadist—and it terrified her. It terrified *her*, who had been the highest-paid whore in Terreille's Red Moon houses as well as one of the best assassins in that Realm. She hadn't been a whore for decades, since she emigrated to Kaeleer, but she still kept all her knives sharp—and she had, on occasion and with great discretion, used them.

All her skills counted for nothing against a Black-Jeweled Warlord Prince. All those skills counted for nothing against the Sadist.

They'd been getting along so well since the Birthright Ceremony. Something in Daemon had relaxed, a common response when a man was granted legal rights to his child. She suspected that relaxation also had its roots in Daemon's brief meeting with some aspect of Witch, who had gifted their daughter with an extraordinary Jewel.

A few days after the Ceremony, he'd said "I love you" for the first time, words that warmed her, that assured her that he wanted to stay married to her.

Now . . .

She shut off the water, wrapped her hair in one large towel, and dried off with another.

She couldn't take Jaenelle Saetien away from school and the daily lessons in Craft and Protocol the girl had begun with Daemon, but *she* could leave for a few days, could use the excuse of checking on the family's other estates as a reason to be away. Nothing unusual about that. Nothing that would raise suspicions or have Daemon asking questions.

Daemon.

She gripped the sink while she remembered the feel of his hands, the feel of his mouth, the feel of his cock filling her, moving inside her. . . .

She climaxed. It wasn't enough. That greedy, desperate need was back.

Not Daemon. The Sadist had done this to her

She needed to get away in order to figure out why.

Half-awake, Daemon reached across the bed. When his hand found cold sheets instead of a warm body, he rolled onto his back and rubbed his hands over his face.

Mother Night.

He hadn't had sex like that, hadn't *offered* to give sex like that, since . . . Well, he hadn't had sex like that since the last time Jaenelle Angelline had accepted his invitation to play. He hadn't thought that anyone else, even Surreal, would agree to play those games of possession with him, knowing she was safe. He hadn't thought he would love anyone else deeply enough to want to play those games again.

The first time he had seen Witch in his bedroom and reacted to her in this way, his father had explained some things about the nature of Warlord Princes that he hadn't known.

"This is emotional—and it's darker, more dangerous when it happens. It's the thrill of being feared while you seduce your lover to the point where she doesn't want to refuse. And at the same time it's the comfort of being able to reveal that side of your nature to a lover and know you're still trusted. . . . It's a potential for violence that is transformed into a kind of ruthless gentleness. . . . It's part of your nature. It's part of your caste. It's in every one of us. . . . You've twisted a part of yourself into a powerful weapon, honed it to the point people have given it a different name."

What had played in his bedroom last night was the Sadist in his mildest form. The Sadist as lover. That didn't come close to what he was when he let that dark, lethal aspect of himself slip the leash. But all that particular knowledge and skill, wrapped in the velvet of love, could give a woman piquant pleasure in ways nothing else could.

He shouldn't have been surprised that Surreal would accept his invitation. After she made her choice, because playing this game with him had to be her choice, he'd shown her what he was without the barriers he'd kept between them—barriers he'd held in place to protect her, thinking they were necessary. She'd shown him last night that he'd been wrong about that.

A brief psychic probe located the Gray, so he slipped out of bed, put on a robe, and opened the window to let the room air out a bit before his valet or anyone else came in.

Belting the robe, he walked into Surreal's bedroom, then stopped, shocked, when her psychic scent hit him.

Surreal SaDiablo, Gray-Jeweled witch and assassin, his wife for the past fifteen years, was afraid of him. Truly afraid of him. Because of last night.

But . . . She'd made the choice. She'd accepted his invitation to play. And if she'd been uncomfortable at any time, she could have stopped the play with one word. Just one word.

"Surreal."

She gave him a brittle smile. "It's time to check the other estates. I wanted to get an early start and didn't want to wake you."

He could read her body, knew her heart was pounding, her breathing too shallow.

Last night, he'd felt that dark possession, had known the woman was his and, equally important, that he was hers. And he'd shown her who he was—a truth he'd shown to one other woman.

But unlike Jaenelle Angelline, who had accepted everything he was, Surreal had seen the truth and now feared him. Oh, she had been afraid of him at other times, and had reason to be. But not here. Not in their home. Not in her bed.

Except they hadn't been in her bed. They had been in his, and for a Warlord Prince, that made a difference. Oh, yes, it made a difference.

He kept his voice gentle, made no move toward her. "Will you have breakfast with me before you go?"

She hesitated a moment too long. "Sure, sugar. Just give me a few minutes to finish packing and I'll meet you downstairs."

Daemon retreated to his room and closed the door. He took a quick but thorough shower, recognizing that any scent of sex would trouble her right now.

Maybe going away would help her, give her time to realize it had been a game, that he would have stopped the instant she asked him to stop. But she hadn't asked. He *knew* she hadn't asked. Just as he knew that the Sadist as lover had known exactly where her line was between sharp pleasure and real pain and hadn't, even for a heartbeat, crossed that line.

Even so, he'd scared her instead of pleasing her. Her going away for a few days might be a good thing. If her fear didn't dissipate, it would become a wall between them.

As he dressed, Daemon worked to restore the leashes on his temper, on his power, on the Sadist, and on the sexual heat. But something inside him had swelled last night, had bloomed, and when he tried to snug the leash on the sexual heat, it felt like a shirt that should have fit but was a little too tight.

Today was not the day to ease up on control of the heat, so he ruthlessly snugged the leash to where it had been the day before, ignoring the nip of pain that came from choking back a part of himself too much.

Having leashed every part of himself as tightly as possible, Daemon went downstairs to do what he could to reassure his wife before she fled from their home.

THREE

Lord Dillon found a dimly lit nook behind a curtain near the main ballroom. He opened the window a crack to breathe in some cool fresh air and give himself a quiet moment before throwing himself back into the bright and sometimes brittle sounds of instruments and voices, the flash of jewels and Jewels and women's gowns. A typical aristo party in a Rihland city. He'd never been outside the Territory of Askavi—not yet, anyway—but he imagined that aristo parties were pretty much the same in every Blood city in the Realm of Kaeleer.

Maybe he should find out. There was no reason for him to stay in Askavi and plenty of reasons to go.

If you loved me . . .

He'd been nineteen years old when he made the Offering to the Darkness and came away with the Opal as his Jewel of rank. He'd been in his second year of training to be an escort who could serve in a Queen's court, and had one more year to go. Many young men received their education in District courts while they served in the Third or Fourth Circle. Youngsters weren't paid for their service, but they were given room and board, which was regarded as sufficient compensation. His father, however, had wanted him to study at a school, claiming that the escorts who served in a court and were responsible for training the young men sometimes undermined those potential rivals for the Queen's attention. Much better to be trained at a school and have the polish necessary to be offered a place in a Second Circle and rise to an important position that much faster.

He hadn't cared about a fast rise through the levels of a court. He had wanted the adventure of going away. His father had wanted him to go to the school, so he went, and at one of the dances that gave escorts-in-training a chance to gain some experience, he'd met Lady Blyte. She'd been a couple of years older than he, the daughter of a Warlord and a witch whose bloodlines were far more aristo than his family's modest claim to that label, and he'd been flattered that she had singled him out for a second dance.

He hadn't realized at the time that she'd chosen him because she hadn't expected him to give her any trouble when she tired of him and tossed him aside.

He'd been dazzled the first time she kissed him—although, at the time, he'd believed he'd initiated that first kiss. He'd believed he'd initiated quite a few things—until she started wanting things that wouldn't do any harm to her reputation but would sully his. He'd balked the first time she tried to get him into bed, not because he didn't want sex but because he wanted to serve in a Queen's First Circle someday, a position that required the ultimate trust not only of the Queen but of her Steward, Master of the Guard, and Consort.

A man who damaged his honor and respectability by having sex outside the marriage bed would never receive that trust anywhere but in the meanest kind of court, where trust and honor could be bought and sold.

But most young men from good families received some formal sex instruction, since learning to be a good lover was considered essential for any man who wanted to serve as a consort in a Queen's court or wanted to please a wife. The men sat through frank discussions and some demonstrations of how to please a lover. That instruction was usually followed by one or two lessons with a woman who was qualified to train young men in the skills required in and out of bed. Despite the marks he'd been spending on Blyte, he'd saved enough from his quarterly allowance to pay for the formal instruction.

When he told Blyte that he had signed up for sex training at a reputable establishment, she had led him to a shadowed spot on the terrace just outside the ballroom and had said the fatal words for the first time. *If you loved me* . . .

If he loved her, he would forget about the training and use the money to take her to . . .

He couldn't remember what she'd wanted that first time, but it had sounded reasonable, and he *had* loved her, so he'd canceled the instruction and taken her to some expensive event.

Then, if he loved her, he would let *her* instruct him in the art of sex and lovemaking. After all, she'd had her Virgin Night, so taking an inexperienced lover wouldn't be a risk to her power or her Jewels. And she couldn't stand the idea of him being with another woman, even for instruction, and if he loved her, he wouldn't ask her to endure that.

When he still balked about having sex—after all, it wasn't her reputation that would be harmed if anyone found out—she asked him to handfast with her, to be her husband for a year. If he loved her, he would do this for her, to please them both.

If you loved me. If you loved me. If you . . .

She taught him a great deal about sex while she stalled about making the handfast official. After all, they were married in their hearts, weren't they?

And then, finally uneasy enough about the delays and Blyte's desire to keep their arrangement secret—for his sake—he told his family that Blyte had asked him to handfast and he wanted to proceed with the ceremony.

When his father met with Blyte's father to negotiate the

terms of the handfast, Blyte hysterically denied making such a commitment to Lord Dillon. She tearfully confessed she'd been having sex with Dillon, but she was entitled to a lover, while he . . .

Scandal. Accusations and counteraccusations. When his father threatened to take the matter to the Province Queen, who, unlike the District Queen who ruled their city, was not related to Blyte's family, Dillon had received "compensation" for the "misunderstanding"—enough gold and silver marks to buy his silence and end the accusations.

His family didn't quite disown him—that would have negated the claim of Dillon being the wronged party—but his parents made it clear that it was in everyone's best interest for him to settle in another city and start fresh. After all, he was twenty now and old enough to stand on his own, and there were his two younger brothers to think about. If he stayed at home, the smear on his reputation might stain his brothers, and he wouldn't want that, would he?

Of course not. But leaving home to serve in a court or to accept a position in another city to do one's chosen work wasn't the same as being asked to leave because he'd made the mistake of believing a bitch's lies.

Deeply wounded when his father, pressured by his mother, had given him a week to find another place to live well beyond their home ground, Dillon hadn't been able to think, hadn't known where to go. He blindly chose a Rihlander city on the coast of Askavi—a place where his family often took a "cottage" for a month in the summer as a way to show they were affluent even if they were a minor branch of an aristo family tree.

The summer visitors had left weeks ago, but the aristos who lived here were easy enough to find, and it hadn't taken more than a couple of days for him to make the acquaintance of a few young Warlords around his age. They'd been sufficiently impressed by his Opal Jewel to show him around, introduce him to other aristos. He was getting a feel for who was who and thought he might be able to wangle an introduction with the Steward of the District Queen who ruled this city. Thankfully, she wasn't the same Queen as the one who ruled the city where his family lived. If he could get an introduction, maybe he could get a court contract to serve in the Second or Third Circle—a position that would allow him to finish his training as an escort while using the skills he'd already learned.

After a year or two to gain some seasoning and polish, maybe he could head out to one of the other Territories. Someplace like Dharo or even Scelt, which was on the other side of the Realm. Or maybe even someplace more exotic like Tigrelan, a Territory that had two kinds of Blood. Both had claws and striped skin, but one race was human and the other feline. Both were dangerous. But wouldn't it be exciting to—

"There you are."

A bright, brittle female voice.

Dillon turned and smiled—a carefully calculated smile that was warm enough to be courteous but not warm enough to be mistaken for an invitation. He'd learned that much before he left the school.

Either the light wasn't sufficient or Lady Carron didn't choose to acknowledge the meaning of the smile. She walked toward him in a way that should have made his body hum, and wrapped her arms around his neck. He kept his teeth clenched to stop her from giving him an open-mouthed, tongue-tangling kiss.

"What's the matter?" she asked, pouting.

"Nothing's the matter," he replied.

"Then why are you being like that?"

"Like what?" Dillon tried to disengage, but her arms tightened around his neck, pushing her body more firmly against his. "Lady Carron, this isn't appropriate."

"*I* heard that you're not a stickler for what's appropriate. That you enjoy a good ride. Plenty of enthusiasm, if lacking the experience to be really good in bed. That's what *I* heard."

His stomach rolled. "You're mistaken."

Her smile had a knife-edge. "That's not what my good friend Blyte told me. I know *all* about *you*, Lord Dillon." She rubbed against him. "And if you don't want *everyone* to know what Blyte told me about you, you're going to be very nice—and very accommodating—to me."

He went hot, then cold. Wasn't it enough that Blyte's betrayal had smeared his honor and caused a rift between him and his family? If Carron told other aristos whatever Blyte had said about him, he would never be granted an audience with a Queen's Steward, would never be allowed to serve in a court, because a Queen wouldn't consider an escort with a stained reputation, not when there were so many unsullied young men for her to choose from.

He had to do something—fast.

"Not here," he said. "Not tonight."

"Make it soon."

He heard the threat behind the words.

Well, he would do something soon. Immediately, in fact.

Burning with a corrosive, careless anger, Dillon walked out of the nook, one hand mussing his russet hair in what looked like some attempt to tame it, while his other hand ran down the front of his evening jacket. His green eyes scanned the edges of the ballroom until he spotted Lord Foley, the acquaintance who might have become a friend. Folly, as he was sometimes called by those who insisted they had sharp wit, loved gossip and couldn't keep a secret to save his life—something everyone in the aristo social circles knew about the young man. And that made Folly the perfect choice.

Dillon rushed up to Folly and pulled him aside. Not too far, not out of earshot of a sharp-eyed Warlord who looked at Dillon, then looked toward the nook where Carron had disappeared.

"Folly, you won't believe this, but I'm going to handfast with Lady Carron!" Dillon kept his voice low, conspiratorial, but just loud enough for the other Warlord to also hear what he had to say.

"What?" Folly yelped. "You're what?"

"I know! We've barely known each other a week, but she said she *needs* me to be her lover. So we're going to handfast so that I can be her husband for a year. And she'll be my wife. Isn't that wonderful? But you can't say anything yet, because she just asked me and I still need to place the notice into the weekly paper that prints these announcements."

"B-but . . . ," Folly stammered, "I heard Lady Carron's father was negotiating a marriage contract with a Warlord from another aristo family."

Bitterness welled up in Dillon. His eyes glittered. "Maybe she's already tried horizontal dancing with the man and decided he wasn't up to her standards since he was willing to oblige her *before* the contracts were signed."

A flash of anger nearby told him his verbal knife had found its mark, and he wondered whether Lady Carron— had anyone else noticed her name sounded so much like "carrion"?—would have to find another potential husband or if the marriage contract currently on the table would become much more expensive.

"I have to go." Dillon clapped a hand on Folly's shoulder. "I want to write to my parents and send the news by special messenger first thing in the morning." He raised his hand and held up a finger. "Remember. Not a word to anyone yet."

Dillon moved swiftly, hoping the Warlord who might have been the intended husband didn't follow him. He'd had some basic training in how to fight and defend—every escort knew that much—but he didn't want to find himself cornered by a man who had more training and skill.

No one followed him. He slipped away and was heading back to his hotel room before Folly shook off the shock enough to start spreading the news—in confidence.

The summons from Lady Carron's father arrived before breakfast, but the meeting was set for midmorning, a time carefully calculated. The balance of urgency and courtesy made Dillon wonder what Carron's father had said to her last night—or what her intended husband had said to her father. Was a marriage still being negotiated? If her father offered him a contract to handfast with Carron . . .

Did he really want to spend a year of his life with her? No, he didn't. Any girl who could be friends with Blyte would be a torment for him.

Nothing was said at first when Dillon was shown into the man's study, but he knew the Warlord took in Dillon's Opal Jewel, weighing that power against his own Summersky and making some adjustments in how this meeting would go.

"There was a misunderstanding last night," the Warlord said, watching Dillon.

"Sir?" he replied politely.

"My daughter couldn't have offered you a handfast. The man she's chosen to be her husband and I have been negotiating the marriage contracts for the past two weeks, so she wouldn't have offered you a handfast."

"But . . ." Dillon looked painfully confused—an expression he'd practiced for an hour last night in anticipation of this meeting. "She asked me to have sex with her. *Insisted* that I oblige her."

The Warlord's face flushed. "Yes. Well. A young woman who has gone through her Virgin Night has . . . needs, and there is nothing wrong with her enjoying a lover."

"You are, of course, correct, sir," Dillon said. "But a young man doesn't have the same freedom, and a young man who obliges before a formal contract is signed can be . . . misunderstood. That's why, when Lady Carron insisted that I provide her with sex, *I* confirmed that she was asking me to enter into a formal contract, because I *know* she wouldn't want a man to do anything dishonorable. After all, if *she* thought it was all right to use a man that way, then that would be like giving other girls permission to pressure her brother into providing them with sex. Wouldn't it, sir?"

The older man's face turned white and his eyes filled with fear at the mention of *that* potential danger to his son's reputation.

Seeing that, Dillon thought that maybe, in time, he could forgive his father for caring more about his brothers' reputations than about him.

"My daughter deeply regrets giving you the wrong impression."

I'm sure of that, Dillon thought.

"I'm told you've recently come to town."

"Yes, sir."

The Warlord called in a thick envelope and held it out. "You're a handsome young man, Lord Dillon, and temptation is easier to resist when a girl doesn't see it every day. I'm hoping you will oblige me by . . . relocating. This should cover your expenses and be some compensation for the inconvenience my daughter caused."

Dillon took the envelope, opened it, and riffled the notes inside. Three thousand gold marks. *Three thousand.* Even more than the compensation he'd received from Blyte's father.

"Yes, sir." His voice sounded brave, sad, and understanding. Sounded perfect. "I wish Lady Carron all the best." He paused. "If you will excuse me, sir, I think the sooner I'm gone, the easier it will be for all of us."

As soon as he left the man's study, Dillon vanished the envelope. He walked a block before hailing a horse-drawn cab and returning to his hotel. Anticipating the need to get out of this city quickly—there was always the possibility that Carron's intended husband would challenge him to a fight—he vanished his already-packed trunks, settled his bill, and went to the Coaching station to buy a seat on a Coach heading for a town he was sure his family hadn't visited before. With any luck, no one in that town would have heard of Carron—or Blyte.

FOUR

Jillian stood outside the front door, taking another minute to breathe in fresh air before she entered the Yaslana eyrie. No school today, so she had planned her arrival for after breakfast— and hoped Prince Yaslana was already out and about.

After a week of discomfort, she was getting used to the feel of the sexual heat washing over her when she was near him, was getting used to the punch of it when she first walked into his home. It was like an odor permeating the eyrie's stone walls, but more intense when he was physically present. No, the diaper pail was an *odor*. Yaslana's sexual heat was a spicy, potent, alluring scent. Not all that different from his physical and psychic scents, actually, but sexual. Definitely sexual.

But not for her. He couldn't help being who and what he was—and who and what he was had gotten her and Nurian out of the service fair and had made it possible for them to live in Ebon Rih, had made it possible for her to go to school and also receive training in the use of Eyrien weapons. If she thought of the sexual heat as being similar to a cologne some men wore to be more appealing to women, then it wasn't any different from the scent Nurian sometimes wore when she wanted to feel more feminine. Wasn't any different from a bowl of potpourri that Marian used to freshen rooms in the winter.

Jillian grinned. Sex potpourri. Something to be enjoyed for a moment and then forgotten as a background scent.

She walked in, hung her cape on the coat-tree, and went to the kitchen. The table had been cleared, but the dishes weren't done.

Marian? she called on a distaff thread.

I'm changing the baby. Again.

Poopy diapers. How fun.

The children are picking up their rooms, Marian continued, *and Lucivar is in his study.*

I'll do the dishes.

There should be a couple of meat pastries in the cold box for you if the men in the house didn't stuff them into their faces the moment I left the kitchen.

Daemonar might have grabbed for another one before they were put away—the boy had a staggering ability to eat—but Yaslana would have stopped him. And to be fair, if told the pastries had been saved for her, Daemonar probably would have left them alone, because taking care of the women in the family was a man's privilege. Of course, not eating something that had been saved was seen as an insult and resulted in hurt feelings.

Boys could be so peculiar.

After filling one side of the double sink with soap and water, she washed the breakfast dishes and was rinsing the bowl that had been used to make the pastry when she heard the eyrie's front door open. Curious, because the family was accounted for and anyone else should have knocked, she grabbed a dish towel to dry the bowl as she walked to the archway between the kitchen and the big front room—and then forgot what she was doing.

She'd seen him plenty of times before, but, Mother Night, he was beautiful! That almost painfully exquisite face and mouthwatering body. The thick black hair was a little long and artfully disheveled, and the gold eyes . . .

Those eyes looked at her, recognized something in her, and started to glaze as the room began to chill in warning.

"Witchling?" Yaslana's voice, coming from the corridor that led to the rest of the eyrie. "Jillian?" Sharper now. Commanding.

She blinked and turned her head to look at Yaslana as he entered the front room. For a moment, for just long enough, the sexual heat that was becoming familiar created a barrier between her and Prince Sadi's darkly seductive sexual heat.

"I . . . I have to do something." Jillian hurried to the pantry, leaned against a shelf, and hugged the bowl she'd been drying. Prince Daemon Sadi was . . . Mother Night! She was pretty sure the bones in her legs had just melted from his heat curling around her.

Potency and power. The darker the Jewel worn by a Warlord Prince, the more potent the sexual heat. Sweet Darkness, he was potent!

She frowned. It was more than that. If you put aside the sexual heat, because only Warlord Princes had that as part of their nature, Prince Sadi was still exciting because he was sophisticated and educated and . . . other stuff that Eyrien males didn't care about at all but that seemed desperately important all of a sudden.

Even if he wasn't married and unavailable, it would take a strong, sophisticated, educated woman to be his lover. And she was too young to be anyone's lover. But . . .

Wouldn't it be wonderful to be courted by a Warlord who was like Prince Sadi in most ways?

Lucivar led the way back to his study. "What brings you to Ebon Rih so early?"

Daemon's psychic scent felt jagged, and that was a worry. Sadi's mind had been shattered, and repaired, twice, and any sign that he might be slipping toward the border of the Twisted Kingdom was cause for concern.

Daemon was Saetan's true heir and, as Saetan had before him, ruled the Dark Realm as the High Lord of Hell—and he was more dangerous and lethal than their father had ever dreamed of being. Since Saetan had once committed genocide, destroying a place called Zuulaman and everyone from that race, anything that threatened Daemon's control of his temper or power needed to be stopped before it went too far.

"I wanted to check the supplies at the cabin," Daemon replied easily. "I'll spend a day or two there once Surreal is back at the Hall and available to be the parent on duty."

Lucivar settled in one of the visitor's chairs instead of the chair behind his desk. "Where is she now?"

Daemon took the other seat. "Checking up on the other estates."

Lucivar studied his brother. Daemon had been different since Jaenelle Saetien's Birthright Ceremony. Happier. Warmer. Closer to the way he'd been when he'd been married to Jaenelle Angelline. Now Daemon felt jagged—and there were shadows in the depths of those gold eyes.

"You okay?" he asked.

Daemon shrugged, a dismissive move. "Have a bit of a headache."

"What's the witchling done now?"

Daemon laughed. "She has been pestering to have a special-occasion cake made. She made a sufficient nuisance of herself that Mrs. Beale came to my study to discuss it."

"Did Mrs. Beale bring her meat cleaver?"

"Of course she did." Daemon crossed his legs at the knees. "Since I have my own kitchen in the family wing, which is still a sore spot as far as Mrs. Beale is concerned, I offered to help Jaenelle Saetien make the cake if she wanted one so badly."

"Sounds fair." His children often made the biscuits while he prepared another part of the meal on Marian's resting nights. The biscuits were edible most of the time.

"I thought so. Despite my explaining how much of each ingredient had to be added, she was a bit . . . slapdash . . . about it, because measuring took time and stirring took time." Daemon smiled. "Then she announced that there was something she had to do and that she would be back in a few minutes."

"Yeah, I've heard that excuse. It's your own fault—and mine—for having bright, clever children."

"Hmmm. Well, my clever child bounced into the kitchen about thirty minutes later to find her papa reading a book and the cake ingredients looking exactly the way she'd left them. When she started to express her disappointment, I reminded her that I had offered to help her make it, not do the work, and since she didn't want the cake enough to put any effort into making it, there would be no further pestering of Mrs. Beale or me or anyone else, because further pestering would result in a loss of privileges."

"Would the cake have been edible?"

"Not likely. But that, too, would have been a lesson." Daemon seemed to weigh something before finally asking, "Did your two behave differently after receiving their Birthright Jewel? I don't remember them being different, but I didn't see them every day."

"Titian shied away from doing any kind of Craft for about a month because, once she had her Summer-sky Jewel, doing even basic Craft was *important* and maybe she'd been doing it wrong. So Marian and I ended up teaching her the same things she'd been doing, because she wasn't a child anymore; she was a *girl*. She was certain she would be held to a higher standard because she wore a Jewel."

"She wasn't wrong," Daemon said.

"No, she wasn't wrong." Lucivar huffed out a laugh. "The *boy*, on the other hand, acted like he'd finally learned some manners when he received his Green Jewel. That lasted less than a week. In the years since then, he seems committed to being more and more of a pain in my ass. He's on the cusp of leaving boyhood behind and embracing the changes that come from being a youth. I figure the pissing contests will start in earnest when he's fully into adolescence." He considered Daemon's question and his mood. "You worried about the witchling?"

Daemon didn't reply. Then, "I'm starting to appreciate how much thought and care Saetan took when he began training a young witch who wore extraordinary Jewels, how firmly he had to draw the lines. Being special is its own kind of burden."

"Maybe it's like the sexual heat," Lucivar said. "The people around you have to adjust to its presence. And then the people who mean the most to you get used to it and you're accepted for who you are."

"What if you're not accepted for who you are?" Daemon asked softly.

Why did Surreal really leave to check on the estates? Being Eyrien and wearing the Ebon-gray, he didn't think twice about making blunt observations or asking questions no one else would dare ask. But the jagged feel of Daemon's psychic scent warned him not to push for answers. Not yet. Instead, he said, "Well, old son, if you ever need reminding of how much you're accepted, just come here and I'll knock you on your ass a couple of times. That should help you remember."

Daemon laughed, as Lucivar hoped he would.

No sign of Jillian when he walked Daemon to the front door. No sign of Marian or Titian either, but Daemonar rushed out to say good-bye to his uncle and convey the news.

"Baby Andulvar made a big fart and sprayed poop all over before Mother got a clean diaper on him," Daemonar announced.

"Don't sound so excited, boyo," Lucivar said. "You and I are going to help clean up the room."

"But, Papa. It *stinks* in there."

Lucivar gave Daemon a lazy, arrogant smile. "Sure you need to go?"

"I'm certain," Daemon replied dryly.

Lucivar watched his brother's gliding walk across the flagstone courtyard in front of the eyrie. Daemon never looked like he was moving fast, but he covered a lot of ground.

"He could have stayed and helped."

Lucivar looked at his son's sour expression. "Oh, I expect he has enough shit of his own to deal with. Come on—we need to help your mother."

A boy had rushed out to make the poop announcement, but it was a young Warlord Prince who was another step closer to adolescence—and the sharper temper that went with maturing—who helped him clean that room so that Marian could deal with the baby.

FIVE

❖

Dillon hunched in his seat on the Rose-Wind Coach, hoping he wouldn't be recognized by any of the other passengers. Then he sat up and called in a book. Better to look unconcerned. Just a young Warlord traveling for business or pleasure, but certainly not involved in anything sordid.

Not many of the Blood were taking this Coach. Its destination wasn't one of the places where the aristos played and courted and pressured the rest of the people in Askavi—Blood and landen—into believing they were too important to follow the Blood's code of honor.

He should have thought it through, should have realized a city where aristos flocked wouldn't be a safe place for someone like him. Carron must have been furious when she learned her father had paid him to leave town. She must have contacted Blyte and the two of them written their vindictive letters to all the aristo girls of their acquaintance as soon as he'd left town. The bitches here had been looking for him, waiting for him. He'd barely settled into the hotel and walked down the street for a meal before they spotted him and the whispers started.

"That one can't keep his trousers zipped. He'll give anyone a ride."

"Amusing enough, but he's from some insignificant branch of some minor aristo family tree."

"Are the knees of your trousers shiny, Lord Dillon? Must be from all the time you spend on them."

They circled around him like a pack of savage dogs until he had no choice but to pack his trunk and flee to another town. Hopefully the aristos in the next town would be from minor branches of a family, more like his own parents. A place like that wouldn't be of interest to Blyte's or Carron's family. Maybe the aristo bitches would leave him alone for a while.

Dillon turned the pages of the book, but he wasn't reading the words. He spent the journey thinking about what he'd been told by the one Warlord who had dared to talk to him after the girls began their vicious whispers about who he was and what he'd already done in girls' beds.

"You think you're being mistreated—and you are," the Warlord had said. *"But at least you're still alive. My cousin got caught by Lady Blyte's 'if you loved me' spell and couldn't get free of her until he didn't have a copper left to buy her presents. Then she destroyed his reputation and his honor, making him sound like a street whore who went with any woman who snapped her fingers.*

"My cousin barely lasted a month after Blyte and her cronies went after him. The young men who had been his friends avoided him, afraid to have their reputations stained by association. His family didn't know how to counter the verbal attacks. The boy had made a mistake with one girl, the wrong girl, but the girl and her friends kept twisting the story, turning Blyte into the victim of an unscrupulous boy. I offered to report Blyte's conduct to the Province Queen, but before I was granted an audience, my cousin took a bath in his own blood.

"He didn't think it through, though. Didn't drain the power from his Jewels before he opened his veins. He made the transition to demon-dead and most likely is in Hell

now, still trying to make sense of why loving a girl had destroyed his life."

Dillon vanished the book and closed his eyes.

Was that all it had been? A bit of Craft that had made Blyte's suggestions sound reasonable? A spell that had him believing that he loved her? Was that all?

If you loved me.

A spell like that would be expensive—maybe not for the spell itself, but sometimes discretion was the most expensive part of a transaction. It would probably take most of the payoff he'd received from Carron's father. And he couldn't go back to the same witch who had taught the spell to Blyte, even if he found out who she was. The *Lady* was probably a favored customer who paid very well for deceitful spells and unsavory brews. However, if one witch knew how to make that kind of spell, it stood to reason that there were others who were as well trained in the Craft and would know that spell or something similar—and would be willing to teach the spell to a young Warlord for the right price.

If you loved me . . .

He could play that game as well as Blyte. If the aristo girls were going to plague him because of things she had said, he should get some compensation for the association—without having to get into a bed.

SIX

Standing behind a table in her sitting room, Surreal sorted her notes and reports for the SaDiablo estates and slipped the pages into heavy paper folders, along with the correspondence she carried from District and Province Queens who wanted to convey information to the Warlord Prince of Dhemlan but didn't want him to think his personal attention—and presence—was required. She didn't have a study like Sadi or an office like his secretary, Lord Holt. She didn't want one. She wrote reports whenever she deemed it necessary and handed them to one man or the other, letting them figure out what to do with the requests, the complaints, and the paperwork.

The arrangement suited her, and the men, wisely, had never asked her to make any adjustments that might have accommodated them better and certainly would have annoyed her.

She'd spent a couple of days at each estate and a couple more talking to residents of the neighboring villages, the District Queens who ruled those villages, and even a Province Queen who must have heard she was in the area and made an "informal" visit to that village. That had left the District Queen's court in a state of controlled panic as her First Circle organized a formal dinner for the Queen who ruled over theirs as well as for the Warlord Prince of Dhemlan's second-in-command.

After spending days doing the work she'd been doing for decades—and still enjoyed—she admitted to herself that she had missed Sadi's company, had missed sleeping with him. Missed having sex with him.

Admitting that much allowed her to consider what had happened with Daemon that last night before she'd fled from the family seat.

Truth wasn't always a comfortable beast to ride.

A Warlord Prince's bedroom is his private place, and he tends to be more possessive when he's there.

She should have heeded Jaenelle Angelline's warning and instruction.

Truth, then, before Sadi and Jaenelle Saetien returned from visiting Manny and Tersa in the village.

She had loved Daemon Sadi for a long time. She still loved him. Had chosen to marry him because he needed to stay connected to the living, and he'd trusted her enough to make the commitment to be her husband. All right, if she hadn't become pregnant, he wouldn't have married again after losing Jaenelle Angelline, but once they'd made a child, she became his wife.

Except she hadn't become his wife. Not the same way Marian was Lucivar's wife. She and Sadi had a partnership—a mutual commitment to raise their daughter, to take care of the family estates and the vast SaDiablo wealth, and to rule Dhemlan. There had been a comfortable distance between them. A *safe* distance between them. Even when they had sex, she had been separate, independent—and always in control of how much she surrendered.

That night in his bedroom, he'd erased that distance, that safety, had drowned her sense of independence and her ability to choose what she surrendered. He'd made her need with a desperation that was almost a sickness.

But that had been in his room, in his bed. That seemed

to be the key that turned that particular lock, so she would take care to stay out of his personal territory from now on.

Surreal knew the moment that the Black returned to the Hall. Minutes later, she felt Sadi approach her sitting room. Moving the folders to the sides of the table, she called in her crossbow, already primed to fire, and set it in the center of the table.

Daemon rapped on the door and took one step into her personal domain before he stopped. He looked at the crossbow, then at her, his lips twitching in what might have been amusement. Or relief?

"Is that on the table because you found out something at one of the estates that you think I won't like?" he asked.

He just stood there. Beautiful. Tempting. His sexual heat flowed into the room, a stealthy coiling around her skin, between her legs. She'd shaken off this damn need while she'd been away, and here it was again, just as fierce, within a minute of her being in the same room with him.

"The estates are fine." Her voice held an edge that should have warned him to back off.

"Surreal . . ." Daemon took another step into the room.

Surreal placed a hand on the crossbow. He stopped. But the heat . . . In another minute, she'd be on him, tearing at his clothes and trying to arouse him in order to get some relief.

No. She was *not* going to surrender to the point of being helpless. Not again. "I accept some of the blame for what happened that night—"

"Blame? Surreal . . ."

"—but I am telling you, here and now, that what happened that night will *not* happen again. You will not do that to me again. Are we clear on that, Sadi?"

A flash of something in his eyes—pain? regret?—before that beautiful face became a mask that revealed nothing.

"You have made your wishes very clear, Lady. I will, of course, respect them." His voice, like his face, told her nothing. "Now that you're home, I need to be away for a day or two. If Jaenelle Saetien pesters you about having a special cake made, the answer is no. I've already had this discussion with her."

She'd been gone for days, and now he was leaving without . . . Well, Hell's fire, she couldn't exactly say that she needed sex, could she? *Wanted*, not needed.

"When are you leaving?" she asked.

"In the morning. I have some things to finish up here before I go."

His psychic scent had an unfamiliar edge, and his physical scent . . .

As he turned away, she snapped, "Leash the damn heat!"

Daemon turned his head but not enough to look at her. "The sexual heat *is* leashed." He walked out of the room.

Surreal vanished the crossbow before she did something that couldn't be undone. She knew what Sadi felt like when the heat was leashed, and he didn't feel like *this*. This was *more*—with something jagged and dangerous mixed in with the heat.

The man who had walked out of the room wasn't quite Daemon Sadi and wasn't quite the Sadist. She wasn't sure what was happening between them, or why, and she didn't know who would come to her bed tonight. But she *was* sure that if she wasn't careful, the man who came to her bed would be something a woman might not survive.

"That's all the immediate concerns," Holt said as he took the signed letters.

"Good," Daemon replied. "I won't be gone for more than a day or two."

"If someone needs to contact you?"

Daemon stared at his secretary. Holt had been a young footman when Daemon had first come to the Hall, but his service to the family had been invaluable. When Prince Rainier retired from the position of being Daemon's secretary, Holt had stepped in. Intelligent and discreet, the Opal-Jeweled Warlord had never betrayed a trust.

"I'll be in Riada," he finally said. "Unless there is an emergency, I would prefer not to be disturbed."

"I'll convey that message if required."

Daemon waited until Holt left the room before he sagged in his chair and braced his forehead against his fisted hands.

". . . I am telling you, here and now, that what happened that night will not *happen again. You will not do that to me again."*

The time away hadn't done anything to ease Surreal's distress about what they had done that night or her fear of him the morning after. So. The barriers between them would be reinforced to keep her safe from the full truth of what he was. Doing anything less would be cruel now that she'd made her feelings so clear.

"Leash the damn heat!"

He couldn't contain the sexual heat more than he was doing now. Surreal should know that after living with him for so many years.

Didn't matter what she should know. He'd made a mistake, and she was still feeling raw because of it. He wouldn't make that mistake again, but he had to give her time to let her feelings settle one way or the other.

Daemon rubbed his temples, trying to ease the pain. Maybe Surreal was right and he wasn't keeping the heat as tightly leashed as he should. It was hard for him to tell when the pain felt like jagged edges of a broken glass being shoved into his brain.

If the pain persisted, he would see a Healer about these headaches when he returned from Riada.

That evening, after he and Surreal had played a board game with Jaenelle Saetien and the bedtime story had been read, Daemon had been surprised when Surreal made it clear she expected her husband to join her in her bed. His headache had subsided, but the echo of pain had lingered, and he would have been content just to cuddle with her.

Surreal needed more. Aggressive and demanding, she took control, riding him hard as he helped her reach a climax that should have satisfied her.

It may have satisfied her body, but sex that night did nothing to soothe her heart or her temper.

Daemon slipped out of her bed at first light and left the Hall before anyone but the earliest-rising servants was awake. Until last night, he had enjoyed being Surreal's lover. Now he felt relief that he wouldn't be required to perform that particular duty for a couple of days.

SEVEN

Weakness washed through Marian Yaslana as she put a pot of beef stew, a bowl of sweet cheese, and a stick of butter into the cabin's cold box. Daemon was perfectly capable of cooking his own meals or picking up food at The Tavern, but when he stayed at the cabin, she liked providing him with one meal as a welcome.

After she closed the cold box, her hand trembled as she pulled out a chair at the kitchen table and sank into it. She stared at one of the loaves of spinach-and-herb bread she'd made that morning because she liked that bread with the stew, and the bakery in Riada didn't make it.

Foolish to think she could do as much as she'd done before baby Andulvar's birth. Foolish to keep trying. But she didn't want to be a semi-invalid who couldn't play with her children or spend time with her husband—or bake bread. She didn't want to watch someone else tend her garden because she didn't have the strength to care for it.

Nurian had told her rest was the only cure, and she did feel a little stronger on the days when she did nothing more than sleep, read, and tend the baby. That had been fine for the first week or two, but she didn't want that to be her *life*. Unfortunately, Nurian's tonics didn't seem to do anything to restore her vitality. Nothing seemed to do that.

Was it time to use Jaenelle Angelline's last gift? It was a healing spell unlike any other—and impossible to duplicate.

"Use it when you need it most."

What if Jaenelle had seen something else in her future? Something that a little more rest couldn't cure?

She knew what Lucivar would say if he was aware of the healing spell, which was why she had tucked it away since the day she'd been given that last, special gift and had said nothing about its existence.

The cabin's front door opened. Marian felt the dark power of a Black Jewel fill the cabin. Daemon was sensitive to any intrusion inside the cabin that Saetan had built for Jaenelle Angelline decades ago. The cabin had been Jaenelle's private place, and then it had been hers and Daemon's, and now it was his sanctuary from all the responsibilities he shouldered.

"I'm in the kitchen," she called.

He appeared in the kitchen doorway, his gold eyes glazed and sleepy—a sign and warning of a Warlord Prince who was a heartbeat away from the killing edge. Then his eyes cleared and warmed. And then he frowned.

"Marian? Darling . . . ?" He moved swiftly, bending over her, one hand on her forehead as if checking for fever.

"I'm fine," she said. "Don't you start fussing too."

He eased back and his lips curved in a hint of a smile as his deep voice—that voice that always held a sexual purr—caressed her. "You know saying things like that is pointless, don't you?"

"It doesn't mean I can't say them."

"I won't fuss." Daemon looked pointedly at the loaf of bread. "And neither should you. I can take care of myself, especially when I don't plan to do or be anything but lazy."

Marian looked at his hand resting lightly on the table. Looked at the slender fingers and the long, black-tinted nails. And remembered why he, like his father, wore his nails that way.

Black Widow. Saetan had been the first male Black Widow, the first to be taught the Hourglass's Craft. Daemon was not only the second male to be trained in that particular Craft; he was the only natural male Black Widow in the history of the Blood.

"Daemon?" She moved a hand to indicate her body. "Could this be caused by something Nurian wouldn't be able to recognize?"

"Wouldn't recognize because . . . ?"

She rested the fingertips of her left hand on the black-tinted nails of his right. "Because the cause began outside my body." She didn't want to accuse anyone. She didn't have any enemies that she knew of, didn't think any of the Black Widows living in Ebon Rih had a reason to harm her. But now that the thought was there . . .

"May I?" Daemon asked.

Marian nodded.

His left hand rested against her neck. His right hand pressed lightly against her chest as he used Craft to undo the buttons of her tunic all the way to her waist. His eyes no longer saw her or the room, because he was focused on something else. She felt the feathery touch of psychic probes exploring her in ways healing Craft didn't do. This wasn't the touch of a Healer looking for illness. This was the touch of a hunter searching for an enemy.

His right hand moved lower, fingers spreading so that thumb and little finger touched her breasts. The hand moved lower to her belly. Then to her womb.

Raising his hands from her body, Daemon took her left hand and used the edge of his fingernail to nick the pad of her first finger. When a bead of blood formed, he licked the skin clean—and waited.

Releasing her, he rested one hip on the table. "I'm not sensing any kind of spell wrapped around you. Definitely no death spell designed to mimic a wasting disease. And there's no taste of poison in your blood."

She blinked. She hadn't considered a slow-acting

poison. Or death spells. "Have you ever created a spell like that?"

She watched his eyes change. The man looking at her now wasn't the man who loved her like a sister and flirted with her gently. The man looking at her now was the man who once had walked into an enemy camp where she and Daemonar had been held captive and who had tortured his own brother in order to provide a distraction so that he could get her and her son out of harm's way.

"Yes," he said too softly. "I have."

A Warlord Prince is true to his nature. You can't expect him to use what he is to protect you and yours and then treat him like an outcast when you're safe.

Jaenelle Angelline had understood the nature of Warlord Princes better than anyone else in Kaeleer—and she had understood the nature of the men in the family. All the men.

"Then you would know," Marian said in her no-nonsense mother voice.

There were shadows in his eyes, but the terrifying side of Daemon's nature withdrew in response to that voice, leaving the man she knew well.

"Darling, what you need is time and rest." He leaned toward her. "But if you ever feel concerned that someone might be using a spell to harm you, you send word to me."

Marian nodded and pushed to her feet. "I'm a hearth witch. I don't like being idle." She sounded petulant, which was foolish.

Daemon smiled, called in a book, held it so she could read the title, then raised an eyebrow.

A new book by one of her favorite authors.

"There is idle," Daemon purred, "and then there is enjoying a self-indulgent—"

"Gimme." She reached for the book.

Laughing, he gave it to her. "A fair exchange for the bread and whatever else you put in the cold box." He kissed her cheek. "Go home, put your feet up, and enjoy a good story."

Her smile faded almost before it formed. Something off

about him. She hadn't sensed it while he'd been focused on her, but now, thinking about the shadows in his eyes, she wondered if he, too, was fighting some kind of illness.

"I think I'm not the only one who could use a lazy day," she said.

"Which is why I'm here."

A breezy reply—and a lie. Whatever need had brought Daemon to the cabin this time was more than wanting a reprieve from responsibilities. He would tell her or, more likely, Lucivar when he was ready to talk about whatever was troubling him.

"Thank you for the book." She let him escort her out of the cabin and had the uneasy feeling that he needed her to be gone. That feeling was confirmed the moment she stepped off the porch and Black shields went up around the cabin. No one could reach him now, not even Lucivar.

She flew home and wasn't surprised to find Lucivar standing at the edge of the flagstone courtyard, waiting for her. Or waiting for something, since his focus remained on Riada even as he held out a hand to her.

"Did you see him?" Lucivar asked.

Marian tucked herself against his side. "I don't think your brother is well."

"Yeah. I know. The question is why."

"He put Black shields around the cabin."

Lucivar exhaled slowly. "I'll give him a day. Then I'll see what I can do."

"He brought me a book."

A laugh. "Does that mean you're going to tuck in and enjoy a quiet day?"

Marian smiled. "Yes, that's what it means."

Lucivar turned them toward the eyrie. "In that case, I'll look after our littlest beast for a while and give you a chance to settle in."

Time and rest. She hoped those would be enough to make her healthy again. If they didn't, if they couldn't, there would be one last thing to try.

✦ ✦ ✦

That afternoon, Lucivar and Rothvar paused for a moment to watch Jillian and Daemonar sparring in the yard before going into the kitchen.

"Coffee is fairly fresh, if you want some," Lucivar said.

"I don't need anything, thanks," Rothvar replied. He leaned against the kitchen's archway and looked toward the big front room. "The girl hasn't come for any sparring these past few days."

Lucivar poured a mug of coffee for himself. He didn't really want it, but it served as a prop. "She's been sparring with Daemonar before she helps Marian with some chores."

"Tamnar has his brains in his pants lately," Rothvar observed, not looking at Lucivar.

"He's at that age."

"You think the boy crossed a line and that's why the girl has stayed away?"

Someone crossed a line. Or broke a rule. He had a bigger concern right now, so he'd give Jillian a little more time to find her backbone and tell him what was going on with Tamnar. And then he would put an end to whatever was going on.

"You think there's something we need to do about it?" Rothvar asked.

"Not us. Not yet." Lucivar studied his second-in-command. "Did you know Hallevar when he was an arms master in the hunting camps in Askavi Terreille?"

Rothvar shook his head. "I was trained by another arms master."

"I had firsthand experience with Hallevar." Lucivar smiled. "Let him deal with Tamnar. He'll get the boy's brains back above the shoulders."

Rothvar chuckled, then tipped his chin in the direction of the yard. "And the rest?"

"I'll wait." Lucivar joined Rothvar, leaning against the

other side of the archway. "Patience is an important part of a hunt."

"For this hunt, better you than me."

Lucivar huffed. "Seems like one day they're cute and cuddly little witchlings, and the next they have female . . . opinions."

"Like I said. Better you than me. I'll make a final sweep around this part of the valley and check in with the camps at the northern end." Rothvar hesitated. "The Black is in the valley."

"My brother is staying at the cabin for a day or two."

After Rothvar left, Lucivar poured the coffee down the sink and rinsed out the mug. If he reached out now, who would answer? Daemon? The High Lord? Or the Sadist?

Bastard? he called on an Ebon-gray spear thread.

Prick?

Thank the Darkness, he felt warmth, not ice, running through the thread between them.

Thanks for giving Marian the book. She's been tucked away in her private room since she got home.

Good.

You want to come to the eyrie for dinner?

Not tonight. Daemon retreated from the link.

Yes, there had been warmth, but there had been something else, too, leaving Lucivar to wonder whether it was physical fatigue or weariness of the heart he'd heard in his brother's voice.

EIGHT

Daemon clenched his teeth and gripped the edge of the examination table as Nyssa, the newly qualified Healer, ran her hand down his bare back—a possessive, inviting touch rather than a professional one. At least, that's what it felt like, but the headaches had become severe enough in the past week for him to seek help, so he could be mistaking her intentions.

He hoped so, for her sake.

"There's nothing wrong with you, Prince," Nyssa said as she caressed his back again. "You're in prime condition."

Too much emphasis on the word *prime*?

Wishing he had waited to see the older Healer who had been taking care of the residents of the village as well as SaDiablo Hall, he wondered why Nyssa had chosen to relocate to a small village like Halaway. She'd been introduced to him upon her arrival in the village, and he'd gotten the impression that Nyssa wasn't a woman who enjoyed village life, that she craved the excitement of the larger towns and cities in Dhemlan.

He could think of one reason why Nyssa would relocate to Halaway, and he hoped again, for her sake, that he was mistaken about that too.

"The headaches?" He tightened the leash on a temper

turning cold—and reminded himself that he could be hearing something that wasn't there.

Her hands rested on his shoulders. Her thumbs pressed into muscles that were painfully tight. "Perhaps you're not getting enough nocturnal exercise."

Daemon exploded off the table. Grabbing his shirt off the chair in the room, he put it on with a grace that didn't betray—or give any warning of—his growing rage.

"Thank you for that . . . illuminating . . . diagnosis." A flash of his temper slipped the leash and turned the air in the room so frigid he could see his breath.

"I didn't mean . . ." Nyssa stumbled away from him until her back hit the wall.

The room reeked of fear. Good. The bitch finally realized she'd gone too far.

"I can put together a mixture of herbs that should help your headache," she stammered. "It will only take a few minutes."

"You do that," he said too softly.

As soon as he gave her enough space to reach the door, Nyssa fled from the examination room.

Daemon finished dressing, giving the bitch enough time to put together the ingredients for a healing brew. Not that he'd trust it—or her—enough to drink any brew made from those herbs, but he wanted to test it. If he couldn't trust the witch who was taking over the Healer's House in Halaway, he would have to make other arrangements whenever anyone in his family—or in his employ—became ill.

As he finger combed his thick black hair into the disheveled style he now preferred, he wondered if Surreal had seen the young Healer recently. Had his wife said something that might lead another woman to think he was open to such an invitation? As for nocturnal exercise, lately he was getting more than he wanted.

He kept the sexual heat leashed as tightly as he could,

but Surreal met him in bed with a blend of hunger and anger, as if she blamed him for making her want him. Keeping his distance didn't please her, and being a considerate lover didn't please her. And the headaches had become severe enough that it was hard to give a damn about making things right between them.

Judging he'd given Nyssa enough time to make up the mixture so that he could take it and leave with limited interaction with her, Daemon walked out of the examination room.

"Here you are, Prince." Nyssa held out a glass jar filled with an herbal mix. "This should help." She held on to the jar moments too long, her fingers brushing against his as he took it from her. "I apologize if there was some misunderstanding during my examination."

There was no misunderstanding, Daemon thought. And her apology was as false as her attempt to sound contrite.

He walked out of the Healer's House before he gave in to the desire to wrap a death spell around the bitch and explode her heart in the middle of the night. The main reason he resisted was that if she made the transition to demon-dead, he'd *still* have to deal with her. Of course, she wouldn't like dealing with him when he stood as the High Lord of Hell. She wouldn't like it at all.

He'd make sure of it.

Shaking off those thoughts, at least for the moment, Daemon vanished the jar and headed for his next stop, letting the crisp afternoon air battle with his cold anger.

Might not be the Healer's fault. Might not. Which was why he intended to get a second opinion.

His gliding walk covered ground with deceptive swiftness, and a few minutes later, he reached the walkway of a tidy cottage. Manny's home. Since he was expected, he knocked on the front door once, walked in—then jerked to a stop as he crossed the threshold.

Manny stood in front of him, her hands on her ample hips, giving him the stare that had warned the boy he had been that he was in trouble. And damn it, that stare could still make him wary, despite the fact that he was the most powerful male in the entire Realm of Kaeleer.

"Where's your overcoat?" she demanded. "How am I supposed to get it into that boy's head that winter is almost here and he needs to wear a coat if you don't set a good example? And don't just stand there looking like a fish on a line. Come in and close the door. You're letting the cold in."

Some things didn't change regardless of age and rank, Daemon thought as he obediently closed the door and followed Manny to the kitchen at the back of the cottage.

Two children sat at the pinewood table—his ward, Mikal, and his daughter, Jaenelle Saetien. Morghann sat next to Jaenelle's chair, wagging her tail in enthusiastic greeting.

Manny bustled about the kitchen, pouring glasses of milk for the children and making coffee for him. And the other adult in the room . . .

"Hello, darling." Daemon held out a hand to his mother. A broken Black Widow whose mind wandered the borders of the Twisted Kingdom, Tersa was unable to grasp what most people called sanity, but she was still gifted in the Hourglass's Craft —and she was still powerful in her own way.

"It's the boy. It's my boy." Smiling, she clasped her hands around his. Then she frowned. "You're cold." Reaching up, she cupped his face in her hands and studied him. "Not well," she whispered. "Not well."

He stepped back, wondering what she had sensed—or seen. "I'm fine," he lied. "I was sufficiently annoyed when I walked out of a meeting that I forgot to put on my coat. That's why I'm cold."

For a moment, he thought Tersa would argue with him. Then her gold eyes filled with the vague look that meant her mind had wandered down another path in the Twisted Kingdom.

"We have nutcakes," she said. "Manny says the children can each have one." She looked at him.

Apparently he'd been demoted back to childhood—at least where nutcakes were concerned. "One is sufficient for a treat." He pulled out a chair opposite Mikal and Jaenelle Saetien and sat, noticing the cautious way Tersa eased into the chair next to him.

When Sylvia, a former Queen of Halaway, had been killed at a house party that was meant as a lethal trap for her sons, Daemon used his positions as patriarch of the SaDiablo family and Warlord Prince of Dhemlan to become Mikal and Beron's legal guardian in order to carry out Sylvia's wishes for her sons. Jaenelle Angelline had worked out the details, and even a century later, the arrangement still followed the intentions of both Queens.

"Since I'm special, I should have *two* nutcakes," Jaenelle Saetien said, putting one on her plate as she reached for another with her other hand.

"Aaaaaahhhhh, no," Daemon replied, using Craft to move the plate of treats out of his daughter's reach. He murmured his thanks to Manny when she placed a large mug of coffee in front of him, and watched his girl pout—and then study him to see if pouting would bring about the desired response of him giving in and letting her have the second nutcake.

Her negotiating to convince him to change his answer when she wanted something wasn't new, but previously she'd argued with logic and provided reasons that were sometimes fascinatingly skewed, coming as they were from a child's perspective, and she usually accepted his final answer with a minimum of fuss. This effort to manipulate his feelings had begun right after he hadn't let her have a special cake—and was an unwelcome ploy. Especially today.

"Something wrong with your lip, witch-child?" he asked mildly.

"I'm special," she said, still working the pout. "I should get two nutcakes."

"You're not that special," Mikal said, rolling his eyes in

a way that was designed to annoy adults—a reminder that the young Warlord had reached the messy years when he was no longer a boy but hadn't quite settled into the long, fraught decades of being a youth.

Pouting forgotten, Jaenelle Saetien turned on the older boy, who was usually considered a friend as well as family. "I am so. Everyone knows I'm special because I wear Twilight's Dawn, and no one else can wear that Jewel."

"Lady Angelline was the first witch to wear a Jewel like that, and *her* Twilight's Dawn was a lot more powerful than yours," Mikal said. "But ever since the Birthright Ceremony, you've been acting like a brat and fanning about like you're better than the rest of us and almost daring the teachers to scold you when you decide you don't have to do your schoolwork because you're *special*." He slipped out of his chair, stuck his butt out, and wiggled it to demonstrate fanning.

"Enough," Daemon said.

Ignoring him, Jaenelle Saetien jumped up, knocking against the table hard enough to slosh milk over the rim of her glass. "You take that back, Mikal!"

"No, I won't!" Mikal wiggled his butt again. "Brat, brat, brat!"

Daemon felt the rise of power driven by his daughter's anger, watched Mikal's eyes widen before the boy wrapped himself in a Rose defensive shield.

The power in Jaenelle Saetien's Jewel ranged from Rose to Green. If she struck Mikal with anything but the lightest end of her Birthright power, she would break the boy's shield at the very least. At the worst, she might break a great deal more than a shield.

That he had to consider the possibility that his girl would do such a thing because of a childish squabble disturbed him. That he might have missed the signs that she felt entitled to use her power against anyone, let alone a member of their family, disturbed him in other ways.

"*Enough.*" Daemon's deep voice, laced with the power of

his Birthright Red Jewel, rolled through the cottage like soft thunder—a warning of a storm gathering on the horizon.

Instantly subdued, the children sat and stared at their plates while Manny wiped up the milk and Tersa . . . He didn't know what his mother was seeing or hearing.

Daemon reached for a nutcake and met Manny's eyes. She had been his caretaker when he was a child, before and after Tersa had been driven away by Dorothea SaDiablo, the High Priestess of Hayll in the Realm of Terreille. Manny had looked after him during the years when Dorothea had used him and trained him to be a pleasure slave. She had been the one good constant in his childhood, and she had never taken any sass from him, even after he'd begun wearing the Black.

That she was looking at his daughter with an expression close to dislike told him he needed to find out what was going on when he wasn't present and make some adjustments.

And at least one adjustment would be made on the way home.

"Are you coming up to ride with us tomorrow, Mikal?" he asked to break the silence.

"Yes, sir, if it's still all right with you," Mikal replied, dropping the Rose shield.

"It is."

"I got a letter from Beron yesterday," Mikal said, the spat apparently forgotten—at least by the boy. "He's auditioning for a new play, but he's planning to come home and visit for a couple of days." The boy's excitement over his elder brother's acting career brightened the room—and calmed Daemon's temper.

"I'll have my guest room made up for him," Manny said. "Make sure he gets a couple of home-cooked meals in him." She glanced at Daemon. "I imagine Mrs. Beale will be expecting to tuck a couple of meals into him as well."

"I imagine she will." He'd check with Holt to find out if

he and Surreal were hosting any particular guests while Beron was in Halaway. If not, Manny and Mrs. Beale could arrange between themselves when and where the young actor showed up for meals.

They discussed the theater and what little Mikal knew about the part Beron hoped to win. Daemon didn't comment about Jaenelle Saetien's big sighs or continued sulking. And he didn't say anything when a nutcake vanished from the serving dish.

I'll handle it, he told Manny on a psychic thread before the woman could make a fuss. *How long has this behavior been going on? There's been little sign of this at home.* No sign of this outside of the cake incident, and no one had approached him about his girl's behavior when she wasn't with him.

Not that long. Like Mikal said, the young Lady has been full of herself since the Birthright Ceremony, Manny replied. *Happens to some youngsters. I expect she'll grow out of it once her Jewel stops attracting so much attention.*

The sooner she grows out of it, the better.

A flash of annoyance from Manny— directed at him for his harsh tone. A flicker of something else from Tersa. That was more of a worry.

I agree, Manny finally said. *Course, I remember what you and your brother were like when you were around her age, even before you had a reason to feel so full of yourselves.*

Daemon looked at Manny. *May the Darkness spare all of us from a child like *that*.*

Too late.

His lips twitched. Dealing with Daemonar's energy whenever the boy came to visit left him exhausted and wondering how anyone survived Eyrien children. And left him wondering what Lucivar had been thinking to have *three* of them. Although Titian really was a darling witchling, and baby Andulvar was still too young to cause too much trouble.

A few minutes later, Daemon—now wearing an overcoat—escorted Jaenelle Saetien and Morghann out of the village, heading toward SaDiablo Hall. Home. His girl's mood had changed from sulky to cheerful, but that wouldn't last long.

He watched girl and Sceltie, not as a doting father but as the Warlord Prince responsible for the well-being of all the Dhemlan people.

Jaenelle Saetien skipped ahead of him, the small brown and white dog trotting beside her. His girl's delicately pointed ears were the visible proof of the Dea al Mon side of her heritage. The other things that were part of the Dea al Mon weren't as obvious.

Surreal had been twelve years old the first time she killed a man with a knife. She'd been justified, but it was whispered by the other races in Kaeleer that the Children of the Wood were born knowing what to do with a knife. Surreal's skill as an assassin was testimony to the truth of the saying.

Her skill had never bothered him. Hell's fire, he'd taught her some of the nastier death spells. But the temperament and power they both had brought to the making of this child . . .

Everything had a price, including privilege. Perhaps, especially privilege.

He waited until they had crossed the wooden bridge that was the boundary that divided Halaway from the Sa-Diablo estate, and changed the public road into the Hall's private drive. Then he snapped his fingers twice and held out his hand. "I'll take that nutcake, Lady Morghann."

But I am supposed to give it to Jaenelle Saetien when we get back to her room, Morghann said.

Daemon stopped walking and looked at his daughter, who poked her lip out in another pout.

"You were told you could have one nutcake," he said.

"But I wanted two!" she protested.

"Because you're special," he said too softly.

She started to agree, then must have realized the words were a warning. "Don't you think I'm special?" she asked in a small voice.

"Yes, I do, but that has nothing to do with the Jewel you wear. I think you're special because you're my daughter and I love you. I imagine every father feels that way about a daughter. I know your uncle Lucivar feels that way about Titian. But being special, regardless of the reason, doesn't give you the right to misbehave or ignore your schoolwork—or convince a witch who is younger than you to do something that you know is wrong."

I did a wrong thing? Morghann asked, alarmed.

Daemon ignored the Sceltie and focused on the girl. "I'm disappointed in you, Jaenelle Saetien. You let Morghann believe it was all right to take a nutcake for you. You tried to cheat by letting someone else take something that you wanted—and take the blame if caught."

Blame? Morghann whined. *There is blame?*

"Is that what you want your little Sister to learn from you? That it's all right to cheat, to take without permission? As long as your hands don't get dirty, it's not your fault and you'll stand back and let someone else take the blame—and the punishment?" The headache, which he'd managed to ignore while he was at Manny's cottage, surged into sickening pain. He had to leave while he could still ride the Winds.

"It was just a stupid nutcake!" Jaenelle Saetien protested.

"Today it was a nutcake," he snapped. "What will you ask Morghann to steal tomorrow?"

Steal? Scelties do not steal. Morghann stared at Jaenelle Saetien and growled.

"Come on," Daemon said. "I have an appointment, and you need to get home."

He started walking, aware that his girl hadn't moved,

was in the throes of some *mood* that was dangerous for both of them right now.

"If that Lady in the Mist had wanted a second nutcake, I bet you would have given it to her," Jaenelle Saetien said, her voice rising in a whiny challenge.

Rage whispered through him, savagely cold, burning him right to the marrow. He turned and walked back to his daughter—and whatever she saw in his face had her taking two steps back.

"If you ever again try to use the Lady as a hammer against me, there will be consequences—and they will hurt. She is my Queen, and *no one* uses her as a weapon. Especially you. Are we clear about that, Lady SaDiablo?"

"Papa . . ."

"Are. We. Clear?"

"Y-yes."

He walked away. Had to walk away.

"Papa!" Jaenelle Saetien wailed as she ran to catch up to him. "I'm *sorry*, Papa."

The tears were probably real, but the headache was a storm pounding his temples and consuming his control, so all he could do was hand her a handkerchief and keep moving until he got her to the Hall and could place her in Surreal's care before he . . .

Surreal, he called on a Gray psychic thread. *Surreal, you're needed.*

He knew she was at the Hall. He always knew where she and Jaenelle Saetien were, not only because he was so attuned to their psychic scents, but because Surreal was the only individual in the surrounding area who wore the Gray, and Jaenelle Saetien's Jewel was unmistakable.

Sadi? Surreal sounded wary. *Where are you?*

We'll be at the Hall in a few minutes. He broke the link between them before she picked up on the pain. He wasn't the only one who was attuned to his partner, and he didn't want her asking questions that might give her cause to worry before he could provide reassuring answers—or at least some kind of answer.

Assuming she still felt enough for him beyond sex to worry.

Surreal wasn't in the great hall when he walked in, but Beale was there. The Red-Jeweled Warlord who served as the Hall's butler looked attentive, as if merely there to follow an order, but Daemon sensed the tight Red shield around the man. Red couldn't survive a strike from the Black, but Beale being prepared for a strike told him his flash of cold anger hadn't been as contained as he'd thought.

He wasn't so steeped in pain that he couldn't appreciate that Beale's response to him was the same as Mikal's had been to Jaenelle Saetien—and for much the same reason—but it made him wonder why Surreal wasn't there, armed and waiting for him. Unless she thought, for whatever reason, that she, and not Jaenelle Saetien, was the reason for the anger?

"Look after Jaenelle Saetien until Lady Surreal is available," Daemon told Beale. "And please convey my apologies to Mrs. Beale for not giving her more notice, but I have a meeting that won't wait and I will not be back in time for dinner."

Beale allowed himself a tiny frown of concern. "A meeting, Prince? Lord Holt didn't mention anything on your calendar this evening."

"It wasn't on my calendar, but it can't be delayed." Daemon backed away from his butler, from his daughter, from the wife who hadn't made an appearance yet. "I will be back tonight."

"I'll convey the message to Lady Surreal."

Convey one other thing to my wife, he said on a Red spear thread, and gave Beale instructions that, even if not understood, would be followed by everyone who worked at the Hall.

As Daemon walked to the stone landing web in front of the house, he noticed Morghann trotting in the direction of the stables.

Morghann, he called as gently as he could.

I did a wrong thing, the Sceltie whined. *There is blame.*

Jaenelle Saetien did a wrong thing. You made a small mistake. We can talk about the correct thing to do when I get back.

She didn't reply, just kept trotting toward the stables.

He'd been too harsh. Being a few months away from her Birthright Ceremony, Morghann was still considered a puppy, which meant she depended on what humans told her was correct behavior, and Jaenelle Saetien telling her to do a "wrong thing" had shaken the Sceltie's confidence— at least for a little while. Morghann would forgive the girl—Scelties were forgiving of human mistakes, as he had reason to know—but she wouldn't forget. And she might never fully trust again. He wouldn't know how deep that break in trust went until he tried to fix it.

But right now something else needed to be fixed.

Tersa returned to the cottage next to Manny's, where she and the Mikal boy lived. The Mikal boy had stayed with Manny to do his schoolwork and help with some of the chores he did around both cottages. No one would wonder about her for a while.

For long enough.

She climbed the attic stairs, then fumbled with the keys she kept on a chain she usually left in a drawer in her dresser. But today she had tucked the chain in a pocket, had felt she'd needed to have the keys handy. She unlocked the door, entered the attic, then locked the door behind her.

Tangled webs were the webs of dreams and visions that were used by Black Widows to see what couldn't be seen in other ways.

Using the second key, she opened the trunk where she stored the tools of the Hourglass Coven—wooden frames and spools of spider silk of various weights, among other less benign tools.

Selecting a frame, Tersa brought it and the box of spools to her worktable. Then she sat on a stool, chose one of the spools of spider silk, and thought about the reason she needed to weave this tangled web.

Her boy was not well. He knew it, but not the cause or how to fix it. Felt the pain that was the body's way of revealing what heart and mind tried to hide. The source of the pain. That was what she needed to find. Not just for him. Not just for him, but for . . .

Her hands stopped moving as she anchored the last strand of the web. Then she took that mental step to the side—a dangerous step for a witch whose power had been broken long ago and whose mind had shattered when she made the choice to regain some of that power. She needed to take that step to help the boy. Her boy. Daemon. Now she opened herself to the dreams and visions—and when she saw what the pain was trying to reveal, she huffed out a sigh of annoyance.

Growing pains. Her boy was trying to hold back a part of himself that had matured so recently he hadn't figured out yet how to deal with it. He'd be more successful trying to hold back the sea at high tide. He could do it for a while, just like he could hold back his own nature for a while. But eventually he would have to yield to what he was. If he didn't, he might damage himself in ways that couldn't be repaired.

Tersa stared at the tangled web. She wasn't seeing everything yet. She'd seen the simple answer, the easy answer. But there was more. Did she want to know about the more?

She followed the threads beyond the simple answer and saw the larger vision, saw what it might cost later if she gave her boy the easy answer now.

If her boy's pain went away, the one person he would need the most wouldn't be there. The one the winged boy would need wouldn't be there.

Daemon's pain was the only key. Could she let her boy suffer now in order to spare him from greater pain later?

"Everything has a price," she whispered as she retreated from the visions.

Using a thin stick of wood, she destroyed the web, carefully wrapping the spider silk around the wood until the frame was clean. Then she used Craft to snap the web-shrouded wood from the rest of the stick and dropped the used portion into a shallow stone bowl. Another bit of Craft created a tongue of witchfire, which she dropped into the bowl.

Tersa watched wood and spider silk burn until there was nothing left, until even the witchfire was extinguished, having used up the tiny bit of power that had created it.

She returned her tools to the trunk and locked it before she picked up the stone bowl and went downstairs. Witchfire burned anything and everything in its path, so even though it looked extinguished, she would keep watch on the bowl for a while longer before burying the ash in the garden.

Once the Mikal boy was asleep, she would ride the Winds to the Keep and hope the one who could save her boy would answer her call for help.

Surreal, you're needed.

Sadi? Where are you? He was supposed to be picking up Jaenelle Saetien after school. Had that much time passed since he'd left the Hall on some unspecified errand in the village?

We'll be at the Hall in a few minutes.

You're needed. Not *Your presence is requested.* Not *Your presence is required.* Those were the phrases of Protocol that were usually used. But this? This sounded like a Warlord Prince summoning his second-in-command.

Which meant she should be heading up to the residential part of the Hall, weapons drawn and ready to meet trouble.

And yet she hesitated as she studied the Black-locked door that she'd discovered at the end of a corridor deep beneath the Hall. She didn't know what was behind that door, but she was sure that few who walked through that door walked out again.

Better not to know. Especially now.

But these walls on either side of the door were also protected by Black shields, and those shields now served a purpose for her. She didn't think Sadi came down here often, and she was sure these shields weren't part of the defensive shields around the Hall. Those Sadi checked every fortnight. But these . . .

Everything had a price. Including power. Especially power. And during a witch's moontime, she needed to channel her power into the reservoir of her Jewels to lessen the pain. Problem was, when everything was peaceful, daily life didn't use much Gray power.

She could ask Daemon to drain her Gray Jewel. He'd done it every month during her pregnancy and several months after that to keep her and the baby safe from her own power. But she didn't want to ask him. She didn't want to be dependent on anyone right now. Especially him. She could take care of this on her own, as she'd done most of her life.

More than anything, she didn't want to be vulnerable around the Black more than could be helped.

Lady Surreal? Beale called.

Did Beale know what was contained behind that door? Did he know about these corridors? Would he think to look for her here? And would he tell Daemon if he did find her here?

She'd lived in and around the Hall for decades, but she hadn't discovered this part of the structure until Daemon had gone to the cabin for a couple of days. She'd been restless and had picked up the feel of the Black beneath the cellars. Curious, she had traced the power to that door and the shielded walls. Still curious, and sufficiently cautious, she had carefully coated her Gray power over the Black—and then pushed just enough for the Black to respond to the "attack" and absorb the Gray. She'd moved to another section of the wall and done the same thing, not pushing too hard in case there was an aggressive shield beneath the passive one. Her Gray Jewel had been drained of some of its power, while the Black shield, though thinned, was still intact. She'd hoped the thinning would be put down to a shield naturally fading over time.

Now there wasn't time for careful draining, not if she didn't want people to start looking for her—and there was one person in particular she didn't want finding her down here.

"Shit shit shit." Surreal unleashed a wash of Gray power along the wall, hitting the Black shield with enough force that she could feel the difference in the shield. If she kept slamming power at that one area until she completely drained the Gray, she *might* weaken the Black, but the power she needed to release prior to her moontime wasn't going to make *that* much difference to the shield.

Couldn't make that much difference. But if Sadi noticed, if he asked why she was trying to break one of his shields . . .

Which side of Daemon Sadi's temper would ask? Her husband? The Warlord Prince of Dhemlan? The High Lord of Hell? Or would it be the Sadist who wrapped his arms around her and played a game of pleasure and pain while he asked questions and waited for answers she didn't want to give?

With any luck, it would take him a while to notice the weakened shield.

He'd notice plenty if she didn't get her ass moving and find out why she was needed.

By the time she reached the entrance hall, the only person waiting for her was Beale. She opened her first inner barrier, then quickly shut it against the stew of emotions filling the great hall.

"Prince Sadi?" she asked.

"He left for a meeting that was not on his calendar," Beale replied. "He will not be home for dinner but will be back sometime tonight."

"Jaenelle Saetien?"

"The young Lady has gone to her room." Beale hesitated. "Nothing was said, but I had the impression that an infraction of the rules has caused some unhappiness between the Prince and the young Lady. Before he left, he gave the order that the young Lady was not allowed any dessert or treats for the rest of today and all of tomorrow."

But he left me to carry out that order, Surreal thought sourly.

"I have informed Mrs. Beale." Another pause. "And Holt."

"Did you inform the Scelties?" she asked.

"I think they already know."

Shit shit shit. *That* didn't sound good. "They're upstairs with Jaenelle Saetien?"

"No. They've gone to the stables to play with the horses."

The girl was upset and the Scelties were not offering company. And Sadi had left for some mysterious meeting. Great. Wonderful. "I'll sort out what I can."

As she turned toward the informal sitting room, which held the staircase that led to the family wing of the Hall, Beale said, "Lady Surreal? It's not my place to say, but the Prince looked . . . unwell."

"He seemed fine this morning." *And more than fine last night.*

"Ah. A passing indisposition." Beale sounded relieved. "I'm sure it's nothing more than that."

Hurrying toward the family wing, she stopped at Daemon's suite of rooms first, relieved when she found Jazen, his valet, hanging up freshly laundered silk shirts in the dressing room.

"Prince Sadi," she said before Jazen could greet her. "If he was ill, would you know?"

Jazen hesitated, and Surreal wondered if it was because the man was considering the question or trying to balance loyalties.

"Some mornings he seems indisposed, but I've thought it was due to stiff muscles, since he seems to shake it off after a hot shower. Should I be watching for something?"

"No. Never mind."

A fully shaved man—mutilated for the entertainment of Dorothea SaDiablo and her cronies—who had had no future until Daemon hired him as a valet, Jazen would be loyal to the Warlord Prince of Dhemlan. While he might not say anything to *her*, if Daemon really was ill, Jazen would say something to someone.

And what she'd told Beale was true: the man had been in fine form last night when he'd come to her bed.

Not finding Jaenelle Saetien in the playroom, she knocked on the girl's bedroom door and went in without waiting for a response. Her daughter sat cross-legged in the middle of the bed, looking sulky.

Surreal sat on the edge of the bed. "I hear you butted heads with your papa and lost." No response. "And the penalty for whatever you butted heads about is no dessert or treats for the rest of today and all of tomorrow."

That got a response. "That's not fair!"

"Why isn't it fair?"

The story poured out. Nutcakes. Mikal. Papa being mean about her wanting a second nutcake even though Manny did say just one each. But she was *special*.

Surreal suspected that the real conflict was buried in the things Jaenelle Saetien didn't say, but she'd work with this. "You're lucky it was your papa and not your grandfather who decided the penalty for this nutcakes-and-sass drama. Your grandfather, like your papa, was indulgent about some things and very strict about other things. *Very* strict. If you'd tried this with him, you'd be lucky if the no-desserts-and-treats order was for less than a week."

She couldn't have shocked the girl more if she'd dumped a bucket of ice water over her head.

"Do you want to know what 'special' really means, my darling? It means more training, more work, more study, more discipline, more rules. Part of the power you wield is at the level of the Green, and that means you wear a dark Jewel. No one can afford to look away from bad behavior and allow you to become a bitch. Too many people died in wars that were started by bitches who thought they were above the laws, above the rules we live by."

"It was just a nutcake," Jaenelle Saetien whispered.

"Was it? Then why aren't the Scelties here with you?"

The girl didn't answer.

Surreal nodded, guessing a bit more of what must have happened. "I used to say your papa had a firm *no* and a soft *no* when it came to something you wanted to do or have. After today, I think you're going to find him drawing a harder line, and no matter how pleasantly he says it, from now on, *no* will mean *no*, and disobeying him will have consequences."

She gave her daughter a kiss on the forehead and headed for the door to let the girl sulk for a while. Then she went to her own suite and locked the doors so that no one would walk in on her while she paced and wondered if the life she'd built around being Daemon's wife and the mother of his child was breaking apart around her.

Prick.

The pained whisper on a Red spear thread had Lucivar calling in his Eyrien war blade as he strode out of his home and tried to pinpoint his brother's location. *Bastard?*

Here.

He spotted Daemon coming up the stone stairs from the landing area below the eyrie—saw his brother sway.

Vanishing the war blade, Lucivar rushed down the remaining stairs and grabbed Daemon before the man could lose his balance and take a hard fall down the stairs—or even fall off the damn mountain. Securing one of Daemon's arms around his shoulders, he wrapped his arm around his brother's waist, closed his fingers around the thin leather belt, and half carried Sadi up to the eyrie.

Nurian! The command, sent out on a general psychic thread, thundered over the valley. *To my eyrie, now!*

"What in the name of Hell is wrong with you?" he muttered as they reached the flagstone courtyard in front of his home. Marian stood in the doorway. She met his eyes, nodded, and disappeared into the eyrie.

"Headache," Daemon whispered.

"Try again, old son."

"Fine," Daemon snapped, sounding a bit more like himself. "It's a wicked bitch of a headache."

Sadi hadn't been anywhere in Ebon Rih until he arrived a minute ago, so that begged the question of why he'd made the journey here instead of staying put until the headache had eased.

And the answer was he'd been someplace where he couldn't afford to be vulnerable.

One thing at a time.

Stay out, boyo, Lucivar said when he hauled Daemon into the eyrie and saw his elder son standing in the doorway leading to the shielded yard. If Daemon was suffering from something more than a headache, he wanted the boy out of the way of any . . . unpleasantness.

Marian had the covers of the bed in the primary guest room pulled down. She also had a basin full of water and a cloth on the wide window ledge, and an empty basin floating on air near the bed.

Papa? Nurian is here, Daemonar said.

Tell her to come back to the guest room. And you stay in the front of the eyrie and keep your sister with you.

What's wrong with Uncle Daemon?

Don't know yet.

Ignoring his brother's grumbling, Lucivar stripped off Daemon's black jacket and white silk shirt, then pushed him down on the bed so that Marian could remove the shoes and socks.

"What . . . ?" Nurian stopped on the threshold, her dark, membranous wings folding tight to her body.

"Prince Sadi says he has a headache," Lucivar said.

"I *do* have a headache," Daemon growled.

"Well, let's take a look." After a moment's hesitation, Nurian entered the room, all brisk efficiency—as if being in the same room with the two most powerful men in Kaeleer when one of them was in pain wasn't the least bit dangerous. "Let's sit him on that padded bench. It'll be easier for me to get a good look at everything."

Nurian and Marian moved the bench from under the window to a spot in the room that allowed Nurian full access to her patient.

"Come on." Lucivar wrapped a hand around Daemon's arm and hauled him to his feet.

"You son of a—," Daemon began.

"I love you too, Bastard. Now sit on the bench before I knock you down."

What he saw in Daemon's pain-glazed gold eyes scared him to the bone—which was why he gave his brother the lazy, arrogant smile that always promised trouble.

After settling Daemon on the bench, he and Marian left the room and walked to the end of the corridor.

"Was he in a fight?" Marian whispered.

"Don't think so," Lucivar replied, keeping his voice low. "But something is wrong." Had been wrong for a while now.

"I have some soup I made the other day for tender tummies. I'll heat some up. Nurian might want him to have some nourishment to help fuel her healing brew."

After Marian headed for the kitchen, Lucivar walked back to the guest room and stood in the corridor, out of sight.

His brother was damaged. Lucivar had known that on some instinctive level from the first time they had met again as youths, neither remembering the childhood years before they'd been taken from their father. Whatever pain and torment he'd endured being a half-breed bastard in the Eyrien hunting camps where he had been trained to fight, it was nothing compared with what Dorothea SaDiablo must have done to Daemon, taking him into her bed while he was still a boy and training him to be a pleasure slave whose service she had sold to the Queens who curried her favor.

Whatever had been done to Daemon during those early decades of his life had shaped and twisted the side of him that became known as the Sadist. Using the sexual heat as an inescapable lure that could seduce anyone, regardless of preference, the Sadist wove pain and pleasure together in a way that broke down his enemies piece by piece. Broke down the mind. Broke down the body. Merciless. Relentless. A raging, brilliant cruelty that lived inside a beautiful face and well-toned body.

He had danced with the Sadist, had been used by the Sadist. Had hated his brother because of those games. But he'd known—on some level he had always known—that the Sadist had shown restraint, had retained a sliver of mercy when they had danced, had tortured him in order to protect him. Had, in fact, loved him.

Surreal thought she had dealt with the Sadist during the times when Daemon's temper turned cold, but she'd seen only a glimpse, had only brushed against that side of Daemon's nature. No one who truly danced with the Sadist in all his raging glory survived.

With one exception.

The Sadist had been in love with Witch, and she had looked at the truth of all that Daemon Sadi was without fear. On the rare occasions when the Sadist had played the lover with Witch, Daemon and Jaenelle Angelline had looked exhausted and dazed for a day or so afterward—and content to just be together, quietly cuddling.

The Sadist had looked at him out of pain-glazed eyes, but the headaches could be a sign of something else. There had been no sign of trouble after Witch had repaired the shattered chalice a second time, no sign that something that had been healed might be breaking again.

Until now.

Sweet Darkness, please let this be something a Healer like Nurian can fix.

Lucivar listened to Nurian asking questions and Daemon answering.

"Did the headaches start after the Birthright Ceremony?" Nurian asked.

"Before," Daemon replied. "More of an annoyance than anything. And not as persistent."

"But a few bad ones since then?"

"Yes."

"Bad as this one?"

"Yes. Several bad ones this past week, but this is the worst."

Not good, Lucivar thought. *Daemon had mentioned having headaches, but he hadn't given any indication they were this bad.*

"Drink this," Nurian said. "Healing brew with a sedative to help you sleep for a couple of hours. While you're drinking that, I'm going to rub some warm liniment into your neck and shoulders. That should help relieve some of the pain. You have a choice of this liniment . . ." She called in a bottle and held it close enough for Sadi to take a sniff.

"Smells like a Lady's boudoir," Daemon complained.

"Or this one." Nurian called in another bottle and held it out.

"Hell's fire! Who would want to smell like *that*?"

"Eyrien warriors," Nurian said dryly.

"Figures." Daemon huffed out a breath. "I'll take the boudoir."

"Good choice. The stink of the other one would probably keep you awake."

Daemon's reluctant laugh had Lucivar's shoulders relaxing enough for him to appreciate how tense he'd been since seeing Daemon on the stairs leading up to his home.

Murmurs. Movement. The sound of someone settling into bed. Then Nurian came out of the room, shutting the door partway.

Lucivar followed her to the end of the corridor, where he could keep an eye on the guest room. Just in case.

"Well?" he asked quietly.

"There is nothing physically wrong with Prince Sadi," Nurian said just as quietly. "There is enough tension in the shoulders, neck, and jaw to make someone's head hurt, but there is nothing *wrong*. Not that I can detect. No signs of damage to the brain or bleeding or anything else. No signs of trouble with his heart or lungs or any other organ. Your brother is a vigorous, healthy man in his prime."

"Who is suddenly suffering from debilitating headaches."

"Yes." Nurian looked troubled. "Whatever is causing the headaches, it isn't physical. Yet. But I'm concerned that if something isn't done, what's bothering him could manifest as more than headaches." She hesitated. "Is there a Black Widow he would trust enough to allow her to look for a cause that isn't physical?"

Lucivar hesitated. "Maybe. But it might not be easy to find her."

"Talk to him when he's feeling better." Nurian held up a jar. "I have to go back to my eyrie for a bit."

"Is that a healing brew for him?"

She shook her head. "This is the mixture the Healer in Halaway gave him. He asked me to test it."

"For . . . ?"

"Anything that shouldn't be in the mixture."

That explained why Daemon was here instead of at home. "Let me know what you find. Marian's in the kitchen, warming up some soup."

"I doubt he'll stay awake long enough to eat it, but he'll need something once he wakes up."

Returning to the guest room, Lucivar used Craft to move the padded bench closer to the bed before sitting down and studying Daemon, who lay on his back with his hands resting on his belly.

"What did she say?" Daemon asked, the words slurred enough that Lucivar wondered just how much of a sedative Nurian had added to the healing brew.

"You have tight muscles and a bad headache."

Daemon snorted. "Already knew that."

"Yeah." Lucivar hesitated. "Will you let me help you?"

The gold eyes that looked at him still held pain, but behind the pain . . . Cold. Brittle. Predatory. "How?" the Sadist asked too softly.

"I could drain some of the reservoir in the Black, give the power a place to go so that your body can rest." Lucivar waited. His Ebon-gray was as dark and deep as that Jewel could get, but Daemon stood deep enough into the Black that there was no chance of surviving an attack by that Black strength.

"You can't spare that much Ebon-gray," Daemon finally said.

Lucivar gave his brother that lazy, arrogant smile. "I can spare enough."

Daemon moved his hands, resting his arms at his sides—unspoken permission. The pendant holding the Black lay on his chest.

Watching Daemon's eyes, Lucivar laid his right hand on his brother's chest, his fingers resting next to the Black as the power in his Ebon-gray ring gently brushed against the power inside the Black. Brushed against it—and was absorbed by it, using up both. An easy draining. Nothing that challenged. Nothing that might provoke an aggressive response.

When he'd drained most of the Ebon-gray reservoir in the ring, Lucivar lifted his hand. "Better?"

"Some," Daemon murmured. "Thank you."

Lucivar stood and used Craft to put the bench back in its place under the window. "Get some sleep. I'm going to put a shield at the end of the corridor to keep my offspring from checking on you every five minutes."

"Good idea." With a sigh, Daemon turned on his side . . . and slept.

By the time Lucivar put the shield at the end of the corridor and made his way to the front of the eyrie, Nurian had returned—and she was pissed.

"Anything?" he asked.

"Nothing."

Not the answer he'd expected. "Nothing?"

"Nothing. Including what *should* have been in a healing brew to help a man in pain." Nurian blew out a breath. "I can understand being stupid and targeting Prince Sadi. Hell's fire, the man is walking temptation."

"Trying to play him is a messy way to commit suicide."

"I'm more concerned that this Healer might be targeting other men in the village to create dependence, or to acquire a lover, or . . . I don't know. But a Healer has to be trusted, and if she's caught doing something like this, it smears the reputation of all of us."

"I'll have a word with the Queen of Halaway. This Healer wouldn't be the first idiot to try to ensnare Sadi, but it's a reason for the Queen to look closer at any disturbance in her court or around the village. One thing is sure—this will be the last time that bitch tends to anyone in the Sa-Diablo household. I imagine the Hall will have its own Healer very soon."

"I'll make up more of the healing brew that the Prince can take with him," Nurian said.

"How much sedative did you put in that?" Lucivar asked.

She hesitated. "I wasn't sure how much to use for the Black, so I used the amount I would have used for you if you were in his place. Should be sufficient to help him relax enough to sleep for a while."

Lucivar nodded. "It was enough." And wasn't too much.

He saw Nurian out and watched her fly to her eyrie. Then he checked on Daemonar and Titian, who were playing hawks and hares, a children's card game. Crouching, he balanced on the balls of his feet, his wings tucked tight. "Your uncle Daemon isn't feeling well and needs to sleep awhile."

"We'll be quiet," Titian said.

"I know you will." He kissed their foreheads before going to the kitchen to talk to Marian.

"Are you going to tell Surreal about this?" Marian asked, taking the soup off the stove.

"Don't you think she already knows?" he countered.

"Did you know he was feeling this bad?"

"Shit." He liked Surreal. Loved her as a sister. Would throw everything he was into protecting her and Jaenelle Saetien. Had been willing to stand against Daemon when Surreal learned she was pregnant and wasn't sure she wanted to marry the man who had become the High Lord of Hell when Saetan became a whisper in the Darkness. But he wasn't blind to the fact that Surreal could be a prickly bitch at times and had her own emotional scars. And he wasn't blind to the fact that, while Daemon and Surreal loved each other, they weren't, and never had been, in love with each other.

The Birthright Ceremony and acknowledging paternity didn't always make things easier between a man and a woman, but he hadn't sensed any serious trouble between them. Just the opposite, in fact. He'd just have to visit the Hall more often over the next few weeks and consider if he'd been wrong about that.

"If it looks like I need to talk to her, I will," he finally said.

He kept an eye on the children and set the table for dinner while Marian fed and changed baby Andulvar. And he wondered what it might mean to all of them if Surreal *didn't* know about Daemon's headaches.

Tersa followed a path only she could see as she wandered the courtyards and corridors inside the massive structure known as the Keep. Built inside the mountain called Ebon Askavi, the Keep was the repository of the Blood's history— and the lair of Witch, the living myth, dreams made flesh.

She was aware of the watchers—the Seneschal, some of the demon-dead, and the shadowy beings that guarded the Keep—but no one tried to stop her as she looked for the place she needed to reach before she said what she'd come to say.

Finally, she found the garden sleeping under a thin layer of snow, in a part of the Keep that was usually inaccessible without an invitation.

Shivering, she closed her eyes and reached out with everything in her—power, mind, and heart—and sent her plea as deep into the abyss as she could.

"I'm here about the boy. My boy. Daemon." Her shattered mind wanted to wander the paths of memory, but she fought hard to stay in the present, fought to find the words that would convey the message she needed to deliver. "He's not well, but he doesn't recognize the signs, doesn't understand the warning. He'll try to chain the reason he isn't well, and the shattered chalice you mended will crack more and more and more, and the High Lord will not be here when he's most needed. And he will be needed. I saw it in a web. He will be needed. Please help him. The cracks have already started, but the girl doesn't see the signs, doesn't understand the warnings, won't be able to help. Please."

Exhausted, empty, Tersa opened her eyes and noticed

the witch who stood in the doorway, watching her. An old woman. A Gray-Jeweled Queen. Demon-dead.

"It's time for you to go, Tersa," the witch said.

An old woman. And then not old as the shards of Tersa's mind formed a new pattern, veiling the old woman with the memory of a younger one with spiky white-blond hair and ice-blue eyes—and legs that had been damaged by poison and the desperate healing that had followed.

"Time to go," the witch said again—gently, because she, too, was a Sister of the Hourglass and understood about dreams and visions.

As Tersa shuffled her feet to take the first step away from her chosen spot, she heard a whisper rising from deep, deep, deep in the abyss.

If he asks for help, I will answer. But only if he asks.

"Thank you," Tersa whispered as she walked toward the Gray-Jeweled witch. "Thank you."

The Keep's Seneschal and the witch gave her food and hot drinks before arranging for a Coach and driver who could ride the Winds and quietly return her to her cottage in Halaway.

"Thank you," she whispered again once she was home and tucked in her own bed. "He'll ask. Perhaps not soon enough to mend all that gets broken, but he will ask."

NINE

Dillon riffled the stack of silver marks and eyed the red-faced, Purple Dusk–Jeweled Warlord who stood on the other side of the desk. If pushed, he could win a fight, since his Opal outranked Purple Dusk. But he'd spent just enough time around the man's daughter to realize winning wouldn't be in his favor. That was no reason to let the man off easy. He had expenses, after all.

Dillon riffled the stack of silver marks again. "Looks like your daughter has played this game so often her value is going down."

"How dare you . . . ?" the Warlord blustered.

"There was a promise of a handfast, which is a binding one-year contract of marriage." Dillon pitched his voice to carry anger and disappointment he didn't feel. "There were two witnesses who heard your daughter invite me to her bed and her subsequent agreement to a handfast when I refused, and we had a Priestess ready to perform the ceremony before you intervened."

"Someone pretending to be a Priestess," the man countered, making a slashing motion with one hand. "The whole thing was a poor jest, nothing more."

"Then I'm the injured party, played by a jade who enjoys compromising men's honor."

"I've heard about you, Lord Dillon. You don't have any

honor." The man looked triumphant when he said the words.

The words cut deep, which only made Dillon more determined to walk away with a full purse.

"If I take this to the District Queen, your daughter will have to explain the 'jest' that was intended to lure me into her bed, and you know how a formal complaint can fuel gossip—especially when it's not the first time a girl has been accused of this 'jest,'" Dillon said.

The man looked at Dillon with equal measures of fear and hate, confirming the accusation. Then he called in another stack of silver marks and threw them on the desk.

So. The girl's father had been hoping to bluff him into taking less to make all the unpleasantness go away.

Dillon picked up the second stack of silver marks and vanished both stacks.

"You got your payment, Lord Dillon. If I hear *anything* that smears my daughter's reputation . . ."

"No one will hear anything from me." *And may the Darkness help the next fool who falls for your daughter's game.* "But I will say, sir, that I've heard you're hoping your daughter marries into another aristo family of equal standing to yours. If that's the case and is one of the reasons you're trying to smear *my* reputation, I hope your daughter ends up with exactly the kind of man she deserves."

The flicker of distress in the man's eyes told Dillon he'd slipped the verbal knife into the right spot. If the daughter married the kind of man she deserved, her life would be a misery.

He walked out of the man's study, walked out of the house, walked several blocks before hailing a horse-drawn cab to take him to the modest hotel that had been home for the past few weeks.

He kept his anger and his growing despair tightly reined during the ride to the hotel and for the few minutes when he was in view of other people. He bade acquaintances a good day, helped an elderly Lady and her granddaughter into the cab he'd just left, smiled at the clerk at the desk.

By this evening it would be all over town, although whispered behind hands, that the handfast had been a *jest* that he had taken seriously. There would be sympathy for someone who had fallen for the ruse, but every young man from a minor aristo family would breathe a sigh of relief when Dillon and his tarnished reputation left town.

No one wanted to sit at a table with a moral lesson.

Once he reached his room, Dillon locked the door and put an Opal shield around the room to assure he wouldn't be disturbed.

He opened a bottle of brandy, settled in the room's small sitting area, and drank straight from the bottle. Drank until he needed to breathe.

After making careful inquiries in a place that aristos didn't frequent for honorable reasons, he had found a witch who could teach him the "if you loved me" spell—and didn't want to know who he was or where he came from. It had cost him almost every mark he had, which made him wonder if the spell had become some kind of fashionable game among the wealthy Blood families because no one else could afford it, and bored aristos might think it amusing to see whom they could coerce into doing something otherwise unpalatable.

For a moment, as the brandy gave him a fuzzy kind of clarity, he wondered if he should report the use of this spell. He had the names of some of the men who had been damaged by Blyte's use of it, but whom could he tell? If this was some fashionable aristo game, how could he be sure that whatever Queen granted him an audience wasn't also playing? And if she was playing and didn't want anyone to know—because, fashionable or not, it was a sordid game—would he live to see another sunrise?

The only thing he could do right now was use the spell on a girl before she used it on him. He'd been one step ahead this time. The girl had known what he'd done, but his Jewel was sufficiently darker than hers that she couldn't resist him. Besides, if she'd said anything, he would have countered that *she* had tried the spell on *him* and it backfired. That would have opened up questions about her previous liaisons—something her father preferred to hide beneath substantial payoffs.

He could continue targeting aristo bitches whose fathers would pay him to disappear, but he was already tired of pretense, tired of lies. He wanted the chance at a real future, not a continuation of these games. He wanted honest work. He wanted a real handfast as a first step to proving he *could* be a good and faithful husband. He needed both those things to restore his reputation and remove the stain on his honor.

He wasn't going to find either of those things in a Rihland city that catered to aristos. If he was going to be successful, he'd have to settle in some out-of-the-way place and find a girl who was sufficient to his needs and then use the spell for a little while—just long enough to make her love him.

TEN

*F*our *pegs, each one as big around as the palm of his hand. A loop of leather went around each peg, one end of the leashes that were attached to the choke collar around his neck. He had to keep the leashes tight, so very tight, to protect the people he loved from what he was. It should have been all right. It had always been all right. Hadn't it? But now, as the leashes tightened, so did the collar around his neck, choking him until he couldn't breathe.*

His heart pounded, pounded, pounded in a way that would damage it eventually. His lungs burned with the effort to draw a breath, but he had to keep the leashes tight because . . .

A hand slapped his shoulder hard enough to sting, and a voice said, "Kiss kiss."

Gasping, Daemon looked at the witch now standing beside him. "Karla."

"Prince Idiot."

A flash of temper. One leash relaxed a little; the strangling collar loosened a little. He sucked in a breath and studied the witch who had been the Queen of Glacia—and one of Jaenelle Angelline's closest friends.

She looked old. She looked the way he remembered her in the last years of her life. White hair, lined face, a body that was still straight-backed yet growing frail. But the ice-blue eyes had never changed. He hadn't been the High Lord of Hell when she made the transition to demon-dead, but he'd known she had settled in Hell near the Gate that was closest to Glacia, in order to keep track of her adopted daughter—Della—and Della's children and grandchildren.

"What are you doing here, Karla?"

"What am I doing here? What are you doing here? This is supposed to be my vision, my dream, my tangled web." She looked at the pegs, at the leashes, at the collar that had bruised his neck. "Then again, you're the one who's in trouble. You need to loosen those leashes before you ruin yourself."

"I have to stay in control," Daemon protested.

"Not this much. You've never held the leashes this tight. No one could for long."

"I can. I will."

The leash that had loosened a bit with his flash of temper tightened again, choking him.

"And what price will Kaeleer pay for this self-indulgence?" Karla asked.

Daemon smiled a cold, cruel smile as one particular leash relaxed around its peg. Unlike the others, this one was leather braided with chain. This one held the Sadist in check.

"You do not want me to slip this leash," he said too softly. "Not this one."

"And you don't want to snap this leash along with the rest of them when you start fighting to survive," she replied, sounding too damn reasonable. "So loosen another one, Sadi."

"They're all there for a reason."

"Yes, yes, yes. Temper. Power. Sexual heat." She waved a hand at the chain and leather. "And whatever that one keeps in check."

"I'm a Black-Jeweled Warlord Prince. I have to keep power and temper under control."

"Not under this much control. Not all the time. But if you truly believe you have to keep power and temper so tightly leashed, at least loosen that one." She pointed to the leash he held on the sexual heat.

"You want me to turn all of that on a woman? You want to see every woman around me begging to be mounted? I don't." Even the thought of it reminded him too much of being a pleasure slave and added cold claws to his temper.

She smacked his shoulder again, making him snarl.

"Dream. Vision. Me, who was never impressed with the wiggle-waggle even when I walked among the living. What's done here won't matter, so do it now."

Allowing that leash to go slack around the peg, Daemon drew his first full breath in . . . How long had it been?

Sweet Darkness, had he really been holding on too tight? And when had that leash frayed to the point of breaking, leaving him in less control than he'd realized? He couldn't be around other people if the heat wasn't under control. He certainly couldn't be around Surreal, since the heat continued to upset her.

"You have your own bedroom, don't you?" Karla asked as if she'd heard his thoughts. Maybe she had. As she'd pointed out, he'd somehow landed in her dream vision, not the other way around.

"I do."

"Breathing room, Sadi. You need it. You're too damn dangerous to indulge in being foolish."

Daemon looked thoughtful. Then he shook his head. "I can control it."

"Until you can't."

Karla blinked. Sat back in her chair and stared at the tangled web of dreams and visions. Uneasy, she pushed away from the worktable and used Craft to glide across the room to the small table that held a decanter of yarbarah and a ravenglass goblet. She filled the goblet, then created a tongue of witchfire to warm the blood wine.

Tersa's plea hadn't been directed at her, but that didn't matter. She had heard, and Tersa's concerns about Daemon Sadi had been troubling enough that she had woven her own tangled web.

The demon-dead were not supposed to interfere with the living. When he'd been the High Lord, Uncle Saetan had held that line. All right, he had smudged the line when it came to his own family, but being Jaenelle Angelline's adoptive father had been necessary, and he'd needed the help of his eldest son, Mephis, as well as Andulvar and Prothvar Yaslana—especially after he ended up being the honorary uncle for Jaenelle's First Circle.

No, the demon-dead were not supposed to interfere with the living. But couldn't the new High Lord of Hell have advisors who no longer walked among the living even if he still did? Couldn't he have the relief of talking to old friends whose only interest in Kaeleer was their concern for him? Couldn't he be allowed the luxury—and necessity—of expressing his feelings to someone who had no reason to fear his temper?

"The time will come when you'll be needed. I hope you can stay in Hell that long."

"Well, Sister, it looks like you were right." Karla raised the goblet in a salute to the friend who wasn't there. Of course, if Jaenelle still walked the Realms, Daemon wouldn't be descending into this troubling state of mind.

How could she tell him his control was slipping when his reaction would be to try to tighten that control even more—which would only fray the leashes of his self-control faster until either the leashes snapped or his mind shattered? If his mind shattered, there was no one in the Realms anymore who was strong enough or gifted enough to heal him.

The sexual heat seemed to be the sticking point, but

why now? And why, if Tersa had seen something similar, had she come to the Keep to beg for help from someone who didn't exist anymore instead of telling her son to ease his control of the sexual heat and put up with the annoyance of women—and men—lusting for him?

Unless Tersa's tangled web had revealed more than Daemon's excess of self-control. Unless Tersa had seen something coming that would require the intervention of someone who didn't exist. At least, everyone believed Witch didn't exist—except, it would seem, a broken Black Widow.

"Song in the Darkness," Karla whispered. "Are you more than that, Sister? If the need is great enough, can you be more than that?"

Which brought her back to the question of what to do about Sadi.

She could tell him what she had seen and let him do whatever he liked with the information. Or she could wait and keep watch. Whatever was coming, Daemon would need some old friends, but he wouldn't go looking for them. She'd just have to be in a place where she would be easy to find—a place where he couldn't avoid finding her.

Having made that decision, Karla drank the rest of the yarbarah, cleared away her tangled web, and went to talk to Draca, the Seneschal, about taking up residence in the Shadow Realm's Keep.

Daemon woke in the dark, heart pounding, throat feeling bruised. Where . . . ?

Feeling overheated, he sat up, tossing aside the bedcovers as he used Craft to create a small ball of witchlight.

His bedroom at SaDiablo Hall. His room.

By the time he'd returned to the Hall from his trip to Ebon Rih, Surreal had retired for the night, and he'd had no desire to disturb her—and even less desire to tangle with her temper. Time enough in the morning to discuss Jaenelle Saetien's misbehavior and the whole nutcake incident.

Getting up, he went to the window and pushed aside the heavy winter drapes that Helene and her staff had hung in the bedrooms recently to keep out the cold. The moonlight shined through the glass—and the chill from the glass whispered over his skin, a refreshing sensation after the bed's heat.

He drank water straight from the carafe Jazen brought up each evening when the valet came in to turn down the bedcovers. Daemon thought it was an unnecessary bit of work, since he slept with Surreal most nights, whether or not they had sex, but he knew better than to interfere with any household routines and requirements. He might own the Hall and pay all the bills, but the place ran according to the dictates of Helene, Beale, and Mrs. Beale—and skimping on one's duties was *not* acceptable.

Leaving the drapes open, Daemon drained the power from the witchlight and returned to bed. He stretched out, ignoring the covers as he tried to recall the odd dream he'd been having just before he woke. Something about Karla? Why would he dream about Karla? Couldn't remember. Besides, he felt languid, lazy, better than he'd felt in weeks.

The feel of cool air against his bare skin was almost as sensual as a lover's caress, and he was just floating back to sleep when the door between his bedroom and Surreal's opened. His mind registered her psychic scent as he breathed in her physical scent—a scent heated by lust.

"Surreal." Too languid and lazy to have any interest in sex, even with a woman who had entered his private domain, he drifted toward sleep again.

Then she climbed on the bed, took his cock in her mouth, and worked him until he swelled to an edgy lust that equaled her own, until he was hard and hungry and needed to be ridden. Spurred by her hunger, he welcomed the pricks of pain from her nails as she impaled herself on him and rode him to a climax that took them both to the razor's edge of marrying pain to pleasure.

When she was done, she didn't settle next to him to cuddle or talk or even sleep. She didn't say a word. She simply dismounted and went back to her room, leaving him to wonder what had just happened—and why.

Surreal washed away the smell of sex—and him—before putting on a fresh nightgown and getting into her own bed. Then she grabbed fistfuls of her hair and pulled, hoping the pain would settle her, would help her think past the wanting that was twisting into something terrible.

Daemon had always been a demanding lover. He wore the Black and was a Warlord Prince, so that wasn't surprising. He'd always been a wonderful lover, enjoying the pleasure he gave almost more than his own. He also liked to play, and while that play never physically hurt her, ever since the night when she'd found herself in bed with the Sadist, having sex with Daemon—even being around Daemon—frightened her, because he made her so needy, so desperate for his touch, his kiss, that she couldn't think past *feeling*.

He swore the sexual heat was leashed, but she knew that wasn't true. It was *more* now, always more, wrapping around her like a cocoon of soft fur that imprisoned, took away choices.

That was what the Sadist did—wrapped his victims in desire that they couldn't escape. Didn't want to escape until it broke them. Ruined them. Destroyed them.

She should talk to him again, should demand an explanation for why he was continuing to play with her like this. Like tonight, going to his own room without saying anything. Then that sexual heat drifting from his room into hers, and her waking with hard nipples and a wet need between her legs that wouldn't be slaked by anything but him.

She had entered his room, ignoring the danger of being there, not sure if she intended to tell him to stop or to take her, but that one word purred in that deep, smooth voice—"Surreal"—took the decision away from her, had her working him, riding him. And leaving him. Escaping before the Sadist woke and decided to play with her.

She should talk to him in the morning and insist that he stop this game. But she was afraid, so terribly afraid, that if she forced him to admit that he had turned sex into an addictive torment, he would apologize with genuine sincerity—and never touch her again. And that was a torment she didn't want to endure.

ELEVEN

Jillian dumped a pile of clean diapers at one end of the wooden table in the laundry room, then started folding the dry baby clothes. Daemonar and Titian were eating breakfast, and Marian was taking care of baby Andulvar. That gave her a little time to complete some chores before she escorted the children to the Eyrien school.

She liked Lord Endar, but she had learned everything he could offer. How much longer did she have to sit in a classroom, listening to the same lessons over and over and over? But if she didn't go to school . . . When she was younger, she'd wanted to be a guard, a warrior, but she wasn't sure she wanted that anymore. And she wasn't interested in the other work that was usually pursued by Eyrien women, so what was there to do? She liked Marian, but she didn't want to be someone's helper forever. She wanted . . . She didn't know what she felt, didn't know what she wanted, didn't know . . .

"What's wrong with you?" Daemonar asked, approaching the table but not getting too close.

"Nothing is wrong with me." What did it say about boys that Daemonar, a Warlord Prince who wore a Green Jewel, could plunge his hands into the guts of a deer but got squeamish about touching a diaper—even a clean one? "If you've finished your breakfast, you should clean your teeth and get ready for school."

"Something is wrong," Daemonar insisted. "You've been acting . . . odd. You've been acting like . . . a *girl*."

Her hands clenched on the little shirt she had just folded. If she didn't say something, he would keep poking at her until she hit him or started crying, so she said the one thing she knew would rout him. "I used to change your poopy diapers, boyo, so don't you get bossy with *me*."

She watched color rush into his face, darkening his light brown skin, before he rushed out of the laundry room.

Bitch, she thought as she finished folding the shirts. She grabbed the pile of little trousers and kept her head down as she felt the return of a male presence. Then, angry with herself for being bitchy and angry with Daemonar for pushing her into being bitchy, she turned and said, "Look, boyo . . . Oh." She pulled her wings in tighter, an instinctive reaction when facing an adult Eyrien male. Lucivar Yaslana had a hot, volatile temper, but it was seldom displayed inside his own home. Remembering that, she offered a wobbly smile. "Is there something I can do for you, Prince?"

Lucivar studied her a moment before he started folding diapers.

Relieved to have some of his attention off her, Jillian folded more of baby Andulvar's clothes.

"You should start thinking of another argument, witchling," Lucivar said as calmly as if he were pointing out something of interest on the mountain. "Right now the boy is of an age where he's embarrassed that he needed diapers and doesn't want to think about who changed them. In a few more months—or years if you're lucky—he'll still be embarrassed, but he'll set his heels down and fight . . . and he'll fight harder for being embarrassed."

"It's none of his business."

"You're probably right." Lucivar gave her a smile that

she knew meant trouble. "But now it's my business. So what's wrong?"

Trapped. Excuses like being late for school or needing to do *something* that would get her away from him wouldn't work. A glance at him told her everything she needed to know—the relaxed wings, the easy stance, the lazy smile. Anyone who didn't know him wouldn't realize he was prepared for a brutal fight. And right now she was the opponent he was focused on.

"I don't know," she said, her voice barely audible.

Lucivar went back to folding diapers. "You must have some idea."

"I don't!"

They folded clothes in silence for a minute before Jillian blurted out, "I broke the permission-before-action rule. I kissed Tamnar. And he kissed me back."

"Oh?" Lucivar didn't look at her, just kept folding diapers.

"It wasn't intentional. It just sort of happened. And that's all we did, so we barely broke the rule."

"And?"

She was down to matching little socks and wasn't sure how long she could spin out the task. "And what?"

"Did you like it?"

Relief that he wasn't roaring at her made her head swim. "It was all right. I think Tamnar liked it more than I did." She instantly felt disloyal. Tamnar was her friend, and it wasn't his fault that kissing him hadn't felt wonderful or exciting. Except . . . "Who else is there to kiss?"

Lucivar folded the last diaper. "That is a question, isn't it?" A beat of silence. Then he looked at her. "Shouldn't you be getting ready for school?"

"Yes, sir." He was letting her go. He wasn't going to push. She hurried out of the room but stopped when he said, "You didn't eat this morning. Get some food in your belly before you leave here, so your legs don't give out. Understood?"

Maybe feeling dizzy wasn't all due to relief. "Yes, sir."

As she passed through the eyrie's kitchen, Marian

handed her a hollowed-out roll filled with scrambled eggs, bacon, and cheese.

"You know he'll ask you if you ate anything, and you know you can't lie to him," Marian said quietly. "If he was willing to use Craft to pin his sister's chair to the table and keep her there until she ate enough to satisfy him, he won't hesitate to do the same to you."

Lucivar's sister had been Jaenelle Angelline, the Queen of Ebon Askavi. Jaenelle could have exploded Lucivar's defensive shields and torn him to pieces, despite his Ebon-gray Jewels, but he still was willing to fight her into the ground if he thought she was ignoring anything she needed to do to stay healthy. Which made no sense, on the one hand, since that kind of fight would have left both of them badly injured—or worse. But knowing he was willing to do exactly that usually had the Queen backing down or negotiating a compromise.

Unlike Jaenelle Angelline, she wasn't powerful and she wasn't a Queen. She'd have no chance to make her own choices if Lucivar started paying that much attention to her.

Jillian took a small bite of her sandwich. Marian smiled in sympathy and shooed her out of the kitchen.

"I'll be back in the afternoon to help with the baby," Jillian promised.

She collected Titian, ignored Daemonar's surly looks, and made them wait—him especially, since he'd been the one who had tattled to his father—until she finished her sandwich. Then they flew to the eyrie that had been converted into a small school.

Lucivar's chest tightened as he watched Marian walk into the laundry room. His darling hearth witch was ill, and there was no denying it even if he pretended along with her that it was just something that happened sometimes after a hard birthing and she would recover.

Pretending because that's what she needed from him

didn't mean he wasn't acutely aware of every aspect of his wife's health—and would fight her with everything in him if that's what he had to do to keep her safe. To keep her with him.

"I don't know what to do for the girl," he said as she wrapped her arms around his waist and settled against him. "How can I help her if she can't tell me what's wrong?"

"She's not a girl," Marian replied. "She can sense the sexual heat now, so she's not a girl."

"Well, as sure as the sun doesn't shine in Hell, she isn't old enough to be considered a woman." He tried, unsuccessfully, to keep temper and frustration out of his voice. Marian didn't need either of those things. Not from him.

She looked up at him and smiled. "Is that transformation from boy to man as hard on your gender as girl to woman is for mine?"

"Not a question I'm going to answer." When she laughed, he rested his forehead against hers. "She kissed Tamnar, which Rothvar and I already figured out. Kissed him without permission, which explains some of her moodiness and the boy's lack of concentration when he's been sparring."

"It was mutual, wasn't it?" Marian sounded concerned. "I can't imagine Jillian taking advantage of a boy—and certainly not a Warlord she's grown up with."

"It was mutual, but I think Tamnar is going to be disappointed if he hopes Jillian will continue to help him practice his kissing technique."

"There aren't any other Eyriens their age," Marian said.

"I know that." Just as he knew how limited the choices were for his own children finding Eyrien partners.

"Did you know what you wanted to be at her age?"

"I wanted to survive." By the time he was Jillian's age, he'd realized that wasn't something he could take for granted. He was a half-breed bastard in the Eyrien hunting camps, and every man in those camps wanted to put him in the dirt, wanted to believe he was nothing. Problem was that the boy was already a better fighter than most of them, and the boy grew up fast and hard and deadly. "I'm a Warlord Prince. We're born to fight—and to kill."

"I had dreams when I was her age," Marian said quietly. "I wanted to get out of the Black Valley, wanted to get away from the drudgery of caring for my mother and sisters, since they made it clear that my being a hearth witch was a family embarrassment and I was beneath their notice—unless I didn't do a chore they wanted done right that instant."

"Bitches," he said just as quietly. He hadn't met any of Marian's family. He still hoped they would be foolish enough someday to come to Ebon Rih and try to contact her. Even if they weren't that foolish, they would die eventually, if they hadn't been swept away decades ago in Witch's purge of the Realms, and then they would end up having a chat with his brother.

"Being a hearth witch, there are skills I've had since I was very young, and there is work that attracts me. So my dreams had a shape. But Jillian is a young witch who hasn't found her passion yet, and I think this valley is starting to feel small. She doesn't fit in with the Rihlander girls who are her equivalent age. She might one day, but she doesn't now."

"What am I supposed to do? Let her be moody and unhappy?"

Marian rose on her toes and gave him a light kiss on the lips. "For now."

Lucivar studied the concern in her gold eyes. "What?"

"Are you going to check on your brother today?"

"Wasn't planning to. I have a full day of work in Ebon Rih. Besides, if I show up today, he'll think I'm worried about him."

"Aren't you?"

He sighed. "Yeah. I am. But that's not something I can tell him." *Just like I can't say how much I'm worried about you.*

"You could tell him that Nurian asked how he was feeling and if he'd like her to make up another batch of those healing herbs for him to take when the headache is just coming on."

"I'm not going to lie to him, Marian."

"It wouldn't be a lie if you actually asked her."

That would give him an excuse to see Nurian and ask about other things as well. "I can do that."

She gave him another kiss and stepped back. "You're lingering and about to start fussing. Go to work, Lucivar."

"I'll bring something from The Tavern for the midday meal." She would "forget" to eat during the day if he wasn't there, so he made sure he swung back home to feed her. She was still nursing the baby and he could see the weight slipping off her—weight she couldn't afford to lose.

He flew to the communal eyrie, where Rothvar and the other men waited for him to review the day's list of duties. Once the other men headed out, he flew to Nurian's eyrie.

"Prince Sadi?" she asked as soon as Lucivar entered the room where she made her tonics and healing brews.

"He's fine as far as I know. I just wanted to check if he could get another batch of those herbs. . . ."

"He's run out already?" Nurian sounded alarmed. "I gave him enough to make up several healing brews. If he's run out—"

Lucivar raised a hand to stop her. "I just wanted to let him know you would do that if he needs more." His eyes narrowed as he watched the tension leave her shoulders.

"Of course," she said. "My apologies, Prince. I made the mixture strong, since his headaches were so severe, and it shouldn't be used in excess." She thought for a moment. "And it shouldn't be used by anyone else. You would be all right with that mixture, but not anyone who wears a Jewel lighter than Ebon-gray."

"I'm sure he wouldn't leave the jar unshielded, but I'll have a word with his valet just to be safe. Right now, I'd like to encourage him to use the stuff, but I'll say something to him if it looks like he's using more than he should." He gave Nurian that lazy, arrogant smile. "Now, Healer, is there something I should know about my wife?"

She hesitated. "I've told you everything I know, Prince. I won't deny that I'm concerned, but Marian isn't the only woman whose recovery after having a baby has taken longer than is usual. It happens. There is nothing for me to heal, nothing to mend."

"She's fading, Nurian. She's hidden it well, but she's fading."

"I know. All I can recommend is food and rest—and time to let her body heal on its own."

He wasn't sure that would be enough, but he knew Nurian was doing everything she could—and he suspected everything she could do wouldn't be enough.

As he stood in front of Nurian's eyrie, he looked toward the mountain called Ebon Askavi. A century ago, there had been someone else he could have asked for help, *would* have asked. But maybe there *was* someone there now who could help. It wasn't his place to challenge visitors who came to the Keep. The vast library and historical records drew scholars and historians from all the Territories in the Realm. However, the appearance of someone wearing a Gray Jewel was bound to catch his attention.

His visit to the Keep didn't take more than a handful of minutes to confirm that, yes, Lady Karla was now in residence and would be staying for the foreseeable future.

He didn't think Draca could actually foresee the future, but considering who and what she was, he wouldn't have bet on it. Didn't matter at the moment. The sun was up, which meant Karla, being demon-dead, was at rest until the sun went down. He would return then, since Karla had not only been a Queen and a Black Widow; she'd been a strong Healer who had learned some of her healing Craft from Jaenelle Angelline.

Nothing he could do right now for Daemon or Marian, so he dealt with the work of ruling Ebon Rih. If worry was the whip that pushed him to work harder, to work until his body ached with fatigue, it was no one's business but his own.

Daemon knocked on the door and waited to be acknowledged before entering Surreal's bedroom. Staying near the door, he tucked his hands in his trouser pockets and watched her transfer the folded clothes on the bed into a trunk.

"Going somewhere?" he asked quietly.

"I'm going to check on the family's other estates," she replied, not looking at him.

"Again?"

"Yes. Again. I'll be back in a few days."

Will you be home and back under my protection before your moon's blood begins to flow? He'd done a quick calculation that morning while he was in the shower and wondered if her mood last night—and apparently this morning—had a simple explanation. While she *should* be safe at any of the SaDiablo estates, she knew it was easier for him to allow other males to be around her during the vulnerable days if she was here at the Hall or staying at the family's town house in Amdarh, where he could count on the staff to assist in protecting her.

He studied her stiff movements, which usually meant she was primed for a fight. It wouldn't be prudent to mention her moontime, but perhaps he could make things easier for her.

"Would you like help draining some of the power from your Gray Jewel?" he asked. Since she couldn't use her power during those first three days of her moontime, her Jewels needed enough of the reservoir of power drained to make room for the power that needed to be channeled out of her body.

"No, I already took care of that." She looked up from her packing but didn't quite look at him. "But thanks for the offer."

She'd already drained the Gray? How?

"Surreal." He took a step toward her, then stopped when she instantly snapped to attention, her right hand curling as if holding a sight-shielded weapon. Which was quite possible. "What's wrong?"

"What could be wrong?" she countered.

That evasion instead of giving him a straight answer confirmed that there *was* something wrong, because Surreal didn't evade. Something wrong with her? Was she hiding a secret from him for the same reason he was hiding the severity of his headaches from her? Because neither of them wanted to add another problem to a marriage that was turning sour?

"You're running away. That's not like you."

"Maybe I don't want to get in the middle of this ongoing pissing contest you're having with Jaenelle Saetien over nutcakes," she snapped.

"It's not about nutcakes. It's about an attitude she's trying on that can't be allowed to continue."

"Whatever it's about, I don't want to deal with it. Is that clear enough?"

"Very." His voice cooled, his temper responding to hers. "My apologies for disturbing you. Have a pleasant journey."

She picked up a stack of underclothes and threw them into the trunk. Then she wrapped a hand around the bedpost, as if she needed help staying on her feet.

Daemon crossed the room and had her in his arms before she drew another breath. They sat on the side of the bed, silent, while Surreal shuddered with the effort to regain control.

"I'm all right." She pushed at him, but he didn't let her go. "Sadi, I'm all right."

"Would you like to try a more believable lie?"

She hesitated. "I don't want to fight."

"Since when?"

She laughed, but it was a reluctant sound. "I just need some time on my own. That's all."

"You would tell me if this was something more?" he asked quietly.

"Of course."

She should have known better than to lie to him when he was holding her, when he was so attuned to her body and her emotions.

He kissed her cheek and left her bedroom, then went down to his study to review paperwork and write a brief note to Beron, warning him that Manny and Mrs. Beale would be expecting him to bring his appetite when he came to visit. He seldom worried about the young Warlord, who had resided in Amdarh ever since Beron had been deemed old enough to live on his own and study to be an actor. Understanding how fast the leash could be tightened if he didn't keep in touch with the patriarch of the family, Beron had always been a good correspondent. And while he had his own lodgings, he took advantage of the SaDiablo town house, staying over at least one night a week, which guaranteed he would be well fed for one evening meal and the next day's breakfast. It also guaranteed that Daemon would hear any significant gossip or concerns about Beron, since Helton, the town house's butler, would report any activity or association that might endanger the young man's well-being.

Daemon hesitated. Should he ask Beron to spend a few extra days at the family's town house when it was most likely that Surreal would be staying there? Helton would defend Surreal with everything in him, but it would be easier on everyone who had to deal with a Black-Jeweled temper if there was a male member of the family in residence during Surreal's moontime.

He felt the absence of the Gray and knew the moment when his wife and second-in-command stepped on the stone landing web in front of the Hall and caught one of the Winds to ride to whichever estate was her first destination. Still, he waited for Beale to enter his study and inform him that Lady Surreal had left.

"Jaenelle Saetien has gone to school?" he asked.

"She has." Beale waited a beat before adding, "The young Lady was keenly disappointed in the lack of breakfast pastries this morning, which I'm sure you'll notice when you come in for your own breakfast."

Daemon set his pen in its holder and sat back. "Is this lack of pastries because of my instructions not to provide dessert or treats, or did Jaenelle Saetien do something to piss off Mrs. Beale?"

"The young Lady made one or two imprudent remarks."

Hell's fire. Maybe Surreal had the right idea when it came to abandoning this particular field of battle. Except he couldn't. Wouldn't.

He also wasn't foolish enough to ignore Beale's warning that the staff had noticed what he was— and wasn't— eating and soon would come to their own conclusions about his lack of appetite.

Pushing back his chair, he said, "I'm sure I won't notice a lack of pastries while I'm tucking in to whatever dishes Mrs. Beale has prepared this morning."

As he followed Beale to the dining room, he noticed Morghann and Khary trotting out the front door.

"They didn't accompany Jaenelle Saetien to school?" he asked.

"They did not," Beale replied.

That troubled him, because Scelties didn't hold on to grudges. Not when they loved the person who had made the mistake.

"Beale." Daemon stopped outside the dining room door. "Was I too harsh? I hadn't intended to cause a schism between Jaenelle Saetien and the Scelties over a nutcake."

"I would not presume to have an opinion about how you raise your daughter, Prince," the butler replied.

"If my father had asked you that question, would you have offered an opinion?"

Beale looked him in the eyes—a reminder that no matter what Beale did for a living, he was a Red-Jeweled Warlord.

"Like your father, you understand the need to draw lines when behavior is inappropriate," Beale finally said. "In my opinion, you were not too harsh with the young Lady."

Relief washed through Daemon. At least he had one ally. But . . . "With Morghann?"

"Whatever you said to Morghann is not the problem." Beale sighed. "Trust betrayed is harder to forgive than a shared mistake."

Yes. "Thank you, Beale."

Opening the dining room door, Beale said quietly, "You can thank me by appreciating the breakfast Mrs. Beale prepared for you."

He felt a little fragile this morning, but the headache wasn't threatening to return in full force, so he found his appetite and appreciated the breakfast sufficiently to please his staff.

Before he returned to his study to deal with more paperwork, Daemon wandered the Hall, checking on the shields that were woven into the building's stones—protection for everyone living there against anyone foolish enough to launch an attack.

All secure. And yet Surreal's comment about having drained her Gray scratched at him. He'd have felt any spell or use of Craft that required that much power. Unless . . .

Down and down and down through the cellars beneath the Hall until he came to the corridor that led to the door to his father's private study. His private study now.

Like Saetan, he was a Black Widow and had the snake tooth and venom sac beneath the ring finger of his right hand. Like Saetan, he had been trained in creating the Hourglass's tangled webs of dreams and visions—and trained in the creation and use of poisons, although most of *that* knowledge he had acquired on his own.

This study deep beneath the Hall was the place for the darker aspects of ruling Dhemlan and its people. It was the place for the creation of the darker kinds of Craft. It was not a place for weakened shields.

His hand moved just above the stone walls on either side of the door. He hadn't been down here for a while, hadn't felt the need to visit the study. An error.

Had Surreal thinned these shields for a reason, or had she chosen this part of the Hall because it was so out of the way that she thought using the shields here to drain the Gray would go unnoticed? It was tempting to follow her to the family estate she intended to visit and demand an answer, to ask why she was choosing this method of draining her Jewels instead of the personal contact he had offered. But he wouldn't ask the question, wouldn't demand an answer. Not until he figured out what was going wrong between them. For now . . .

Black power flowed into the shields, replenishing them and wiping away all trace of the Gray. The next time Surreal came down here, she would realize he had discovered her secret. And he might discover one or two other things as well, based on what she did—or didn't—say.

Marian opened a secret drawer in the sewing cabinet Lucivar had given her when she'd still thought she was his housekeeper and nothing more. The cabinet held fabrics and skeins of yarn and all the other tools and supplies she used for the handcrafts and weaving that she enjoyed doing in her spare time.

It also held a simple wooden box that contained Jaenelle Angelline's last gift: a piece of a clear Jewel no bigger than her thumbnail. A special spell inside the Jewel made it look translucent black.

"I made this for you, so don't use it for anyone else," Jaenelle said. *"It won't work for anyone else."*

"What is it?" Marian asked, studying the Jewel.

"It's a healing spell. Put the Jewel in a mug and pour hot—not boiling—water over it. The hot water will release the spell. Let it steep for five minutes to release the whole spell and turn the water into a healing brew. Five minutes. No more. Time it carefully and make sure you drink all of it. This isn't meant for something as simple as a head cold or a fever. It can be used only once, so keep it until you need it most. You'll know when that day comes."

Marian lightly pressed a hand against her belly. Had Jaenelle seen this in a tangled web of dreams and visions? Had she known there would be complications from a birth that would occur years after she was gone?

The pregnancy might not have happened. Lucivar had agreed to put aside the contraceptive brew because she'd wanted one more child, but this particular pregnancy might not have happened if he'd been away from home during that cycle of fertile days. A different pregnancy, a different outcome. And whatever Jaenelle had seen wouldn't be more than a vision of what might have been.

But Jaenelle had seen something, had known a day would come when something would go wrong inside Marian and had gifted her with a way to make things right.

Was this the time? There were fewer and fewer days when she had the strength and energy to do more than take care of the baby. There were fewer and fewer nights when she wanted more from Lucivar than the warmth of his body and the unspoken assurance that she wasn't facing this unknown illness alone.

Was it time?

"Don't leave it too late, Marian."

Even when it took a while, women recovered from hard birthings. Maybe she was expecting too much from herself.

Maybe she was afraid to make a choice because she didn't know what to expect—and all Jaenelle could tell her was the healing would depend on why the spell was needed and would continue for as long as required. Which meant she might be bedridden for days, caught in whatever way the healing manifested.

Was it time?

Winsol was a few weeks away, a time of happiness and celebration. A time when the family gathered together. She didn't want to shroud the Blood's most important celebration with however the healing would manifest itself.

"Admit it," Marian whispered. "You're scared. You don't want this to be serious enough that you need Jaenelle's gift."

She'd give her body a few more weeks to recover by itself. If she was still unwell after Winsol, she would use Jaenelle's gift and make the healing brew—and hope that postponing this decision wasn't going to be a fatal mistake.

TWELVE

Anticipating his father's arrival, Dillon set the box of carefully wrapped gifts next to the trunk of clothes. He hadn't been able to afford much and had spent more than he should have for these Winsol gifts.

During the weeks leading up to Winsol, he had gone from one town to the next, reluctant to use the "if you loved me" spell on girls whose families couldn't afford a decent payoff and might agree to a handfast because even a minor aristo would enhance their social standing. He couldn't see himself spending a year with any of those girls—and their families. And the aristo girls he might have targeted for money looked at him like cats looked at mice—something to play with until it was too broken to be amusing.

He'd ended up in a small village where he'd found work in a sweetshop, of all places, and had settled in to do some honest work. The owner of the shop, a Warlord heading into his twilight years, had been pleased by his enthusiasm and glad to have employed a young man who wanted to learn all aspects of the trade.

Then the bitches found him. Not the girls from merchant families who had thought he was shy because he didn't flirt. No, it was the bitches from the handful of aristo families in the village, who must have talked to someone who had talked to someone. Oh, the first couple of times they came in, they bought the chocolates and other sweets. Then they made it very clear to the owner that they expected to be able to buy something else as well—and if they couldn't buy the services of that particular sweet, well, a shop depended on the perceived quality of its merchandise, didn't it?

He didn't blame the owner for dismissing him. After all, one of the bitches was a second cousin to the District Queen who ruled that town. The owner couldn't even lodge a complaint about a verbal threat when it would have been his word against an aristo's. And for what? To defend a young man who might have been a good worker but whose reputation was already sullied?

Now he was back to counting coppers and needing a new place to live. If the bitches had found him at the shop, it wouldn't be long before they found his lodgings. Whether he opened the door or barricaded it against them, the result would be the same. He would be shunned by the other tenants, and the landlord would want him gone before a respectable place to live became smeared with a reputation for being a kind of brothel.

A quiet knock. Dillon's pulse raced until he recognized the psychic scent of the man on the other side of the door. Filled with relief, he rushed across the room. His father was here, responding to the letter he'd sent. He was going home for Winsol.

He'd barely opened the door before his father slipped into the room.

"Cold out there," his father said.

"Yes. Well, it's Winsol." Unease began to replace the relief when his father wouldn't look him in the eyes. "Let me take your coat."

"No, no. I won't be long."

"Of course. I'm all packed."

His father looked at the trunk and the box of gifts. "Ah."

"Sir?"

"I'm sorry, Dillon, but we can't have you staying with us over Winsol."

The room spun once. "What?"

"Some of our social engagements are with families of quality. Those are important connections for your brothers."

"All right." Dillon swallowed bitterness. "I don't have to attend any parties or—"

"Just you being in the house might give some people the wrong idea." His father's voice took on a wheedling tone. "You understand."

"But it's Winsol." It wasn't about going to parties. It was about taking quiet walks and being with family. "If I can't come home, where am I supposed to go?"

His father smiled sadly. "If it was my decision . . ."

Except you haven't made a decision in a lot of years, have you?

"We have to think of your brothers," his father added. "We have to protect their reputations."

Dillon felt something break inside him. Felt some part of himself die—and wanted to inflict an equal amount of pain.

"Like father, like son," he said quietly.

His father looked puzzled—and nervous. "I don't—"

"I can count, *Father*. Early baby?" Dillon shook his head. "I don't think so. I think my being born seven months after you married Mother proved to everyone that you were doing more than cuddling before the marriage contract was signed."

His father paled.

"While it might have proved sufficient vigor to sire offspring, it also showed a lamentable lack of restraint." Dillon smiled. "How much did your father pay her father to get that marriage contract signed so that your actions wouldn't smear *your* brothers' reputations?"

"Now see here!"

Bluster without power. Why hadn't he realized that until now?

"If a whisper were to start in certain circles that your moral weakness was a flaw you had passed on to your sons—*all* your sons—what do you think would happen to those promising invitations?"

"You wouldn't!" His father stared at him. "You would ruin your brothers?"

"If you had stood up for me the way your father stood up for you, would we be having this discussion?"

His father sputtered. Dillon smiled and waited.

"You're no son of mine."

He'd expected that verbal thrust and blamed the sentiments of the season for the words hurting so much. "In that case, *sir*, let's discuss what your sons' reputations are worth to you."

Dillon counted the gold marks. One thousand in the first envelope. That was the one his father had brought as "compensation" for his not being allowed to come home. The three thousand gold marks in the other envelope had arrived an hour ago. Which of his uncles had been tapped for the loan? Didn't matter. His uncles had sons, too, and four thousand marks wasn't a high price to pay to keep the reputations of all the males in the family from getting dirty. A scandal from a generation back shouldn't have caused that much worry, so maybe his brothers and cousins weren't quite as pristine as his father wanted him to believe.

He'd find a quiet village and use a different name. He could be a young widower whose cherished wife had died after a swift illness that the Healer was unable to identify in time. He could take those quiet walks and avoid people. He could purchase a stack of books and spend his evenings reading. He could smile sadly when invited to participate in festivities. He could do that.

And no one would wonder why he wore loneliness like a heavy cloak.

✦ ✦ ✦

Surreal stood beside Daemon as he listened to another Province Queen struggle to find things to say in order to keep his attention a little while longer. He gave no indication that he knew why these women were struggling or why women whom he'd been on good terms with a year ago now looked like they wished to do nothing but rub themselves against him.

She could have told them to be careful of such wishes.

Since the Province Queen had to deal with Daemon in his role as the Warlord Prince of Dhemlan, she would be cautious. She would be wary. And she would wonder if the Prince was meting out some subtle form of punishment.

Lately, Surreal wondered the same thing.

Despite his insistence that the sexual heat was leashed, it continued to smother her, made her helpless and desperately needy—and resentful. An hour ago, he'd humiliated her by arousing her so fiercely that she'd come when he'd done nothing more than brush his fingertips across her palm. No matter how hard she'd tried to hide her response, she was sure everyone in the room had recognized what had happened. Some of the women might have thought it was terribly romantic to be so consumed by a lover, but it wasn't romantic. Not anymore. Now it was just terrible. And the cruelest part was the baffled look he gave her, as if he didn't know what he'd done.

She hadn't been paying attention to the words, but she heard the sharpness in Daemon's reply and knew the Queen's unwitting—and, most likely, unwilling—sexual interest had honed his temper.

"Let's dance," she said abruptly, slipping her arm through his. "If you'll excuse us, Lady?"

"Of course." The Province Queen looked relieved, as if she'd been pulled away from a steep cliff that had been crumbling beneath her.

Surreal swore silently when she realized the dance was

a waltz. Better for the rest of the people in the room—
certainly safer for them—but a misery for her. Still, she
smiled at the women who looked at her with envy and
greed and ambition and let her smile say: *Look at that
beautiful face, that body. Listen to that voice so deep and
dark and luxurious, and imagine what it's like when he
comes to your bed and whispers all the things he'll do to
you. You may look but never touch, because he's mine. I
won the prize, and I'm going to keep him.*

"Another hour should be enough to fulfill our official
obligations, don't you think?" Daemon asked as they
moved with the other dancers.

"It's up to you." She gave his face a quick study when
he looked past her. "You all right, Sadi?"

"I have a headache."

"That's usually the woman's excuse." She wanted to
kick herself when he looked at her, confused. "The clash
of perfumes is making my head a bit achy too."

Maybe he wouldn't want to sleep with her tonight.
Did she want that when this need for him was building
again?

She'd loved him for decades—centuries, even—and
had never thought she could have him as a lover. Had never
expected to be Daemon Sadi's wife.

Lately, as she tried to endure this game he was playing,
she didn't know if she loved him or hated him. Sometimes
she wondered what would happen if hate became the dom-
inant emotion. After all, when she'd lived in Terreille, she
had been a very good assassin and sex had always been the
best bait.

*Karla studied the crystal chalice. It had been shattered
twice and expertly repaired.*

*More than repaired. It had been healed with a skill that
no longer existed in the Realms. Oh, the seams between
the individual pieces were still visible, were, in fact, filled*

with a hairline of power that didn't come from anything as simple as the Black.

"It can no longer hold what it was meant to hold. Not completely."

Karla looked over her shoulder and watched Tersa walk into her web of dreams and visions. She turned back to the chalice. "If it shatters . . ."

"He will fall into the Twisted Kingdom beyond reach," Tersa said. *"The Black gone mad will bring terror to the Realms."*

"Will bring war."

Daemon Sadi, raging and insane, against armies of Warlords and Warlord Princes. And leading those armies . . .

"The winged boy will not turn against his brother," Tersa said. *"Even if the boy falls, the winged boy will stand with him."*

"Then may the Darkness have mercy on the living," Karla replied. *"And the dead."* Lucivar and Daemon at war with the rest of Kaeleer. The cost would be staggering. *"There must be something we can do."*

"Pain will lance the wound, but the blade isn't sharp enough yet."

Tersa walked around the chalice, then studied the four leashes that were wrapped around posts at one end and secured to the chalice's stem at the other. She pointed to something at the base of the chalice.

Karla looked closely to find the pinprick hole. As she watched, a tiny bead of Black power oozed out of the hole, hung for a moment, then fell on one of the leashes. Thank the Darkness it wasn't the leash braided with chain, but two of the other choices wouldn't be much better.

As she watched, the bead moved down the leash to the post. Or what should have been the post. What had been the post when she'd seen it in another vision not that long ago.

Now that post looked bloated, and the leash, instead of giving Sadi some measure of control, was being covered, like a tree might grow over a wire wrapped around its trunk. Except the spillage, the excess . . .

"He's fighting to survive," Tersa said.

"I told him he was holding on too tight. I told him to relax his hold on that leash." But when she'd said that in a dream, she hadn't seen *this*. Hadn't realized he was channeling Black power he couldn't hold and transforming it into more sexual heat than anyone could want or need.

"He doesn't know." That realization staggered her. "He thinks he's still holding the leash, that the sexual heat that surrounds him is the same as it's always been."

"Yes," Tersa agreed.

Karla went back to studying the challice. "Mother Night, he can no longer survive what he is. The only way for him to get through this is if he could somehow dilute the Black power that is an essential part of who and what he is so that he wouldn't stand so deep in the abyss." She looked at the mad Black Widow who was Daemon's mother. "Could he do that?"

"No," Tersa replied.

"Is there anyone who could do that?"

They looked at each other.

"Until he's the one who asks for help, there will be no answer," Tersa said softly.

"Even if he asks, how can he get an answer from someone who doesn't exist anymore?"

It disturbed her that Tersa didn't reply. Made her wonder again if, in her madness, Tersa knew something the rest of them didn't know.

"Could you tell Surreal?" she asked.

"The girl sees the warning signs but does not trust herself or the boy enough to speak. She has chosen not to listen."

"Can't you tell Daemon?"

"Tell him what? That madness will break him, and the price will be the destruction of Kaeleer? Should I tell him this when there is nothing he can do to stop it or change *it? Even his physical death won't stop this. Only one thing can stop this."*

"For the pain to become so great that he asks for the impossible."

"Yes."

"And Surreal? This will leave deep wounds in her too."

"Yes. But she could ask for help, for guidance, for counsel—and has not."

The air shimmered. The vision faded.

Hell's fire, Mother Night, and may the Darkness be merciful!

Karla poured a glass of yarbarah and drank it cold.

These weren't typical dreams and visions. She didn't usually interact with other people, didn't have these conversations.

Then again, the two individuals who had invaded the past two visions were also Black Widows, and one was broken and always lived in the Twisted Kingdom, and the other was starting to break and slide into madness.

According to Tersa, telling Daemon would be pointless, but maybe that just depended on who did the telling.

Prince Yaslana, she called on a Gray thread. *Your presence is required.*

She'd barely had time to pour and warm another glass of yarbarah before Lucivar walked into her suite. He gave her one sharp look, then scanned the room, stopping when he saw the tangled web still connected to its wooden frame.

"Problem?" he asked.

"How is your brother?"

"Still getting bad headaches. The herb mixture Nurian makes for him relieves the pain to some degree, but she can't find a physical reason for the headaches."

No, she wouldn't, Karla thought.

Lucivar closed the distance between them, his eyes never leaving her face. "You know why this is happening." It wasn't a question.

"I know there will be a price to pay before this is resolved, and it may be steep."

"I won't sacrifice my wife or children, but anything else . . ."

The Tersa in her vision had been right. If Daemon fell, Lucivar would go with him—and Kaeleer would lie in ruins by the time it was done.

"How is Surreal? Are things all right between her and Sadi?"

A flash of hot anger, swiftly controlled, filled the room.

"This hunt would be easier if you told me what kind of quarry I'm looking for," Lucivar said.

And this is why the dead shouldn't interfere with the living. And why Black Widows shouldn't meddle in other people's lives unless asked. We have no stake in the consequences of our words.

"I think Daemon's headaches are being caused by his keeping the sexual heat leashed too tight," Karla said.

Lucivar looked pointedly at the tangled web, then at her. "That's it?"

No, that wasn't all of it, but if Tersa was right about the rest and Daemon had to reach an unendurable threshold of pain in order to keep his mind from shattering, relieving any of the pain could be a mistake. She still felt Lucivar should know at least some of it. Since he wore Ebon-gray, he might see the warning signs of deterioration in Daemon faster than anyone else.

She sighed. "There is some indication that Sadi has . . . damaged . . . his ability to control the heat, and that might be causing some trouble between him and Surreal."

"Shit." Lucivar blew out a breath. "Well, it's Winsol, and in a couple more days all our official obligations will be met and the family will gather for a private celebration. I'll see if he and I can go off on our own for a few hours during that time. Or as alone as we can be with children and Scelties underfoot."

Lucivar took a step toward the door.

"I'm sorry I couldn't be more help."

He turned back. "I've known you since you were seventeen. I saw you through your Virgin Night. I know I'm the only man who has ever touched you that way. And I know when you're lying. Telling me about the sexual heat? You're just throwing ash in my face, making it hard for me to see the rest. You always talked straight, Karla. The fact that you're not doing it now means whatever you saw in that web scares you, and there is nothing you or I or anyone else can do about what's coming. So Daemon and I will do what we've always done: wait until we recognize the face of the enemy—and then fight."

And if the enemy's face is the one you see in the mirror?

"Let's hope it won't come to that."

"You go ahead and hope. I'm going home to sharpen my knives."

Once Lucivar was away from the Keep, Karla disposed of the tangled web.

Bad choice. Shouldn't have told him anything, especially during Winsol.

Nothing she could do now except hope that Daemon asked for help before the fighting began, because once it began, help, even if it came, would come too late.

THIRTEEN

Did I leave it too late?

Marian carefully set the clear Jewel that held the healing spell into a large mug and poured hot water over it. She immediately turned the five-minute hourglass timer, then struggled to think clearly for a few more minutes.

She'd made it through Winsol, feeling more frail with each passing day. She hadn't wanted to upset everyone during the Blood's most important celebration of the year, but she hadn't fooled the adults in the family. Lucivar, Daemon, and Surreal had said nothing, but they'd all watched her.

Someone should be here to watch her. Why hadn't she thought of that?

Lucivar? She should have said something before he'd left to check on the villages in Ebon Rih. She should have . . . *Lucivar!*

He was beyond the range of a Purple Dusk communication thread.

Nurian, then? But what if Nurian tried to stop her from taking this healing brew because the Healer didn't understand what it was and Marian didn't have time to explain?

She wasn't thinking clearly. Wasn't thinking . . .

Lucivar. Had to tell him, explain, something . . . in case the healing took a while.

She reached for a square of paper and the pencil she used to leave notes for her family. She looked at the sand running in the hourglass. Almost time.

Unable to hold the pencil properly because her fingers didn't work right, she tried to form letters, tried to think of what to tell him. *Lu . . . ci . . . var . . .*

No time to explain, no time to call for help. Either Jaenelle Angelline's healing spell cured the fading that had begun at baby Andulvar's birth or . . .

She wouldn't think about the alternative. Jaenelle had made the spell, so it would work.

As soon as the last grain of sand fell, she fished the Jewel out of the mug, wrapped it in a kitchen towel, and put the towel in a bowl. Taking bowl and mug with her, she retreated to her workroom. Besides the sewing cabinet, a worktable, and her loom, there were a daybed and a chair where she could rest or read. This was her private space in the eyrie, where she could enjoy solitude when she needed some. Lucivar insisted that no one was allowed to enter without her permission—and that included him.

The room, which usually felt cozy, now seemed impossibly long as she took step by shuffling step to the daybed. She drank the healing brew. When she tried to use Craft to vanish the bowl and mug, she discovered she couldn't do something even that basic, so she pushed the items under the daybed to keep the room tidy. Had to keep things tidy, had to . . .

She lay down on the daybed, got as comfortable as she could, and pulled up the two quilts she hoped would help her fight the sudden chill that seemed to wrap around her bones.

Then she felt herself fall into rivers and night skies and cold winter winds. Falling, falling, falling. Couldn't get her wings to open, couldn't stop the plunge.

She didn't think she was supposed to feel these things. Which meant she had squandered Jaenelle Angelline's last gift by waiting until it was too late.

✦ ✦ ✦

Lucivar finished his monthly review with the Master of the Guard in Agio, the Blood village at the northern end of Ebon Rih. A fist of Eyriens who worked for him was assigned to help defend Agio and the landen villages and farms that were under the hand of Agio's Queen, and he had no reason to doubt their loyalty or their willingness to stand and protect. But even the short-lived Rihlanders hadn't forgotten the stories about the Eyriens who had given their allegiance to Prince Falonar, Lucivar's former second-in-command, and who hadn't given any assistance to Agio's guards when the Jhinka had attacked. So he sat with the Master of the Guard once a month and listened to what was said—and what wasn't said.

"Sure you won't join me for the midday meal?" the Master asked.

"I appreciate the offer, but I have other stops to make," Lucivar replied.

"Well, then, I'll see you—" The Master's eyes narrowed.

Turning, Lucivar watched Rothvar fly toward them. Flying fast.

Rothvar backwinged hard and landed a man-length away, gave Agio's Master a curt nod as he approached them, then focused on Lucivar. "Anything else that needs doing here, I'll do it. You need to go home."

The tone, so close to a command, grated against Lucivar's temper—and he wondered if Rothvar was starting to turn against him, like Falonar had done.

"I still need—," Lucivar began.

Rothvar gripped Lucivar's arm hard, a fast move that had Agio's Master calling in a fighting knife.

"Lucivar," Rothvar said with quiet intensity. "You need to go home. Now."

Lucivar read the concern, the sympathy in Rothvar's eyes—and felt chilled.

Marian, he called. *Marian!* An Ebon-gray communication thread could reach far beyond the borders of Ebon Rih, but that didn't help him reach a hearth witch who didn't answer.

"Nurian?" he asked Rothvar.

"She's already at your eyrie. She sent me to find you."

He understood the message. Rothvar could have reached him on a Green psychic thread, could have told him to come home. But a Healer had sent a Warlord to find the Warlord Prince he served and deliver the message in person. That told Lucivar more than the words themselves.

"Go," Rothvar said.

Lucivar launched himself skyward, caught the Red Wind, which was the darkest Web within easy reach, and flew toward home and the woman who held his heart.

Jillian walked with baby Andulvar from one end of the front room to the other. Back and forth. Back and forth. The playroom or the family room would have been more comfortable—certainly warmer—but she needed to keep an eye on the other children while Nurian tried to heal Marian, and Daemonar wouldn't budge from the eyrie's front room. He just stood there, tears running down his face as he stared at the door, waiting for his father. And Titian clung to her elder brother. So no one was going anywhere until Lucivar returned or Marian . . .

She didn't know what had happened to Marian. Daemonar had shown up at Nurian's eyrie in a panic, saying the baby was crying and his mother wouldn't wake up. While Nurian rushed to Marian's side the moment they arrived, Jillian had been left to deal with a baby, a frightened girl, and an anguished Warlord Prince who had taken a long step away from being a boy.

As the minutes crawled by, Jillian watched Daemonar Yaslana age and harden, understood that this moment was one of the forges that would shape the steel and hone the blade of the man he would become.

As he met her eyes, she also understood that he would never again back down from a fight. Any kind of fight.

Lucivar entered the eyrie with a blast of controlled temper and cold air.

"Papa!" Daemonar took a step toward him.

Lucivar glanced at the boy and kept going, heading deeper into the eyrie. "Give me a minute, boyo. Then we'll talk."

He stopped at the doorway of Marian's workroom and took a moment to leash his temper, his fear, his everything. If Nurian was performing a healing, his power could overwhelm her efforts and destroy a healing web. And that might make the difference in whether Marian survived.

He entered the room carefully. So carefully.

Nurian knelt beside the daybed. She waited until he, too, knelt at his wife's side.

"I don't know," Nurian said. "It's like she's fallen into a deep healing sleep, but it doesn't feel like any kind of healing sleep I could create. It's more—and it's powerful."

"An attack of some kind?" he asked.

"I don't think so."

"Can you break it?" Lucivar watched Marian breathe. He wrapped his fingers around her wrist and felt the slow beat of her heart. Too slow?

Nurian shook her head. "Right now there's a chance she'll come out of this on her own. I just don't know what would happen if I interfered with this . . . living death." She sucked in a breath. "My apologies, Prince. That wasn't what I meant to say."

Wasn't what you meant to say out loud, but it was what you meant, what your Healer's instincts are telling you.

"Is there anything you need from me?" he asked. "Fresh blood for a healing brew?"

Nurian shook her head again. "Maybe when she wakes, but not right now."

"Then I'll see what I can do for the children."

He left the room as quietly and carefully as he had entered it, but he didn't go to the front of the eyrie, where Daemonar waited. Instead he went to the bedroom he had shared with Marian since the first time they'd made love. He closed the door and locked it.

Then he gathered everything in him and sent it on an Ebon-gray spear thread to the one person he needed right now.

*Daemon! *Daemon!** A hesitation before he admitted who might really be needed. *High Lord. Please.*

Looking at Morghann's hopeful expression and wagging tail, Daemon regretted that he hadn't used Craft to fetch the novel he'd intended to read for a few minutes before he returned to the stack of reports, post-Winsol social invitations, and a smattering of requests and complaints that were couched as backhanded compliments—not to mention deciding what he wanted to do about a few personal, and highly inappropriate, invitations. But he'd wanted to move instead of using Craft, wanted to stretch his legs by walking up to his suite in the family wing of the Hall.

He hadn't expected to be ambushed by a different kind of hopeful witch.

Play? Morghann asked.

"I can't, Morghann. I have to work."

More work? Big sigh.

"Why don't you go out and play with Jaenelle Saetien and Khary? They're playing in the snow. You would have fun."

Head down. Tail down. *I might do a wrong thing. There might be blame.*

You're still fixated on that?

Daemon stifled a sigh and swallowed a hefty measure of guilt. He'd lost count of how many generations of Scelties he'd helped raise, educate, and train, but this was his first experience with an insecure Sceltie. Or was she an overly sensitive Sceltie? Whatever the reason, that one incident with the nutcake a few weeks ago had seriously damaged the friendship between Morghann and Jaenelle Saetien and had made the pup fearful of doing *anything* without his prior approval.

She was young—that's what she was. She wouldn't go through her Birthright Ceremony until spring, so maybe she felt vulnerable.

She felt betrayed—that's what she felt. He knew it every time Morghann abandoned Jaenelle Saetien in favor of his company. He was the Prince, the power, the adult male who would teach her properly and wouldn't tell her to do a wrong thing. He made sure his instructions were clear and within her current abilities—and any correction was carefully phrased to rebuild her confidence while still teaching her.

If Morghann had made this choice earlier, he would have let it play out differently, would have accepted Morghann as a friend and companion in the same way that Ladvarian had been a friend and companion—and so much more—to Jaenelle Angelline. But Morghann was clinging to him now because she didn't trust his daughter, and he needed to help restore that friendship and at least some of that trust if he could.

He sank to his knees, sat back on his heels, and held out a hand. "Come here, little Sister."

She rushed to him, climbing into his lap and into his arms, happy to be held by the person she trusted more than anyone else.

He petted and soothed until her psychic scent told him she was calm enough to listen.

"Learning to play is important," he said quietly, continuing his soothing strokes. "That's why you should go outside and play with Khary and Jaenelle Saetien while I take care of the work I need to do in my study."

Ladvarian knew about human kinds of work, she said

timidly. *Ladvarian learned a lot of things when he lived with the Lady.*

Ladvarian was a legend among the Scelties—the first among them to know Jaenelle Angelline, the first to serve in her court. And he was the Warlord who had gathered the kindred who had stubbornly, and against all odds, saved Witch and brought her back to the living.

Brought her back to him.

Was Morghann's attachment to him just a sign of insecurity, or was she one of the Scelties who was inclined to learn about the human rules of business in order to help him with the school in Scelt that Jaenelle had created decades ago and he still oversaw?

She was young, but he could show her simple things—addition, subtraction—and see if she had any interest. Today, though, she needed a different kind of lesson.

"I would like you to go out and play," he said. He felt the resistance in her body. "Khary knows how to play in snow. He knows games you can play with human children. You go outside and learn from Khary."

Khary will not do a wrong thing.

"No, he won't. And after you play, you can come back and keep me company while I work. I'll show you one of the things Ladvarian learned from the Lady."

Her confidence momentarily bolstered, Morghann trotted out of his bedroom.

Feeling the Gray presence in the next room, he wished the trouble with his wife could be fixed as easily. He knocked on the door between their rooms and waited for Surreal's permission to enter—and wondered if he'd receive that permission. She finally used Craft to open the door in silent invitation.

"I have a meeting in Halaway," Surreal said as she tossed a dress with its matching calf-length coat on the bed.

He almost said that a meeting wasn't listed on the schedule of engagements that Holt kept for both of them, but he didn't want her making up an excuse for why the meeting wasn't listed or, worse, lying to him about whom she was meeting.

He didn't understand what was happening with her. The woman who hadn't hesitated to aim a crossbow at him a few months ago to make sure she had his undivided attention when they needed to talk was now unwilling to give him a straight answer about anything that touched on her thoughts or feelings. Her emotions were a maelstrom, especially in bed. She hid it well on the surface, but he'd always gone below the surface to gauge the mood of a lover, and she was anger coiled with lust. She didn't want tenderness anymore, even when he wanted to give it, needed to receive it. She still wanted—still *demanded*—sex, but she didn't want to make love.

"I hope the meeting isn't too tedious." He stepped close to her, bent his head to give her a light kiss on the lips— and felt her flinch.

Daemon! Lucivar, reaching for him.

He raised his head and noted Surreal's furious relief, but he focused on his brother.

Daemon!

He took a step back. Lucivar sounded upset. Frightened. Nothing could frighten the Ebon-gray except . . .

"Sadi?" Surreal said.

"I have to go to Ebon Rih." He hurried to his bedroom, intending to grab some clothes, aware that Surreal had followed him to the doorway. Then . . .

High Lord. Please.

Daemon stopped. Let his brother's fear and those words—*those words*—settle as a weight on his shoulders. Only one reason why Lucivar Yaslana, reaching out and afraid, would request the High Lord of Hell.

"Daemon, what's wrong?" Surreal entered his bedroom and grabbed his arm. She studied his face, his eyes. "Marian?"

"I think so."

"What can I do?"

At least in this they were still partners. "Have Jazen pack a couple of changes of clothes for me, and tell him to add additional clothing suitable for staying at the eyrie. And fetch Manny. Tell her she's needed at Lucivar's home."

"There are Eyrien women who can handle the children."

"I'm sure there are, but none of them will be able to handle Lucivar."

Daemon rushed through the corridors. The servants who saw him must have alerted Beale and Holt, because both were waiting in the front hall.

"Prince?" Beale asked.

"My presence is required at Prince Yaslana's eyrie," Daemon said as Holt helped him into his winter coat. "I may be there a few days."

"Prince Yaslana asked for your presence?" Beale asked quietly.

He looked his butler in the eyes, understanding Beale's question. Very few people knew for sure that he had become the High Lord of Hell when Saetan embraced the final death and became a whisper in the Darkness, but Lord Beale, the Red-Jeweled butler at SaDiablo Hall, was one of them.

"Not his brother's presence," Daemon replied just as quietly. "Mine."

Beale dipped his head in acknowledgment.

Daemon walked out of the Hall, went to the landing web, and caught the Black Wind to ride to Ebon Rih.

The land looked bleached of all color to the point that there were barely shades of gray. It looked . . . faded. It looked like Marian felt, like all the vitality that had once filled the land had been siphoned off, leaving little more than a failing memory of what it had been.

She remembered falling, but she didn't remember landing. Didn't remember how she'd come to be in this lost, fading place.

Then she heard the voice, the song. The song wasn't familiar, but she remembered that voice. Recognized that voice.

Not knowing what else to do, Marian followed the voice until she reached a cascade of black water spilling into a warm pool.

Surreal wasn't sure what to say when Tersa walked into Manny's cottage carrying a cloth travel bag. Since it wasn't likely that Tersa would think to pack clothes, the Darkness only knew what was in the bag.

"My boy will need me," Tersa said. "The winged boy will need me."

She couldn't argue with that. If Lucivar's call for help was an indication that Marian's illness had taken a turn for the worse, she would need all the assistance she could get to deal with Yaslana's emotions. She'd been too caught up in her own grief—and the aftermath of the first night she'd spent with Daemon—to remember what Lucivar had been like when his father died. By the time she'd seen him, her pregnancy was the paramount concern, and Lucivar had been Lucivar—arrogant, demanding, and ready to stand on a killing field if that was what it took to protect someone who was a member of their family.

Manny walked into the front room with her own cloth travel bag, looked at Tersa's, and said, "Mikal."

Hell's fire. She'd forgotten about the boy. Not forgotten, exactly, but she hadn't known Tersa would be coming with her, so no provision had been made for the boy.

Holt, she called. *Mikal needs to stay at the Hall for a few days. Tell him Manny and Tersa have gone with me to Ebon Rih.*

We'll take care of him, Holt assured her.

She hustled the two older women into the small Coach

she'd chosen for this trip. It was meant for short distances and didn't have a toilet or sink. Hopefully no one would need such amenities.

Or was she hoping for an excuse to delay their arrival by needing to set down in a village somewhere to accommodate an older woman's personal needs?

When had she become a coward?

When? It had happened on the day she'd realized that Daemon Sadi changed into the Sadist every time he saw her, spoke to her, made her desperate for him to take her.

Tortured her.

Lucivar knew the moment the Black arrived in Ebon Rih, knew by Daemon's psychic scent that his brother had understood the message. By the time he reached the front room, the High Lord of Hell walked into his home—but it was his brother who reached out and held him.

"Bad?" Daemon asked.

"She's unconscious. We can't wake her. Nurian says it feels like a healing sleep, but it's more, and it's powerful, and it's like nothing she's seen before. She thinks if we try to break whatever this is, Marian won't find her way back." Lucivar rested his forehead against Daemon's. "If the worst happens . . ."

"If her body dies, I will take care of her. If Marian no longer walks among the living, your children won't lose their mother. It's not like our family hasn't included the demon-dead before. Daemonar might not remember Andulvar, but he's old enough that he would have memories of his grandfather. We'll adapt."

"Right now, there's just a body in that room, not their mother. If the body dies before Marian returns . . ."

"Then I will find her. Whatever I have to bend or break in order to do that, I will find her and bring her back." Daemon's hand closed around the back of Lucivar's neck, both comfort and warning. "Do you understand me?"

Lucivar eased back enough to look at the man who held him. It didn't matter what the rest of the Blood called Daemon—Prince, High Lord, Sadist—for him there was one word that meant all of those things and more: brother.

"I understand you." He stepped back. "I'd better check on the children. Jillian's been looking after them, but I've left her on her own long enough."

As he turned to head for the playroom, Daemon fell into step beside him.

"I'll check the food supplies, bring in what we'll need," Daemon said.

Lucivar snorted. "Give it a couple of hours. Rothvar came to find me when Nurian was called to the eyrie. By now all the Eyriens in the valley and most of the Blood in Riada know Marian is very ill. I expect the casseroles, cakes, and other offerings will be arriving anytime now."

"Then I'll handle that while you concentrate on the children." Daemon hesitated. "You feel easy about Rothvar taking charge while you tend to things at home?"

"He's a good man—and an honorable one."

Lucivar knew why Daemon asked the question, and he knew Rothvar's life depended on his answer. Prince Falonar had been sent away to serve in a Rihlander Queen's court and had disappeared soon after. Most people assumed he'd gone into hiding somewhere in the Askavi mountains or, more likely, had returned to Terreille. Lucivar had always suspected that the man walking beside him was the only person who knew exactly what had happened to Falonar after he vanished from Lady Perzha's court.

They heard the baby fussing before they walked into the playroom. Jillian looked frazzled as she rocked the baby, and Titian rushed over to them the moment they entered the room.

As Lucivar hugged his daughter, he scanned the room. "Where's Daemonar?"

"He left a while ago to use the toilet and said he was going to wait with you until Prince Sadi arrived," Jillian said.

Lucivar looked at Daemon.

He wouldn't do anything foolish, Daemon said.

He found Marian, and he's upset. And the mountains could be a dangerous place, especially for a boy preoccupied with worry about his mother.

Daemon walked out of the room. By the time Lucivar untangled himself from Titian and offered half-assed reassurances to her and Jillian, Daemon met him in the corridor.

"The boy's not here," Daemon said.

"I am going to kick his ass all the way down the mountain for leaving and not telling someone," Lucivar snarled.

"Let's find him first. Why don't you fly over the mountains and see if you can pick up his psychic scent? He's probably tucked in a hidey-hole somewhere. I'll check the Keep and Riada."

"Let's try one thing first." Lucivar gathered a measure of the Ebon-gray and let power and temper thunder from one end of the valley to the other. *DAEMONAR!*

They waited. There were queries from the Eyrien men—some startled by his summons, some wary, and many responding with concern—but as the minutes passed, his son didn't answer.

If the boy had done something fatally careless, it could take a few hours for him to make the transition to demon-dead. He wouldn't be able to respond until then.

Cursing himself for not paying enough attention to Daemonar's whereabouts, Lucivar left the eyrie to fly over the mountains in search of his son.

Daemonar looked around and breathed a sigh of relief. He had reached the Misty Place. He never knew when it would happen, couldn't say what combination of need and feelings brought him here. He'd come to realize that if he wanted to be here but didn't *need* to be here, the problem was something he could, and should, figure out for himself—or ask for more ordinary help with.

But he always found this place when he really needed to talk to her.

"Auntie J.?"

The sound of a delicate hoof striking stone.

Daemonar turned, keeping his eyes focused at about knee height. Hooves came into view. Knees. Halfway up the thighs was the hem of a sapphire garment. That provided enough reassurance—and disappointment—for him to look at the rest of Witch, who had been the living myth and dreams made flesh. Still a myth. Still a dream. But no longer flesh. And never like this in the flesh. Except here.

He'd begun wishing that he hadn't been such a prudish little boy the first time he'd seen her in this form. She'd been naked that first time, unconcerned about a shape that revealed the Self that had lived within the flesh. Amused and a little baffled by his reaction, she'd created a garment to cover what the boy hadn't wanted to see.

He wasn't interested in the titties or the thatch of hair between her legs. He figured all girls had those things. But here, in this place, her golden hair was more like fur, and her hands had a cat's retractable claws, and there was the small spiral horn on her forehead. And there was that faun's tail visible through a back slit in the garment. Along with the delicately pointed ears, those were the things he could see, but what else was now hidden under cloth that he hadn't observed that first time?

Tiger and Tigre, Arcerian cat and unicorn, satyr and centaur, Dea al Mon. So many races had yearned so long for this dream that her Self reflected all of them. But the eyes, those ancient sapphire eyes, were the same as they had been when she'd walked among the living.

More than his beloved Auntie J., she was his Queen, always and forever. He knew it—and she knew it. That was why she allowed him to come here when he needed her.

"What's wrong, boyo?" Witch asked.

"Mother is sick. She's really sick, and she won't wake up. I found her."

She studied him, then turned her head as if listening to something only she could hear. Back to him, frowning. "Didn't Marian use the healing spell I left for her?"

"What?"

"A last gift. Did she use it?"

"I don't know."

A stone bench appeared. Witch sat and waited for him to join her.

He sat and leaned toward her. What he could see was nothing but a shadow, an illusion created by Craft and power. If he leaned against her, he would fall right through the shadow. If she, on the other hand, leaned against him, she felt real and skin touched skin. He didn't know why it was true; he just accepted. She had never been like everyone else when she had walked among the living. He saw no reason for her to be like everyone else now.

She leaned just enough for their arms to brush.

"When you found Marian, did you see anything that looked like this?" Witch asked. A black translucent stone floated in the air in front of them. "Or this?" The stone became clear.

Daemonar thought for a moment, then shook his head. "I wasn't paying attention to anything but Mother, but I don't remember seeing anything like that."

"Look around as soon as you can. If you find the stone and it's clear, then Marian used the healing spell, and that's why you can't wake her. She's in a healing sleep, and she'll wake when the healing is complete."

"What if I find the stone and it's still black?" Daemonar asked.

Sorrow in her eyes. "That means she left it too late and didn't have a chance to make the healing brew."

"Could we give it to her now?"

"No."

He didn't ask why. If Witch said it wouldn't help now, then it wouldn't.

She nudged him. "Your mother is not a fool. She wouldn't have wasted the gift by not using it when she needed it." She pursed her lips. "Where is your body, boyo?"

"At your cabin in Ebon Rih."

"Inside?"

He shook his head. "Only Uncle Daemon goes inside. He stays there sometimes. And Mother goes in once a month to clean. But no one else is allowed to go in."

"So you're outside?"

"Yes."

"In the cold. It's winter there, isn't it?"

"Uh-huh."

Hell's fire. She was getting that look—the one she got just before she whacked him upside the head for being stupid.

"Did you at least remember to put a warming spell around yourself so your body doesn't freeze to death while you're here?" Witch asked sweetly.

Sweetly was bad. Very, very bad. She didn't sound like syrup unless she was really pissed off. Of course, her sounding cold was even worse. Potentially deadly.

Fortunately, he had the correct answer. "Yes, I did. I put a warming spell on my cape and another one around me. And a bubble shield for protection."

Her lips twitched. "Worried about getting your ass kicked?"

He was more worried about her preventing him from visiting her anymore if he got careless with his body. "Maybe."

"Go inside next time. Or stay in your own room, where you'll be safe—and warm."

"Yes, Auntie," he said meekly.

Her silvery, velvet-coated laugh rang through the Misty Place. "Meek does not suit you, boyo."

He grinned.

When she stood, so did he, knowing this visit had come to an end. He always wished to stay longer, but he understood that the Misty Place stood so deep in the abyss it wasn't a safe place for him. For anyone. Except Witch.

"If I find the stone and it's clear, can I tell Papa? He'd want to know that Mother will get better."

Witch looked away and he wondered what she could see. Or what she had already seen.

"If you find the stone and it's clear, let someone else explain it to him."

"Who?"

"Oh, there are one or two people around who could explain it to him without getting into trouble—or having him ask awkward questions when it isn't time for him to hear the answers." She smiled. "Time for you to go, boyo."

He bowed, a Warlord Prince acknowledging his Queen. "Lady."

"Try to stay out of trouble."

"But I only get to visit when I'm in trouble."

She faded away, but her laughter lingered, surrounding him as the Misty Place also faded away.

Daemon stopped at the Keep to inform Draca and Geoffrey that Daemonar was missing and asked that they let him know if the boy turned up looking for shelter or a hot meal. If the boy was still missing by sunset, Draca would inform any of the demon-dead currently in residence and they, too, would join the search.

He didn't think it would be necessary. He knew where he would have gone for the illusion of comfort—where he still went several times a year.

He dropped from the Winds and landed in front of the cabin Saetan had built for Jaenelle Angelline when she was an adolescent—a solitary place on the outskirts of Riada where she could be Jaenelle instead of Witch or the Queen of Ebon Askavi. During the years when he and Jaenelle had been married, whenever they needed a couple of quiet days to be nothing more than a man and woman in love, they came here. Since her death, on the nights when he stayed here, he still dreamed that he slept with her, still smelled her unique scent on the sheets when he woke, even though he knew that wasn't possible. It didn't matter if it was self-delusion; the nights when he dreamed of nothing more than Jaenelle being there with her body lightly pressed against his back quieted something inside him that nothing else could—not even being with Surreal, despite his love and respect for the woman who was now his wife. In those dreams he felt that he could stretch a part of himself that was usually coiled and tightly leashed, could purr and show the claws he usually hid from the rest of the Blood.

In those dreams he could be everything he was in all of his terrible glory.

Sometimes he caught Lucivar looking at him, studying him, and knew his brother feared the day when the dreams stopped and nothing would quiet all that he was.

Pushing those thoughts aside, Daemon tried the front door and frowned. Still locked. He scanned the porch, letting a touch of his Birthright Red power drift over the floor and furniture in case the boy thought a Green sight shield would keep him hidden.

Nothing on the porch, but he did sense the Green nearby.

Since he wasn't about to wade through knee-deep snow to go around the cabin, Daemon used Craft to air walk above the snow, a neat trick Jaenelle Angelline had taught him long ago.

He found the boy curled up against the back door, unmoving. Taking the step that brought his foot just above the narrow back porch, he reached out, relieved to feel the Green shield—and frustrated, because he didn't want to destroy the shield unless the boy was hurt.

"Daemonar."

Daemonar raised his head and looked at him with eyes that held a familiar mix of emotions—grief, guilt, and, most of all, relief. And that made him wonder if, in this place, he was the only one who dreamed.

"Am I in trouble?" Daemonar asked.

"Let's just say your disappearance has exercised your father's temper."

"Everything has a price," the boy muttered as he stood up, his movements stiff from the cold.

Relieved that the boy hadn't done himself any harm, Daemon allowed annoyance to fill his voice. "Hell's fire, why didn't you go inside instead of staying out here to freeze?"

"No one is allowed to use the cabin."

The boy had a point. Daemon welcomed no one to this cabin, not even Lucivar, and barely managed gratitude and grace when Marian cleaned the cabin or left food for him. Of course, she didn't give him any choice. Cleaning the cabin had been one of the services she had performed for the Queen of Ebon Askavi. As long as the cabin stood, Marian would continue performing that service.

Daemon pointed to what looked like a slice of a tree trunk nailed to the side of the cabin. He pressed his fingers to the center. Using basic Craft, he lifted the inside half of the trunk, the separation skillfully made along one of the tree's rings so that it went unnoticed. He took out the key hidden in the back of the removed section and held it up.

"Key to the back door. Next time, use it." Daemon looked at his nephew and let some of his power whisper between them. "But only you. Understood?"

"Yes, sir."

Satisfied that the boy really did understand, Daemon replaced the key and fit the center piece of the trunk back into place. "You used a warming spell?" He hadn't sensed any Craft except the shield, but the warming spell could have been used up.

"Yes, sir. Two of them."

Since the boy was all right, it was time to contact Lucivar. *Prick? I found him. He's fine.*

He won't be when I kill him flatter than dead.

Flatter than dead had become a family catchphrase that indicated annoyed relief rather than true anger at a child's misbehavior.

We're going to stop for a hot drink and something to eat before returning to the eyrie, Daemon said.

Going to fortify him for the scolding when he gets home? Lucivar asked dryly.

As an indulgent uncle, what else would I do? Why did he get the impression that Lucivar was relieved to have him away from the eyrie a while longer?

No questions about where the boy had been found. There was no need. Lucivar would know everything when they talked later that day.

"Come on, boyo," Daemon said. "We'll stop at The Tavern for some soup."

"And hot chocolate?"

He should withhold the treat as a penalty for upsetting the adults, but today an occasionally indulgent uncle would learn more than a strict one. "And hot chocolate."

Surreal hung her clothes in the wardrobe and tucked her underwear in one of the dresser drawers before turning to Tersa. "Would you like me to help you unpack?"

Tersa dropped her travel bag next to the dresser. "The boy is sleeping in another room?"

"Yes. You and I are sharing this room." And a bed, since none of the guest rooms at the eyrie had two beds. She could squeeze a daybed into the room, but those were being used by Manny, who was staying in the baby's room, and Jillian, who was staying with Titian. Lucivar had said nothing when she told him she would stay with Tersa.

Maybe he had his own concerns about a broken Black Widow staying in an unfamiliar place without someone close by who would know if she woke up and wandered out of the eyrie. They were on a mountain, after all.

Lucivar hadn't asked why she didn't intend to sleep with her husband, an indifference she put down to his being preoccupied with Marian's illness and Daemonar's disappearance. She wasn't sure what Daemon was going to say about the sleeping arrangements.

She found out an hour later when Daemon and Daemonar returned.

"Is Daemonar all right?" she asked, staying just a step away from the door of the primary guest room while Daemon hung up the clothes Jazen had packed for him.

"He just needed some private time to think," Daemon replied.

He didn't look at her, but she could feel that sexual heat drifting toward her—a lure to compel her to give in to something she wanted to resist while they were at the eyrie. They weren't here for him to play his games. They were here to help his brother.

"You're sleeping elsewhere?" he asked mildly.

"Tersa came with us. Someone needs to keep an eye on her, and Manny is looking after the baby."

"You should do what you think best."

Something under those bland words. Something that might be dangerous.

"I do think it's best while we're here," she said, her voice sharp before she regained enough control to remember that courtesy was the way most of the Blood survived interacting with the most dangerous among them. "I'll let you finish unpacking while I figure out what to do with all the food that's arriving."

He turned and looked at her. She couldn't interpret what she saw in his gold eyes, but the door closing as soon as she stepped into the corridor—and the click of the lock—expressed his feelings quite well.

✦ ✦ ✦

Dressed in the flannel sleep pants he occasionally wore on cold winter nights, Daemon put a warming spell on the sheets before settling into bed. Just as well that Surreal had chosen to sleep elsewhere. If she'd stayed with him, she'd want sex, and he wasn't in the mood to oblige her.

His smile was sharp and a little bitter when someone knocked on the Black-locked door. Then Lucivar said, *Bastard?*

After creating a dim ball of witchlight that floated near the ceiling, he released the Black lock and sat up as Lucivar walked into the room and closed the door.

"Problem?" he asked.

Lucivar stared at a spot on the wall just past Daemon's shoulder. "I can't sleep in that bed. Not tonight."

His arrogant Eyrien brother seldom hesitated, but they both knew who had to extend the invitation.

Daemon lay back and raised his right arm. Lucivar came around to that side of the bed and tucked in beside him, laying his head on Daemon's shoulder. How many times had they slept this way over the years when one of them was wounded in body or heart? Protection and comfort. A silent promise that the one who was hurting more could rest because the other would keep watch.

Tonight that was Lucivar.

Daemon said nothing. Whatever was happening to Marian they would face together. As his fingers drifted through Lucivar's hair, he added a soothing spell that would ease his brother into needed sleep.

Once Lucivar fell asleep, Daemon allowed himself to drift toward his own rest. Then the door opened and Daemonar hurried in. The boy didn't even blink when he saw his father and uncle together. If anything, he looked relieved—and piled onto the bed, fitting himself against Daemon's other side.

"All the girls have someone to sleep with," Daemonar

whispered. Then he yawned, made a snuffling sound, and went alarmingly limp.

Before Daemon could decide if the boy was ill or really fell asleep that fast, Lucivar reached across and wrapped a hand around the boy's arm, a move so ingrained that neither Eyrien woke—and Daemon relaxed.

When Lucivar took Daemonar hunting on the mountain, he probably allowed the boy a lot of freedom to learn—and to make small mistakes. But at night, when they both needed sleep and the boy might make a potentially fatal move? Daemon imagined Lucivar kept a hand on his son as protection and would wake immediately if he sensed anything wrong.

Someday, when baby Andulvar was old enough to join them, he would sleep between father and elder brother, protected by both.

And hopefully, when that day came, they would return to the eyrie after a hunt to find Marian working in her garden or reading a book, whole and healthy and able to welcome them home.

Marian stood under the cascade of warm, soft black water. The song, that familiar voice, seemed to fall with the water, seeping into her skin, down into her muscles, through her bones right into the marrow.

She wasn't sure how long she stood under the water before she felt something trickle between her legs. Alarmed, she started to reach for herself when she noticed a fine black silt dripping from the ends of her fingers.

Stay, the voice sang. *Stay until the water runs clear. Stay until what doesn't belong is washed away.*

She felt a tickle, a trickle along her scalp, and tipped her head back to let the black water wash more silt away. And as she listened to the song, she stayed beneath the black water that washed away what didn't belong.

FOURTEEN

Propped on one elbow, Dillon watched the woman sleep.

He hadn't been looking for anyone during the days of Winsol, and it had taken him a couple of days to realize the witch who was a decade older than he had focused on him for more than brief conversation. He hadn't thought much of her interest in him until she began sharing her sad tale about the lover who had jilted her. They had been handfasted and were going to marry, were going to have children and be together forever. But he'd abandoned her, had packed up his things and had left *one minute* after the handfast expired.

After being with her a couple of days, Dillon didn't blame her former lover for running. He'd accepted her invitation for "company"—which, it turned out, had meant sex—because he was lonely and still hurting from his own family's rejection during the days of the Blood's most important celebration. In the days since then, he'd likened her to one of those plants that ensnared its prey and then sucked the life out of it.

She constantly compared him with her previous lover. Favorably, yes, but he felt like she was ticking off boxes on a list. Or, worse, was simply desperate to acquire another lover to prove the other man was wrong about her and whatever had been said wasn't true. What had, at first, seemed like a need for reassurance now felt smothering.

She'd asked too many questions about the cottage and village where he claimed to live, had pouted when he hadn't leaped at her suggestion of coming for a long visit, and had started making "teasing" remarks about him having another woman as the reason for his lack of enthusiasm. She'd mentioned too many times how she longed to have children, making him glad that he kept the contraceptive brew he used hidden and shielded. He wondered if she'd tampered with the brew her former lover used, intending to get pregnant and hold a child for ransom to ensure the man would dance to her tune until the Birthright Ceremony, when he would either gain legal rights to his child or be denied forever.

He'd told himself he wanted a handfast, wanted a way to begin restoring his reputation and honor. But not with her. All he could see with her was a year, or a lifetime, of misery.

He did want a handfast, but he didn't want to be the one feeling the knife's edge. Not again. He needed someone he could control.

His thankfully temporary lover opened her eyes, smiled, and reached for him.

Her fingers were skilled. But the desperation and calculation in her eyes confirmed that he needed to convince her to let him leave. Time to find out how well that spell worked and whether it was worth what he'd paid to learn it.

If you loved me . . . If you loved me . . . If you loved . . .

Surreal dreamed of hands that caressed her until she felt helpless with pleasure, dreamed of long black-tinted nails that were sharp as a razor slicing her thighs. She dreamed of her husband pleasuring her as he watched her bleed out—and woke in a panic, on the verge of a savage orgasm.

Using her own hand would take away the worst of the need, but it wouldn't satisfy. She'd learned that the hard way. Everything else was a pale substitute for Sadi's touch.

Tersa wasn't in bed, wasn't in the room. Surreal had no idea how long the Black Widow had been gone, but she'd find Tersa later. Right now her husband needed to fulfill one of his duties. The bastard.

Daylight but still early. She hurried through the eyrie's corridors to the primary guest room, grateful she hadn't run into anyone—and wondered why Lucivar, at least, wasn't up and about yet.

She didn't knock on the door. She just walked in and took a step toward the bed before she stumbled and stared.

Daemon in the middle of the bed, his chest bare, his face turned away from the door, his cheek resting against Lucivar's head. And Lucivar, asleep, his head on Daemon's shoulder, one arm draped across Daemon's belly.

Sadi and Yaslana didn't talk about their past—especially not their past with each other. She'd been a whore for decades before coming to Kaeleer, had accommodated the kind of sex play that required discretion. As she stared at them, she didn't wonder what they had been to each other in the past; she wondered if they still . . . indulged . . . on occasion.

Then, finally, she noticed Daemonar tucked in with them.

No matter what Daemon might do with his brother, she couldn't see either man playing any kind of sex game when the boy was in the room.

Realizing they'd slept together for comfort and not sex, when she desperately *needed* sex, made her furious with both men.

She didn't know how long she'd stood there, staring at them, when Tersa said behind her, "Puppies in a basket." Then Manny let out a huffing laugh and said, "Huh. Some things don't change." As if seeing Lucivar and Daemon together was nothing special—was, in fact, ordinary.

She'd been distracted by the older women for a moment, just a moment. When she looked back at the bed, Daemon still slept, but Lucivar's gold eyes were open and fixed on her—a predator assessing a potential adversary.

Surreal backed away. Turned and ran to her own room.

As she dressed, she tried to decide if she was distressed or relieved that the sexual heat that pumped out of Sadi these days had ensnared the Ebon-gray, even if it was for nothing more than comfort. What chance did she have of escaping if someone as strong as Lucivar could get pulled in?

Daemon pulled casseroles out of the cold box. One had eggs, ham, and some vegetables. Suitable for breakfast. He put that dish and another one in the oven to heat, then started making the coffee.

Marian's condition hadn't changed overnight. At this point, he'd take no further decline as a good sign—just as he recognized Lucivar's temper running sharp and hot as a sign of trouble. Something had sparked that temper. Or someone.

He'd picked up a hint of Surreal's psychic scent in the room when he woke. He didn't know who had still been in the bed or in the room when she walked in, but he suspected that her coming in and looking for a morning ride was the reason for Lucivar's temper. Not because she wanted the ride but because she didn't want to share a bed with her husband for any other reason.

Or had she seen them and said something? *Sweet Darkness, please don't let her say anything to Lucivar. If she wants to stick a verbal knife into someone, let it be me.*

Tersa wandered into the kitchen. He managed to get half a slice of toast into her and a couple sips of tea before she wandered off again. Lucivar had an Ebon-gray shield around the eyrie, effectively locking everyone in, so Daemon wasn't worried about Tersa beyond the usual worry of coaxing her into eating enough.

When Jillian entered the kitchen, with fatigue smudging the skin under her eyes, he said, "Scrambled eggs for the children?"

She blinked at him, and he watched her effort to wake up. "I can make them."

Daemon smiled. "No, darling, I can make them if you think the children will eat them. What about you? Do you want to eat the casseroles I'm heating for the adults, or would you prefer to eat scrambled eggs this morning?"

Being included with the adults perked her up. He poured coffee for her and spooned out generous portions of the casseroles for both of them. Her cheeks pinkened with pleasure over his attention. After finishing her own breakfast, she took a tray for Nurian so that her sister, who had arrived a few minutes ago to check on Marian, could have a quiet meal before resuming the duties of a Healer; then she returned a few minutes later to make up a tray for Manny, who was watching the baby.

Daemon stood at the counter, eating the food out of necessity but not enjoying it. Right now, food was just fuel for the body, and he needed to be at his strongest to deal with Lucivar today.

Daemonar entered the kitchen, looking not as worried as Daemon expected the boy to be but more than willing to reduce the amount of food currently hot and available.

Except the boy set his plate on the table and made no move to eat.

"I guess you got squashed with me taking up space last night," Daemonar said, staring at his plate.

"Your aunt Jaenelle and I used to share a bed with an eight-hundred-pound Arcerian cat. Compared to Kaelas, you don't take up much room."

Daemonar took a bite of the ham-and-egg casserole. "All that fur must have been nice in the winter. Warm."

"Yes, it did provide warmth." Daemon sipped his coffee, wondering if the boy was fishing for something or just making an observation. "Arceria is so cold and has so much snow in the winter, the Arcerian cats build dens under the snowpack, and there is still enough snow above the dens that a grown man could walk over them and not fall through. Despite that, the damn cat used to whine about Jaenelle's feet being cold."

Daemonar grinned. "Did you whine about Auntie J.'s cold feet?"

"Husbands do not whine about cold feet."

"If they're smart, they put a warming spell around their legs before their darlings scramble into bed and put those feet on them," Lucivar added, walking into the kitchen.

"How do you learn things like that?" Daemonar asked.

Daemon looked at Lucivar. They looked at the boy and said, "Experience."

Daemonar pushed away his plate, the food uneaten. "I want to help watch over Mother."

"No," Lucivar said.

"Of course," Daemon said at the same time. "All the Warlord Princes in the family should take a turn. If you're finished with breakfast, why don't you take the first watch?"

As he expected, Lucivar turned on him as soon as the boy left the kitchen.

"He's too young to see his mother like that," Lucivar snarled.

"He knows something, Prick," Daemon said softly. "He found out something yesterday and he's been searching. When he volunteered to dry the dishes last night, he tried to be subtle—"

Lucivar snorted.

"—but he was looking through the cupboards for something. He didn't find it. I think he wants to look around Marian's workroom without us asking questions."

"What could he be looking for?" Lucivar asked.

Daemon filled a mug with black coffee and handed it to his brother. "We'll know that when he finds it."

Daemonar opened the doors and drawers of the cabinet that held all of his mother's sewing and weaving supplies. A Jewel the size of the one Auntie J. had shown him could be hidden anywhere, tucked into a skein of yarn or hidden in folds of cloth. It could even be in a jar of buttons. He couldn't sense any power, so he'd have to take everything out, and if he couldn't put it back as she'd had it, his mother would kill him flatter than dead.

If she ever woke up.

"Looking for secrets?" Tersa asked.

Daemonar suppressed a yelp. He hadn't thought she'd noticed him when he entered the room. She'd been staring at Marian and hadn't responded when he'd greeted her, leaving him free to poke around.

He approached the chair next to the daybed and considered what he could say. You never lied to Tersa. That was one of his father's and uncle's strictest rules, because Tersa's hold on the world as the rest of them saw it was tenuous. But she *was* a Black Widow, and Witch *had* said there was one or two people who could explain things to his father once Daemonar found the clear Jewel. Could Tersa be one of them?

"Yes," he said. "There is something I need to find. A gift Mother might have used before . . ." He looked at Marian.

"Nothing on, nothing over. What is left?" Tersa looked at him expectantly.

Was she seeing this room or some other place? Was this a riddle or an actual question?

Nothing on. Nothing over. He scanned the furniture around the daybed. Someone would have checked the covers already and there was nothing above the bed. So what was left?

"Under." Daemonar dropped to his hands and knees and looked under the bed. "Found something."

As his hand closed around the mug, it occurred to him that his mother might have needed to use something as a chamber pot if she'd been too ill to move or call for help.

The mug was empty, a dried stain at the bottom that looked like some kind of tea or witch's brew. The bowl had one of the kitchen towels. Since it was dry and didn't smell, he sat back on his heels and had started to unwrap the towel when the door opened and his father and uncle walked in.

"What did you find, boyo?" Daemon asked.

He glanced at his father, who stood behind his uncle, as if not daring to come closer. Better to talk to Uncle Daemon, who knew lots of things about the Hourglass's Craft. "I'm not sure. It depends."

Daemon went down on one knee beside him. "Open it."

He unwrapped the towel and breathed a sigh of relief.

"A clear Jewel." Daemon sounded puzzled. "Why have a clear Jewel here? They're only used as beacons on landing webs."

"They can have other uses," Tersa said. "Can hold a different kind of beacon."

"A trap or a spell of some kind?" Lucivar asked, sounding like there were shards of glass in his throat.

"Not a trap." Tersa stared at the clear Jewel. "A beacon holds special kinds of healing spells. This one . . . Dark water washes away what doesn't belong. Dark water—and a song in the Darkness."

Lucivar sucked in a breath. Daemon tensed, and the room suddenly filled with a yearning that made Daemonar want to cry—or reveal a different secret.

"Tersa?" Daemon said softly. "You've seen something like this before?"

"She gave me some beacons before she left the Realm

of the living. Like but not the same. A special brew that helps Tersa find the path back to the boy and the winged boy and the Mikal boy when Tersa wanders too far. She saw. She knew." Tersa laid a hand over Marian's. "Once the black water washes away what doesn't belong, the hearth witch will be shown the path home."

"So we wait," Lucivar said.

"We wait," Daemon agreed.

Tersa pointed at the clear Jewel. "The beacon must be returned to the Keep. That is part of the bargain."

Daemon rewrapped the Jewel in the towel, vanished it, then tapped Daemonar's shoulder. "Come with me." He looked at Lucivar.

Daemonar wasn't sure what was said on a psychic thread, but as he walked out of the room with his uncle, he looked back to see his father kneel beside the daybed.

Daemon kept a hand on Daemonar's shoulder as they walked through the eyrie toward the front room, where Lucivar would join him in a few minutes. There were so many questions he wanted to ask, *needed* to ask. But he couldn't ask any of them.

Did you talk to her? Can you see her?

Witch had told him after Jaenelle Saetien's Birthright Ceremony that she wouldn't come to him again, because he needed to stay connected to the living. But when he stood in the Black at his full strength, she was a song in the Darkness, a reminder that he wasn't alone. He had to accept that was all she could—*would*—give him.

He wouldn't jeopardize whatever gift Witch had granted the boy, but there might be a way to find specific answers to this particular puzzle.

"You probably saw one of those clear Jewels when you were younger," he said, keeping his tone conversational. "You would have seen them used in village landing webs and could have wondered what other use might be made of these smaller pieces. Your aunt Jaenelle might have explained that pieces of clear Jewels could be used to hold spells for a long time."

Daemonar said nothing, but he felt the boy tensing under his hand.

"Things you'd been told, memories of seeing Jewels like that, might have woven themselves into a dream, which is how you thought about looking for the thing that had contained an unconventional healing spell. Does that sound possible?"

"Yes, sir."

"That's what I thought." Daemon felt the boy relax a bit. "Why not tell your father and me? We would have helped you look for it."

Hesitation. He and Lucivar needed to get to the Keep before the sun got much higher, but he hoped his brother wouldn't walk into the front room just yet.

"I didn't want to tell him unless the Jewel was clear again," Daemonar finally said.

"If it wasn't clear?"

"It meant Mother didn't have a chance to use the healing spell and it would be too late."

"You've got balls, little Brother, to carry the weight of that knowledge in order to spare your father." Daemon leaned down enough for them to be eye to eye. "But we share the weight in this family. If you can't tell one of us, think about telling the other. Understood?"

"Yes, sir."

Did you talk to her? Can you see her?

Before he could ask a question that might break the boy's willingness to tell him anything in the future, Lucivar walked into the front room and Daemonar bolted.

"You think we'll get any answers at the Keep?" Lucivar asked as they put on their outer garments.

"That will depend on whether we get there before Karla retires for the day," Daemon replied.

✦ ✦ ✦

Lucivar solved the problem of Karla's needing to retire to conserve the reservoir of power in her Gray Jewel: he opened a vein and filled a small cup with fresh blood.

Accepting the cup, she took a sip and made a face. "Next time, consider doing this when you're calmer."

He wasn't sure if temper really changed the taste of blood or if she was simply commenting about the emotions she felt pumping in him. "We have questions. We need answers."

She drank the rest of the blood. Two swallows. Setting the cup aside, she said, "Marian?"

"In a way," Daemon replied. He called in a kitchen towel, unwrapped it, and held up the clear Jewel. "Whatever was in this Jewel is the reason Marian fell into a healing sleep unlike anything Nurian had seen before. We're hoping that, being a Healer and a Black Widow, you have seen something like this."

Karla took the Jewel, rubbed a thumb over the surface. "If you're asking if a Healer like Nurian could create a healing spell and place it in a clear Jewel to lie dormant for decades, the answer is no."

"What about other kinds of spells?" Daemon asked. "We can wrap spells into objects. Death spells and witch-fire are a couple that come to mind."

"Yes, but power fades over time and the potency of a spell fades with it. If the spells you mentioned fade, someone may survive the death spell, or the witchfire might burn out quickly. A healing spell has to *work* when it's needed and be as potent as when it was made."

Daemon nodded toward the Jewel. "Could you do this?"

"Not even when I walked among the living." Karla studied both of them. "But you already know there was only one witch, one Healer, who had figured out how to do this."

Lucivar felt like his heart would explode in his chest. "Jaenelle could have warned us. Warned *me*."

Karla held up the Jewel. "This was between Marian and Jaenelle. I'm guessing they didn't tell you because neither of them knew when the spell would be needed, and both of them knew that when the time came, there was nothing you could do to change the outcome for good or ill. Not saying anything to you before she drank the brew? That's something to discuss with your wife when she's feeling better."

Oh, yes, they would have a *discussion*. "Tersa described the spell as dark water that washes away what doesn't belong. Dark water—and a song in the Darkness."

"Tersa also said that Marian would be shown the path home," Daemon added.

"Are you sure Jaenelle did this?" Lucivar asked. If his sister had created the spell, then Marian would survive. But if this was an attempt to kill his wife and leave her Self imprisoned somewhere . . .

"Do you remember when I was poisoned and Jaenelle did the healing that saved me?" Karla asked.

Daemon shuddered. He had assisted Jaenelle during that healing. "I remember."

"When a Territory's stability depends on the strength of its Queen, the Queen cannot afford to appear fragile. Cannot afford to *be* fragile. Injured, yes, but not susceptible to things like cold winters. I wasn't going to hide the damaged legs or the need for a cane or the wheeled chair, but the rest of the damage the poisons had done to me? That was a secret between Jaenelle and me. She tried to teach me the particular healing brew and spell that helped me stay as healthy as I could be. I could get close to what she made, but not quite close enough. Every six months, when we'd gather, she would make that brew and weave the healing spell she combined with it. And I could take care of my people for a while longer."

Lucivar huffed. "No one knew?"

"Not even Gabrielle, and she was the other side of the Golden Triangle."

The Golden Triangle had been Saetan's term for Jaenelle, Karla, and Gabrielle—the three Queens who were also natural Healers and natural Black Widows. The only witches in Kaeleer with the triple gift.

"The last Winsol we celebrated together, Jaenelle gave me a pretty container that held pieces of clear Jewels." Karla smiled. "She told me she wouldn't be able to do complex healing spells much longer, but these would be enough. When there were two left, it would be time to put my affairs in order. It would be time to decide what I wanted to do when I made the transition to demon-dead."

"All of the First Circle had made the transition before I . . . before Saetan became a whisper in the Darkness," Daemon said. "I often wondered how all of you seemed to know and were ready." He took a step back. "Thank you for your assistance, Lady."

Lucivar watched Daemon walk away, then turned back to Karla. "Did everyone who mattered receive a last gift?"

"I'm sure they did. But not every gift was stored in a piece of clear Jewel, Lucivar, and some won't appear until they're truly needed."

If Marian recovered, that was the only gift he needed. Jaenelle probably knew that too. But Daemon? Was his daughter the last gift, or was there another one waiting for him? And what would be the trigger that would indicate the gift was truly needed?

Jillian opened the glass doors that led to the snow-covered lawn and outside play area and breathed in the fresh air. The eyrie felt stuffy, or maybe it was the additional psychic scents and so much emotion that had her wishing she could locate one of those cleansing spells Marian used after Prince Yaslana slipped into the rut and spent a few days doing nothing but having sex with his wife. Afterward, you could almost taste the sex in the air.

This wasn't the same, but the . . . swamp . . . of feelings

made her a bit ill. She didn't want to tell Yaslana about her reaction to whatever was going on with the adults, but maybe Manny would know a similar cleansing spell.

Until she could talk to Manny, cold fresh air would have to do.

Prince Sadi had treated her like an adult this morning. Like a *woman* instead of a girl. She understood the danger of thinking his actions were anything other than the courtesy he would offer any woman, but this morning, she'd seen him as a *man*. Beautiful, intelligent, powerful. Educated.

She'd been aware of him in a way that made her tingle. That, in itself, wasn't dangerous as long as she kept thoughts and feelings to herself. He was married, and a married Warlord Prince didn't welcome invitations from anyone who wasn't his wife—would, in fact, defend his marriage vows with a savagery no other caste of male could match.

That didn't mean she couldn't enjoy his attention, couldn't talk to him about books and other things that were of interest to her and of no interest to Eyrien males.

Why couldn't she find someone like Prince Sadi? Maybe someday. Right now her education wasn't sufficient to hold the interest of a man like him.

"Where is everyone?"

Jillian smiled at Lady Surreal as the Gray-Jeweled witch walked into the front room. Educated, sophisticated, beautiful. Knowledgeable about so many things, including how to use a knife. Just the sort of woman who could be the wife of a powerful Warlord Prince like Sadi.

"Daemonar is in the playroom with Titian. Tersa is sitting with Lady Marian, and Manny is feeding baby Andulvar. Prince Yaslana and Prince Sadi went to the Keep to find out about the healing spell that Daemonar found. Well, he found the container for the spell, but it sounds like Marian will be all right once the spell is completed."

Looking at the tight way the other witch held herself,

Jillian wondered if Surreal had quarreled with Prince Sadi. She hadn't been around for breakfast. Maybe her moontime was approaching and she wasn't feeling well?

"Would you like me to make some fresh coffee? Or some tea?" Jillian asked. "There is plenty of food. I can heat something for you."

Surreal hesitated, then said, "Thank you. Would you like to join me?"

Before Jillian could reply, the front door opened and Yaslana and Sadi walked in.

"Did you find out anything?" Surreal asked.

"Healing spell," Sadi replied, removing his winter coat and hanging it on the coat-tree near the door. "A powerful one. Marian will wake once the spell has completed its work."

"But you don't know what it's doing or who made it?"

"We don't know what it's doing," Lucivar said. Using Craft, he removed his heavy wool cape, handed it to Daemon, then fanned his dark, membranous wings to clear the snow off them.

Jillian bit her tongue to keep the scold behind her teeth.

Lucivar looked at her. "I'll wipe up the floor in a minute."

"I didn't say anything," she replied.

He huffed out a laugh. "You didn't have to, witchling. You learned that look from Marian."

She studied the men. Relaxed now. Conserving their strength while they waited for the next battle, whatever it might be.

"Coffee?" she asked.

Sadi smiled at her. "That would be welcome."

"I could heat up some food." Jillian was painfully aware of Yaslana's sudden stillness, so she was also aware of the moment he let go of some weight he'd been carrying since Marian fell into this mysterious healing.

"Yeah," Lucivar said quietly. "Yeah, I could do with some food now."

Feeling like she'd suddenly flown into stormy air over jagged rocks, Jillian hurried to the kitchen, leaving the adults to sort things out for themselves.

Surreal waited until Lucivar went into the kitchen to choose a meal from the mounds of food that had been delivered since the news of Marian's illness reached the Blood in Riada. Then she turned to Daemon. "You know who did that to Marian."

Something cold and lethal flickered in the back of his gold eyes before he hid it. "*That* is a powerful healing spell, something no Healer now in the Realms could duplicate. The Queen's last gift to Marian, to be used when it was needed."

The Queen. Jaenelle Angelline. That explained why Lucivar had relaxed, and it explained Daemon's cold response to what he had heard as criticism. But it was her job to push—not as Daemon's wife but as his second-in-command. "You're sure it came from her?"

"Two Black Widows recognized the use of a clear Jewel as a container for such a spell, and one of those Black Widows is also a Queen as well as a Healer. Or she was a Healer when she walked among the living."

Surreal blinked. "Karla? You talked to Karla?"

Daemon nodded. "She's now in residence at the Keep."

"That's good news, then."

"Yes." He took a step toward her, then asked softly, "Are you all right?"

"I'm fine," she lied.

"Of course." He waited a beat, then added casually, "Once Marian wakes, I'll return to the Hall. There's always a lot of work to be done after Winsol."

"I'll see what needs to be done here. Maybe stay an extra day or two."

"Whatever you think is best."

He walked into the kitchen, and Surreal wondered if

the disappointment she heard in his voice was real or something she imagined because she needed it to be real.

The black water ran clear. No silt running off her scalp or her fingers or between her legs.

Marian climbed out of the pool and spread her wings, fanning them until they were dry.

The path that had led to the pool was overgrown now. Gone. But there was another path, barely discernible. There were no familiar landmarks, nothing to tell her if the path would lead anywhere. Except the song, that voice in the Darkness.

As Marian followed the voice and the path, she noticed the land changing. She walked and walked, and with each step, what had been fading and failing regained color and vitality. Then she walked around a curve in the path and stepped into her own garden in the full bloom of summer . . .

. . . and opened her eyes.

"Marian." Lucivar's voice. Soft. Strained. "Marian."

She turned her head and looked at him, wondering why tears filled his eyes.

"Welcome back, sweetheart." He kissed her lips, and she felt him tremble. "Welcome back."

FIFTEEN

❖

The following day, Marian was bathed, fed, and moved to the family room to spend an hour with her children before being tucked into the bedroom she shared with her husband. Lucivar retreated to his study to give the children that time with their mother. He listened to Rothvar's report and gave his second-in-command orders for the next few days so that he could keep a sharp eye on Marian's recovery.

When Surreal saw Rothvar escort Nurian out of the eyrie, she judged it was time to have a chat with the Warlord Prince of Ebon Rih. The study door was open, so she walked in and found Lucivar staring at a basket overflowing with letters as if it were his fiercest enemy.

"Problem?" she asked, knowing perfectly well why he was scowling at the basket.

Lucivar could read, and did when it was required, but it was a struggle for him. Marian usually sorted the mail, winnowing down the stack to the pieces the Warlord Prince of Ebon Rih had to see. If Marian wasn't available and Lucivar needed help with a document, he requested assistance from the other person he trusted above all others.

She approached the desk but stayed out of reach. Which didn't mean anything when dealing with Lucivar, but it made her feel easier. "Couldn't Sadi help you with that?"

"He left at first light."

And hadn't said anything to her before leaving.

"I saw the two of you yesterday." She had decided not to mention it, but the words tumbled out anyway.

"I saw you too."

"You and Sadi . . ." Did she really want to know?

"Wasn't the first time. Won't be the last." Lucivar shook his head and growled. "Look, witchling, if I'd needed to spend the night walking around the mountain, he would have gotten dressed and gone with me. If I'd needed to scream until my throat bled, he would have put aural shields around a room and listened. If I'd needed to feel flesh and bone under my fists, he would have said whatever would spark my temper, and we would have beaten the shit out of each other. Because that's what we have always done. Even when we hated each other, that's what we've done. Last night, I needed to sleep, so I went to my brother for help."

Lucivar walked around the desk, stood so close she wanted to take a step back, except she couldn't. Wouldn't.

"Sugar, if you don't want a knife between your ribs, you'll step back now."

There was some anger in his smile, but he stepped back. "Now, that's the Surreal I know. So tell me, little Sister, why are you and Sadi at odds?"

"We're not."

His smile took on a knife-edge. "Liar."

She couldn't deny it.

"At the Birthright Ceremony you were worried that Daemon would back out of the marriage once he had legal rights to his daughter. But he didn't back out. Never occurred to him. And it seemed like the two of you had come to a . . . richer . . . understanding, at least for a little while." Lucivar studied her. "He loves you. You love him. Or you did."

"Still do," she snapped. "And even if we were at odds, it's none of your business."

"For now. When it does become my business, you'll know."

Warning? Threat? "I thought we were friends."

"We're more than friends. You're my brother's wife, which makes you my sister. Even before that, you were family, and I would do almost anything for you."

"As long as it's not against him."

"Yeah. As long as it's not against him."

He'd drawn the line. He wouldn't bend it.

"Surreal?" Lucivar's voice softened. "Until that moment, I will do everything I can to help you. You just need to tell me what's wrong."

He'd slept in the same bed with Sadi. If he couldn't feel what was wrong, how could she explain it? And damn it, now that Sadi wasn't here, now that the sexual heat that poured out of him wasn't creating a need in her that was also a misery, she missed him. Wanted him.

"There is nothing wrong." She pointed at the basket. "You want me to sort those for you?"

"Sure. Thanks." As she reached for the basket, Lucivar said, "Has he told you about the headaches?"

Surreal frowned. "Headaches? Sadi?"

"For months now. Bad ones. Nurian makes a blend of herbs for a healing brew that reduces the pain and helps him sleep, but it's not as effective as it was in the beginning, and she says it's not safe to make the brew any stronger."

Surreal put the basket back on the desk. "Why is Nurian making this healing mixture?"

"Because the Healer in Halaway was more interested in having Daemon come back to her for help than actually helping him."

Now she understood why he'd insisted that she and Jaenelle Saetien be seen by the Healer in Amdarh who served in Lady Zhara's court. Did Sadi believe the Healer in the village would be so foolish as to do something to his wife or daughter in order to insert herself into his life? Could the headaches be the reason for his cruelty in bed?

"He didn't tell me."

"And I wasn't supposed to tell you."

"Why not?"

"You'd have to ask him."

For months now. Months. "Does Nurian know what's causing the headaches?".

Lucivar shook his head. "She can't find any physical reason. But I know this: Daemon can endure a lot of pain. If this gets bad enough to break something inside him, nothing and no one will be safe."

Surreal swallowed hard. She'd married him because she was pregnant and he wouldn't let her walk away with his child. She'd married him because she'd loved him for a long time. And she'd married him because he needed to stay connected to the living, and she'd felt strong enough to do that. Had been strong enough until sex with him had become a demoralizing addiction.

"If Manny and Tersa aren't ready to leave . . ."

"I can get them back to Halaway." Lucivar stepped close, rested his hands on her shoulders, and kissed her forehead. "Sometimes you can't fix things once they're broken."

"Are we broken? Sadi and me?" she whispered. Was he talking about her marriage or the man she'd married?

"I hope not. If you need help, I'm here."

Manny and Tersa wanted to stay another day, so Surreal left the small Coach for whomever Lucivar assigned to take the older women home. Catching the Gray Winds, she rode toward Dhemlan and home.

At the last minute she altered direction and went to Amdarh instead of going all the way to SaDiablo Hall. She needed an evening alone to think. She needed a day at the family's town house, away from Sadi and Yaslana.

Sadi had been in pain for months and had hidden it from her. Until the headaches were under control, she would have to endure the sexual addiction he'd created in her.

✦   ✦   ✦

Daemon stepped off the landing web in front of SaDiablo Hall and found himself surrounded by snow-covered children and Scelties.

"Papa!" Jaenelle Saetien flung her arms around him in welcome, transferring a fair amount of snow from her coat to his.

"Hello, witch-child." He hugged her, grateful for the welcome. "Mikal."

"Sir."

Daemon! Morghann, wild with excitement, scratched at his legs for attention.

Khary, his gray and white fur blending with the snow and shadows, just wagged his tail and leaped into another snowbank, disappearing until Mikal lifted him out of the snow.

"Aren't you cold?" Daemon asked. "I'm cold. Let's go inside and you can tell me what you've been up to."

"Lots of things!" Jaenelle Saetien sounded gleeful.

Ah, Hell's fire. Since a quick scan of the Hall didn't reveal any broken walls or windows or holes in the roof, the children couldn't have caused *too* much trouble. He hoped.

When they walked in, they were met by Beale and a dozen maids and footmen armed with towels for drying off Scelties and children, and baskets to carry the snow-encrusted clothes to the laundry rooms, where they would be dried.

Divested of his own coat and promising to meet the children in the family room to hear all the news, he waited until he was alone with Beale and Holt, who had come out of the study when he'd heard the commotion.

"Marian was wrapped in a powerful healing spell," Daemon said quietly. "She rose out of it yesterday evening and will recover."

"That's good news," Holt said.

Daemon nodded. "For all of us." He looked at Beale and raised an eyebrow in question.

"There were a few . . . spats . . . but differences of opinion were resolved," Beale said. Then he added blandly, "Some teeth were involved."

Whose teeth? Noting the steely look in his butler's eyes, Daemon said, "Was a Healer required?"

"No, Prince."

"Then I don't need to know."

"That would be for the best."

Sweet Darkness. Daemon turned to Holt, who said, "I have nothing that can't wait for an hour or two."

"In that case, I'll be up in the family room."

It had once been a private sitting room used by adults and visiting children. Now, as the family room and Jaenelle Saetien's playroom, it still had a lived-in shabbiness seen nowhere else in the Hall. Overstuffed bookshelves held children's books and stories for the Scelties. Cupboards held games and toys. A hodgepodge of comfortable, worn furniture that was no longer suitable for the public rooms ended up here, where rough use by children and Scelties didn't matter.

"We're helping Morghann and Khary learn how to count," Jaenelle Saetien said as soon as she and Mikal and the Scelties piled onto a sofa with him.

"They're as smart as some of the boys at school," Mikal said. "Smarter."

One, two, three, four, five, Morghann said.

"Yes, there are five of us on the sofa," Daemon agreed.

"Lord Marcus helped us," Jaenelle Saetien added.

He smiled at the thought of his man of business teaching the Scelties how to count. "Well, Lord Marcus does know his numbers."

No one mentioned any spats. In fact, Jaenelle Saetien and Mikal seemed to have reached a new understanding and a renewal of the friendship they'd had before she acquired her Birthright Jewel.

After Daemon assured Mikal that Marian would get well—a subject that worried the boy, since he'd lost his own mother when he was very young—boy and Scelties left, giving Sadi time alone with his daughter. He ran a fingertip over the outer edge of her delicately pointed ear and thought she looked more like her mother every day, a fact that, today, caused him pain and joy in equal measure.

"Your mother is staying at Lucivar's eyrie a little longer to help out, but she'll be home in a day or two." He wondered if that was true.

"Papa?" Jaenelle Saetien climbed into his lap.

"What is it, witch-child?" He wrapped his arms around her, an unspoken promise of protection.

"Beale said that the Lady had to follow the house rules even though she was a Queen and the most special witch in the Realm."

"That's true. Your grandfather followed the Old Ways of the Blood, as I do, and he insisted on proper attire for dinner. Ladies wore gowns when there were guests at the Hall, or a simpler dress or a skirt and blouse if it was just family and close friends at the table. If someone came to the table dressed in a way he didn't feel was appropriate, he would hold the meal until that Lady changed her clothes."

"Even if it was *the* Lady?"

"Yes, even if it was *the* Lady. She wasn't just his daughter—she was also his Queen, and he still wouldn't budge when it came to the house rules."

Jaenelle Saetien crinkled her face. "But she was special."

"Very special. But Saetan knew that her being special left her feeling isolated and alone sometimes, and he didn't want her to feel apart from the rest of the Blood. So even though she was special, he treated her as if she were ordinary and insisted that she follow the same rules as the Queens who were her friends and also lived at the Hall. He did that because he loved her."

"Like you love me?"

He kissed the top of her head. "Exactly like I love you."

✦ ✦ ✦

"Yeah, yeah, I know it's not your mother; you'll just have to make do, boyo." Lucivar teased the bottle's nipple into his baby's mouth. "She doesn't have any milk to give you, but losing the milk now is a small sacrifice in order to have her in your life for all the years to come."

After a minute of fussing, baby Andulvar settled down to the business of getting his meal, his eyes focused on his father's face.

Lucivar smiled. "We'll take care of her. All of us."

"Papa?"

His smile warmed even more. "You need something, witchling?"

Titian shook her head as she joined him. She leaned on his shoulder and watched him feed the baby. "Mama will get well?"

"Yeah, she will."

"I was scared."

"Me too."

Titian looked at him as if seeing someone a little different. "Papas don't get scared."

"Yes, we do. But when things get scary, the people we love need us to be brave, so we're brave."

"Who do you have when you need someone to be brave for you?"

"I have you, witchling," he said softly. "I have you and your brothers. I have your mother. I have your aunt and uncle." *And I have memories of a very special Lady.*

They remained in companionable silence until the baby finished the bottle, but Lucivar sensed there was something on his girl's mind. The past couple of days had been an emotional beating for all of them, and he just didn't have the strength to pry right now. Fortunately, Titian, his quiet, somewhat timid little witchling, didn't require prodding. It might take her a while, but eventually she would tell him whatever was on her mind.

He was about to get up and change the baby's diaper when she said, "I think Uncle Daemon needs someone to be brave for him."

Lucivar settled back in the chair. "What makes you think that?"

"Even when he smiled at me, he looked sad. Like Mama did before she fell asleep. When she smiled at me and Daemonar today, she didn't look sad anymore."

A chill went through him. "I'll keep an eye on your uncle Daemon."

"Promise?"

"Promise."

Satisfied, she helped him change the baby's diaper and tuck the boy in for a nap.

He took care of children and chores, encouraged Jillian to go home and rest—and have some time to herself. He waited until Daemonar was playing a quiet game with Titian, and Manny had settled in for a nap. Then he went looking for the one person he hoped could give him some kind of answer.

He *felt* Tersa's presence in the eyrie, but he couldn't find her in the common rooms or the laundry area or the bedrooms or the room that had a pool fed by a hot spring. He even checked his weapons room. Finally, he began searching the storage rooms that were deep in the eyrie—rooms that held the things that weren't needed but Marian didn't want to discard yet.

Feeling the chill in the corridors, he realized it had been a while since he'd replenished the power in the warming spells he'd put around these rooms, and made a mental note to do that once everything settled into some semblance of normal.

He opened the door to the last room . . . and walked straight into an illusion created by a tangled web of dreams and visions.

A crystal chalice on a stone altar. Leashes were attached to the stem, leading to four posts.

A Queen holds the leash.

His temper frayed the leash.

He'd used those phrases all his life. Here, in this vision, the leashes were physical things. He studied the leash that was leather braided with chain and instinctively knew what it controlled.

So. These weren't the leashes that held him.

"Daemon," *he whispered.*

Three of the leashes, including the leather and chain, looked normal—looked like he suspected his would look if they were made of something more than discipline, training, and self-control. But the other . . .

"The chalice is breaking again." *Tersa stepped up to the altar.* "The vessel can no longer contain all it was meant to contain."

That other leash cut into the fourth post, which looked soft, bloated. Sick. Pus oozed from splits and created a kind of carapace. Once it covered the whole post, he wasn't sure anyone would be able to break through without breaking . . .

No. He couldn't think of that. Wasn't going to consider that.

"He fights to survive," *Tersa said, pointing to the bloated post.* "He fights with instinct, not knowledge."

Couldn't someone provide the knowledge?

"Will he win?" *Lucivar asked.*

"No. The sand is running in the glass." *An hourglass appeared on the altar, the sand draining into the lower half.* "When the last grain falls, not even she will be able to save him."

"She? You mean Surreal?"

"It is too late for the girl to save him."

"Then who . . ." *Lucivar stared at Tersa. Felt his heart soar for a moment before he considered the danger.*

Had the trouble started between Daemon and Surreal when Witch made an appearance at Jaenelle Saetien's Birthright Ceremony? He'd had the impression that the meeting between Daemon and his Queen, the love of his life, had eased something inside him, had been responsible for Daemon's ability to be a warmer, more loving husband.

But a onetime meeting wasn't the same as Witch's continued presence—assuming that was possible.

How could it be possible?

"Dreams made flesh cannot become demon-dead," he said. "Saetan was sure of that."

Tersa watched him.

A presence, but not flesh. They had all believed even that wasn't possible. Daemon had certainly believed it wasn't possible.

"If Witch comes back in any way, it will change things between Daemon and Surreal," he said.

"Everything has a price," Tersa replied. "And things have already changed. That is why it's too late for the girl to help him."

Lucivar studied the bloated post. He'd call in his biggest knife and slice through that leash without giving a damn what would come afterward, but he suspected breaking that leash wouldn't help anything now. "Who did this to him?"

"He did it to himself. First he did it to help the girl, but everything he could do wasn't enough. Now he does it to survive."

He considered every person standing on this particular battlefield—and what it might cost each of those people. Then he considered what would happen to Daemon and to the Realm of Kaeleer if they lost this battle.

Only one choice, no matter the price. "How do I find Witch?"

"If the boy asks for her help, she will answer. But only if he asks."

"Then we have to tell him."

"We have tried to warn him. He isn't ready to listen."

"Then I'll explain it to him." With a brotherly fist to the ribs if that was what it took. "He has to ask."

"What will he ask of her?" Tersa set a bloody knife on the altar. "What will he give, thinking that is the path back to her?"

Lucivar eyed the knife. "He wouldn't hurt Surreal."

"Not to ease his own pain, no."

He felt hemmed in, chained in a way that was far worse than anything he'd endured while he was a slave in Terreille.

"What do we do, Tersa? What can I do?"

"The girl can't help him now, but she will free him to ask."

He swallowed frustration. "So we wait and watch them both suffer?"

"Wounds must fester before they are lanced."

A flash of his temper, hot and pure, filled the room.

Lucivar staggered, spread his wings for balance, and breathed in air that felt like needles of ice stabbing his lungs.

Hell's fire, it was cold!

And dark.

Creating a ball of witchlight, Lucivar lobbed it toward the center of the room and looked around.

Tersa wasn't in the room. Not anymore. But there were footprints in the dust, and a tangled web, crumbling to ash now, sat on a table that had been moved to the center of the room.

Tersa had told him what she could.

"We have tried to warn him. He isn't ready to listen."

Daemon might not be ready to listen, but he was—and there was another Black Widow within easy reach who might be able to give him answers.

Late that night, while everyone slept, Lucivar flew to the Keep to have a chat with Karla.

"Seeing a problem in a tangled web isn't the same as being able to fix the problem," Karla said. She'd hoped Daemon would be the one looking for answers, because Lucivar was *not* going to accept the unpalatable truth.

"You're a Gray-Jeweled Black Widow," Lucivar snapped as he prowled a reception room at the Keep. "Why can't you fix the problem? If it's a matter of convincing Daemon to let you do some kind of healing, I will haul his ass to the Keep and hold him down for you."

"I can't fix this because I wear Gray and he wears Black. He's beyond my reach, Lucivar. He's beyond yours. He's beyond everyone's reach except his own." After Lucivar's description of the vision Tersa showed him, she wasn't sure that was true anymore. What should have been light, and natural, self-control had turned into something ugly—a kind of self-mutilation. Every tangled web showed Daemon's condition worsening with frightening speed.

"Tersa said Surreal couldn't help him now, but she would free him to ask for the help he needs." Lucivar's eyes held a cold and bitter look. "Assuming he survives long enough to ask for that help."

"You can buy him some time by convincing him to drain some of the reservoir in his Black Jewel and keep it drained," Karla said. "Surreal would be able to help that much unless he's already draining her Gray prior to her moontimes. You can help him find more ways to use the Black."

"Sure. He could turn a city or two into rubble. He'd probably sleep much better for a few weeks after unleashing that much of the Black."

"You could teach him that trick you have of making wood tapers."

Lucivar didn't scoff at the idea, which she found encouraging.

"Everything that uses the power Sadi is currently transforming into unneeded sexual heat will slow down the physical damage, maybe even reduce the headaches."

"Yeah," Lucivar said. "Slow down the damage, reduce the headaches. Until the thing that pushes him over the edge."

Karla floated to a spot in front of him. "If he asks for information, for advice, for anything, I will do what I can. For him. For all of you."

"Is that why you're here at the Keep now?"

"Yes."

The sharp smile that started to curve his lips faded.

"Things were seen and promises were made, Lucivar."

He looked away. "Did she see this?"

"No, I don't think so. I think what Witch saw was fairly simple and didn't require help from any but the living. But Sadi turned it into something complicated. Not on purpose."

"Instinct, not knowledge."

Karla nodded. "What I don't understand is why Surreal didn't call him on it. She must have seen some change in him."

"I don't know. She says nothing is wrong." Lucivar started to walk away, then stopped. "If you see another warning . . ."

"I'll let you know."

The way he looked at her, he seemed to be searching for something. "Do you see Witch, Karla?"

"No. Regardless of what happens, I don't expect that to change."

"Would you want it to?"

"Yes, I would. But I don't expect it will change."

She didn't ask if he would want to see Witch again, but she wondered what answer he would give.

Pain was a familiar and faithful lover.

Daemon lay in bed, his eyes closed, and waited for the healing brew to ease the headache that had started as a dull ache during dinner and then turned savage soon after Mikal and Jaenelle Saetien had gone to bed.

No physical reason for this pain, which meant the cause

lay beyond the flesh. A spell of some kind? Or a stealthy attack on his inner barriers? No. He would have recognized the attempt even if he didn't immediately home in on the source.

"Breathing room, Sadi."

He'd had a dream about Karla a while ago, but he couldn't remember what it was or why it occurred to him now. Something to do with posts and leashes and the . . . wiggle-waggle?

He huffed out a soft laugh. Trust Karla to make a man's cock sound like an embarrassing toy.

"You're too damn dangerous to indulge in being foolish."

How was he being foolish? How . . .

A sheet as soft as a wish covered his body, whispering pleasure with every small movement. Sensual, not sexual. Inviting him to relax, to rest, to let go of his fierce control just a little. Just enough.

He couldn't get a sense of the sexual heat, couldn't tell if it was banked or burning, but the collar attached to the leashes—the collar that had become a tight metal band— relaxed, letting him breathe again. Letting him rest.

"Sadi."

A warm hand caressing his chest. Warm lips brushing against his.

Sensual, yes, but gaining the tang of sex. Pulling him away from the place where he could rest.

"Sadi."

Daemon shook off the dream as his body responded to Surreal's touch, to her need.

"I love you," she said as she kissed his mouth, his face. "I do love you. Don't go away."

He gathered her in his arms and returned her kisses, her caresses. "I'm here, Surreal. I'm right here. Easy, love. Easy."

She couldn't be easy. It was like she was caught up in a female version of the rut, barely catching her breath after

one orgasm before she was on him again, wanting more—
needing more. Relentless.

He obliged her with sex for hours before she fell into an
exhausted sleep. And he wondered what it was about him,
about them, that she wanted so much from him and yet
wept in her sleep.

PART TWO

SIXTEEN

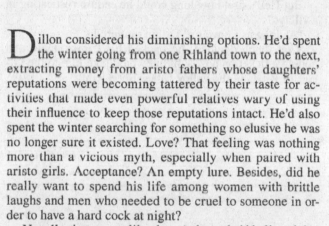

Dillon considered his diminishing options. He'd spent the winter going from one Rihland town to the next, extracting money from aristo fathers whose daughters' reputations were becoming tattered by their taste for activities that made even powerful relatives wary of using their influence to keep those reputations intact. He'd also spent the winter searching for something so elusive he was no longer sure it existed. Love? That feeling was nothing more than a vicious myth, especially when paired with aristo girls. Acceptance? An empty lure. Besides, did he really want to spend his life among women with brittle laughs and men who needed to be cruel to someone in order to have a hard cock at night?

Not all aristos were like that. At least, he'd believed that until he'd made that one life-changing mistake. Now he couldn't seem to find anyone who wasn't brittle or a bully.

Maybe he needed to go somewhere less fashionable. Somewhere where the minor branches of aristo houses went to live because they could be the important somebodies in a place full of nobodies.

In fact, there were some distant cousins on his mother's side who lived in a place like that. The valley where they lived was famous, but the village itself was rustic at best—at least according to his mother. Those cousins had come for a visit once. The boy, Terrence, had been about his age and they'd gotten along well. And he remembered Terrence's mother as a kind woman. Even if she'd heard about his sullied honor, he didn't think she would close the door in his face once she knew he had nowhere else to go.

Unlike his own mother.

A last chance. He needed to pick the right girl, someone young enough to be flattered by his attention, connected enough to provide him with some status when they handfasted, but not *too* connected. He'd had his fill of aristo bitches.

But Hell's fire, how long could he endure rusticating in a village?

"As long as I have to," Dillon muttered.

That much decided, he packed his trunks again and bought a ticket on a Coach that would take him to the village of Riada in the valley called Ebon Rih.

SEVENTEEN

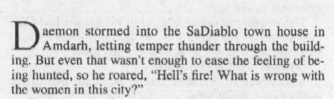

Daemon stormed into the SaDiablo town house in Amdarh, letting temper thunder through the building. But even that wasn't enough to ease the feeling of being hunted, so he roared, "Hell's fire! What is wrong with the women in this city?"

He knew one of the things that was wrong with the Ladies in Amdarh. For months now, he and Surreal had maintained a careful schedule that kept them from residing under the same roof for more than a couple of days every fortnight. On those days they would attend social gatherings together in the evening, and at night, in private . . .

They satisfied their carnal needs for hours—*her* carnal needs more than his. There was heat in that collision of bodies, but little warmth, and he felt less and less enjoyment being with the woman who was his wife and lover.

But this assault by women who should have known better! At every social duty he fulfilled on his own, they surrounded him like starving cats around a succulent—and wounded—bird, and not even meeting defensive shields cold enough to freeze skin deterred them.

He had the sexual heat leashed so tight it was a surprise that he hadn't emasculated himself, and that *still* wasn't enough. Of course, the headaches, which had gotten more and more savage over the past few months, had done a good job of killing his libido, so the limited sex with Surreal was more than sufficient, even excessive.

And still the bitches kept pushing him. Pushing and pushing. Didn't they realize they were going to push him too hard one of these days and snap his control? *Then* he would play with them. Sweet Darkness, how he would play!

"Prince?"

Daemon looked at Helton, the town house's butler. The man's face maintained a professional demeanor, but the eyes were full of fear.

The struggle to regain control of his temper had Daemon sweating. He didn't want to fight this battle. Wasn't sure how much longer he would win this battle.

"Prince?" Helton said again.

Somewhere in the town house, he heard one of the maids weeping. Terrified.

Daemon swallowed hard. Tasted a hint of blood.

He walked into the sitting room, then waited for Helton to join him.

"My apologies, Helton. It's been a trying day, but that is no excuse for bringing temper into the house and distressing the staff."

Helton took a step toward him. "Is there some way I can be of assistance?"

For a moment, he considered asking if Surreal was having an affair. If other witches had reason to think the marriage was breaking, they might also think he would be amenable to ignoring his vows. That could explain their otherwise inexplicable behavior. But asking the question would put Helton in an untenable position of conflicting loyalties, so he didn't ask. Besides, he owed Surreal a great deal, including the gift of his darling daughter.

He would be back at SaDiablo Hall tomorrow, dealing with Jaenelle Saetien's latest effort to test his rules. At least she was a female he still understood.

"No, thank you," Daemon said, then changed his mind. "Yes. I'm not available to anyone for the rest of the day."

"Very good, Prince." Helton turned to leave, then turned back. "I hope things improve for you."

"So do I." It was a shame neither of them could put a name to what those things might be.

EIGHTEEN

Jillian flew down to Riada's main street, full of nervous anticipation. Not wanting to call too much attention to herself, she wore her usual daytime trousers, but she'd paired them with a new top that had a more daring neckline than anything she'd worn before. She wasn't a little girl anymore, so it was appropriate to wear clothing that suited a woman in love.

After taking a couple of deep breaths and resisting the urge to fuss with her hair and clothes, she began perusing the merchandise on display.

Market day in Riada. You could always go into the shops to purchase greens and fruits, fish and other seafood, and all kinds of meat, but as soon as the weather warmed up, merchants hauled out carts and tables and displayed their goods in the open air, turning the chore of shopping into a festive celebration. That one morning a week was as much about chatting with neighbors as it was about selecting the food for a couple of days' worth of meals.

Even when she didn't have to buy anything, Jillian looked forward to market day. The street swirled with color from the cloths that shaded the tables and the clothes worn by the men and women who were buying or selling. Voices mingled, rose, and fell in their own kind of music. The sound of a village, a community.

Keeping her wings tucked to protect them from the people jostling to see the merchandise, she wandered from one display to the next, looking at everything but buying nothing. Not yet, anyway. Marian had given her a shopping list but told her to purchase the ingredients for a meal she would like to learn how to make. Being a hearth witch, Marian was a wonderful cook—unlike Nurian, who was an excellent Healer and made healing brews that people actually *liked* drinking but, somehow, could make even an overspiced roast taste bland.

"Your basket is empty, Lady Jillian," one merchant said, his voice a genial scold as he pointed at her basket. "Eyriens love the air, but even you can't eat it."

"First I have to decide what to eat. Then I'll buy the ingredients," she replied, smiling.

"What about seafood?" the fishmonger called. "I have fish fresh from my brother's nets, brought to me just this morning. Or shrimp. What about lobster? I have some right here. I can put one in the pot and cook it for you if you don't want to do it yourself."

"You have a brother who catches fresh fish *and* lobsters?"

"My brother catches the fish. I have cousins who tend the lobster pots and also catch the shrimp. Lucky for you, huh? You won't find fresher fish in all of Ebon Rih."

Laughing, Jillian started to move on, then stopped. Marian had taught her how to make a spicy-sweet dressing for cold seafood served over fresh greens. Marian circled the plate with a couple of different kinds of sliced fruit and served it with crusty bread.

An easy dish to prepare for today's midday meal, especially if the fishmonger cooked the lobster for her while she selected the other ingredients. And if Nurian didn't get back from visiting her patients exactly on time, Jillian could put the meal together quickly once her sister got home, and nothing would overcook and spoil.

After checking Marian's list, she said, "Two cooked

lobsters and a pound of the shrimp." That would be enough for everyone.

"Do you want to select your own lobsters?" The fish-monger gestured to the tank of water behind him.

"You can choose." She wasn't squeamish. She was Ey-rien after all, and she'd seen enough game being dressed for the table. But lobsters were different. Even when they were dead, their beady eyes had an accusing stare that made her want to apologize while she ripped off their claws and broke open the shell. If she didn't point to one, then they all had a chance to live a little longer—or at least live until the next customer made a selection. "I'll make my other purchases and come back for them."

Moving with purpose now, she purchased the other items that Marian wanted for the Yaslana household, then selected the fresh greens and other vegetables that she wanted for the salad, as well as the items she needed to make the spicy-sweet dressing.

She stood by the fruit cart, her eyes closed as she held up a piece of fruit so that she could breathe in the scent.

Then a male voice said, "Luscious, sweet, and deliciously ripe."

Feeling heat stain her cheeks, Jillian opened her eyes and smiled. "Yes, it is."

"I wasn't talking about the fruit."

She looked at the Opal-Jeweled Warlord standing beside her and felt butterfly wings in her belly. He had the dreamiest green eyes and stylishly disheveled russet hair that looked so striking compared with the black hair and gold eyes of the Eyrien race.

"Lord Dillon." She knew she sounded breathless. Unsophisticated. She always did when she was around him.

"Lady Jillian." A pleasant voice. A cultured voice with just a trace of an accent that, like his hair and eyes, made him so different from an Eyrien male.

A Rihlander from an influential family who lived in the eastern part of Askavi, Dillon had come to Riada to visit some cousins. She had met him a couple of weeks before at the lending library when he'd noticed her selection of books and asked her opinion of one he had chosen for himself, then apologized for being so forward and speaking to her without a proper introduction. It was such an aristo attitude, no doubt polished for fancy dances held in ballrooms or serving in a Queen's court, and yet she didn't get the feeling that he thought of her as a rube—a sentiment some of the aristo girls in the village managed to convey without saying anything that could get them into trouble with Prince Yaslana.

Since then, she and Dillon had met a few times—most often at the lending library, but also while she ran errands for Nurian or Marian. Sometimes she had Titian with her and the meeting was brief—barely a greeting in passing. And sometimes when she flew down to Riada alone, she and Dillon slipped away for a few minutes to talk, to have a few precious minutes in private to . . .

It wasn't the open-mouthed kind of kiss she'd read about in the romance novels she hid from Nurian and read only in her room at night, but it wasn't the dry brush of lips she'd experienced with Tamnar either. Dillon's kisses were *romantic*, full of promises and desire.

Too much desire wasn't good, wasn't safe before she was old enough to have her Virgin Night, the ceremony that would remove the risk of her power and her Jewels being broken by her first experience of sexual intercourse. Dillon was old enough to have made the Offering to the Darkness and was now considered a grown man who wore the mantle of his full power. He was old enough to want a lover, and she couldn't oblige. But how could she resist a few kisses when he told her he was dazzled by her because she was such a strong woman? How could she say no when he asked for a few minutes alone with her? It wasn't like she was from an aristo family that required girls to have an escort when they spent time with a male friend.

As she selected the fruit and picked up loaves of crusty

bread for herself and Marian, Dillon walked along with her, polite enough not to give offense but not chatting with the merchants. He seemed impatient, even a little aloof—until they passed a wide alleyway that led to the backs of the shops and the fields beyond.

"This way." Dillon grabbed her arm as he took the basket and dropped it a few steps inside the alleyway.

"Dillon," Jillian protested, looking back at the abandoned basket of fresh food. "You can't leave the basket. The village cats will be all over the meat I picked up for Lady Marian!"

"She can wait." He pulled her into the alleyway a few more steps.

"Well, let me put a shield and cold spell around—"

"You're not her servant, Jillian. Why do you act like one?"

She blinked, confused by his sharp tone. "I don't. I help Marian, and I get paid for it, but that doesn't make me a servant."

"Hired help, then."

Tears stung her eyes. Why would she get all weepy just because Dillon didn't understand that she had a role in the Yaslana household?

A spurt of temper and defiance made her lift her chin. "There is nothing wrong with serving someone or working for a living."

He studied her, then looked contrite. "I know. I'm sorry. I don't know why I said that. It's just . . . We haven't had any time together in days." His hand slid down her arm and closed over her hand as he looked deep into her eyes. "If you loved me, you'd want to spend time with me." He bent his head and leaned toward her, whispering, "If you loved me, you'd want to kiss me as much as I want to kiss you."

His lips brushed her mouth, asking for permission. How could she refuse when she wanted to kiss him with everything in her?

She felt the wall at her back and his erect penis poking at her through their clothing as he pressed himself against her.

That made her nervous, made her feel trapped. She pushed at his arms, tried to break the kiss to tell him she didn't want this, it didn't feel good, not when she felt trapped. Then his hand closed over her breast, something he'd done once before, but that time she'd had room to pull away.

No, she thought, trying to push him back. Permission before action. That was the rule. Kissing might be overlooked, but she didn't know how to explain *this.*

Breathing hard, Dillon broke the kiss. "If you—"

She felt the dark power and hot fury a moment before Prince Yaslana grabbed Dillon by the throat, swung him around, and slammed him into the side of the building.

"No!" Jillian cried as Lucivar's hand tightened around Dillon's neck, choking him. Killing him. "No!"

She threw herself at Lucivar. She wasn't sure he noticed her when he straightened his left arm, turning it into a barrier. She wrapped her hands around that arm, tugging and crying as Dillon, his toes barely touching the ground, struggled against an unyielding hand backed by Ebon-gray Jewels and a vicious temper.

"He didn't do anything!" she cried.

"He had his hand on your tit in view of anyone who walked by," Lucivar snarled. "So I say he did plenty."

"Please."

Lucivar was the law in this valley, and there was no one in the whole of Askavi strong enough to stand against him.

"Please," she pleaded. "He didn't do anything."

Lucivar opened his hand and took a step back as Dillon slumped to the ground. Then he turned glazed gold eyes on Jillian. "The next time he doesn't do anything in that way, I will rip off his cock and shove it down his throat. And then I'll snap his neck. Are we clear?"

Glazed eyes were a warning that a Warlord Prince was riding the killing edge, primed for slaughter. So this wasn't an idle threat. Lucivar never made idle threats.

"Are we clear?" he snarled softly.

"Y-yes."

"Then go to my eyrie and wait for me."

"I h-have to . . ."

"My eyrie. Now!"

She bolted out of the alleyway and leaped for the sky as soon as she had room to spread her wings.

Never breaking stride as he left the alleyway, Lucivar grabbed the handle of the basket and kept moving. Had to get away from the market, from the people who were scrambling to avoid him. They looked at him and knew he was riding the killing edge and that something as simple as the wrong inflection on a word might be enough to snap the leash on his formidable temper.

"Prince." Rothvar, his second-in-command, took a step toward him.

"No," he rasped, the only warning he could give before he spread his dark wings and flew home.

Something wrong. Too much fury burning in him. Why so much fury? He'd come across other youngsters taking advantage of the illusion of privacy, whether it was someplace in the village or a favorite spot by a stream. When it happened, he simply grabbed the back of the boy's shirt— or girl's, if she had the boy pinned—and hauled one youngster away from the other. That was sufficient to make any libido go limp.

Except this time . . . Because it was Jillian in that alleyway? Was that the source of his fury? Or something else?

The moment he walked into the big front room of his home, he heard the weeping coming from the kitchen. He couldn't be inside, couldn't let his temper stay inside with his family. Couldn't.

"Papa." Daemonar rushed forward, then skidded to a stop, his wings spreading for balance.

Couldn't be around another male right now, not even his son.

"Keep the other children in the playroom," Lucivar said, fighting to stay in control. When the boy hesitated and looked toward the kitchen, he snarled, "Get away from me. *Now.*"

Daemonar didn't run. Knew better than to run. He backed away for a few steps, looking toward his father but not meeting the glazed eyes, not issuing any kind of challenge. Then he turned and walked down the wide corridor, just as Lucivar had taught him.

Breathing a little easier, Lucivar walked into the kitchen and dropped the basket on the table, momentarily silencing Jillian's weeping.

"Lucivar." Marian tightened her hold on the girl.

"I'll be outside. When she's taken care of things, she and I are going to have a chat."

He saw the understanding—and sympathy—in Marian's eyes.

Walking out of the kitchen, he crossed the big front room and went out the glass doors that opened to the yard, bordered by a stone wall enhanced with a Red shield that kept frisky children from tumbling off the mountain. Since the shield rose to twice his own height, that was enough protection for Daemonar and Titian when they played out here on their own. Once baby Andulvar started walking, and fluttering, he'd reshape the Red walls into an air-cushioned Red dome.

He paced the long length of the yard, tightening the leash on his temper with each step.

Shouldn't have been that angry, not over something that, while not exactly prudent, wasn't unexpected. Except . . .

Hell's fire! She knew his rules, and she wasn't helpless. Wasn't usually helpless.

As he reached the far end of the yard, Lucivar felt the presence of a male intruder. Pivoting, he headed for the eyrie, calling in his war blade despite recognizing the psychic scent. Not an intruder, as such, but Rothvar should know better than to come here without being summoned.

Then again, being Nurian's lover, Rothvar also had an interest in Jillian.

As he strode toward the eyrie, he watched Marian cross the big room to reach the front door. His steps lengthened, then slowed when Marian crossed the room again, carrying another shopping basket—and Rothvar flew away without crossing the threshold.

Lucivar vanished the war blade. A moment later, when Jillian walked out of the eyrie, her eyes puffy from crying but her chin up—a sure sign of temper—he settled into a fighting stance, ready for a different kind of battle.

Jillian walked through the open glass doors to have this "chat" with Prince Lucivar Yaslana. It didn't matter that he was the Warlord Prince of Ebon Rih, that he was the *law* here. It didn't matter that he was the second most powerful male in the whole Realm of Kaeleer. It didn't matter that almost from the day she and Nurian had arrived in Ebon Rih, she had run tame in the Yaslana household, helping Marian with Daemonar when he was a baby, and later helping with Titian and now baby Andulvar. It didn't matter that Lucivar had defied Eyrien tradition and had given her the training in weapons and fighting that she'd wanted, while insisting on her participation in traditional education—something no ruler in the Realm of Terreille would have done for a young witch who wasn't from an aristo family.

What mattered *today* was that he had treated her like a little girl, humiliating her and hurting Dillon. Terrifying her wonderful Dillon.

All right. Prince Yaslana wanted to have a "chat"? Had a few things to say? Well, so did she. She just didn't know where to start, so she stared at him, waiting for all these boiling feelings to shape themselves into words.

"What in the name of Hell were you doing?" Lucivar shouted, breaking the silence.

"We weren't *doing* anything!" Jillian shouted back, wanting to turn words into daggers.

"Witchling, I saw enough to know that *he* was doing something! And I didn't walk into that alleyway by chance. 'Prince, Lady Jillian went that way. I don't think she's feeling herself.' 'Prince, I saw Lady Jillian's shopping basket on the ground in that alleyway.'"

Oh, that was more than humiliating that someone had tattled so that she and Dillon would get into trouble.

"I love him, and he loves me! We haven't seen each other in days and just wanted a few minutes alone. There is nothing wrong with that."

Lucivar took a step toward her. "He had you pushed against a wall on a day when you're vulnerable. There is plenty wrong with that, witchling."

Dillon couldn't have known her moontime had started. Hell's fire, *she* hadn't known. The fact that Lucivar *had* sensed the physical change just made the whole thing even worse.

"You're done with him," Lucivar said.

"No." Panic filled her, immediately replaced by fury. "No! I love him and—"

"I don't doubt *your* feelings, but I have a lot of doubts about his. Either way, the decision's made. You're done with him."

"You don't get to decide that!"

"Yeah, I do."

"No, you don't! You're not . . ."

. . . *my father.*

The unspoken words hung between them.

Jillian saw Lucivar brace for a blow he couldn't dodge. In that moment, despite the anger she felt toward him, she understood that if she said the words, it would shatter what was between them in a way that could never be mended. He would accept the line drawn by the words, and she would never deal with Lucivar again, the man who taught her to handle weapons, who listened to her, who laughed with—and sometimes at—her. If she said the words, he would distance himself from her, and she would be like almost everyone else in the valley and surrounding mountains, dealing with and answering to the Warlord Prince of Ebon Rih.

Until that moment, she hadn't realized how much it had mattered to her that he had treated her like one of his children rather than the girl who came over to help Marian by watching the little ones.

Until that moment, it hadn't occurred to her that they were both about to fly into some stormy winds.

". . . being fair," she finished lamely.

The tension in his shoulders eased, but the bright temper in his gold eyes didn't fade.

"I don't have to be fair, not when being fair interferes with my vow to cherish and protect. If I see a threat coming at me or mine, I deal with it."

"But Dillon isn't—"

"Enough."

Defeated, brokenhearted, she stared at the tear-blurred ground between them.

"Hell's fire, Jillian. He's just—" Lucivar turned away from her. He swore quietly but with frightening intensity. Then he turned back. "Go home, witchling. *And stay home.*"

"Yes, sir." She blinked away the tears but was careful not to look at him. Crying in front of the Warlord Prince of Ebon Rih was something little girls did.

She flew back to the eyrie she shared with Nurian. Once she was safely in her own room, she let the tears flow.

"What did Rothvar want?" Lucivar asked when he stepped into the kitchen.

"Jillian had left without the lobsters and shrimp she'd purchased," Marian replied calmly as she cracked the shells of two large lobsters. "Rothvar wasn't sure if she had purchased them for me or for herself and Nurian, so he brought the food here. I think she was intending to make a simple meal of seafood on a bed of greens, so I'll shell one lobster and half the shrimp and take it over to her."

He moved away from the kitchen archway, then back again, wings rustling, hands tightening into fists. She wasn't afraid for herself—Lucivar believed what his father had taught him, that a Warlord Prince leaves his temper at the door—but she gave Daemonar a psychic tap and reinforced Lucivar's earlier order to remain in the playroom with his sister and baby brother. That Lucivar couldn't shake off the anger, had brought it inside their home, worried her.

"What was I supposed to do?" Lucivar snarled. "He had her in an alleyway. His hand was on her breast! Even if she could have used Craft, she wears Purple Dusk and he wears Opal. She couldn't have held him off if he wanted to do more. And despite what she might have said to you, she *was* trying to push him away."

Of course she was, Marian thought. *It hurts to have a breast squeezed when it's already tender from the onset of moon's blood.* The fact that Lucivar knew even the gentlest touch could be painful some days had to have fueled his temper when he saw Jillian with the young Warlord.

She stopped trying to prepare the midday meal, since the man she'd adored through decades of marriage filled up her kitchen with his temper and body, unable to stand still.

"Would you have been so angry if Jillian's moontime hadn't started moments before you saw her?" she asked quietly.

No one was ever quite sure if it was psychic scent or physical scent that alerted Warlord Princes to a woman's moontime, but any female under the protection of a Warlord Prince was *protected* during the three days when she couldn't use her own power and was, therefore, vulnerable. The annoying part was that those men were so attuned to the women who were a part of their lives that they usually knew before the women—and reacted violently to anything that might possibly be a threat. The men in Riada had learned long ago to treat her with special care during her moontime whenever she ventured beyond the family eyrie—and Lucivar had learned that nothing more than a snarl from him was needed to have every man backing away. But before he had learned to trust enough, there had been times when even the Eyriens who worked for him had felt his war blade resting just above their skin—a blade honed so sharp that just pressing against it by taking too deep a breath was enough to slice through leather and cloth to reach skin.

Jillian wasn't a stranger to her moon cycle. She might have rolled her eyes at the required three days of rest at home, but she had never disobeyed that rule. She hadn't disobeyed today either. This was just unfortunate timing, but Marian feared the conflict between Lucivar and Jillian would escalate if something wasn't done. More than that, whatever lines were drawn with Jillian would also apply to Titian when she reached an age when boys became interesting as a different kind of playmate.

"I think we should get a second opinion," she said.

"Why in the name of Hell should we get a second opinion?" Lucivar demanded. "His hand, her breast. I should have ripped off his damn arm instead of giving him a warning choke."

Mother Night. "We need someone on the outside who can look at this young aristo Warlord without prejudice."

"Fine. I'll ask Daemon to come and look at the little prick-ass. Then he can help me bury that whelp in a deep, cold grave."

"You'd kill him for—"

"I didn't say we'd kill him."

Marian swallowed, aware of every muscle that moved in her throat. For everyone's sake, she needed to jolt Lucivar out of the fury that hadn't quieted.

"I think we need someone who would make more of an impression than your brother," she said.

That stopped him. He just stared at her for a long moment. "Hell's fire, Marian. Who makes more of an impression than Daemon Sadi?"

NINETEEN

◆

Surreal placed her underwear in a dresser drawer, then turned to face Marian. "Tell me again why I'm here?"

"Because Lucivar needs a second opinion."

"Why doesn't he ask one of the other Eyriens? They usually have opinions about everything."

"In this instance, their opinions are useless, because they're male, they're Eyrien, and they work for Lucivar, so of course they will agree with whatever line he draws."

"Uh-huh." She put her nightclothes in another drawer. "You know, sugar, it occurs to me that you were very careful to phrase your message in a way that indicated I needed to visit as soon as I could get here, but you didn't actually say why you needed me." She studied Marian. "Is there a problem between you and Lucivar?"

"No, nothing like that."

Thank the Darkness. I'm dealing with a big enough problem of my own.

"It's just . . ." Marian hesitated. "Whatever boundaries are drawn now will also apply to Titian."

"Exactly what are we talking about?"

"We're talking about Jillian and the way Lucivar reacted to catching the scent of moon's blood the other day. We're talking about a boy kissing Jillian and putting his hand on her breast."

"And Lucivar, being such a calm, mild-tempered man, bounced off the ceiling?"

"He slammed the boy into the side of a building and choked him a little. At least, I was told it was a little."

Shit. "Where did this happen?"

"In Riada, around the open market."

"Where were the boy and Jillian?"

"In an alleyway between two of the buildings."

"Uh-huh. And you don't see anything wrong with that?"

"I see a lot of things wrong with that," Marian snapped. "For one thing, him touching her that way in public was disrespectful. If Lucivar had heard about it from someone else, he wouldn't have been happy, and he would have let Jillian know in no uncertain terms exactly why he wasn't happy, but I don't think he would have gone looking for the Warlord."

He might have, if whoever had told him about the incident had known the boy's name. Lucivar had strict rules about anyone touching the children without his permission, and he didn't make exceptions just because the person doing the touching was also young. Which didn't make it easy to indulge in a little romantic exploration.

Then again, Lucivar's father had had the same "no permission, no sex" rule when anyone was under *his* roof.

"But because *Lucivar* was the one who walked into that alleyway and saw them, he reacted as if Jillian were under attack," Marian continued. "I don't want Jillian or Titian to avoid getting acquainted with boys because they're afraid Lucivar will seriously injure those boys." She pulled clothes out of Surreal's trunk and hung the trousers and dresses in the wardrobe.

Surreal shook out the blouses and handed them to Marian. "Can you finish unpacking for me? I think I should have a chat with your husband."

"It's Jillian who needs your opinion. You're not going to change Lucivar's mind."

"Wanna bet?"

Marian paused. "Are you going to call in a crossbow and threaten to shoot him?"

"Our most productive chats always start with me threatening to pin his balls to the wall. Doesn't change his opinion about anything. It just makes sure I have his full attention."

Marian finished hanging up the blouse and reached for another. "Twenty gold marks and I'll bake your favorite pie while you're here."

"I can't bake a pie, but I'll put up twenty gold marks and a box of that salty dark chocolate that's made by the best chocolatier in Amdarh."

"Deal."

Surreal walked out of the guest room. When she reached the eyrie's main corridor, she found Daemonar waiting for her.

"Hey, boyo. Why aren't you out kissing sky?"

He eased up next to her and whispered, "Something is wrong with Papa and Jillian."

"People don't always see eye to eye." She brushed a hand over his black hair and realized they were almost the same height. Damn. When had that happened? She'd seen him just a few weeks ago when he'd come to SaDiablo Hall for a visit, and would have sworn he hadn't been this tall. "I'm sure it's nothing serious."

"I think it is. Papa is really unhappy." Daemonar paused. "He's in his study, doing paperwork."

Not good. Lucivar often viewed sitting behind a desk doing paperwork as a form of self-punishment.

"Keep the little beasts occupied, okay? I'll see what I can do to help your papa."

"Thanks, Auntie Surreal."

She thought he was going to say something more, but he shied away from it, so she went to the study to tackle the volatile problem.

"Pretend I brought my crossbow to this meeting," Surreal said, taking a chair in front of the big blackwood desk. The desk wasn't as big as Daemon's back at the Hall, but it was sufficiently expansive. "I'm pointing it at you. Threaten, threaten, blah blah blah."

Lucivar eyed her, then put the pen in its holder with an insultingly slow move. "Am I supposed to know what that means?"

No emotion at all in his voice, which meant he was so unhappy over whatever this was that he wasn't feeling anything at all or he was holding on to his explosive temper so tightly he couldn't afford to let anything show. Either way, she had to get him to respond before he would really listen to her.

"Blah blah blah. An annoying little phrase Jaenelle Saetien picked up at school. I gather it's supposed to mean 'we've covered this ground before and don't actually have to say the words again.' Imagine her surprise when she wanted permission to go on an outing with some friends and rushed into her papa's study minutes before she was supposed to be meeting those friends and gave him the 'blah blah blah' as an explanation of where they were going and who would be the chaperons."

"Oh, Hell's fire."

Hearing that tiny bit of interest in his voice, Surreal nodded. "Yeah, it went over as well as you'd expect. And not the way Jaenelle Saetien intended, because Daemon looked at her and said that since 'blah' meant dull and uninteresting, the reasonable conclusion to her saying 'blah blah blah' was that this outing was going to be exceedingly dull and uninteresting, and since that was the case, he would provide her with the excuse to get out of going by not giving his permission. By the time she convinced him that she *was* interested, the friends had already left."

"Bet that went over well."

"It did. There were lots of tears and a few words said in a tone that bordered on pure bitch—which Daemon, surprisingly, didn't comment on. But when the foolish girl began slamming doors to indicate her extreme displeasure, he quietly informed her that since words spoken quickly could be misinterpreted, any requests to visit friends or go on outings in the foreseeable future would have to be submitted in writing, using proper spelling, full sentences that provided the necessary information he would need in order to make a decision, and, of course, good penmanship."

Lucivar's lips twitched.

"A couple of days later. Another outing. When reminded that requests had to be submitted in writing, she dashed off the note—which Daemon returned with a gentle apology, saying that the note was too illegible for him to decipher and needed to be resubmitted."

"She didn't make it to that outing either, did she?"

"No. More weeping, more complaints, more slammed doors—and for every slammed door, Daemon added a week to the time when written requests would be required."

Lucivar leaned forward. "That's brat behavior and doesn't sound like Jaenelle Saetien. Something wrong with the witchling?"

"Lately she has felt the need to test boundaries and rules." Surreal sighed. "Her friends continue to be impressed by her Birthright Jewel—and her teachers tend to be indulgent, despite the chats they've had with her father about being indulgent. But no one at the Hall is impressed, because they saw the first Twilight's Dawn, the darker one. And the person who is least impressed by the Jewel itself is Jaenelle Saetien's papa. I salute Daemon for his patience. He let the girl slam against his will until she finally understood that he would not allow her to become a brat or a bitch, that he would draw the line and hold it as much out of love for her as out of duty to all the people of Dhemlan."

"They're okay?" Lucivar asked.

Surreal nodded. "She snapped out of her current brat mood, and they're fine. They don't need me as a buffer, if that's what you're wondering."

"I wasn't wondering, but that's good to know. So you're here because . . ."

"You need a second opinion. I'm here because of you, Jillian, and the little prick who was feeling her up in public. I might like him for being so ballsy. It's not quite like whipping out his cock and pissing on your boots, but it's close." She waited a beat. "I heard you choked the shit out of him."

"Nah." Lucivar dismissed that with a wave of his hand. Then he considered. "Did choke the piss out of him."

She started to laugh, then realized he was serious. Shit shit shit. "Why did you do it?"

Lucivar shook his head. "You'll be influenced by what I say and will no longer provide an impartial second opinion."

Well, Hell's fire, he was serious about that too. "You and Jillian. Was anything said that can't be forgiven?"

He shook his head. Didn't even hesitate. She breathed a sigh of relief.

"All right, then. I'm going to go talk to Jillian and arrange a time when she and I can meet with this young Warlord."

Feeling wary, Jillian eyed Surreal SaDiablo. Not only was Surreal a Gray-Jeweled witch, but she was Daemon Sadi's wife—and his second-in-command. She was also half Dea al Mon, which meant she was skilled with a knife.

"Why do you want to meet Dillon?" she asked.

"Do you like him?" Surreal asked in turn.

"Yes."

"You want to spend time with him?"

Jillian nodded. She wasn't sure Dillon would want to get anywhere near her again, but just the thought of him still filled her stomach with butterflies.

"Then I, as the intermediary, need to meet him so that I can form my own opinion."

"What if you agree with Prince Yaslana?"

"Then you're out of luck. But if I don't agree with him . . ." Surreal leaned toward Jillian, and there was a wicked twinkle in her gold-green eyes. "Why him? What is it about him that makes this so important to you?"

"He's so pretty!" Jillian felt her face heat. She hunched her shoulders. "You think that's stupid."

"I'm married to a man who is so beautiful, women stop on the street and stare at him, and if he were to give them even the mildest look of encouragement, they would follow him around like he was a juicy steak and they were starving puppies. So I can appreciate why a woman would be attracted to a man because he's pretty."

She called me a woman, Jillian thought. *She understands.* "It's not just that." She was testing an emotional cliff edge, not sure the ground would hold, not sure she would be able to get out of the way if the ground crumbled beneath her and started a rockslide. "He's smart and has a proper education and he reads all these books and knows social etiquette and how to do more than country dances, and he makes me feel . . ."

No. She couldn't talk about how he made her feel. Not yet.

"First kiss?" Surreal asked.

She shook her head. "Tamnar and I did a little kissing." Kisses that had barely broken Lucivar's rule.

"But Dillon is the first to give you a lover's kiss?"

She nodded. *Those* kisses had definitely broken the rule. Not something she would say to anyone.

"You didn't feel what you wanted to feel when Tamnar kissed you? And you feel that way when Dillon kisses you?"

"Yes."

At least, she *had* felt that fluttery excitement until Dillon had thrust his tongue in her mouth as if letting him do it once a few days ago meant he could keep doing it anywhere and anytime. And yesterday, his hand on her breast had hurt, changing the pleasure of seeing him into uneasiness when he wouldn't stop. But if her moontime had started an hour earlier, she wouldn't have gone to the market and she wouldn't have seen him while she was feeling so tender, and he wouldn't have hurt her.

Surreal smiled. "Then this is what we'll do. From what Marian told me, tomorrow is still a quiet home day for you, so write a note to Dillon and invite him to join us at the Sweet Tooth the day after tomorrow at three o'clock. Do you know the place? It's a cake shop located in the aristo part of Riada and is supposed to have the very best treats."

"That place is expensive." Yaslana had taken her and Nurian there for her birthday last year. She'd been impressed by the pretty, delicate decor that was in keeping with the intricately decorated cakes. And while she hadn't seen the actual bill that had been eased onto the table, she had seen the number of gold marks Yaslana had left on the table to pay for the outing.

"I imagine it's the kind of place Lord Dillon visits all the time." Surreal stood. "Now let's see what you have in your wardrobe that would be appropriate for an afternoon outing."

Lucivar stared at Surreal and wondered how he had allowed himself to be cornered this way. "You've arranged an outing with the prick-ass. Not just a meeting, an *outing*."

"Yes," Surreal replied with maddening calm. "The three of us—meaning me, Jillian, and the prick-ass—are going to the Sweet Tooth for coffee and cakes. A perfectly respectable public place."

"Why there?"

"It's pretty?"

He prowled behind his desk and snarled, "Pretty isn't the same as good. You know why they make the cakes look so fancy? So you won't notice the damn things are dry and don't have much taste."

He needed to fly. He needed a fight. He needed to tear into someone who wouldn't—couldn't—be hurt, who could handle not just the temper but the power. Mother Night, how he missed his sister at times like this. Jaenelle Angelline could have fought him into the ground, slammed strength against strength until he could put what he understood instinctively into words.

His beloved sister and Queen wasn't here, hadn't been for a lot of years now.

But Surreal *was* here, and she didn't back down either.

He shot her a hostile look. "Daemon wouldn't sit down in a place like that, no matter how many aristos filled the tables."

"Of course he would, for the same reason you did—to please someone else. And if he shared your opinion about the cakes, he would look around for another place that had the same exterior feel but served better food. Something you might want to look into before you take someone out for the next special occasion. Doesn't have to be in Riada, you know. There are plenty of cities in Askavi where you could go to the theater or have a fancy meal. You could use a Coach to ride the Winds so no one's dress gets rumpled during the journey."

"You're a pain in the ass."

"Love you too, sugar." She studied him. "Had you met Dillon before the moment when you were choking him?"

"No." As far as he was concerned, that was a serious tactical error on the boy's part.

"Then this little outing will be very interesting."

TWENTY

❖

Dillon studied his reflection in the mirror and nodded, satisfied that he would make a good impression on Lady Surreal SaDiablo.

"You don't know that family," Terrence said, worrying a button on his jacket until it hung by a thread.

"Do you?" Dillon turned away from the mirror and focused on his cousin, curious. He'd never met an Eyrien until he saw Jillian at the lending library and decided she was the answer to his future.

"Only by reputation. I've seen Prince Yaslana around the village, but I've never spoken to him. Dillon, Eyriens are a warrior race, and even among them, Yaslana is a law unto himself. He isn't someone you want to cross. They say he slaughtered an entire army of Eyriens once when they turned against him and tried to take over the valley."

He could believe that. What he couldn't believe was the way Yaslana exploded over him being friendly with a girl who worked for the man's wife. Jillian's sister was a Healer, and that gave her good social standing, but they weren't aristos. Unless Jillian was an unacknowledged daughter, he couldn't figure out why Yaslana paid so much attention to the hired help.

Until he received Jillian's note, he'd thought his efforts had been wasted. Yaslana's display of temper had been too public for him to try again with another girl anywhere in this valley. Thank the Darkness he was being given another chance.

"And no one even dares whisper anything about Yaslana's brother," Terrence added.

"Who is married to the Lady who invited me to this outing?" Dillon brushed nonexistent lint from his sleeve. Older women usually looked favorably on a young man who paid attention to them and made them believe they were interesting—a sentiment that would have earned him a reprimand if he'd still been training to serve as an escort in a court. Oh, he wouldn't aim too much attention in Lady SaDiablo's direction. Just enough for her to think favorably about him handfasting with Jillian.

"Why are you so focused on this Eyrien girl?" Terrence asked.

"Because I like her." That realization surprised him. He *did* like her. More important, she liked him and listened to him with a shining and apparent belief that he was wonderful and intelligent and educated. He could see himself living with her for the year of a handfast and enjoying the experience of being both lover and mentor.

What surprised him even more, he could see himself living in Riada for a year. Terrence had turned out to be a lively companion, if a little shy, and his parents had been gracious about having a distant relation show up on their doorstep, looking to visit for a few weeks.

Until the collision with Yaslana, he had felt safe here in a way he hadn't felt safe since Lady Blyte and her family had set out to ruin him. Even before he'd met Jillian, he'd begun thinking of what sort of work he could do in order to stay in Riada for a while.

Of course, now living here with Jillian would mean bumping up against Yaslana for that year. He'd never dealt with a man who thought killing someone was more expedient than handing that person an envelope of gold marks to encourage that person to go away.

"Everything will work out," Dillon said. "You'll see."

"You don't know that family," Terrence said again. "You don't know *him*."

No, he didn't. But he was about to find out everything he could over coffee and cakes.

Jillian was right about the young Warlord. He was certainly pretty. Brown hair leaning toward red complemented the green eyes and the skin that had received just enough sun to look healthy instead of pasty. He was trim and moved with confidence, but the trimness came from youth rather than the work a man put in to toning his muscles, and that made her wonder what he'd look like with his shirt off. She didn't think he would be quite so appealing without his clothes.

Superficially, he reminded her of Rainier, the Warlord Prince who had been her companion for decades. They had been friends who had loved each other and had shared a house, but they hadn't been lovers. Yes, similar coloring and a graceful way of moving reminded her of Rainier, but there was something about this boy that lightly scratched her temper.

Maybe she was a bit influenced by Lucivar's dislike of the young man. Or maybe it was the hint of something in his psychic scent that made her study him like a Warlord Prince's second-in-command—or like an assassin assessing her prey.

Yes, he was definitely pretty, and he knew it. Surreal watched the way he smiled at the somewhat attractive girl waiting tables—and the way he smiled at the beautiful girl working behind the counter, taking care of customers who wanted to bring home a treat. Something going on between those two? No. At least not yet. But the beautiful girl was signaling quite clearly that she would like more than a smile and a bit of flirting from him.

Would Lord Dillon have responded differently if he hadn't been meeting her and Jillian that day?

Then Jillian saw him and lit up, a flower opening for the sun. And the smile he turned on Jillian when he noticed her standing in the doorway . . . She'd expected a calculated smile, but the boy seemed genuinely pleased to see the girl. A point in his favor.

"This is my lucky day," Dillon said, getting to his feet as they walked over to the table. "I get to sit with two beautiful women."

That, however, sounded like every man she'd met who wanted to ingratiate himself enough to ask for a favor—usually a favor that required some assistance from her husband.

"Lord Dillon, this is Lady Surreal SaDiablo. She's visiting from Dhemlan."

Surreal held out her right hand. She had chosen to wear the ring and pendant that held her Birthright Green Jewel. Being one rank darker than his Opal Jewel, it wouldn't make him as cautious as seeing her Gray. And she didn't want him cautious; she wanted to let him play his game—if he was, in fact, playing a game.

Dillon bowed over her hand, almost, but not quite, touching his lips to her skin. When he looked up, she saw his anxiety, quickly hidden.

She'd seen that look plenty of times before, but usually from young men when they were testing their training in a social setting: *Am I making a good impression? Am I sufficiently pleasing?* In a court, it was understood that men Dillon's age were practicing and that the witches in the court would offer gentle correction when required or acknowledgment of lessons well learned.

Had he received formal training to serve in a court? If he had, why wasn't he trying for a position in a small court where he could acquire some polish and experience? Had he been wounded in some way during the training and was now too damaged either emotionally or physically to serve in a court?

Why invest so much time on a girl Jillian's age?

"I'm delighted to have this opportunity to meet Jillian's friend," Surreal said once they were seated.

He winced at her choice of words, but he was smart enough not to claim to be something more.

The somewhat attractive girl approached their table and handed out menus that were written in a script with so many curlicues it was almost impossible to make out the words. Surreal knew ornate writing. Saetan had never written anything in any other way. But the flourishes that had been natural for him never interfered with a person's ability to read the message.

"We'll have the variety platter—the large one," Dillon said. "And three coffees?" Now he looked at Surreal and Jillian.

"Sounds lovely," Surreal replied. Was there a reason he had placed the order before she had a chance to look at the menu?

"My treat," Dillon said, giving her a smile that made her itch to call in her stiletto. His smile, his manners, made her think of someone singing just a little off-key—nothing deliberately malicious but still grating.

"That's not necessary," she said. "Meeting here was my idea."

"I insist."

She inclined her head, noting how Jillian looked at him, as if offering to pay were the most brilliant thing a boy could do.

The platter of cakes and the coffee arrived. Dillon included her in the conversation, but the effort was heavy-handed. Not that Jillian noticed. Then again, when he focused on the girl, he sounded at ease. It was like watching someone sliding on ice—moments of grace followed by flailing limbs. It made her think again of young men trying out social skills and revealing their lack of experience. It would seem Lord Dillon's polish was still superficial, and that made her wonder *why* it was still superficial.

Surreal took a sampling of the cakes on the platter—nothing excessive and less than a third. Jillian, following her example, made different choices but took the same number. After a moment, Dillon took the same amount.

She wasn't trying to read his thoughts, because that would be a serious breach of the Blood's code of honor. But emotions flowed beyond a person's inner barriers. Some people were better at self-control and concealing their feelings, or stood so deep in the abyss their feelings couldn't be read. This Warlord had neither the power nor the control, and the flash of annoyance that followed her taking the selection of cakes made her wonder what game he was really playing—and what role he thought Jillian filled in that game.

Then he seemed to shrug off the annoyance and entertained them with talk about books he had read and plays he had seen.

"I saw Lord Beron in a play recently," Dillon said. "He's worked his way up to second male lead and was quite good in this new part." He nodded sagely. "Quite good."

"We go to see him whenever one of his plays comes to the theater in Riada," Jillian said.

"I doubt he'll be playing small theaters like the one in Riada for much longer. When we had dinner after his last performance, he hinted that he'll have the male lead in the next production."

"Really?" Surreal put a seed of doubt in her voice. "That seems a bit presumptuous, since he hasn't auditioned for the role yet." She gave Dillon a puzzled look, as if she wasn't quite smart enough to understand him. "I'm sure if Beron was on the threshold of such a significant step in his career, he would have mentioned it to my husband. After all, Prince Sadi *is* Beron's legal guardian, and the Prince also had dinner with Beron recently." She took a sip of coffee. "Since he knew I was coming to Ebon Rih, I'm surprised the Prince didn't mention you. He makes it his business to know about all of Beron's friends, so he would know that you're currently staying in Riada."

"We're not *friends*, exactly," Dillon said hurriedly. "More like acquaintances who have some friends in common."

"But you had dinner together." She didn't look at Jillian. The girl still looked at Dillon as if he were the yummiest cake in the shop—which she could believe, having tasted one of the cakes on her plate—but there was a hint of bafflement under the adoration. Good.

"A group of actors and aristos went out to dinner together, so we didn't have more than a minute or two to talk," Dillon said.

Surreal nodded. Now she turned to Jillian and smiled. "We know how those dinners go, don't we? There's barely time to congratulate the boy before he's swept off to be hugged by someone else."

"That's because he's brilliant," Jillian said. Her eyes shone as she focused on Dillon. "One of the reasons Beron is so graceful and can do those athletic moves on the stage is because Prince Rainier taught him how to dance. Rainier served in the Queen of Ebon Askavi's court."

"He was also Lady Angelline's dance instructor when she was an adolescent," Surreal added. Then she laughed. "When Jaenelle and Rainier danced together, you could watch them all night. They didn't just dance; they soared." A bittersweet memory, one she hadn't meant to share.

Dillon abruptly changed the subject.

Surreal listened to the boasting, the bragging, and the subtle sneering at anyone who wasn't a member of the aristo class—no, more than that, who wasn't a member of Dillon's exalted clique, which now, curiously, seemed to exclude Beron. She wanted to gag, but Jillian soaked up every word, as if her life had been nothing but a dull and boring gray, and Dillon had presented her with a palette of colors that dazzled the eyes.

Jillian was right about Dillon. The boy was pretty to look at, as long as you didn't look beyond the surface. Then again, the boasting, bragging, and sneering hadn't started until he'd made the mistake of claiming to be one of Beron's friends and been called on it. Maybe those things were an attempt to hide his insecurity and regain some ground.

Lucivar was right about the cakes. They were awful and could be part of the reason she wanted to gag.

Four cakes were left on the platter and Surreal was more than ready to leave. Then Jillian reached for another piece and Dillon blocked her hand, pushing the platter away from the girl—or as far away as he could, considering it was a small table.

He smiled and shook his finger playfully. Jillian blushed and looked unhappy.

"Thank you for the cakes, Lord Dillon," Surreal said, pushing her chair back as a signal that the outing was over. "It has been an interesting afternoon."

"I hope I was able to entertain you in some small measure," Dillon replied. He turned to Jillian. "And I hope we can do this again."

"Are you sure I can't settle the bill?" Surreal asked. "This place was my choice, after all."

He waved her offer away. "No, it's my pleasure. You two go along, and I'll take care of things."

"In that case, good day, Warlord."

"Lady SaDiablo. Jillian."

Surreal walked out of the shop and took the first side street, moving swiftly until they reached open land and were far enough from the buildings in Riada that nothing that was said would be overheard.

"Lady Surreal?" Jillian sounded worried. "Aren't we going back to the eyries?"

"I need to walk for a bit. And we need to talk."

✦ ✦ ✦

Jillian waited, but Surreal continued to walk and remained silent. Finally, she couldn't stand waiting.

"What did you think of Dillon? Isn't he lovely? He's so smart, and he went to all these fine schools, so he knows *everything*. Well, not everything. He doesn't know about weapons or fighting or things like that, but Dillon says those skills aren't as important as they used to be."

Surreal just kept walking.

"What did he say to you?" Surreal asked suddenly.

"What?"

"When he stopped you from taking that cake. What did he say to you?"

"It was nothing."

"You were having an enjoyable afternoon until that moment, so it wasn't nothing."

"It was just a tease, but sometimes I get self-conscious and too sensitive."

Silence. Surreal walked. Jillian followed half a step behind, wondering how things had gone wrong.

"If you want me to tangle with Lucivar to give you opportunities to spend time with this boy, you will tell me what he said." Surreal sounded cool, distant, not the indulgent chaperon she had been at the cake shop.

Marian and Nurian would do whatever Lucivar said. Surreal was the only one who might stand up to him. If she lost Surreal's support, she would never see Dillon again.

"He said if I ate another cake, I would be too plump to fly."

"I see," Surreal said.

"Haven't you ever felt this way?" Jillian cried. "Haven't you ever thought your heart would burst out of your chest because it was beating so hard when you caught sight of a special boy, or would break if he didn't send you a note when he promised?"

Surreal walked. She appeared to be heading for the old cabin on the outskirts of the village.

Before Jillian could point out that the cabin was out of bounds to everyone, Surreal stopped walking, as if she could sense the boundary that shouldn't be crossed.

"My mother was murdered when I was twelve," Surreal said. "I came home from lessons one day and found her on the floor with her throat slit. She was a Queen and a Black Widow who had been broken by a man who had lusted for a girl who looked exotic. Being Dea al Mon in the Realm of Terreille certainly made her exotic.

"I ran because that was what she wanted me to do—get away, hide from her killer. I was raped a few days later. I wore Birthright Green, and sometimes raw power makes up for the lack of experience or training. That man violated my body, but he couldn't break me, couldn't break my Green Jewel.

"I let men use me in order to have enough coins to buy food, to keep going another day. And then a man used me and refused to pay. I rammed a knife into him and began my second profession. Even at that age, I was good with a knife. I whored on the streets for a few years until Sadi found me and arranged for me to train in a high-level Red Moon house."

"Why didn't he help you get out of being a whore?" Jillian asked softly.

"I wouldn't let him, and he knew that. So he made sure I received the best education available for the skills I wanted to acquire. I was the most sought-after, and expensive, whore in Terreille, but I was even better as an assassin." Surreal looked at Jillian. "I never felt that rush, that tingle of anticipation, that heightened level of nerves because every knock on the door might be that special boy. Because of that, I will help you have opportunities to spend time with Dillon and get to know more about him— and give him a chance to know you. But my rules aren't negotiable, Jillian. If you break them, even once, you had better hope that Lucivar gets to that boy before I do. Are we clear on that? If you can't, or won't, follow my rules, you should write a note to Dillon telling him you can't see him again—and warn him not to try to see you."

Jillian hesitated but couldn't see another choice. "What are your rules?"

Surreal nodded, as if Jillian had asked the right question. "Dillon can visit you at your sister's eyrie or at Lucivar's eyrie, as long as one adult is present. When you go into the village, you go with a chaperon."

"I've been allowed to go into Riada on my own since I was a child!"

"And you were safe," Surreal agreed. "But that kiss and grope in the alleyway changed things."

If Dillon had given her just the kiss instead of doing more, they wouldn't have been caught and Prince Yaslana wouldn't be angry and she wouldn't have these restrictions on where she could go and whom she could see.

"There will be opportunities for kissing, but there won't be time for him to take the play and petting beyond what is acceptable to me—and what I can persuade Lucivar to agree to."

"But I love Dillon!"

"I don't doubt it. But he's reached the age of majority, and you have decades ahead of you before you reach yours. So a chaperon is required when you go down to the village. An adult has to be home if Dillon comes to visit—and if you're not within sight of that adult, you have to be visible to anyone who might fly past the eyrie. That way, if Dillon's hands, or anything else, end up where they're not supposed to be, no one will wonder why an Eyrien war blade sliced through his wrists."

The wind changed direction. Surreal finger combed her hair away from her face and used Craft to twist it into a casual knot at the back of her head.

"You want time to think about it?" Surreal asked.

"I'll follow your rules," She wasn't sure how Dillon was

going to react when he heard what was required in order for them to see each other, but she would deal with that later.

"Then it's time we got back to the eyrie."

The thought was there and the words were out before Jillian had time to consider. "I think you did have a crush on a boy once, before the bad things happened. I think you did feel that tingle of anticipation, of waiting for him to visit and notice you."

Surreal gave her the queerest look. "Maybe. And maybe I also know what an impulsive, imprudent action can cost a girl and don't want you to carry that same kind of regret."

Sobering words. But Dillon would never ask her to do something she would regret.

When they reached the open ground outside her home, Jillian thanked Surreal for the outing and hurried into the eyrie. As she set the table for dinner and cleaned the vegetables, she wished she had thought to ask the waitress to box up the remaining cakes so that she could bring them home and share them with Nurian.

Not looking at Surreal because it would piss him off if he looked at her right now, Lucivar picked up one of the chunks of wood on his desk and blasted it with power and temper, then watched the sawdust drift into a pile on his desk like sifted flour.

"You want me to back off, let him court her."

Surreal nodded. "Yes, I do. Allowing men the opportunities and space to court young women is part of being Blood, regardless of race."

He picked up the next chunk of wood and blasted it, watched it dribble onto the desk. "That's true for Warlord Princes, not the Blood in general."

"No, Warlord Princes are given a clear field once they express interest in a woman to avoid having their potential rivals splattered all over the walls. But all social gatherings allow people to meet and get to know one another—and see if the attraction one person feels for another is friendship or romance."

"You think I overreacted, that my instincts about that little prick-ass are wrong."

"Oh, no," Surreal said with a tight smile. "There is nothing wrong with your instincts. If we were still in Terreille, I would have been tempted to gut Lord Dillon in a way that would have had his intestines spilling into the street when he walked out of the cake shop this afternoon. But we're not in Terreille, so while our instincts about Dillon aren't wrong, they might not be quite right either. He's . . . Hell's fire, Lucivar, if you take away Dillon's veneer of polish, Daemonar has better social skills than that Rihlander Warlord."

He'd been reaching for the third chunk of wood. Now he stopped and looked at her—and was glad the desk was between them and her hands were in sight and empty.

"There's something off about him."

"Yes, but I can't decide if he really is an arrogant prick who deserves a knife in the guts or if his social maturity is stunted for some reason. He wants to be fawned over and admired. Not just wants it. *Needs* it. I suspect that's what he finds so appealing about Jillian. She's young enough not to see his flaws—or recognize his subtle cruelty," she added softly.

Wondering if she was still talking about Dillon, Lucivar picked up the chunk of wood, came around the desk, and held it out to her. Her right hand slipped off her lap, then came up fast. Lucivar saw the glint of a blade and released the wood, jerking his hand out of the way at the same time he created an Ebon-gray shield around himself.

The big hunting knife she'd commissioned from Kohlvar several years ago flashed up, then left to right.

Four smaller pieces of wood hit the floor.

"Impressive speed," he murmured. She had always

been good with a knife, and he knew better than to be careless around her.

"He's new and exciting," Surreal said. "He's pretty on the outside, and he talks a good game. He's every aristo thing you despise, but if you stop this now, all she'll remember is that you stopped her from spending time with the boy she loves."

"Loves?" Lucivar bared his teeth. "*Loves?* How can she love that piece of walking carrion?"

"She doesn't know him." Surreal slid the hunting knife into its leather sheath and vanished it. "Let her discover who he is while she's standing safely in your shadow."

He blew out a breath. "She'll get hurt."

"Better a skinned knee than a broken wing."

He rubbed the back of his neck, trying to ease the tension. "We still have a wolf pack on the mountain. I can ask them to keep a discreet lookout at my eyrie and Nurian's. They won't be seen, but they'll sound a warning if the prick-ass crosses a line."

"Discreet watchers are good," Surreal agreed. "But you don't want to be that subtle. Not this time. So I was thinking of chaperons who will be overlooked by the inexperienced but will be louder, faster, and more insistent about announcing any wrongdoing than a whole pack of younger siblings."

Lucivar paled. "Oh, Hell's fire, no."

"They'll just come for a visit. Then they'll go home."

"Swear to me on your Jewels that they will go home."

Surreal blinked. Then she laughed so hard she gasped for breath. "I swear, Lucivar. I swear I will never tell anyone that you're afraid of Scelties."

Since he wasn't going to admit it, he hauled her out of the chair—and hoped the dogs let her keep her promise.

TWENTY-ONE

Someone kept pounding on his front door. Swearing, Lucivar secured the loin wrap around his hips as he hurried through the eyrie to stop the damn noise before it woke up the children.

He yanked the door open. A rock from the decorative rock garden Marian and Daemonar had made last summer dropped in the space between his bare feet and six little furry front paws.

He looked at his brother, who carried his sleepy niece. *I hate you.*

Daemon's smile held a brittleness that spoke of more than one kind of pain. *As Karla likes to say, kiss kiss.*

Lucivar looked at the three Scelties. He recognized Morghann, the brown and white witch who now wore a Purple Dusk Birthright Jewel, and Khary, an Opal-Jeweled Warlord who was dark gray with white legs, chest, and tail tip. The third Sceltie, a black and white Warlord with tan patches on his face, must be the puppy Daemonar had met when the boy had visited his uncle a few weeks ago.

Bright eyes looked back at him. Tails wagged. Tiny movements brought those front paws just a wee bit closer to the threshold of his home. Before they had a chance to start offering opinions about everything, he offered an opinion of his own. "If you leave the rock there, Marian will be unhappy with you."

The rock instantly rose two fingers off the ground and scooted toward the empty space in the rock garden. It did one roll and would have settled dirt side up if Daemon hadn't added mildly, "The bottom of the rock already has dirt on it and should go back in that way. It will matter to Lady Marian."

Morghann gave Daemon an anxious look before focusing on her task. Using Craft, the Sceltie turned the rock right side up, then let it settle back into the dirt. But that wasn't enough, because she continued to make small adjustments until the rock exactly matched its previous position.

"Perfect," Daemon said quietly.

The joy that blasted out of the little bitch made Lucivar glad he didn't have to deal with her on a daily basis. He looked at the last member of this party and smiled when Daemon set her on her feet. "Morning, witchling. Have you got something for me?"

"We brought Scelties!" Jaenelle Saetien said, now awake and as bright-eyed as the damn dogs.

"Anything else?"

"I brought Papa!"

Daemon kissed the top of her head. "I think Uncle Lucivar is looking for a hug."

She took a step, avoided putting a foot on any Sceltie tails, and launched herself at him.

Not enough height and too much distance.

Lucivar stepped forward, caught her under the arms, and lifted her so that she could wrap her arms around his neck and give him a hug—and tried not to wince when her leg gave him a light whack where a man didn't want to be hit.

"Aahhhh, that's better." He returned her hug before he put her down.

"Is Titian awake?"

"Not yet. Why don't you go wake her?"

Jaenelle Saetien rushed past him into the eyrie.

The Scelties looked at him.

Giving in, Lucivar stepped back. "Come in."

Khary raced after Jaenelle. Morghann waited for Daemon's nod before running to catch up. The third one immediately began exploring the front room.

You know Morghann and Khary. This one is Lord Tagg. Daemon stepped into the eyrie. "Is there any coffee?"

"Not yet," Lucivar replied. He closed the door and headed for the kitchen. So much for getting another hour of sleep. "I'm not even going to ask what time you got up in order to get here this early."

Daemon removed his black jacket and laid it over the back of a kitchen chair. Moving around the kitchen, he took eggs, bacon, and butter out of the cold box. "Would you like an omelet?"

Lucivar measured out coffee and put the pot on the stove. "That's good for me. The children will want scrambled eggs when they wake up."

"I can do that." Daemon broke eggs into a bowl. "You look tired."

So do you, old son. "Baby Andulvar has been fussy. Took a while to get him settled last night." He pulled out a frying pan to cook the bacon.

"How is Marian?"

Daemon asked that question every time they saw each other, as if needing the reassurance that one of them was still loved and happy.

"She's doing fine. She regains a little more strength and energy every day, but she's occasionally frustrated because it's been months since that healing and she still doesn't have the stamina she had before the . . . illness. Nurian looks in on her a couple of times a week, mostly because no one has any experience with the kind of healing spell Jaenelle Angelline gifted to Marian. Of course, having three children can sap the stamina from anyone."

How much longer can you endure this, whatever this is? How much longer can I wait and watch you suffer? And how can I let you know there is someone who can give you answers without losing you?

Putting the pan down, Lucivar braced his hands on the counter.

"Lucivar?" Daemon moved to stand beside him. "What is it?"

"I don't think I can tell you."

"You can tell me anything."

He wanted to believe that. All right, then. A hint. A clue. A rope thrown to a man trying to save himself from a deadly fall and holding on to the cliff with one broken finger because that was all he had left. "I think Daemonar sees Witch once in a while."

"You mean he dreams about her when he visits the cabin? I did give him permission to go inside."

"No, I think he sees her. Talks to her."

Daemon didn't move, barely breathed. Finally he whispered, "Are you sure?"

Lucivar shook his head. "I'm not sure of anything, but I've been noticing some things since the day Marian fell into that healing sleep and he disappeared for a while. Since then, when we butt heads and he goes away to sulk . . . sometimes he'll come back and argue his point from a different angle—an angle I'm sure his boy brain would not have considered. Sometimes he comes back looking like he'd gotten the sympathy he wanted—someone taking his side against his mean old father—but also received a whack upside the head along with the sympathy. And sometimes he comes back and apologizes for being a brat—and then we talk about his behavior and my reaction. Bastard, those things aren't coming from him. Not on his own."

"That doesn't mean Witch is his confidante," Daemon said.

Something in Daemon's voice. Something that sounded too much like desperate hope.

"No, it doesn't. I know Chaosti keeps an eye on the boy, and some of that might be coming from him." While he had walked among the living, Chaosti had been the Warlord Prince of the Dea al Mon. For the past few months he had divided his time between helping his own people when they made the transition to demon-dead and residing at the Keep in Kaeleer.

Silence. Then Daemon said, "Jaenelle Saetien hasn't mentioned seeing her special friend since the Birthright Ceremony. Does Titian talk to Witch?"

"No. Titian never knew Jaenelle Angelline."

"Well, the boy always doted on his Auntie J." Daemon cleared his throat and went back to preparing the omelet while Lucivar cooked the bacon. "Tell me about this trouble with Jillian."

"Didn't Surreal tell you?"

Another silence. "She sent a note to the Hall asking that someone escort three Scelties to Ebon Rih, but didn't say why they were needed." He hesitated before adding, "She didn't ask *me* to bring the Scelties, but Jaenelle Saetien wanted to spend time with her cousins, and I wanted to spend some time with you." Another hesitation. "Surreal won't be pleased to see me."

"Are you telling me I should put you in a separate guest room?" Lucivar asked quietly.

"That's up to Surreal. I could stay at The Tavern in Riada or at the Keep. That should be sufficient distance."

Sufficient distance for what?

Quietly descending to the level of his Ebon-gray power, Lucivar picked up a whisper of fragility at the level of the Black along with the jaggedness in Daemon's psychic scent that had appeared around the same time as the headaches. And something else, something that Daemon was trying fiercely to control.

What in the name of Hell was going on?

Couldn't meet this battle head-on. He'd let Surreal handle things with Jillian for the most part and find reasons that he and Daemon needed to be away from the eyrie, find distractions until his brother was willing to talk to him.

While they ate breakfast, Lucivar told Daemon about the incident that had set off his temper—and set all the rest of this mess into motion.

"What do you know about Lord Dillon?" Daemon asked as he refilled their coffee mugs.

"Comes from an aristo Rihlander family. He's visiting family in Riada. That's all anyone here knows about him."

"Maybe that's all anyone is willing to say about him, but I doubt that's all anyone knows."

Lucivar shrugged. "I don't like him, and Surreal thought there was something off about him. But this is first love, so I'm expected to be fair about this." He bared his teeth in a smile.

"Uh-huh." Daemon sipped his coffee and studied his brother. "Now that we've agreed to respect the mantles of our authority and be adult and fair about this, who is your best source for gathering gossip?"

"I stop at The Tavern for that," Lucivar said. "Same as I've been doing ever since I first arrived in Ebon Rih."

"That tells you about Riada. Maybe Doun and Agio, too, since the Masters of the Guard for those Queens' courts know they can drop by and share a few unofficial observations that will be followed up by the Warlord Prince of Ebon Rih making an official visit to their village. No, we need someone who knows the gossip about aristo families throughout Askavi."

Lucivar put his mug down and eyed Daemon. "There is one person who might know. But if you really think I need to ask her, you're coming with me."

"Why?"

"Because being demon-dead hasn't made Lady Perzha any less eccentric."

✦ ✦ ✦

Surreal tightened the belt on her robe before she unlocked the guest room's door and stepped back to allow Daemon to enter.

His sexual heat washed over her, making her nipples harden and her body throb with need.

Bastard. Couldn't he have given her a couple of days of peace while she was helping his brother?

Daemon studied her for a moment, then slipped his hands in his trouser pockets and said in a voice stripped of emotion, "Jaenelle Saetien wanted to visit her cousins. I thought that would provide them with a distraction while you dealt with Jillian. If staying in another guest room here inconveniences you, I can take a room at The Tavern or stay at the Keep."

And have everyone in Riada whispering behind their hands the way the Blood in Amdarh were doing? Have Lucivar back her into a corner and demand to know what was going on? If she'd thought for one minute that he would understand, that he might be able to rein in the games Sadi was playing to torment her, she would have told him. But it was more likely that Lucivar would side with Sadi. Not only side with him, but think that she was the one in the wrong for not being willing to accommodate her husband's needs because Daemon had these damn headaches—which didn't seem to trouble him when they were in bed.

"There's no reason for you to stay elsewhere or to stay in another room here," she said.

"Very well," he replied. "Lucivar and I are heading out. There's someone who might have information about Lord Dillon, and Lucivar doesn't want to go by himself."

He would be gone for a few hours, and she could breathe again. Thank the Darkness.

She locked the door before stripping off her night-clothes and getting dressed. Then she waited until she felt the Black and Ebon-gray leave the eyrie before venturing out to the kitchen to get something to eat.

Little Weeble was often described as quaint or original. Those were the kind words that were used, although the tone in which they were said was often less than kind. Not that the citizens of Little Weeble cared what outsiders thought or said about their village. After all, outsiders were outsiders and weren't required to deal with the citizens except for business ventures—were, in fact, gently encouraged to go away.

As he and Daemon walked from the landing web to Perzha's sprawling patchwork home, Lucivar noted how many merchants who were just opening their shops froze at the sight of them—and how many stopped working and followed them at a distance calculated not to provoke a challenge.

He had visited Little Weeble once or twice a year for decades and had never seen the people react this way. They had never worried about *him* showing up. Which meant Daemon was the reason for their barely contained panic and fear.

By the time they reached Perzha's house, her First Circle was there. Most were old men—still vigorous and mentally sharp, but there was no denying that most of them had grandchildren. But there were younger men who hadn't been there the last time he visited, men in their twenties who might have been serving their first full contract in a court.

The old men's eyes were filled with fear. The younger men stared at Lucivar and Daemon with defiance that wasn't quite a challenge.

"You'll have to excuse them," a woman said from behind the wall of men. "They can be overprotective." An age-spotted hand thumped the shoulder of a young Warlord Prince who was too close to making a lethal mistake. Reluctantly, he lowered his eyes, no longer on the point of challenging two Warlord Princes who would have destroyed him if he started a fight. Even more reluctantly, he stepped to the side to make room for the woman who jingled and jangled into sight.

Lady Perzha had freckles, buckteeth, rusty red hair heavily threaded with silver, and a face that was so homely it was oddly attractive. She wore shirts and skirts and shawls in colors that clashed as often as they coordinated. Her jewelry was a mishmash of seashells and glass beads, pearls and rubies, diamonds and emeralds. And somewhere under all of it was a Red Jewel, making Perzha as powerful as she was eccentric.

"Is this an official visit?" she asked politely, looking at Daemon.

Being demon-dead, she was the only one facing them who wasn't holding his breath waiting for an answer.

"Not on my part," Daemon replied mildly. "Prince Yaslana needs your help, and I tagged along to keep him company."

"Do you mind if we sit out in the garden? I do love the early-morning hours when I can be outdoors and look after my flowers." Perzha turned to one of the older men. "Lord Carleton, will you see to refreshments?"

"But . . ." Carleton, who was the Steward of Perzha's court, slanted a look at Daemon before hurrying into the house.

"This way." She led them through a gated archway that divided the house into two sections and provided access to the enclosed lawn and gardens. "Even if one works from a single room, it's important to be able to separate business from one's personal life, don't you think?"

"My study may be my main place of business, but it's also my sanctuary from household drama," Daemon replied as they took seats at a round table on a terrace overlooking flower beds that followed the same color schemes as Perzha's wardrobe. "That's why it has a thick door and a stout lock."

Perzha gave them a sympathetic smile. "When children reach a point of having opinions of their own, family is often about drama."

"Mine have been voicing opinions since before they could say actual words," Lucivar said, happy to see a woman wearing an apron approaching the table with a coffeepot, followed by a younger woman carrying a tray that held plates of pastries and sandwiches. Carleton brought a ravenglass goblet and a familiar kind of decanter.

"May I," Daemon said, indicating the goblet and decanter. It wasn't a question.

Carleton set the items next to Daemon's place at the table and retreated, along with the two women from the kitchen.

Ignoring his coffee, Daemon removed the crystal stopper from the decanter and poured the dark liquid into the goblet. As he tilted the goblet, he used Craft to create a tongue of witchfire. He turned the ravenglass slowly over the flame until the liquid warmed to the correct temperature. Extinguishing the witchfire, he moved the goblet back and forth under his nose, breathing in the scent before he took a taste—and made a face as he set the goblet on the table.

"Hell's fire, woman," he said. "What kind of blood wine is this? Why aren't you drinking proper yarbarah?"

"Proper yarbarah, as you put it, comes from the SaDiablo vineyards in Dhemlan," Perzha replied. "A few other places produce some yarbarah for ceremonial purposes, but the best vintages come from your vineyards. Having my court ordering bottles on a regular basis would have caught your attention."

"So?"

"So you are more than the Warlord Prince of Dhemlan, and my people have feared the day you would come calling."

Lucivar chose a sandwich. He wasn't hungry, was rapidly losing his appetite for a lot of things since realizing what their arrival might mean for this village, but lazy arrogance was a useful tool—or weapon. "Is there a reason they've been concerned about Prince Sadi coming here? Something your court should have reported to me?"

"You know full well the reason for their concern. I told my First Circle—the First Circle who was with me then—that I should go to Hell. I was demon-dead. I died of natural causes, of an illness this old body couldn't overcome. It was swift, and I died in my sleep, which is why, when I made the transition to demon-dead, I still had the reservoir of power in my Red Jewel as well as my Birthright Green." Perzha leaned toward Daemon. "I told them I should report to the High Lord of Hell and they should look for another Queen. I told them Prince Yaslana wouldn't allow Little Weeble to go to another Queen without considering what the people needed. But the First Circle pleaded with me to stay until they could find the right Queen to take my place. As long as a Red-Jeweled Queen ruled here, the village couldn't be claimed by some ambitious twit—their word, not mine—who looked at Little Weeble as a place to gain credentials for something better. As if there could be any place that was better."

"I wouldn't have allowed a twit to take over the village," Lucivar growled. "They should have known that."

"They should have," Perzha agreed quietly. "Especially considering who you still serve."

He didn't look at Daemon. The commitment they had made to the Queen of Ebon Askavi was a lifetime commitment of service—their lifetimes, not hers. So he understood why the people in this odd yet productive village would have resisted bringing in anyone who couldn't be another Perzha.

"Do they actually look for another Queen?" Daemon asked.

"Yes, they do." Perzha hesitated. "Every year, the First

Circle collects a bucket of sand from our beach. Then the men use a screen and carefully sift the sand. On the day they find a diamond among the grains, they'll know there is a Queen out there who is right for Little Weeble and they should let me retire, even if retiring means going to the Dark Realm."

"You really think there is a diamond somewhere on that beach?" Lucivar asked.

She smiled. "Yes. That's why I have stayed. It's there. They just haven't found it yet."

His heart gave an odd flutter. Daemon, he noticed, looked pale.

"Who told you?" Daemon asked quietly.

"A few days after I made the transition to demon-dead, the living myth came to Little Weeble with the previous High Lord. She was the one who told the First Circle about the sand and the diamond. She saw it in a tangled web of dreams and visions—the diamond found in the sand would herald the arrival of the new Queen. Until that day, everyone agreed that I should stay here and take care of my people."

Daemon rested his hand over hers. "If my father and my Queen agreed to this arrangement, then I will honor it. But if you tire of duty, if you want to go whether the people find the diamond or not, all you have to do is send a message, and I'll return for an official visit." He sat back and took a sip of now-cold coffee. "Until then, we came for some gossip."

Perzha blinked at Daemon, then looked at Lucivar.

"Yeah, gossip," he said.

"The more titillating, the better." Daemon gave Perzha a smile that would have made her blush.

"Oh, my." She patted a hand over her heart, looking flustered. "I've never heard of you being much of a flirt."

"I only flirt with those who would appreciate it for what it is and not expect anything more."

Because anyone who expected more would find them-

selves facing the Sadist, the cruelest and most lethal side of Daemon's temper, Lucivar thought.

"Well, gossip that reaches a coastal town is a bit like storm wrack," Perzha said. "A lot of debris gets thrown onto the shore, but not much is worth anything unless it happens to be the thing you're looking for." She gave them a brilliant smile. "Who do you want to know about?"

An hour later, when members of Perzha's First Circle kept showing up every five minutes, broadly hinting that their Queen needed to rest, what with her having an allergy to the sun and all, Daemon and Lucivar walked back to the landing web at the edge of the village.

"Hell's fire," Lucivar said. "How does she know so much about aristos in other villages? *Why* does she know so much?" She hadn't known anything about that prick-ass Dillon, but he felt confident now that she would find out everything he wanted to know.

"She's an eccentric Queen from a little village with a weird name, so people forget that she wears a Red Jewel and can wipe the floor with most of them." Daemon called in a pen and a thin leather binder that held a sheaf of paper. "Want to bet the gossip about this place is that there have been other Queens over the generations since Lady Perzha ruled here, but a condition of a First Circle forming an official court around the new Queen is that she take the name Perzha, at least for her public identity, and use an illusion spell to *look* like the late beloved Queen?"

"No bet. It sounds like something the people here would do."

"Since they would want sufficient warning if someone figured out the deception, I would also wager that some of her court are very good at ferreting out information about anyone of interest anywhere in Askavi."

If they were that good, they should have remembered that I knew Perzha was demon-dead, Lucivar thought.

They should have known that Daemon wouldn't force her to go to Hell. Our family, more than anyone, understands the difference between refusing to let go and still being needed.

Then he felt a chill when he realized Daemon was making notes about this visit. "What are you doing?"

"That yarbarah Perzha was drinking is the equivalent of rough whiskey made in a still. Worse, the stuff was putrid. If she's going to stay in Little Weeble, she should be drinking something better to sustain the flesh and her power. So I'm giving Holt instructions to have regular deliveries made from the SaDiablo vineyards." Daemon looked at Lucivar. "Do you have any objections?"

He shook his head. "If I'd known she was sustaining herself by drinking swill, I would have supplied her with yarbarah myself. Hell's fire, if it mattered so much for her to stay, why did her court give her shit to drink?"

Daemon finished making notes and vanished the pen and leather binder. "They probably never tasted it and didn't know how disgustingly bad the stuff was—and Perzha didn't tell them because they were afraid of losing her. The First Circle who had been serving her when she died knew that Saetan knew about her. He would have insisted she consume properly blended yarbarah. But that would have been what? Two, three Rihlander generations ago? The oldest men serving her now would have been boys, if they'd been born yet."

"So after Father returned to the Darkness, they didn't continue whatever arrangement was made." Lucivar swore softly. "Even if she didn't want to approach you, she could have said something to me."

"Maybe this is a very recent decline in the quality of what they are purchasing—or in the quality of what they are now receiving—but they still believe they're providing her with a decent vintage."

They looked at each other.

Daemon called in the binder and pen and made another note.

It wasn't for show. Holt would be given part of the assignment to gather information about any vineyard making yarbarah. But the High Lord of Hell had other sources of information, and if someone had been substituting a bad vintage for a good one, Lucivar would kill the bastard's body—and Daemon would take care of the rest.

TWENTY-TWO

───────────◆───────────

Jillian walked into the Yaslana eyrie as Titian and Jaenelle Saetien dashed out of the kitchen. Titian looked equal parts curious and alarmed, but Jaenelle Saetien said in a singsong voice, "Daemonar's in trouble."

"Sounds like it," Jillian agreed. Must be a morning for high drama, judging by the sounds coming from the kitchen.

The girls dashed down the corridor toward the playroom.

"I didn't know Mother was saving it for something special," Daemonar said, trying to sound like he had done something perfectly reasonable and not coming close. "And they were hungry."

We're very hungry, a young-sounding male voice said.

And we didn't want eggs and toast, another male said.

And we already ate the oatmeal the girl pups didn't want. That voice was female.

"Which doesn't excuse going into the cold box and taking a roast," Daemon said sternly.

We didn't take the roast, the second male voice said. *Daemonar took the roast.*

But he took it because we are very hungry, the other male said.

"At home we have rules about taking things out of the cold box without asking," Daemon said. "Not being home doesn't mean you can forget the rules."

We did a wrong thing? The female sounded alarmed.

"No, *you* didn't do a wrong thing. *Daemonar* made a mistake," Daemon said.

Jillian tiptoed toward the kitchen. Not that she needed to get closer to hear everything. But she was curious about whom the voices belonged to. Young-sounding didn't always mean young.

She peeked around one side of the archway that opened onto the kitchen.

Prince Sadi and Prince Yaslana were staring at Daemonar and three small dogs who were bunched around the boy's feet.

Scelties. The ones who were vessels for the power that flowed in the blood were called kindred, and they wore Jewels and learned Craft just like the rest of the Blood.

She'd seen Scelties before, but that was years ago, and although she'd observed how the dogs had herded Mikal and Daemonar to keep the boys out of mischief, she'd never interacted with the Scelties herself.

"We'll put it back." Daemonar sounded sulky. "I was just trying to be a good host."

A beat of silence. Then Yaslana blew out a breath, a sound full of annoyance. "You can't put it back. Your mother isn't going to want to cook it now."

We're sorry we are hungry. That was the larger male, a gray and white dog with black markings on his face . . . who wore a *dark Opal Jewel*?

Jillian blinked, but that didn't change the rank of the Jewel mostly hidden in the white chest fur. *Mother Night.*

"No, you're all sorry for taking the meat without asking, and you should apologize to Marian, since this is her kitchen in the same way the kitchen at the Hall is Mrs. Beale's territory," Daemon said.

Mrs. Beale said she would make puppy pies out of us if we took anything from her kitchen without asking, the smaller male said, pressing closer to Daemonar's legs.

Mrs. Beale is scary, the female said. *Marian isn't scary.*

"Mother can be scary when she's really mad," Daemonar said in a loud whisper. "But it takes a lot to get her that mad." He eyed his father and uncle. "We'll go without supper."

No food? *We don't get food?* *But *we* weren't bad.*

Jillian put a hand over her mouth to hold back the laugh. Yaslana looked over his shoulder at her. Either he'd sensed the movement or, more likely, he'd known she was there all along.

"You feel up to doing some shopping at the market?" he asked.

"Yes, sir." She hadn't been down to Riada since the outing to the cake shop, so she hadn't had a chance to talk to Dillon and tell him about being able to see him. Sort of. "Is it all right if I go to the library too? I have some books to return."

Yaslana stared at her a moment too long. "All right." Still looking at her, he crooked a finger at Daemonar. "Bane of my existence, come here." When Daemonar came up beside him, Yaslana wrapped a hand around the back of the boy's neck. "You are standing escort for Jillian while she does the shopping and runs her errands. That means you don't go wandering off to talk to friends. You keep each other in sight. Got that?"

"Yes, sir."

She could convince Daemonar to give her a few minutes to talk to Dillon. Not out of sight or anything, because Dillon would be in trouble if they did that, but with Daemonar far enough away for them to have a private conversation.

"And you three are chaperons for both of them," Lucivar finished, turning his head to stare at the Scelties.

Well, that wouldn't be so bad. The dogs would obey her. Wouldn't they?

"Lady Marian is feeding the baby," Yaslana said, looking at her again. "Lady Surreal is with her. Go ask if there is anything they need while you're at the market."

"Yes, sir," Jillian said.

Yaslana gave Daemonar an easy push. "You go clean your teeth and wash your hands."

As Jillian walked past the kitchen, she saw Prince Sadi crouch and the Scelties gather around him.

"You think they'll be all right?" Lucivar asked when Jillian and Daemonar flew down to Riada while Morghann, Khary, and Tagg caught the Winds down to the village. They would meet up in front of the butcher's shop.

"They'll be fine." Daemon looked at the roast that had three chunks torn out of it and shook his head as he set it on a cutting board. "This was a fine piece of meat." Taking a large kitchen knife from the block on the counter, he cut up the rest into small chunks.

Opening one of the lower cupboards, Lucivar selected a container with a tight lid. "A couple of weeks ago, I wouldn't have worried about the children going to the village on their own. But that damn Warlord sniffing around Jillian changes everything."

Daemon scooped up the chunks of meat and put them in the container. While Lucivar closed the lid, he washed his hands. Then he took the pencil and one of the squares of paper Marian used in order to pin information on the family message board and wrote *Sceltie food*. He used Craft to fix the paper to the lid, then put the container in the cold box.

"There was going to be a boy sooner or later," Daemon said, returning the pencil.

"I expected any boy interested in Jillian to know better than to piss on my boots."

"I would have expected the aristo family who is hosting him to know better. After your initial reaction and his accepting Surreal's invitation to join her and Jillian at the cake shop, they have to know he's expressed interest in the girl. Why haven't they told him to come up to the eyrie and introduce himself? If that's too intimidating or if they're concerned that might indicate more interest than is felt, especially considering the difference in Jillian's and Lord Dillon's ages, there are ways to make a casual introduction."

"The Eyriens who settled in Ebon Rih didn't come from aristo families."

"You do," Daemon said quietly. "I know it doesn't mean much to you. That sort of thing never did. But sometimes, brother, reminding someone of just how aristo your bloodlines are can be a very sharp whip."

Lucivar smiled and shook his head. "Perzha wearing all her clattering jewelry. Me wearing the leathers that are suited for a working Eyrien warrior instead of looking like the ruler of this valley—of the whole damn Territory, even if I haven't officially claimed it. A truth about who we are, but also a disguise."

"I know a bit about using one kind of power to conceal another."

Yes, he would. There still weren't many among the living who knew Daemon Sadi was more than the Warlord Prince of Dhemlan—was, in fact, the High Lord of Hell.

It took Jillian less than a minute after landing in front of the butcher's shop to learn that Scelties were bundles of information—especially when it came to themselves.

The female Sceltie was Morghann, a Purple Dusk–Jeweled witch. Khary was a Warlord who wore an Opal in the deeper range of that Jewel, and Tagg, a black and white youngster with tan markings, was also a Warlord, but he was too young to have gone through the Birthright Ceremony, so he didn't have a Jewel. Normally he wouldn't have been brought along for a visit in another Territory, except a visit to Scelt, but Daemon had decided that Tagg should come with the other two because it would be educational and the Scelties would be with members of the Sa-Diablo family.

Jillian interpreted that explanation to mean that the three dogs had put up such a fuss about Tagg being left behind that Prince Sadi hadn't wanted to return home to deal with whatever trouble one unhappy Sceltie could cause at the Hall. So he brought the trouble with him.

It wasn't the day for the full open market, but the grocer had carts of fruits and vegetables set up outside. Before she could walk into the butcher shop and buy a replacement roast, Tagg dashed toward a cart full of vegetables and leaped—a move that would have landed him in the middle of the produce. Daemonar caught him in midair, swinging the Sceltie out of reach a moment before Tagg grabbed a crown of broccoli.

"What's going on?" The grocer dashed outside, holding a broom in a fighting stance.

"Sorry, sir," Daemonar said, struggling to hold the excited dog. "This is Lord Tagg. He likes broccoli."

Greens are good! Tagg whapped Daemonar's leg with his tail.

Hello, Morghann said. *We are Scelties. We live at the Hall with Prince Sadi and Lady Surreal, but we are visiting Prince Yaslana and Lady Marian.*

The grocer blinked. Then he pursed his lips as Jillian and Khary rushed up to join the kerfuffle.

Honestly, it was like dealing with fast-talking, four-legged toddlers who dashed off to look at, sniff, and taste whatever caught their interest.

Well, she'd been helping Marian deal with children since Daemonar was a baby, so she could, and would, deal with this too.

"Yes, we do need some greens for tonight's dinner, but

I'm going to select them, and there will be no tasting until we get home and Lady Marian decides what she wants to use."

Morghann and I can help choose the fruits, Khary said. *We're good at sniffing out the ripest fruit.*

"That's all—," Jillian began. Then she—and everyone else—stared as the two Scelties rose until they were standing on air level with the cart bed. They walked above the mounded fruit, their paws never touching anything as they sniffed the offerings. Their selections rose above the cart to float on air.

I can help! Tagg struggled to get out of Daemonar's arms. *I want to help.*

Move away from the carts, Jillian told Daemonar on a psychic thread.

I'm supposed to stay with you.

*If he manages to get away from you, he'll land right on top of all the vegetables in the cart. Do you want to explain *that* to your father?*

I'm not moving out of sight.

Just out of range of getting us both into trouble.

Daemonar grinned and walked to the next shop, which had brooms in a barrel just outside the door. Nothing much there to tempt a Sceltie—she hoped.

They were drawing a crowd. She heard a woman asking, "What about the melons? Can you pick out the ripest melon for me?"

Jillian gave the grocer an apologetic smile. "They're just visiting."

"What about this one?" Another woman held up a different melon.

Morghann sniffed it. *Not ripe for eating today, but soon.*

"That's good. I wanted it for a couple of days from now." She went past the grocer and entered the shop with the chosen melon and the rest of the produce in her basket.

"So those are Scelties," the grocer said quietly, talking

more to himself than to Jillian. "You hear stories about them, even here in the valley. Didn't expect to see one."

Jillian scanned the list Marian had provided. She swiftly chose the fruits she was supposed to buy, taking her selections from the fruit floating above the cart. "I have all the fruit we need. You should—"

"Oh, couldn't they help a little more while you finish your shopping?" That was another woman. With a little shiver of dread and fascination, Jillian realized they had drawn a *big* crowd, and the grocer was looking a bit bemused by the entertainment value being provided by his fruit and vegetable carts.

You should finish up before the grocer offers one of them a job, Daemonar said.

She hoped he was teasing, but just in case he wasn't, she selected the vegetables using touch and her own nose.

Broccoli! Tagg said. *Is Jillian buying broccoli for us?*

"The last time I visited the Hall, Uncle Daemon said you weren't allowed to have broccoli, because it makes you fart," Daemonar said.

Tagg whined and gave the grocer a pleading look.

"I might risk Prince Yaslana's displeasure," the grocer said, "but I'm not going to do anything that could stink up Lady Marian's home."

Reminding herself that boys thought farts were an acceptable topic of conversation no matter where they were, Jillian ignored the chuckles from the men and *tsk*s from the women as she took her basket inside and had the purchases added to the Yaslana household account.

"Come on, everyone," she called as she headed back to the butcher shop. "We don't have all day."

We have to go now, Morghann said, trotting between the shoulders of two customers. *We are chaperons today.*

Approving nods from the women, along with a few "Come back and visit again" remarks.

Jillian vanished her basket. Without the broccoli being

right in front of him, Tagg settled enough that Daemonar could put him down.

When they reached the butcher shop, she saw a flash of movement in the alleyway, there and gone.

Jillian. The whisper of her name was so unexpected, she almost gasped. Dillon didn't like using psychic communication. He said it didn't convey half of what could be heard in a real voice—the difference between corresponding with a person and meeting face-to-face.

She looked at Daemonar. "Do you know what to purchase?"

"Jillian." Daemonar's voice held a warning.

A Warlord Prince was the most amenable he would ever be in his entire life during those years just before he began the change from boy to man—unless that boy had almost lost his mother and would no longer back down from a fight. "Five minutes. Right next to the shop in plain sight. I just need to tell Dillon about the arrangement I made with Lady Surreal." When he didn't respond, she added, "Please?"

"Out in the open, in full sight of people on the street," he finally said, reluctantly yielding to her plea. "You promise?"

She should have agreed immediately. Making a promise to someone so much younger rankled enough to have her hesitate.

"Jillian, whatever you're planning to do? Don't," Daemonar said. "You've already made a promise to Auntie Surreal, and she's half Dea al Mon. Your friend's life won't be worth anything if you break your promise to her."

Jillian swallowed the lump of fear that suddenly blocked her throat. "I won't break my promise to her or to you."

She watched him walk into the shop. A boy had given a prime roast to the Scelties for breakfast, but the young Warlord Prince who walked into the butcher shop didn't sound like a boy.

Jillian.

She rounded the corner and stopped, checking that she would be seen easily by anyone walking along the main street. "Dillon?"

He appeared in front of her. Then he grabbed her hand a moment before she felt a whisper of power surround them.

"Sight shield," he said. "Should have thought of it the last time."

Before she could protest, before she could warn him, he pushed her against the wall, covered her mouth with his, and thrust his tongue between her lips. Startled, she did nothing, not sure if she liked the sensation or not.

Then fear cleared her head. She pushed him away, breaking most of the contact between them. But he still held her hand.

"Stop it," she said, keeping her voice low. "You have to drop the sight shield *now*."

"It's all right." He moved in on her—or tried to.

She pushed back, her hand on his chest.

"Don't you want to be with me?" He sounded hurt, vulnerable. "If you loved me, you would want to be with me as much as I want to be with you."

She felt the gentle brush of his thumb over the knuckles of one hand. Of course she loved him, wanted to be with him. But . . . She shook her head, struggling to remember why it would be wrong to have this private moment. Why it would be dangerous. "There's not much time. You have to listen."

"Kiss me first."

Dark Opal power slammed against Dillon's Opal sight shield. That power struck again, breaking the shield.

"What in the name of Hell . . . ," he began.

No touching! Khary's voice boomed in the alleyway for everyone to hear.

He was touching! Morghann's voice, equally loud.

Bad dog! Grrrrr. Tagg's barks were loud enough to start a rockslide.

That brought a whole lot of people running to find out what had upset the Scelties—including Daemonar. And standing in the street, his hand around the hilt of his fighting knife, was Lord Rothvar.

"We're fine." Jillian gave Daemonar a pleading look and then glanced in Rothvar's direction, but she didn't dare meet the Green-Jeweled Warlord's eyes. "Just a misunderstanding with the Scelties."

Daemonar turned and went back to the butcher shop. Rothvar studied her a moment longer before continuing on his way. Everyone else went back to their own concerns, since she didn't need help.

Everyone except the Scelties.

"Lord Dillon was just touching my hand. That's allowed." At least, that was all he'd been doing when Khary broke the sight shield and everyone could see them.

Daemon said no touching, Morghann said stubbornly. At least she wasn't telling the whole village now. *He didn't say no touching except for hands.*

"I need to speak with Lord Dillon."

They stared at her.

"Privately."

No, Khary said.

It wasn't lost on her that Khary outranked everyone standing in that alleyway right now, and if provoked, the Sceltie Warlord could hurt Dillon.

"You three stay here. Dillon and I are going to walk down there and talk for a minute." Jillian pointed to the end of the alleyway.

Turning, she walked away. Dillon trailed behind her.

"Hell's fire, Jillian," he hissed. "What's going on? What *are* those things?"

"They're Scelties. They're chaperons."

"You're joking."

She shook her head. "Everyone is upset about what happened the other day."

"I thought that was settled when I made nice at the cake shop." Dillon did not look or sound happy.

"What was settled was that we can see each other and spend time together. Public outings with a chaperon present." She gave him a wobbly smile.

Dillon stared at her.

"You can come up to the eyrie," she said.

Now he smiled. "Oh, yeah?" When he reached for her, she took a step back.

He looked hurt. And maybe something else. "I thought you wanted to be with me."

"I do."

"You can't let Yaslana dictate your life. He's not your father."

The words made her uneasy, even though she had almost said the same thing to Lucivar herself. "But he is the Warlord Prince of Ebon Rih, and everyone who lives in this valley lives under his hand. And that includes visitors."

"If I don't kowtow, what's he going to do?"

Dillon sounded defiant. That he would be willing to defy an Ebon-gray Warlord Prince to be with her was thrilling— and terrifying. Had Dillon ever had personal dealings with a Warlord Prince before, let alone a man as powerful as Lucivar Yaslana? "He is the law in Ebon Rih. He could banish you from his Territory. Or he could kill you."

"For a *kiss*?"

She wasn't sure Yaslana wouldn't, so she said nothing.

Dillon sighed. Then, tossing a defiant look at the Scelties—and Daemonar, who now stood with them—he held out his hand.

Feeling like she had to draw her own line of how much she would let someone interfere with her choices, she took his hand.

Dillon stepped a little closer, turning his back on the Scelties and the boy. Warm excitement filled her.

"I'm sorry I . . . Well, the thought of not being able to spend time with you made me a little crazy."

"I told you. As long as we follow Lady Surreal's rules, we *can* spend time together. You can visit with me at the eyrie when there is an adult present, or we can have a public outing together, with chaperons. But, for your sake, we *have* to follow Lady Surreal's rules."

He nodded. "Fine. I'll make nice. But that's not what I wanted to talk to you about." Now he looked embarrassed. "Remember when I paid the bill at the cake shop? I wanted to make a good impression because I didn't think Lady Surreal thought much of me. And now I have a bill that I have to pay, and I can't." His thumb rubbed across her knuckles. "Do you think you could . . . ? Just to tide me over."

"Oh," she said when she finally caught on to what he was asking. Pulling her hand out of his, she called in the embroidered pouch she used as a wallet and removed all the marks. "This is what I have. You're welcome to it."

He started to smile until he ruffled the marks. "This isn't enough to cover what I owe. Is there any way you could get a bit more? Maybe borrow a bit from your sister's cashbox? Or from the Yaslana housekeeping money?"

She felt as if he'd thrown ice water into her face. "That would be stealing."

"If they're as rich as everyone says, they wouldn't notice if a few gold marks went missing." When she took a step back, he laughed and touched her hand. "Hell's fire, Jillian. I was only joking. If you loved me, you'd know I was joking."

Of course he was joking. He wouldn't ask her to steal from her sister or from Marian. And since his family was aristo, he would know that things were put on account, not paid for immediately, so housekeeping money wouldn't be lying around.

Of course he was joking. "I have some money saved. I could take some of that if it would help."

"That would—"

"Jillian," Daemonar called. "If you want to stop at the library, it's time to go before someone comes looking for us."

A warning, since they both knew who would come looking.

Dillon vanished the marks and gave her a warm smile. "Will you give me the honor of escorting you to the library, Lady Jillian?"

"Thank you, Lord Dillon. That would be pleasant."

She took the wrapped roast from Daemonar, relieved that the butcher had put a cold spell in the paper to keep the meat fresh. Then she vanished it and strolled to the library with Dillon beside her and Daemonar and the three Scelties trailing behind.

Rothvar stepped into Lucivar's study, then nodded to Daemon before focusing on the man he served. "If you could spare a minute, Prince?"

"I'll get out of your way." Daemon started to push out of the chair but settled again when Rothvar raised a hand to stop him.

"Appreciated but not necessary," Rothvar said. "Figured you would know about it anyway—or hear about it."

Daemon sighed. "What did they do, and who should I compensate?"

Lucivar said, "Shit."

Rothvar laughed. "Nah. If you're talking about those Scelties, they caused a stir, but no trouble came of it. They were just helping some of the grocer's customers select the best fruit, is all."

Daemon groaned. "He'll start thinking, 'How clever. If I had one of those dogs around all the time, customers would flock to my shop instead of the fellow on the other side of the village, because who else would have such a unique helper?' But Scelties *herd*. That's what they do with unflagging passion. First the Sceltie will help customers select fruits. Then he'll want to know why they didn't buy fruit one week, and the person will brush off the question as they might do with another human. And because he's small and furry, people forget about the Jewel he's wearing, mostly because it's hidden in the fur, and they forget that the nose that can pick out ripe fruit also picks up all kinds of interesting things. And if he's helping that person select fruit and he can tell she's unhappy, he'll want to know why. So he'll start digging into why she's unhappy, and if he can't do it by himself, he'll have some Sceltie friends help him—or some of the kindred horses that come from Scelt, or an Arcerian cat, because, despite their having distanced themselves from humans once more, the cats have maintained a bond with the Scelties. And a Sceltie will *not* hesitate to publicly scold a man—or woman—for indulging in sex outside of the marriage bed and will not hesitate to announce, loudly, who the person slept with, because, of course, he can smell that too if the other person gets within range. But if the unhappiness is caused by someone else hurting one of his chosen people . . . Like I said, the Scelties and Arcerians still work together, and a big cat who is hungry doesn't see any point in wasting the meat."

"Mother Night," Rothvar breathed. Then he shook his head and laughed. "You're having me on."

Lucivar wagged a thumb at Daemon. "He co-owns a few businesses with Scelties on the Isle of Scelt here in Kaeleer and a couple of farms in Dena Nehele and Shalador Nehele in Terreille."

"Why?" Rothvar sounded horrified—a sentiment Lucivar shared wholeheartedly.

Daemon's smile was bittersweet. "I continue what my Queen began, and in this way I serve."

"If you're not here because of the Scelties, that leaves the two children," Lucivar said.

He listened to Rothvar's account of seeing some "buzz"

around the grocer's and gliding in to take a look. Then Jillian walked into an alleyway and disappeared for a minute before the Scelties voiced their disapproval loudly enough to bring merchants and customers running to find out what was wrong.

"Things are still new with Nurian and me," Rothvar said. "She hasn't allowed a man to cross the threshold that way since Falonar hurt her and Jillian, so I'm careful around the girl. Not that Jillian is any trouble, but it's not for me to be drawing any lines, if you know what I mean."

"I do," Lucivar replied.

"Nurian said Lady Surreal had laid down some rules so that Jillian could spend time with this boy?"

Lucivar nodded.

Daemon crossed one knee over the other and steepled his fingers. "If you toss Dillon off a mountain or kick him out of Ebon Rih, he'll be a romantic, tragic, flawless figure—the boy who would have loved her like no other boy ever will, if the grown-ups hadn't been mean and sent him away. Right now he dazzles her and she believes she's in love."

"She's not a child anymore, but she's not grown up enough for any of *that*," Rothvar said hotly.

"Physically, she's not yet ready," Daemon agreed. "Emotionally?" He raised an eyebrow. "Which is why Jillian is accompanied by chaperons."

"You can't square off with Jillian," Lucivar told Rothvar. "That would bring up bad memories for her and for Nurian. If any rules get broken, let the girl argue with Surreal. But you should spend more time at Nurian's eyrie, in case someone is thinking about enjoying some private time with Jillian. And if that boy shows up at the eyrie when he thinks an adult won't be there . . ." He smiled that lazy, arrogant smile. "Nothing says you can't draw the line with *him*."

"Where is Jillian now?" Daemon asked.

"Last I saw her, they were all walking toward the library."

"I hope she remembers she's carting around the meat for tonight's dinner," Lucivar said.

"Finished my sweep around Doun, but I can do another," Rothvar said.

He shook his head. "No need. Go home. Sharpen some knives."

Rothvar smiled. "I'll do that." He nodded to Daemon. "Prince."

Lucivar waited until he no longer felt Rothvar's presence in the eyrie. Then he looked at his brother. "Well?"

"Who else knows about the money you put aside for Jillian?" Daemon asked softly.

"You, Marian, and your man of business, since you and he helped me set up the trusts for all the children. I should tell Nurian at some point. But Jillian can't use any of it until she reaches her majority, and you set things up so she could take the interest but couldn't touch the principal without your permission or mine." Discussing money always gave him a headache, which was the reason he'd asked for Daemon's help when he made provisions for his wife and children—including the child who had no actual connection to him except for heart. "There is no reason anyone would think Jillian had money beyond what Marian pays her for her help around the eyrie, so that can't be a lure."

"Young aristo males think all kinds of things. But I don't think it's occurred to Dillon yet that he'll be old enough to be a grandfather, maybe even a great-grandfather, before Jillian is old enough to have her Virgin Night and take a lover afterward." Daemon paused. "He could have genuine feelings for Jillian. Affection rather than lust."

"But you don't think so."

"I haven't met him. However, based on how you found out about him, no, I don't think so. Which makes me wonder why he's playing this game."

✦ ✦ ✦

"I told you," Terrence said. "I told you not to tangle with Prince Yaslana."

Dillon slouched in a chair in the parlor, feeling everything sliding out of control. Again. "She's not related to him. Why is he making such a fuss about me courting the girl? And those damn dogs!"

"Scelties." Terrence leaned forward, looking eager. "You hear stories about them. Are they really bossy and opinionated?"

Dillon gave his cousin a sour look. "Why don't you come with me to that part of the village and see for yourself."

"All right." Terrence hesitated. "But I thought you didn't want company."

He didn't. Since he wasn't going to have a choice, Terrence's presence might reassure everyone that his intentions were honorable. If nothing else, it would divide the damn dogs' attention between them.

Of course, Terrence's presence would interfere with a business arrangement, but he'd been reluctant about that from the start and wouldn't have agreed to it if he hadn't needed the "commission" he received. Having his cousin with him would give him an excuse to withdraw from the arrangement.

Terrence was a young man with an unblemished reputation, and, in truth, he still had an innocence when it came to the distaff gender that Dillon felt oddly compelled to protect. "I would be glad of your company."

TWENTY-THREE

❖

Flustered by the past couple of days and the sharp scrutiny of everything she did and everywhere she went—an unsettling experience that made her feel tethered when she'd been free to come and go as she pleased for so many years—Jillian needed a few quiet minutes to herself before she helped Marian prepare breakfast for the children. Juggling an armload of books, she used Craft to open the glass doors that led out to the yard and was so focused on reaching the small table and two chairs that were used for "quiet play" that she didn't notice Prince Sadi until she almost dropped her load of books on his mug of coffee.

The mug lifted and slid to one side, so smoothly the coffee didn't slosh.

"My apologies, Prince," Jillian stammered. "I didn't realize anyone was out here. I just wanted to . . ."

"Look at your books without being pestered?" Daemon said with a smile. "If one child can ask a thousand questions in a day, how many can three children ask?"

"A million. When questions overlap, they spawn new questions that are usually unrelated to anything that was initially asked."

He laughed. Then he moved his own stack of books and retrieved his mug of coffee. "Why don't you sit down? I take it you'll have your hands full the rest of the morning."

She took the other seat—and felt a bit daring. He, at least, seemed to recognize that she had a woman's heart and feelings without hemming those feelings in with rules and yappy chaperons like Lady Surreal had done. Would he be amused if she confessed that one of the things that attracted her to Dillon was the fact that Dillon reminded her of him? Just a little. Just enough.

Now Prince Sadi was sitting out here without his jacket, which, despite the white silk shirt, made him appear to be casually dressed, and she felt like they were just two people who could chat as equals. Because of that, maybe she could talk to him about things that Nurian and Prince Yaslana didn't want to hear.

"What are you reading?" Daemon asked.

"This and that." Remembering how Dillon had made fun of some of her selections, she cringed when Prince Sadi turned the stack to read the titles.

"You like stories with gore and danger?"

That was one of the books Dillon had mocked. He'd even held his nose as if it smelled bad. "It's just for fun."

Daemon pulled out a book from his own stack. "Have you tried this author? Same kind of thing but the characters are less embellished. Not that there is anything wrong with a character having hidden skills that are suddenly required. Those can be good stories for times when, as you said, you want to read something just for fun. But I think this author's characters feel more real, like someone I could meet in a dining house or in a shop."

She called in a pencil and the small notebook she used for things she didn't want to forget and wrote down the author and title of the book.

"This is an interesting choice." Daemon tapped the spine of another book.

The words came out in a rush. "Dillon says it's a brilliant account of the service fairs and the choices people made when they came to Kaeleer. The author's ancestor emigrated through the service fair, and he wrote the book based on personal accounts of those days." Daemon's odd smile stopped the flow of words. "Have you read the book?"

"I have."

"Did you think it was brilliant?" *Please think it was brilliant.*

"I thought it was pretentious. But I'll be interested to hear what you think of it."

Jillian blinked. "Why?"

"Because you were there."

The words were said so gently, it took her a moment to absorb the meaning.

"You were a girl during that time, but you weren't a young child," Daemon said. "While time may have softened some of those memories and details because you haven't thought about those days until now, you probably remember far more than you realize. You and your sister were among those who fled from the witches who had their claws in Terreille. Nurian signed a contract with Lucivar during the last fair." He sat back. "No matter how faithfully that author recounts what it was like to come to Kaeleer, he can't remember, can't reproduce how it felt the way you can. Those feelings are in your heart and your blood and your bones. History to him. Personal memory for you."

Such an obvious thing, but it hadn't occurred to her.

"May I make an observation?" Daemon asked.

"Yes."

"There is no easy comparison between the long-lived and short-lived races when it comes to age equivalents. We have spurts of development followed by long plateaus. Lord Dillon is a Rihlander who has reached his majority and is considered an adult. If you were a Rihlander, you would be about fourteen or fifteen, and when you turned twenty and reached your majority, Dillon would be in his late twenties. But you're Eyrien, and it will be decades before your age of majority is within sight."

"What are you saying? I don't understand what you're saying."

"He's your first romantic love, and that's special," Daemon said gently. "But it's not forever, even if you'd like it to be."

She almost snapped at him, almost asked him how he would know. Then she realized he did know. He had married Jaenelle Angelline, and even after decades of being married, her death almost destroyed him.

But he was talking to her, really talking to her, instead of telling her what she could and couldn't do.

"Can I ask you a hypothetical question?"

"Yes."

"If two people really love each other and want to be together, you know, physically, intimately, and one of them hadn't reached the age of majority . . . what would happen?"

"That would depend," Daemon replied. "If the man recognized his responsibilities when seeing a young woman through her Virgin Night, there might be disapproval but no other consequences. However, if she was damaged in any way, if he became intent on his own excitement and pleasure, which can happen with a young man, and as a consequence broke the girl, stripping her of her Birthright Jewel and destroying the potential power she might have had at maturity; if she becomes pregnant, especially if she is broken that night and can never have another child . . . The debt he would owe would not be tempered with much, if any, mercy."

"But if she really loved him . . ."

Daemon slid out of his chair, went down on one knee, and took her hand, rubbing his thumb over her knuckles—a gesture so like the way Dillon held her hand.

"Darling, you're forgetting the other half of that statement. If she really loved him and he wanted sex, yes, she might be tempted to give in to please him because he desperately needs her, and her giving in, despite the risks, is the only way he'll believe she loves him. But if *he* really loved *her*, he would acknowledge that she was too young for more than some romance and kisses. If he really loved her, he would respect her decision when she refused to do something he wanted; he wouldn't keep pushing until he got his way. When that happens, it's been my experience that the man doesn't really love the girl for herself; he only loves what he can get from her."

Jillian stared at that beautiful face, listened to the voice that wrapped around her—and felt as if she'd walked out of a hot, stuffy room and breathed in crisp, clean air.

"What if she's already given him some things?"

"Are we talking about material things or her body?"

"Material things."

"If the loss causes some discomfort but no long-term consequences, then it's a mistake that bruises but doesn't destroy, and the person will recognize the signs and not step into the snare the next time." Daemon looked toward the eyrie. "I think it's time to go in for breakfast."

"Hell's fire." Jillian leaped to her feet, almost knocking Daemon over. Fortunately, he got out of the way, although she wasn't sure how he'd managed it. She vanished her stack of books, turned toward the glass doors, then hesitated when she saw Prince Yaslana watching her. Watching them.

Yaslana stepped aside to let her pass.

Glancing back before she went into the kitchen to help with breakfast while Marian fed baby Andulvar, she saw Prince Sadi step into the front room. He smiled at her as he and Yaslana headed deeper into the eyrie instead of coming into the kitchen.

For a moment, Jillian stared at nothing. Daemon Sadi was more beautiful than Dillon and was the patriarch of the most powerful aristo family in the whole of Kaeleer. If Sadi talked to her as if she was intelligent and interesting, why did Dillon leave her with the feeling that she had to prove she was worthy of his attention?

✦ ✦ ✦

Lucivar followed Daemon into the study and closed the door. Then Daemon turned, wrapped a hand around the back of Lucivar's neck, and drew him close.

Glazed, sleepy gold eyes. A sweet, murderous smile. Lucivar knew the warning signs, knew what would happen if he made the wrong move, said the wrong thing.

The Sadist's black-tinted nails were honed as sharp as a knife and could slice a wrist or nick a jugular vein deeply enough for a man to bleed out in less than a minute—and then have his Jewels shattered in the last moments he struggled to survive.

He felt his brother's breath on his skin before the Sadist said too softly, "That little bastard has been using a seduction spell on your girl."

Fury blazed through him, creating a fire beneath his skin. His hands closed into fists. But Daemon's hand was still on his neck, warning him to keep still.

"I won't insult you by asking if you're sure," he growled.

Daemon's eyes were still glazed but no longer sleepy. His smile now held an edge that was no longer murderous but definitely cruel. "Good." Moving his hand, he stepped back—and Lucivar sprang to the other side of the room, needing to move.

"I should have ripped the little prick's arms off when I caught him touching her." Lucivar turned toward the door, but Daemon sidestepped, getting between him and the easy way out of the room.

"You can't do that now for the same reason you didn't do it then," Daemon said with a mildness that ripped away a little more of Lucivar's control. "If you squash him, Jillian will always believe he was a wonderful boy and you were the cruel surrogate father who killed her true love."

"How is a seduction spell true love?" Lucivar shouted, not caring if anyone heard him. Then he took a moment to check the room and realized Daemon had put an aural shield around the walls so they could shout, argue, fight, even destroy the whole damn room and every stick of furniture in it, without anyone hearing them.

"Seduction spells can be used for all kinds of reasons. Don't tell me you haven't used a seduction tendril now and then to make things more exciting for Marian."

Lucivar swore fiercely, a low rumble of sound as he continued pacing. "That's different."

"Completely different. One kind is meant to please; the other kind tries to smother choice."

Daemon knew all about playing games with seduction spells, knew how much to use to. add a bit more persuasion to a request without taking away a person's choice—and knew how to strip a person of any choice at all.

Lucivar glanced at his brother, then stopped moving. Daemon stood there, staring at his own hand, his thumb moving back and forth as if caressing something.

"Bastard?"

"Not just a seduction spell," Daemon said thoughtfully. "There was something else entwined with it. Something hidden."

Lucivar approached warily, his attention split between looking at Daemon's hand and watching for any sign that the Sadist might suddenly return.

"Compulsion spell, maybe," Daemon continued quietly. "Damn good one if it is. Subtle. Enough to influence thoughts and actions and have the influence linger without the spell being obvious enough to detect. Which means there has to be a particular action or phrase that triggers the spell."

"What kind of action?" Lucivar asked, keeping his voice just as quiet. Not that he didn't want to charge out the door and voice his displeasure in a way that would shake the whole damn valley, but he didn't want to distract Daemon from figuring this out.

"I think you'll find that Jillian has 'loaned' her true love whatever she's saved from the wages Marian pays her."

"And you're going to stand there and tell me I'm supposed to do *nothing*?"

"She has to discover the truth about him for herself." Daemon looked into Lucivar's eyes. "And I've already done something. You won't like it."

Oh, Hell's fire. "Tell me anyway."

"I wrapped a different sort of spell around your girl."

Lucivar bared his teeth but stopped himself from ramming a fist into Daemon's ribs. "What kind of spell?"

"When Jillian and I were talking, I detected the seduction spell when I took her hand and rubbed a thumb over her knuckles. So I drained that spell and wrapped her in one of my own. She'll never feel it, Lucivar. It won't interfere with her own power or her ability to use Craft, and it will fade in a few weeks. But during that time, any spell anyone tries to use on her will wash over her and be absorbed by my power without Dillon or anyone else realizing he no longer has the ability to control what Jillian thinks or does. She'll be able to view his actions and words without the veil of seduction or the compulsion to believe what he says."

Lucivar stepped away and prowled the room again, rolling his shoulders to relieve some of the tension. "Titian."

"No," Daemon said. "She's much too young to weave that kind of spell around her."

"Now she's too young. But once she reaches Jillian's age, if I suspected that someone, some boy, was trying the same thing, would you . . . ?" He looked at Daemon.

"Of course. You have only to ask."

Lucivar nodded. Having him as a father wasn't going to be easy for his children as they got older, and he'd figured that his reputation for being volatile and violent would be a layer of protection against anyone trying to make a play for any of them. But Daemon was a different kind of fighter with a different arsenal of weapons, and having *him* as another layer of protection allowed Lucivar to step back a little.

"Come on," he said as he swung around Daemon to reach the door. "By now the yappy horde will have cleared out and we can make our own breakfast."

"Just don't use any bowls on the counter unless you took them out of the cupboards yourself. Scelties will lick the last bit of oatmeal—or most anything else—out of a bowl and use Craft to set the bowl next to the sink so that the adults can't tell who did, or didn't, eat the breakfast they were supposed to eat."

Lucivar thought about the bowl he'd used yesterday morning to beat the breakfast eggs and said, "Shit."

Laughing, Daemon opened the door and led the way to the kitchen.

TWENTY-FOUR

✦

That night, Surreal felt Daemon's sexual heat the moment she opened the door of the guest room. It wrapped around her, smothered her. Frightened her, because the need to have him became so overwhelming she would let him do anything to her. He had shown some restraint for the first couple of days after he'd arrived at the eyrie, leashing the heat enough that she could pretend that sleeping with him wasn't an ordeal. But it seemed even being a guest in his brother's home wasn't a sufficient deterrent for his games tonight.

He lay on his back, his eyes closed and one arm over his head, completely relaxed. The sheet was carelessly bunched just below his waist, showing her his naked, beautifully toned upper body. Looking at him, someone would swear he wasn't doing anything. *He* continued to swear he wasn't doing anything whenever she lashed out at him.

She knew better.

As she looked at him, her heart raced, her nipples tightened to the point of pain as they stood at attention, begging for the feel of his hands, his mouth. And need that threatened to strip her of any choice pulled at her, a liquid heat between her legs.

Had to fight this. Had to hold on to what was left of

herself before she became nothing more than need he would come to despise while he denied any responsibility for this sexual addiction.

Daemon turned his head and opened his eyes. Warm gold. Sleepy. Waiting.

"Everything all right?" His seductive voice wrapped around her, creating a different kind of need.

"Fine." She stripped off the robe and wished the nightgown was one of the modest ones she'd taken to wearing at the Hall instead of the silky gown she'd packed because she'd expected to be sleeping alone while she was Lucivar and Marian's guest. Getting into bed, she added, "Just not in the mood for sex tonight."

She knew her physical scent would shout the lie, at least to a Warlord Prince. She turned on her side, her back to him.

She felt him move, could tell he was now propped on one elbow, studying her. One warm hand settled on her hip.

"Surreal?" The bastard actually sounded concerned.

Push down the sheet, pull up my nightgown, put your hand between my legs, and play with me until I beg for your cock. "I'm tired."

Daemon kissed her shoulder and settled back on his side of the bed. "Sleep in tomorrow if you can."

He extinguished the candle-light. A minute later, Surreal heard the slow breathing that meant he was already asleep. Knowing he would wake the instant she got out of bed, she waited with gritted teeth until she couldn't stand it a minute longer.

She'd barely eased her legs over the side of the bed when she felt his hand on her arm.

"Bathroom," she whispered.

The hand slid down to the bed, the man recognizing the word to mean he could go back to sleep instead of waking fully to meet a threat.

She hurried into the bathroom that accommodated the guest rooms in this part of the eyrie and locked the door.

Then she pulled up her nightgown and tried not to cry as she gave herself some relief.

Pain lanced through his head as Daemon tried to tighten his control of the sexual heat. Nausea, the new companion to the headaches, made him grit his teeth and swallow hard. He could hide the pain, had been hiding its severity for months, but the smell of vomit would be much harder to hide no matter how fast he disposed of the basin.

He hoped, with sick desperation, that Surreal meant it about not wanting sex tonight. She remained convinced that he was responsible for her increased sex drive, and telling her he couldn't—*wouldn't*—oblige . . . Putting a Black shield around himself for protection might break what little affection they still had for each other. Putting a shield around himself would acknowledge the Dea al Mon side of her heritage—and admit that he no longer trusted the assassin who slept with him.

As he struggled for control of the pain and nausea, knowing he had only another minute or so before she returned, he heard the song drifting up from somewhere deep in the abyss. Heard it. Focused on it. There were no words—at least, none he recognized. But he understood the message.

Sleep, the song coaxed. *Rest.*

The nausea subsided. The headache still raged, raping his brain, but moment by moment, it felt more like a storm seen through a window—powerful and potentially dangerous but not immediately threatening.

Sleep, the song coaxed. *Rest.*

Daemon stretched out on his side of the bed and followed that beloved voice down, down, down into the Darkness, where pain was barely a memory.

Surreal stared at the man so deeply asleep that her return to their room hadn't roused him at all.

The sexual heat was banked. Not just leashed, *banked*. Which just proved the bastard *could* control the heat if he wanted to be considerate.

She eased into her side of the bed—and wondered if this was a new form of torture.

TWENTY-FIVE

Marian felt the sexual heat wash over her a moment before she heard Daemon's deep, rich voice purr, "Good morning, gorgeous."

Over decades of marriage, she had adapted to the heat that poured out of Lucivar. Not that it didn't still arouse her, but she'd gotten used to what she thought of as the everyday sexuality of her man. Despite her being used to Lucivar, that first minute around Daemon was like bracing against a dangerous wind that was strong enough to knock a person off her feet. Letting it roll over her, she would acknowledge—to herself—that her body responded to that unspoken promise of sex that was as much a part of a Warlord Prince's nature as a volatile temper and being born to kill, and then she forgot about it. He was Daemon, her husband's brother, and he would never do anything inappropriate. Not with her. Especially with her.

But this wasn't the first punch of everyday heat. This was like being wrapped in layers of satin while floating safely in a deliciously warm lake. It was a heady, overwhelming feeling—and sensuous enough that she felt her nipples harden, felt the sudden wetness and need between her legs.

Uncertain of his intentions because he hadn't been quite himself since the headaches that had started several months ago, Marian pulled the biscuits out of the oven and set them on the cooling rack on the counter before she looked at him.

Not seduction. Daemon looked totally relaxed, even a little bit sleepy, with nothing holding back the sexual heat he usually kept tightly leashed in any public setting—heat he kept leashed even in his own home to protect the servants, male and female, from acting inappropriately toward him and provoking a lethal response. But here, now, he had walked into her kitchen with no barriers, no chains, and she didn't think he was aware that he'd done that.

He feels safe, she thought, stunned by the revelation. *Safe enough to let down his guard around me, to be vulnerable around me.*

She hadn't known how much he trusted her until that moment.

"Oh," she said. "I have to kiss you." She hurried up to him, grabbed the lapels of his jacket, rose up on her toes, and gave him a hard kiss on the mouth. "You're too beautiful not to kiss."

"What? Marian . . ."

She felt him pulling back and waking up, could actually feel him tightening the leash on his sexuality to lessen the impact he had on other people. Could even feel a hint of panic that she might be responding to him, might want something from him that he would never give his brother's wife. In another moment he would pull away from her, violently, and if she didn't say the right thing right now, he might never allow himself to feel safe or comfortable around her again.

"But you know what's better than the way you look first thing in the morning?" She gave him another, lighter kiss and felt his muscles tighten. "You are always willing to help me fix breakfast."

He didn't move. Barely breathed. Then he let out a rough laugh so filled with relief it broke her heart. "You were teasing me."

"Not about helping me fix breakfast."

"What's this?" Lucivar walked into the kitchen, his eyes on Marian.

Lucivar would catch the scent of lust and know he hadn't been the reason for it. She just hoped that when he woke up more, Daemon would assume the scent was because she hadn't washed thoroughly enough after morning sex with her husband.

"Daemon is making his special scrambled eggs for breakfast. You can cook up some chicken strips and beef. I've already made the biscuits, and I'll get the coffee started."

"That will get food on the table, and we might even get something to eat before the yappy horde descends on us." Lucivar moved past Daemon to reach the cold box and remove the meat.

"Are you referring to the children or the Scelties?" Daemon asked, slipping off his jacket and folding it over the back of a kitchen chair.

"Take your pick." As he passed her on the way to the counter, Lucivar added on a psychic thread, *We're going to talk about this.*

Yes, they were. But not for the reasons he expected.

As soon as the yappy horde was fed and herded outside to occupy themselves with their own business, Lucivar followed Marian into the laundry room. When she turned to face him, he put his hands on either side of her, trapping her against one of the laundry tubs.

"Want to tell me what that was about?" he asked.

"Not what it looked like."

"I know you, and I know *him*, so I'm sure it wasn't what anyone else would assume."

"Is he ever like that when it's just the two of you spending an evening together?" she asked.

"Like what?"

"Completely relaxed." She rested her hands on Lucivar's chest, feeling the warmth of his skin through the undyed shirt with the sleeves he'd cut off to form a short cap over each impressive arm. "For some reason, this morning he trusted me enough to show me who he is without any barriers."

"He's potent." Lucivar rested his forehead against hers. "It's what made him so dangerous when he'd been a pleasure slave forced to serve the Queens in Terreille. He could turn pleasure into agony when he wanted to hurt someone. Even now, it's the side of him a person rarely sees unless they're about to dance with the Sadist."

Marian hesitated, then asked a question she'd held back for a lot of years. "And when he was married to Jaenelle?"

"He gave her everything he was, held nothing back. He could do that with her." He laughed softly. "And meeting him first thing on some mornings was reason enough to dive into a cold mountain lake."

Her husband was here, and who knew how much longer they would be alone? Marian pressed against Lucivar and didn't care that she probably wasn't the reason his cock was so hard. "I know something better than a cold lake."

He freed himself from his trousers before she could take another breath. She vanished her underpants and trousers before he ripped them off. Then he was inside her, his cock so hot it felt like a fever as his arms locked around her back and hips and he thrust into her with all the power of a warrior and none of the finesse of a lover. She wrapped her legs around his waist and dug her short nails into his shoulders, remembering just in time not to set her teeth in his neck where he'd have to try to explain a fresh love bite to the children.

Fast. Hard. Hot. Explosive. Responding like a man pleasuring a needy woman instead of a husband taking care of a fragile womb. Responding to her like he used to before the illness that came after birthing baby Andulvar had sapped her strength.

Her climax pushed him over the edge. She bit his shoulder to stifle the scream that would have brought everyone running to find out what had happened.

"Mother Night, Marian." Lucivar balanced her on the edge of the laundry tub

They were shaking and panting and still connected, so she was grateful he hadn't dropped her.

"You should let go of me," he said.

"I'm not sure I can move my legs yet."

He made a pleased sound that was abruptly cut off when he turned his head as if listening to something nearby. "Try."

Happy barking, which meant children and Scelties playing—and the horde could rush into the eyrie at any moment searching for at least one of them, wanting attention, snacks, something.

Lucivar pulled out of her and made sure she was steady on her feet before he grabbed a couple of washcloths from the stack she kept in easy reach and ran them under the water tap.

"We should clean up a bit," she said, accepting one of the cloths.

"You think?" Giving her an amused look, he washed quickly, tossing the used cloth into the laundry tub before tucking himself back into his trousers. "I'll distract them." He gave her a light kiss and left. Moments later, she heard his voice mingling with the children's—and Daemon's.

Blowing out a breath, Marian finished washing herself, straightened her tunic, and called in the underpants and trousers, hurriedly pulling them on. Nothing she could do about flushed skin or the rest. The adults would recognize the signs of hot, fast sex, but hopefully the children wouldn't notice.

As she hurried out of the laundry room, aiming to get

to her bedroom and have a few minutes in private to put on other clothes and get settled, it occurred to her that she had no idea how much these Scelties might notice—and share with everyone else.

She reached one of the eyrie's branching corridors. One way led to the master suite of rooms. The guest room Daemon and Surreal were using was in the other direction. Realizing that she hadn't seen Surreal yet, Marian headed for the guest room and knocked on the door. "Surreal?"

No answer.

Worried, Marian opened the door enough for her voice to be heard by anyone inside the room. "Surreal?"

"Yeah."

Taking that as an invitation, Marian slipped into the room, leaving the door partway open in her haste to reach the other woman. Surreal looked feverish, upset. And she looked like she'd been crying, which was so unusual Marian jerked to a stop. Could this be nothing more than moontime moodies, or did she need to send for a Healer?

To heal what? Her friend had been well when she'd arrived in Ebon Rih. "Should I send for Nurian?" she asked.

"I doubt she has a cure for this." Surreal moved around the room in a restless manner.

"So there is something wrong." There had been something wrong for months, but maybe Surreal was finally ready to talk about it.

Surreal stopped moving, her back to the partly open door. "I love Daemon. I do. And I want to stay married to him because, for all our sakes, he needs to be married. But more often than not lately, I can't stand to be around him. Sometimes I even hate him. When he plays games with me, when he uses that sexual heat on me, I *hate* him."

Marian couldn't move, shocked into stillness. *Oh, Surreal.*

"I feel smothered. His heat rolls over me and I can't think about anything except having his cock inside me. It's a fever that has burned inside me for so many months it's become an addiction. I make excuses to spend time away from the Hall just so I can breathe, just so I can remember who I am when I'm not a sheath for his cock. I feel so damn helpless, and it scares me. *He* scares me."

Mother Night. "You've never felt this . . . need . . . before? You've never seen Daemon act like this?"

"Even when Sadi is in rut, it's not this bad. Or it is, but it's three days and then it's done. This is . . . relentless."

How to say this? "Men relax after the Birthright Cere mony. They don't feel vulnerable, don't feel they could lose the right to be a father to their children, so they let their guard down, allow themselves to be more fully themselves."

"What are you saying? That this is Sadi as he really is?"

"I think that's at least part of it." When Surreal stared at her, Marian tried to find words to describe her encounter with Daemon in the kitchen. "I felt some of that this morning . . ."

"Mother Night, Marian." Surreal looked horrified.

". . . and I realized I was seeing him without any barriers. For the first time in all the years I've known him, I was seeing Daemon when he wasn't leashing his power or sexual heat. It was . . . potent." She flushed with embarrassment but pushed on. "I jumped Lucivar in the laundry room as soon as we fed the children and dogs and booted them outside."

"No," Surreal said sharply. "It's more than that. This started after the Sadist played with me one night . . . and I told Daemon the next morning that I never wanted him to do that to me again. But every time I'm near him, the heat coils around me until I can't think, can't breathe, can't *live.* This is the punishment for refusing to play his games. That monster has gotten me addicted to sex so that he can torture me every night."

Marian ached for her friend. For both friends. "I don't think Daemon would deliberately hurt you. He hasn't been well, Surreal. The headaches. Maybe he doesn't have as much control as he did before."

"It has to be more than that." It sounded like a plea.

"Have you talked to him? Have you told him the sexual heat is causing a problem for you?"

"Yes, I've told him!" Surreal cried. "I can't count how many times I've told him. He insists he has the heat leashed. I *know* he doesn't. Hell's fire, I was a whore for most of my life, so I know about sex. And I know Sadi well enough to know he's using sex to torture me until I agree to let him do anything he wants."

Lucivar had told her enough about Daemon's past—and the warning signs that indicated the Sadist had come to call—that Marian didn't doubt for a moment that, as the Sadist, Daemon didn't distinguish between sex and torture. But what Surreal was saying didn't sound right, didn't fit the man she knew.

Assuming Daemon was still sane.

Chilled by that possibility, Marian said, "You're his wife. That means something to him. Surreal, talk to him before he comes to some conclusions about your marriage that you might not be able to change. Talk to him before it's too late. Or ask someone to intercede for you and find out why things have gone so wrong."

"Who would dare challenge the Sadist?" Surreal said bitterly.

Marian caught the scent of coffee and looked past Surreal. Lucivar stood in the fully open doorway, holding a mug. But he was looking back down the corridor, and Marian realized he wasn't the one who had brought the coffee.

Lucivar retreated, making no sound. Marian wrapped her arms around Surreal and felt the weight of her friend's head on her shoulder as one of the strongest women she'd ever known wept like a heartbroken child.

"Bastard?" Lucivar crossed the flagstone courtyard and caught up to his brother as Daemon reached the stairs leading to the landing web below the eyrie. "You heading somewhere?"

There was nothing for him to read in Daemon's gold eyes, and that lack scared him. It meant Sadi had retreated deep into himself, no longer allowing anyone to see what he was thinking or feeling. It was the mask Daemon had worn when he'd been a pleasure slave in Terreille.

It was the look Daemon had worn just before the Sadist annihilated a Queen and all the bitches who served in her court.

"Just down to the village to walk around," Daemon replied.

A rational, reasonable answer to the question which didn't mean a damn thing.

Lucivar tipped his head to indicate the eyrie. "What are you going to do?" No need to clarify the problem. He'd found Daemon standing just outside the guest room, had seen the pain and sorrow on his brother's face, had heard enough of what Surreal had said to understand the danger if Surreal truly couldn't accept the Black-Jeweled Warlord Prince she had married.

All these years of living around and with Daemon. Living around and with the sexual heat. Living with the cold, dark power of the Black Jewels. It surprised him—and disappointed him—that a woman as strong as Surreal, a witch who wore Gray Jewels, had lasted less than two decades around the Black. Despite what Surreal thought, she *wasn't* dancing with the Sadist, wasn't the focus of the Sadist's cold, cruel rage.

The chalice is breaking.

The girl would free him to ask for help.

Was it finally time? Was this the moment that Tersa and Karla had seen in their tangled webs?

"What are you doing to do?" Lucivar asked.

"Nothing." Daemon's voice, like his eyes, held no emotion. "It was my mistake. I'll fix it."

How? "Maybe someone at the Keep could help."

"If the Gray-Jeweled witch who is my wife can't stand to be around me anymore, I don't think the Gray-Jeweled Queen at the Keep can do anything to help."

Not the Gray, but . . . If Tersa and Karla were wrong about the help that could be found at the Keep, and he persuaded Daemon to ask for help that would never come . . .

"So you're going down to the village?" he asked.

"I am. For a while."

"You want some company?"

"No. Thank you." Daemon went down a few stairs before looking at Lucivar. "Everything has a price, and I have no illusions about what I am." He walked down to the landing web.

I have no illusions about what I am.

Lucivar had never heard Daemon say anything that had frightened him more, because there had been times when he'd heard Saetan say much the same thing.

TWENTY-SIX

———❖———

Dillon walked to his appointment and wondered how to extricate himself from a couple of arrangements now that he had a chance for the exact thing he had struggled to achieve.

He'd been imprudent the last time he'd seen Jillian, caught off guard by her four-legged chaperons. He'd also been caught off guard by what Jillian had said. Public outings with chaperons? Visits to her home—or Yaslana's home—as long as an adult was present? No sneaking around? No need for lies?

This was . . . courtship. This was a chance to show the most powerful men in the Realm that he knew how to be an escort, even if his training hadn't been completed.

He shouldn't have been dismissive of Jillian's thoughts about books and other things. It had become a habit—or a need—to undermine an aristo bitch's trust in her own opinions in order to keep her believing that he was superior. He'd stop doing that. And he'd start listening, really listening, as he would listen to a respected friend.

He'd forgotten what it felt like to have a friend like that.

Jillian might not even notice the difference. Not at first. But he would. And the first thing he needed to do was stop doing things that added smudges to his honor.

✦ ✦ ✦

Pain was a faithful, predictable lover. Unlike the woman he had married, the woman who had given him a precious daughter. The woman he had trusted to be honest with him.

Daemon walked down the main street of Riada, pretending not to see how people scurried out of his way, their faces filled with a fear he'd like to carve into their skin so it would never be forgotten.

No. He didn't want to do that. These people had done him no harm, had offered no challenge. Were not the reason for his pain.

He flicked a glance toward the other side of the street, where Lord Rothvar kept pace with him. Was the Eyrien so foolish—or arrogant—as to think he could survive the Sadist?

He spotted Lord Zaranar up ahead and expected Rothvar to cross the street and come up behind him. But, no, Rothvar remained on the other side, keeping Riada's citizens away from him, giving him a clear path—the same as Zaranar was doing on this side of the street.

Lucivar's orders, no doubt. Yaslana would know better than anyone the need to avoid any kind of challenge.

Crack.

He'd get out of this village, get away from this valley if he could. But he wasn't steady enough to ride the Winds any distance. Getting down to the village had proved that much.

Surreal had seen the truth of who he was and called him a monster who tortured her. The rest of the Blood might see him as a monster, too, but he hadn't tortured his wife. He'd respected her wishes, had understood he'd made a mistake the night she came to his bedroom, had done everything he could since then to keep the heat leashed so that it wouldn't distress her. Had endured this unrelenting pain in his effort to keep the heat leashed. For her. But *she* was the one demanding sex every night they slept together.

Could he stand sleeping in the same bed with her anymore? Maybe . . .

Crack.

. . . she could live in the family town house in Amdarh. Or purchase a town house for herself if she preferred. Jaenelle Saetien could go to school . . .

The taste of sickness and blood filled the back of his throat—and cold rage pushed against the icy calm that provided the last illusion of control.

She wasn't taking his girl. Surreal could leave, if that was what she needed to do, but she wasn't taking his daughter. Monster or not, *no one* was going to take his girl away from him.

CRACK!

He felt Rothvar walking toward him. He turned his head and looked at the Green-Jeweled Eyrien Warlord—and smiled at the terror he saw in Rothvar's eyes.

Yes.

Then something brushed against his senses. A ripple from one of his own spells. He focused on the female psychic scent and reached out until he located her.

Emotions in turmoil. That wasn't right.

Cherish and protect.

Turning away from Rothvar, Daemon followed the psychic scent to a village garden between some shops.

Cherish and protect. Even the Sadist, in his own way, valued those words.

This isn't the way to the library, Khary protested as he trotted beside Jillian. *You told Marian we were going to the library. This is not the library.*

"We *are* going to the library," Jillian said. "But first we're going to the shop over there to buy some cakes for Nurian."

Cake? Scelties like cake.

No matter what Khary said, Jillian suspected that Sceltie

tummies didn't react well to cake, and she didn't want to clean up the result. "This cake is for Nurian and Rothvar. It's a present."

Presents are good. We will go find cake for Nurian. Then we will go to the library, which is where we are supposed to be. That settled, Khary fell a half step behind, and Jillian could feel him eyeing her calf, ready to give her an encouraging nip to pick up the pace.

As they approached the Sweet Tooth, Jillian looked in the window and saw an older, elegantly dressed woman kiss her male companion's cheek before turning to leave. Jillian stopped so fast Khary ran into her leg. Without conscious choice, she put a sight shield around both of them.

*Jillian . . . *

Hush. She stepped closer to the big windows and felt something squeeze her heart. Dillon, there in the shop eating cakes with another woman. An *older* woman.

Too old, surely, to be a . . . lover? Maybe a woman from the family where he was staying? That made sense. He would want to do something to repay their hospitality.

She could drop the sight shield and go into the shop. After all, it wasn't like she was *spying* on Dillon. She had a reason to be there. Maybe, after she bought the cakes for Nurian, Dillon would walk with her to the library. Khary was with her; he'd be enough of a chaperon. More than enough. Too much. Still, she and Dillon would be able to talk and spend a little time together. Now that they could meet openly, as long as there was a chaperon present, he seemed less eager to be with her, and that didn't make sense.

She'd almost dropped the sight shield when she saw him pick up the plate with the four remaining cakes and bring it to the counter. He said something to the girl behind the counter—the beautiful girl who made Jillian feel like a grubby child. They both laughed when the girl licked her thumb and pressed it against the side of one cake, marring the frosting. Then the girl boxed up the four small cakes, hiding the damage on the one cake by placing that side in the center. She put the box in the glass case where new cakes were sold.

Disturbed by what she'd seen, Jillian hurried away, remembering to drop the sight shield after Khary got his teeth in her trousers to stop her from running into a Warlord who couldn't see her.

You are upset! Why are you upset? Khary asked.

"I need to think. I need to sit down and think."

There is sitting for humans over there.

Khary led her to a simple bench located on a little island of green between a couple of shops. Flowers bloomed in a square stone planter. On the other side of the planter, there were a small metal table and chairs that would accommodate wings better than the bench.

Jillian collapsed into one of the chairs. There was an explanation. There had to be. Dillon wouldn't do something so unkind.

"Lady Jillian?"

She looked up. "Prince Sadi." She hadn't heard him approach the table, and Khary had given no warning. Had Sadi noticed her, or had the Sceltie alerted the Prince that something was wrong that required another human?

She felt Khary against her leg, trembling. *Khary?*

The Prince smells sick. Be careful.

Gold eyes that looked sleepy—a danger sign in a Warlord Prince—but those eyes also held a feverish glitter.

"Darling, what's wrong?"

The look in Prince Sadi's eyes, for one thing. The odd note in his voice for another. Brittle. Pained. Chilling.

He's riding the killing edge . . . and something more. Which meant *anything* could snap Sadi's control and start a slaughter.

But there were ways to help a Warlord Prince step back from the killing edge. She remembered Lady Angelline stopping by Yaslana's eyrie one afternoon when Lucivar was with the other Eyrien men and Marian had been at the market. Daemonar had been down for his nap, so Jillian had been out in the garden, weeding the herb beds. And there was Lady Angelline, her gold hair heavily silvered, kneeling next to her, chatting about nothing and everything.

Not nothing. It was never nothing, but Jillian hadn't appreciated that at the time, although she remembered those chats, those quiet lessons. Knowledge passed on from one witch to another. About Warlord Princes.

"Sometimes a Warlord Prince needs assistance to step away from the killing edge," the Lady had said. *"Ask for his help. Give him something to do, some safe way to channel all that power and temper."*

"Won't he realize you're trying to distract him?"

"Of course, but it's part of the give-and-take between the distaff gender and the spear. Don't make up something ludicrous. That will insult him and do you no good. The task can be small as long as the need is genuine."

What she saw in Sadi's eyes as he waited for a response terrified her. Did she have the courage to do this? "I . . . I need to talk, but . . ."

Sadi settled into the other chair with a grace that suddenly seemed predatory. "You need to talk through something, but it's not something you want to explain to Yaslana because he'll react and you just want someone to listen."

"Yes."

"Then I'll listen."

Was listening enough of a task? "You won't tell him?"

He hesitated. "If you're at risk, I can't promise that. If that's not the case, I can tell him as much or as little as you want him to know."

She wanted to ask for a promise that he wouldn't hurt anyone, but she suspected that request might snap his control and start something no one could stop.

Slowly, measuring each word as if she were walking down a steep, treacherous mountain path and the next step could start a rockslide, Jillian told Sadi what she had seen through the shopwindow,

"I don't know why Dillon laughed," she said when she finished. "It wasn't funny to do something mean. And it was wrong for the girl to put the damaged cake into a box and sell it as fresh cake—especially since it had been on someone's table already."

"That upsets you." A quiet statement spoken in a voice closer to his normal tone.

"I know how I would feel if I had bought that box of cakes and brought it home, thinking it would be a wonderful treat for Nurian. And then to open the box and see that one of the cakes had someone's thumbprint in it, as if someone was saying that the people who buy the boxes with the four small cakes don't deserve to have the best the shop can offer because they aren't important enough to deserve the best . . ."

"It would have hurt your heart to give someone who matters to you the best you could offer and then realize you failed," he said.

She nodded—and then wondered who had thought that the best he could offer wasn't good enough.

"We can't know why Dillon laughed. He could have been embarrassed by what the girl had done but didn't feel it was his place to say anything. However, we *can* confirm if cakes are being sold as new that shouldn't be."

"How are we going to do that?"

He smiled. "I'm going to treat a young friend to a plate of cakes."

As they walked the short distance to the Sweet Tooth, she mentioned stopping at the library and he asked her about the books she intended to pick up.

Now that Prince Sadi had started backing away from the killing edge, Jillian couldn't help comparing Dillon and Sadi. That wasn't fair. Prince Sadi was older *and* a Warlord Prince, but hadn't she been comparing them all along? She'd thought they were similar, but she wasn't so sure anymore. Dillon would have made fun of her book selections, and then said . . . Well, it didn't matter what he would have said. But Sadi asked questions, expressed interest in *why* she chose a book, even if she was sure it wasn't anything he would want to read.

As they walked into the shop chatting like old friends, Jillian noticed the look on the beautiful girl's face when she realized who Jillian's companion was. Despite the flutter in her own belly that was caused by being close to him, Jillian suddenly felt protective because she was sure girls looked at him that way all the time—or tried to do more than look—because he was beautiful and sexual, like some kind of dream lover. But when a Warlord Prince married, he was never unfaithful to his wife, and he would kill anyone who tried to compromise his honor. Only foolish women would respond to the lure of that sexual beauty, because it wasn't meant to be a lure. And with him still so close to the killing edge, she didn't want anyone upsetting him.

"What should we order?" Sadi asked when the girl pranced up to their table, her blouse pulled lower than it had been when they'd walked in.

Did women do that when Prince Yaslana went into shops? Maybe a Warlord Prince's sexual heat wasn't as noticeable in an Eyrien, because Eyrien males were warriors, bred and trained, and quick to fight. So the sexual heat could be masked by temper.

"Jillian?"

She blinked, then realized Sadi had asked a question and had been waiting for an answer. "My apologies, Prince. I was distracted by another thought."

"Must have been a good thought to distract you from cake," he teased.

She felt the heat in her face and said nothing.

"We'll take the large plate of assorted cakes and two cups of coffee," Sadi said.

"That's all you want?" The girl licked her lips—and the room instantly turned cold.

"Yes, that's all I want," he replied too softly.

The girl hurried back to the counter to fill their order. The room returned to its previous temperature.

"What are you reading now?" Jillian asked, hoping to draw his thoughts toward something other than the girl's inappropriate invitation. "For fun, I mean?"

For a moment, Sadi stared at her with gold eyes that looked sleepy and glazed. Then he released a breath and returned from whatever dark place he'd been in for that moment.

As they ate some of the cakes and drank coffee, he told her about the books he was reading. Some sounded terribly dull—not that she would say that—but she called in her small notebook and pencil and wrote down the titles of some mysteries that sounded like fun. Then . . .

"You read romances? Why?"

He raised one perfectly shaped eyebrow. "Why not?"

"But you know about lovemaking and all that stuff." Jillian blushed.

Sadi leaned closer. "I saw a copy of the book on Beale's desk in the butler's pantry." His voice felt like a warm breath against her cheek. "And while I shudder to imagine the Hall's butler and cook doing . . . *that* . . . I confess to a macabre curiosity as to why Beale is reading it."

"Maybe it's too . . . informative . . . for some of the younger servants at the Hall, and Beale saw one of them reading the book and confiscated it?"

"Oh, Mother Night, I hope so."

He sounded so relieved she had to laugh.

"Have you had enough to eat?" he asked.

Jillian looked at the last four frosted, fancily decorated cakes. "Yes. Plenty."

"In that case . . ."

She saw the small gold coin he held between thumb and forefinger. Then it was gone.

He paid the bill and escorted her out of the shop.

"Now what do we do?" Jillian asked.

Spotting two Rihlander Warlords walking down the street, Sadi met their eyes. Jillian saw no gesture, heard no command, but the men changed direction and joined them at a point on the sidewalk where they wouldn't be seen by anyone looking out the shop's windows.

"We need your assistance," Sadi said. He took his wallet out of an inner pocket in his black jacket and handed each man several silver marks. "Please purchase two of the boxes of cakes—the four-cake size." He turned to her. "Do you remember the color of the decorations on the cakes we didn't finish?"

"Two had blue flowers and two of the cakes had yellow trim," she replied.

"If you see a box with that combination, buy that one in particular," Sadi said.

"What if someone asks why?" the scruffier-looking Warlord asked.

"Because your auntie is visiting and the blue flowers look like the ones in her garden," the other one said. "I'll look for that box." He hesitated. "Then what do we do?"

"Wait for us." Sadi gave them a smile that had them hunching their shoulders.

Jillian and Sadi waited a couple of minutes before strolling back to the shop.

"You can wait out here with Khary," Sadi said.

I am waiting outside? Again?

The Sceltie sounded more relieved than disappointed. Since Khary lived at the Hall and knew the man better than she did, Jillian took it as a sign that Prince Sadi wasn't as calm as he seemed.

"Yes." Sadi looked at Jillian.

"I was the one who started this," Jillian replied. "If there is an explanation, I would like to hear it."

"Very well." Sadi opened the shop door and escorted her inside. He stepped up to the counter. Jillian lagged behind, not eager to draw attention to herself. She could have been wrong about what she'd seen. If she was, she was causing trouble for people. Dillon would say she was acting like a child.

"I'd like to speak to the owner of this shop." Sadi's cold civility was as much of a warning as a blade being pulled from a sheath.

"She's not available, but . . ."

Jillian could see the girl's face, but Sadi's body blocked the rest of her. The girl didn't say anything—at least not out loud—and Jillian didn't know what she might have done. But the next instant, Sadi smiled a cold, cruel smile—the kind of smile that Jillian had never seen before and hoped never to see again.

The girl backed away from the counter.

"She's not available? Really?" Sadi said too softly.

A moment later a roll of thunder filled the building. The two Warlords set the boxes of cakes on a table. They looked at her, then at the door.

Yes, Jillian thought, viewing everything as if she were on the edge of a violent, terrible storm. If the warning turned into something more, the Warlords would do their best to get out of the shop alive—and would do their best to take her with them. But the girl behind the counter, being the target of that cold rage, would be forfeit.

A woman rushed out of the back of the shop. "What's going—" Seeing Sadi, she froze.

Jillian?

Recognizing Rothvar's voice, she looked over her shoulder. He stood outside the shop, his Eyrien war blade in one hand, a fighting knife in the other. If he walked into the shop right now, he would die. She knew it. So did Rothvar. But he would walk into the shop and try to protect her because she was Nurian's sister.

I'm all right.

"P-Prince?" the woman said. "Is there something I can do for you?"

Jillian was sure everyone could feel the effort Sadi was making to step back from the killing edge. Again.

"You can explain why you've been selling cakes left by the customers eating here as if they were fresh and untouched," he said.

"You're mistaken, Prince. We always offer to box up anything that is left for our customers to take home. If they don't want the cakes, they're set aside on that glass-covered tray and sold as remainders at a steep discount at the end of the day. Or my employees are permitted to take the remainders home with them."

Sadi stared at the woman, then looked at the girl. "It would seem you weren't informed of a change in policy."

The two boxes of cakes the Warlords had purchased floated over to the counter. The lids opened. The cakes rose out of the boxes and settled gently on the counter. Raising his right hand, Sadi flicked his index finger with his thumb, then made a motion as if the black-tinted fingernail was a small knife. He didn't touch any of the cakes, but the eight small cakes were cut cleanly in half. He moved the first two fingers of that hand apart, and the halves of each cake separated.

Jillian and the two Warlords moved closer to the counter.

The woman stared at the gold coin sticking out of the middle of one of the cakes. "I don't understand."

"I had heard your shop was reselling cakes as new that had already been on the table. My young friend and I came in to find out if the rumor was true. I put the gold coin in one of the cakes that we didn't eat. We weren't given the option of taking the cakes with us. From what you say, the cakes should have been put with the remainders. But these Warlords just purchased as new a piece of cake that had a gold coin inside—a coin I put in as a test." Sadi pointed to a cake that had been in the other box. The thumbprint the girl had put on the cake was clearly visible. "Cakes that were already purchased by customers eating in the shop are being resold at full price. Someone is pocketing the profit of selling the same food twice."

The woman squared her shoulders. "Clearly, I haven't been paying as much attention to the front of the shop as I should have been. That error will be rectified."

Sadi tipped his head in the slightest of bows, walked out of the shop . . . and disappeared.

"Come along, Lady." One of the Warlords touched Jillian's elbow, gently urging her to get out, get away, even though the danger was past.

As she reached the door, she looked back and met the eyes of the girl. Shaken by the hatred she saw in those eyes, she rushed through the doorway.

"My thanks, Warlords," Rothvar said to the two men. "I'll see Lady Jillian home."

They glanced at her but didn't challenge the Eyrien Warlord. Either they recognized Rothvar and knew he was Yaslana's second-in-command, or they realized they had no chance of surviving a fight with him.

"You all right?" Rothvar asked, leading her away from the shop. "You look pale."

"I'm all right," she said weakly.

No cake? Khary asked. *Why is there no cake?*

"I changed my mind." She wanted to run home, wanted to hide. But she was Eyrien, and she had a connection to the Yaslana household—and no one connected to that name hid from trouble. She looked at Rothvar, who had asked no questions, made no demands for her to explain the part she had played in a Black-Jeweled Warlord Prince rising to the killing edge. "I still need to make a stop at the library."

Rothvar studied her. "Do you need an escort?"

I am standing escort, Khary said with a growl.

"A second escort," Rothvar amended.

"No, thank you. We'll be fine. I'll be going home right after the library." When Rothvar started to walk away, she said, "Why was Prince Sadi so angry about the cakes? It wasn't right for the shop to sell the cakes twice at full price, but he seemed . . ." He would have killed the women in the shop. She was sure of it. Should she tell Rothvar that Khary thought the Prince was unwell?

Rothvar returned, standing close to her. She braced for a slap, then realized he stood that close to speak quietly.

"Something else was already riding his temper, and something besides the cakes pushed him to the edge. Yaslana asked us to keep an eye on him. I would have stepped in when he approached you, but it seemed to calm him."

"He looked"—*like a man in agony*—"upset when he sat down to talk to me."

"The thing to remember is that, even upset, Sadi didn't lose control. A man who stands so deep in the abyss can't afford to lose control of his power or his temper—not until he steps onto a killing field." Rothvar looked puzzled. "If you suspected there was a problem at the shop, why did you tell Sadi instead of telling Yaslana?"

She couldn't meet his eyes. "I didn't want to cause trouble."

TWENTY-SEVEN

Pain coiled around his chest, an ever-tightening chain that squeezed his heart and smothered every effort to take a full breath. But he didn't ask for help. If he asked, help would be given. Maybe this pain, and where it would take him, would make things easier. After all, sexual heat was a burden placed on the living, not on the demon-dead.

Daemon glided through the corridors of the Keep, shrouded by pain. He saw no one, which wasn't unusual. He was well-known to Draca and Geoffrey, the Keep's Seneschal and historian/librarian respectively, and his presence didn't attract the attention of whatever guarded Ebon Askavi.

Eventually he approached the airy metal gate that blocked the corridor leading to the rooms reserved for the Queen and her triangle—Steward, Master of the Guard, and Consort. He pushed one side of the gate and was surprised to find it unlocked and swinging open at his lightest touch. That *was* unusual. The gate to those rooms had always been locked. But, perhaps, since there was no longer a Queen in residence, there was no need for that symbolic protection.

How many years since he'd walked this particular corridor, opened the door of the Consort's suite, stood in the room that had been his personal territory in this sprawling place? Thirty-five years? More? He'd expected dustcovers over the furniture and the bed stripped of linens and covering. But it looked no different from what he remembered. Looked as if he'd been gone no more than a week or two. Looked as if the years between today and the last time he'd made love to Jaenelle Angelline in the Queen's suite hadn't existed at all.

He wasn't sure how much longer he could breathe, how much longer his heart would beat. Wasn't that why he was here? Assisting Jillian had dulled the pain just enough for him to be able to catch the Winds and reach the Keep. Here, in this place where he'd been accepted, his heart could beat for the last time and he could step away from the pain he caused the living—and the pain the living caused him.

That's a fair dose of self-pity, old son. Lucivar would kick your ass down the mountain and up again if he heard any of that.

Which didn't make the truth any less true. Surreal might breathe a sigh of relief once the High Lord of Hell—and the Sadist—resided in Hell.

Crack.

"Prince?"

Turning, he saw Draca standing in the doorway.

"I'd like your permission to move back into this suite for a while," he said quietly. He didn't mention that he doubted he would need the rooms for long.

She who had once been the last Queen of the dragons, the ancient race that had created the Blood so long ago, took a step toward him. "A Conssort cannot entertain a wife in thiss room."

At least, not a wife who wasn't also his Queen. "I'm aware of that." He looked around the room. "I need this, Draca. It's the only place I can be who I am. Everything I am. It's the only place where I can stand at the full measure of my strength and not frighten people who don't deserve to be frightened by what I am."

She didn't ask who now feared him that he wanted to protect. Maybe she already knew. Maybe she'd always known this day would come, and that was the reason she had kept the Consort's suite ready for him.

"Very well. Would you like ssomething to eat?"

"Not right now. I'd like to be alone for a while."

Draca walked out of the room. The door closed behind her.

He removed his black jacket and hung it over the clothes stand before exploring the room. Nothing in the closet or the chest of drawers except . . . He smiled when he opened the bottom drawer and saw all the pieces that made up the game called cradle. He should purchase the original game, not this labyrinthine version Jaenelle and the coven had devised—and, all right, he'd added a few layers and rules of his own to the damn thing over the years—and teach Jaenelle Saetien how to play.

Would he have the chance to teach her how to play?

Crack.

Flinching at the pain scraping the inside of his skull, Daemon closed the drawer. Checking the bathroom, he found new bars of soap and fresh towels. Then he approached the door that connected the Consort's suite with the Queen's suite. He turned the handle, half expecting it to be locked. But the door opened for him, as it had for seventy years.

He could smell her in this room. Jaenelle Angelline. His wife. His life. His Queen. Oh, the physical scent was gone after so many years, but her psychic scent still filled the room—a room that, like his, looked ready to receive the living myth, as if she were traveling through Kaeleer and would be back any day now.

Tears stung his eyes. He had set aside the misery of living without Jaenelle, had focused on ruling Dhemlan and Hell, had made the commitment to be a good husband to Surreal and a good father to Jaenelle Saetien. He had leashed everything he was as tightly as he could, had done everything he could to protect and please Surreal during these past few months while he battled the debilitating headaches and tried to understand why she had turned away from him in every way except for sex. Now he knew why. She truly believed she'd been bedding the Sadist. Her inability to tell the difference meant she couldn't accept what he was, despite how many years they had known each other and the years they had already spent together. Her words had sliced him deeper than any knife, and that pain had reopened the wound of missing the love of his life, and he didn't know how to heal that wound a second time.

He didn't want to heal it a second time. He wanted to bleed from that wound. Bleed and bleed until he was hollow, until he was nothing more than intellect and power. Until Daemon Sadi disappeared and there was only the High Lord of Hell—and the Sadist.

Maybe someone at the Keep could help, Lucivar had said.

Who could help a man who wore Black Jewels?

Removing his shoes, Daemon stretched out on the bed he had shared with Jaenelle most of the nights they had stayed at the Keep. Bunching a pillow under his head, he squeezed his eyes shut, denying the tears, while his heart pounded, pounded, pounded, and his breathing became more pained and shallow.

Maybe he could sink into a dream of being with his Queen and never wake, leaving the body behind.

Except there was still the child. His daughter. She would need him to teach her and protect her for many years to come. He couldn't walk away from his daughter even if his wife saw him as a monster.

"Jaenelle," he whispered. "If any part of you is still here, please help me. Please . . ."

The headache pounded, pounded, pounded like a hammer breaking bone—or breaking a crystal chalice. His heart clenched—another kind of pain.

The tears fell, and he couldn't say if he wept for himself or wept for his father, who had also worn the cold, glorious Black, had also been thought a monster by some, and had also felt the same terrible loneliness.

CRACK!

The bed felt cold and hard enough to pull him out of sleep.

Rolling to his side, Daemon struggled to sit up. Then he looked around.

It had been a long time since he'd seen the Misty Place, even in dreams.

And there, drumming her claws against the stone altar, stood Witch. The living myth, although no longer among the living. This form was the Self that had lived within the flesh, the Self that had been shaped by the dreams of so many of Kaeleer's races.

The joy of seeing her was almost as sharp as pain.

"Jaenelle," he whispered. "Jaenelle."

He couldn't interpret the look in her sapphire eyes before she returned her attention to something on the altar.

"Hell's fire, Daemon," she said, shaking her head and sounding perplexed. "I can guess *how* you did this, but what I don't understand is why."

"Did what?" Grabbing one end of the altar, he pulled himself to his feet—and wondered if he'd be able to stay upright.

Witch pointed to the crystal chalice. He recognized it as the representation of his own mind. It had shattered twice and been repaired—by Witch. He could see the mends, the veins of power that held the pieces together. But the chalice had many new cracks; it even had a small hole in the bottom that was oozing . . . something.

Four leashes were looped around four posts. Three were simple leather. One was leather and chain. The last time he'd seen these images in another dream, the leash that kept his sexual heat under control . . .

He couldn't see the loop beneath the hardened pus and rot.

"I didn't do this," he said, looking away from the damage.

"No one else could have done this to you. The pain must have been hideous. If someone else had tried to do this, you would have fought back long before you reached this point."

He stared at the posts, at the damaged chalice. "The headaches."

"Clearly a warning you didn't heed."

The snarl under her words gave him a weird kind of comfort. "I went to Healers. More than one. None of them could find a reason for the headaches."

"*That* was the reason!" She pointed to the post encased in hardened pus and rot. "You tried to leash the sexual heat tighter than your current maturity could tolerate. You're a man in your prime, Daemon. You were never going to succeed in choking the heat back to a less mature stage of your life, but you gave it a damn good try and this is the result."

The love and concern he saw in her eyes almost broke him.

"Why, Daemon?" Witch asked. "Why did you do this?"

"I made a mistake."

"And this was your way of punishing yourself for that mistake?"

He might have believed the mild tone of voice if thunder hadn't rolled through the Misty Place, if the lightning of fury hadn't flashed and sizzled over the chasm that held a web that spiraled down and down and down into the Darkness—a web that was the reservoir for the vast power Jaenelle Angelline had set aside when she had dreamed of having an extraordinary ordinary life.

"Show me," Witch said.

"What?" He knew what she was asking; he just didn't want to do it.

"Show me." A Queen's command.

"I can show you what happened as I remember it, felt it. Surreal's feelings are very different." Jaenelle was no longer his wife, but she was still his Queen. He flinched at the idea of sharing a memory of himself with another woman.

"Show me."

She wouldn't ask again. If he didn't obey now, he would have to walk away from the Queen whose will was still his life.

Opening all of his inner barriers, he offered the memory of the night Surreal had walked into his bedroom and he'd thought, *Mine.* He offered every word, every touch, every taste, every sound. Then he offered the memory of the following morning when he'd realized Surreal feared him because of the way they had played the night before, even though staying had been her choice. Finally, the memory of Surreal telling him it would never happen again and to leash the damn heat.

He closed his inner barriers, and his mind, damaged as it was, was his own again.

"She kept saying I was playing with her, kept demanding that I leash the sexual heat and wouldn't believe me when I said it *was* leashed."

Witch sighed. "Well, Surreal is right in one way, and this is why she was very wrong in another way."

She called in four brass rings and placed them on the altar. First, she arranged them in a row from smallest to largest. Then she nested the rings, making the difference in sizes apparent. The difference between the first and second brass ring was significant. So was the difference between the second and third. Not much difference between the third and fourth, but enough that the third fit into the fourth.

Witch pointed to the smallest ring. "Like other traits that are part of a Warlord Prince's nature, the sexual heat begins to manifest at puberty."

Oh, Hell's fire. They would have to deal with Daemonar when the boy reached that age.

"When a Warlord Prince reaches the age when he makes the Offering to the Darkness and comes into his mature power, the sexual heat becomes more potent." She pointed to the second ring, then went on to the third. "And then he reaches physical maturity, a man entering his prime."

"Which is where I was when we were married. Which is where I am now."

"Not quite." She tapped the fourth ring. "A century ago, you were just coming into your prime. Your sexual heat hadn't reached its peak yet. Now you are solidly in your prime, and I'm guessing the last phase of sexual heat happened right around the night you had invited Surreal to play, and by the following morning, it had settled into where it will be until you reach your autumn years, when it starts to decline."

Horrified by the thought, he shook his head. "It can't stay at this level."

"It can—and will. But you'll adjust, and so will the people around you."

"Jaenelle, no. You don't know the misery this has already caused."

"Daemon," she said gently. "This is part of who you are."

"How am I supposed to cope with that?" Was Lucivar going through this too?

"For one thing, you're going to stop hurting yourself. For another, you're going to use that brilliant mind to recognize that every Warlord Prince goes through this. You've seen men go through this. Clearly it didn't make much of an impression."

"I would have noticed."

"Really? Chaosti. Rainier. Aaron. Elan. You knew every one of them before he reached his prime and went through this last phase of the sexual heat. Every one of them, Daemon. You knew their wives or, in Rainier's case, a woman he lived with for decades. The difference is the depth of power. Like so many other things about the Blood, the potency of the heat is connected to the power that flows through the veins." She reached out and tapped the pendant that held his Black Jewel. "That little bit more that might go unnoticed in a Warlord Prince who wore a lighter Jewel is going to be felt by everyone who is dealing with the Black."

Surreal would never want to endure that.

Witch vanished the four brass rings. "You went to Healers who couldn't help you. Why didn't you talk to someone else?"

"The only other man who wore the Black and went through this is gone," he said bitterly.

"Yes, Saetan is gone, but there are two people at the Keep who knew him when he was your age. And there is a Black Widow who might have supplied some answers—"

"Oh, *she* was a lot of help. Cryptic dreams about the wiggle-waggle."

"Which you ignored."

She said it with a sweetness that made his balls want to tuck up inside his belly. Just in case.

"There is also a Warlord Prince currently residing at the Keep, at least some of the time. If you had bothered to talk to him, he would have recognized what was happening and why." Witch looked back at the posts and the chalice on the altar. "You tried so hard to repress your sexual heat, you've actually done some damage to your heart and lungs. It may be centuries before you feel the effects, but what you've done here will extract a price."

Daemon studied the posts and chalice. "The headaches won't abate, will they?"

Silence. Finally, she looked at him. "Not while this remains as it is. I can try to fix what is broken."

A broken vessel mended again. Did he want that? If he wanted to be there for Jaenelle Saetien while she grew up, there wasn't a choice. "Will that relieve the pain?"

"That will depend on how much of the damage I can repair." Witch hesitated. "Daemon, this healing will hurt."

"Everything has a price. Do what you need to do."

Pain washed over him, through him, became him.

Beyond the pain, he was aware of nothing but her voice. Sometimes she sang cadences of healing Craft. Sometimes she swore at him viciously in several languages as she carefully broke through carapaces of pus and drained swellings created by his attempt to please Surreal and subdue the sexual heat.

Hours? Days? A lifetime? He didn't know how long she worked, how long he endured the healing, before she finally said, "It's done. Look. And *learn*."

Daemon climbed to his feet, having no memory of sinking to the floor next to the altar.

The crystal chalice—his mind, his sanity—had been repaired. Again.

The three posts and leashes that represented his control over his power, his temper, and the Sadist looked as they had before. The fourth post, his sexual heat . . . Cleaned and back to its normal size. But the loops that should have snugged the leashes to the posts were loose, and when he tried to tighten them, he discovered a ring of Witch's darker power forming a cushion between loop and post, making it impossible for him to tighten the leashes all the way.

"Jaenelle . . ."

She pointed at the chalice. "I did what I could, but even I can't mend this a fourth time. Daemon, you can't afford to risk your sanity by being careless with yourself. You wear the Black. If you slide into the Twisted Kingdom, you could be a weapon powerful enough to destroy Kaeleer."

"Could you break the Black?" As soon as he said the words, he felt everything in him resist the idea. Give up the Black without a fight? Never.

Witch gave him a look that would have shriveled his balls if this wasn't a dream. "It doesn't matter if I could. It will *not* be done, because the Shadow Realm is going to need the Black. Your family, your daughter, are going to need the High Lord."

He swallowed hard. "War?"

"I don't know, Daemon. Even I can't see everything."

"But enough," he said quietly.

"Enough to know that the man you are will be needed. *Everything* you are will be needed." Her hand moved around the chalice, not touching it, but he still felt her nearness like a caress. "You need to keep the reservoir in your Black Jewel drained enough to make room for the power your body and mind can no longer hold."

"Not an easy thing to do."

He saw the question in her eyes. He waited for her to ask why he wasn't helping Surreal drain her Gray Jewel before her moontime. But Witch didn't ask. Maybe she already knew.

"I have some thoughts about that." She pointed at the posts. "As for these . . ."

"They're too loose."

A hesitation. "Everything has a price, remember? It may take decades of slow healing before you can hold the leashes as tightly as you used to. It may be never. Your mind is too fragile to exert that kind of force on any part of you right now."

"At least tighten that one." Daemon pointed to the leash made of chain and leather.

"I can't. I'm sorry, Daemon, but I can't. Not if you are going to stay sane and whole."

"The Sadist . . ."

"A little more easily provoked, but there are things you can do to help yourself and the people around you."

She seemed to be struggling to find the words, and that wasn't like her. "Tell me."

"You should arrange to have a . . . sanctuary . . . at the Hall, a place different from your bedroom suite. You need a place where you can retreat when people's response to the sexual heat starts to scrape your temper, because now the aspect of yourself most likely to respond will be the Sadist. You should discuss this with a few people you trust without question, and it must be without question.

You will give them an agreed-upon phrase that they will speak if they notice your control slipping. If you hear that phrase, you will not challenge their reason for saying it; you will retreat to your sanctuary and maintain solitude until your control gently returns. If you want a phrase in a language that wouldn't commonly be spoken, I can help you with that."

"Maybe the language of the Dea al Mon." That language wouldn't be known to many outside the borders of the Territory ruled by the Children of the Wood.

How much of that language had Surreal learned over the years?

"Who should know the phrase?" Witch asked.

"Beale and Holt at the Hall. Chaosti here at the Keep. Lucivar."

He considered Tersa, since a woman might sense something in him a man wouldn't, but that would be too much weight for her broken mind to bear. Besides, Tersa would tell him in her own way if she saw trouble. If he'd talked to her all those months ago when she'd first noticed he wasn't well, maybe he wouldn't have endured so much pain.

And he wouldn't be in the Misty Place now, feeling a joyful sorrow at being with Jaenelle again, even in this limited way.

"And Marian," he said. She had seen—and accepted. He could trust her.

Witch made no comment about him not including Surreal in the list.

He didn't know what she searched for as she studied his face, looked into his eyes, but she must have found it, because she said, "You need to stay among the living, Prince. You need to stay *connected* to the living. Do you understand?"

Daughter. Brother. Maybe still a wife. Maybe. "Yes, I understand."

"If you give me your word that you will do your best to stay connected, I'll make you a bargain."

"What bargain?"

"When you've set up your sanctuary and talked to the people you named, then we'll discuss the bargain and what to do about the Black."

Suddenly he was furious. Coldly, savagely furious. "What difference does any of this make?" He waved at the chalice, at the leashes, at the posts. "Dream. Vision. What difference does it make? The pain will still be there when I wake up. The misery will be there. But I'm expected to survive another day and the day after that and after that for centuries to come."

"If I am still your Queen, then my will is your life, and, yes, Prince, I expect you to survive. To do more than just survive."

"Bitch." Wondering why his temper had slipped the leash—and wondering why it should matter—he turned away from her.

"You asked for my help—and I answered."

"You're usually kinder when I dream about you."

A freezing silence. Then, too softly, "You think this is a dream?"

Something lightly brushed against his upper arm. Then he felt the shivering sensation of his skin parting moments before he felt the pain and . . .

Daemon tumbled off the bed.

Panting, he looked at his right arm, at the sleeve of his white silk shirt turning wet and red.

Witch's midnight voice thundered up from somewhere deep in the abyss. *Remembrance. Reminder.*

Shocked, he stumbled into the Consort's suite, turned on the light in his bathroom. No slices in the shirt.

Stripping off the shirt, Daemon stood in front of the mirror and stared at the four bleeding wounds that had been made by Witch's claws.

Remembrance. Reminder.

When Jaenelle Saetien was born, Surreal had ripped his arm with a taloned gauntlet, but those wounds had healed, leaving no scars.

He looked at his left wrist, at the only scar he carried. Tersa had given it to him on the day she told him that Witch walked among the living. And now . . .

Daemon sat on the edge of the bathtub and pressed the bloody shirt to his arm.

Not a dream. He'd been back in the Misty Place, talking to Witch. Arguing with Witch.

He didn't know what sort of bargain she would make with him, but it meant he would see her again. Until then, he would set up his sanctuary, do what he could to repair his marriage, and help Lucivar deal with Jillian and her suitor. He would prove to his Queen that he was willing to do more than survive.

Swaying on his feet, Daemon washed his arm, then used healing Craft to close the wounds. Calling in the small cabinet he kept filled with healing supplies, he spread an ointment over the wounds before wrapping his biceps in gauze and putting a protective shield over the whole upper arm.

He knew with absolute certainty that those wounds would leave scars, because they were a reminder from Witch that he wasn't alone. They were the message that he would see every single day for the rest of his life.

TWENTY-EIGHT

———◆———

Still shaky from her crying jag and confession to Marian, Surreal finished dressing moments before Lucivar barged into the guest room, grabbed her left arm, and pulled her toward the door.

"We're going to talk," he snarled.

"Get your hand off me," she snarled back as her right hand curled in preparation for calling in her favorite stiletto.

He turned on her, his hand tightening on her arm. "You call in a weapon, you'd better be ready to fight. And you'd better be ready for the pain that will follow, because I'll hurt you, Surreal. Today, right now, I will hurt you."

Mother Night. He means it.

She didn't resist as he hauled her through the corridors. She caught a glimpse of Marian's startled expression before Lucivar shoved her into his study and slammed the door. Ebon-gray shields barricaded the room. She couldn't get out and no one could get in.

"You want to tell me—," she began.

"Pretend I'm holding a weapon," Lucivar said. "I'm pointing it at you. Threaten, threaten, blah blah blah."

That stupid phrase sounded a lot more terrifying when he said it.

"We've already concluded the part where you threaten me, so what is this about?"

"You tell me. What in the name of Hell is going on between you and Daemon?"

"That's none of your business."

"Considering what I heard this morning, it damn well *is* my business."

"You . . ." Surreal felt the blood drain out of her head. She wanted to sit down but couldn't afford to show any weakness. "Did you tell Daemon?"

"I didn't have to."

Hell's fire, Mother Night, and may the Darkness be merciful.

"You don't know what it's like to have the Sadist in your bed night after night!" she cried.

"Neither do you." Lucivar spread his wings, then folded them halfway. "You have brushed against that side of Daemon's temper over the years, and you have seen what he can do. But believe me, Surreal, you have *never* danced with the Sadist when he has been focused on *you*."

"How would you know?"

"Because I *have* danced with him. If that's what you'd been facing every night for the past few months, you would not have survived this long."

She shook her head. She knew what she felt. "He's been different since the night I stayed with him in his bedroom."

He folded his wings all the way and stepped closer. "How has he been different? And why didn't you say something? I told you I would help you."

"What was I supposed to say? That I can't think of anything but screwing him whenever he gets near me? That some days I feel like I'm nothing but a sheath for his cock?"

"Why didn't you say something if his sexual heat was making you uncomfortable?"

"I did! Over and over again. What could I have said that he would *hear*?"

"Something like, 'Sugar, I need to rest tonight. Could you bank the heat?'"

She snorted. "Could Marian say that to you?"

"She does. Only she doesn't call me sugar."

Surreal blinked. Using different words could have stopped this? No. Not possible. "I have been dealing with the Sadist." She had to believe that, needed to believe there hadn't been a choice.

Lucivar shook his head. "I'm not saying there isn't a whisper of the Sadist or an edge to the way he sometimes plays in bed. Daemon likes to play. But you're his friend, his partner, his lover, and his wife. When he plays with you, he knows exactly where the line is between pain and pleasure, and he will *never* cross it. Not with you." He thought for a moment. "Well, he *used* to know where that line was, but neither of you told the other that something had changed, so I'm thinking both of you have crossed a few lines you wouldn't normally cross—and there are wounded feelings on both sides because of it."

Annoyed by the scold, Surreal shrugged off those words and concentrated on something else Lucivar had said. "The Sadist crossed that line with you." Daemon and Lucivar had a complicated history, but her stomach started flipping at the thought of them doing . . . what?

Lucivar's smile was bitter. "Even when we were younger and both wore the Birthright Red, he would hit me with that sexual heat and wind his particular kind of seduction spells around me, and there was nothing I could do. He played with me in front of an audience of bitch Queens. Do you have any idea what it's like to be so mad with need, to have so little control over your own body, that your own brother could make you come in front of all those bitches?"

Lucivar walked away and stood for a minute with his back to her, before returning.

"I hated him for what he did to me during those entertainments. It took years before I figured out that he did it out of love. He offered those bitches an entertainment they couldn't resist as a substitute for whatever they'd intended to do to me. Because what they'd intended would have been permanently disfiguring. I could have lost my balls or my wings. Lost my eyes, my ears. They wouldn't have killed me and brought Saetan's rage down on their heads, but they could have maimed me to the point of being a helpless lump that they could continue to torture. I'd seen them do that to other men. But the Sadist offered them a game that was entertainment and lesson—a lesson because he made it clear that if they touched me after he was done, he would do the same to them . . . without any mercy."

"Mother Night," Surreal breathed.

"I don't know what it cost him to play those games." A pause. "Well, I broke his ribs a couple of times when I beat on him afterward. But playing those games did things to him in here." Lucivar tapped his chest. "He's a lot more powerful now than he was then, and so is the Sadist. If you truly believe that's who is coming to your bed, I need to know. If he's acting oddly toward you, I need to know. If you're thinking of leaving him, I need to know. You help him stay connected to the living, Surreal. But if something happens and he goes cold and the Sadist starts sliding into the Twisted Kingdom, I need to know because I'll have to choose to join him in the destruction or stand against him."

"You couldn't stand against him," she said wearily. "He would kill you."

"Yes, he would."

She stared at him. He said the words so simply, with such acceptance.

"Despite the past, or maybe because of it, I love him and I enjoy spending time with him. But I also keep an eye on him for the same reason that Andulvar kept an eye on Saetan, especially after what happened with Zuulaman. Men that powerful have to be protected in some ways, have to know there is a hand that will reach for them if they flounder, have to know someone will say 'stop' before they're out of reach and *can't* be stopped. That was true for Andulvar and Saetan. It's true for me and Daemon. More so for us, because Daemon is a lot more dangerous than Saetan ever thought to be."

Surreal pushed her hair away from her face. "What do you want me to do?"

"What do you want to do?" he countered.

"I don't want to leave him." And she didn't want to leave Jaenelle Saetien alone with Daemon without a buffer. Not permanently. No one needed to tell her that if she walked away, the High Lord's daughter wouldn't be coming with her. "I'll talk to him, explain why I can't handle being around the Black every night."

Lucivar looked past her and frowned. "Come on. We have other things to deal with." He dropped the shields and hurried out of the study.

She hurried after him, not sure what he'd heard that made their discussion end so abruptly.

"Marian?" She looked at Marian's pale face and the way one hand clung to Lucivar's arm as soon as he reached his wife.

Marian sighed, a shuddering sound. "Surreal. Jillian asked if you could meet her at her home. Apparently something happened and she needs to talk."

"All right." She looked from Marian to Lucivar. "Something else?"

Marian's hand tightened on Lucivar's arm. "Rothvar needs Lucivar down in the village. There was some trouble. Daemonar . . ."

"I'll take care of it," Lucivar said. "You look after yourself and the baby. Let Morghann keep watch on the girls."

Marian nodded.

The tender way Lucivar pressed his lips to Marian's forehead made Surreal's heart ache.

She followed Lucivar out the front door of the eyrie.

He looked toward the far end of the valley. "You'd

better go if you're going. That's a wicked bitch of a storm heading this way, and everyone with any sense is going to go to ground until it passes."

"After I talk to Jillian, I'll talk to Daemon," she said.

He watched the sky. "Well, that might be difficult, witchling. I don't feel the Black in Ebon Rih anymore, and Daemon isn't answering my call. Right now I have no idea where he is."

Lucivar flew down to Riada as fast as he could, aiming for the knot of people and the scattered debris in front of one of the shops. He glided toward Zaranar, Hallevar, and Rothvar, who was holding Tagg. Backwinging, he landed lightly on the street just beyond the debris and the crowd, which was divided into such distinct groups he wondered if this was the start of a fight between Eyriens and Rihlanders or an isolated problem. On one side stood the three Eyrien Warlords. On the other side stood a dozen guards who served the Queen of Riada, including her Master of the Guard, who looked furious.

Between the two groups of warriors were five young men and the man who owned the shop. Four of the young Warlords were bloody—black eyes, split lips, a couple with broken noses. And two of them were cupping their balls and groaning, their clothes spattered with vomit. The fifth young Warlord looked rumpled, but Lucivar saw no sign that he'd been in the fight. A couple of men carried a sixth youth out of the shop on a stretcher.

"Need to get this one to the Healer," they said. "He was thrown through the shopwindow, and the defensive shields he had around himself didn't hold. His back and legs are cut up pretty bad."

Lucivar nodded, giving unspoken permission.

When we arrived to break up the fight, Daemonar ran off, Rothvar said on a psychic spear thread. *Don't know where he is right now. He's hurt. Can't say how badly.* He put a hand on the puppy's head. *This one was told to stay out of the fight, but he started barking loud enough to bring us and the Queen's guard running.*

"Something has to be done about that brat!" one of the young men shouted as soon as the men carrying the stretcher headed down the street with their injured friend. "Who does he think he is?"

"He thinks he's the son of the Warlord Prince of Ebon Rih," the Riada Master of the Guard replied. He waved a hand, drawing everyone's attention to where Lucivar stood. "So why don't you tell his father why all of you got into a fight with one boy?"

Two of the Warlords who had been in the fight and the one who had stayed out of it looked at Lucivar and turned sickly pale, confirming that they lived in Ebon Rih, even if they didn't live in Riada. The other two were stupid enough to look defiant.

"The brat started the fight," one of the fools said. "We were just having a little fun."

Lucivar smiled a lazy, arrogant smile. "And what was said that provoked that first punch?"

"We didn't say anything," the second fool said.

Bitch, Tagg said, squirming in Rothvar's arms. *Whore. Suck cock.*

Lucivar watched as fury filled Rothvar's eyes. Zaranar's and Hallevar's too. What surprised him was feeling the same level of fury pumping out of Riada's Master of the Guard.

"What do you want done with these curs, Prince?" the Master asked.

Thunder rumbled. Lightning flashed. The storm would reach the village in minutes.

Lucivar looked at the shopkeeper. "You figure out the cost of repairing or replacing everything that was damaged in this fight, then double it. Give the figure to the Master of the Guard and Lord Rothvar. Everyone who was involved in the fight—and that includes my boy—will each pay a share of the cost." He looked at the Master. "Get them cleaned up and have the Queen's Healer deal with whatever needs healing. Then hold them until I find out if the debt's been sufficiently paid or if they're going to forfeit their tongues."

He ignored the young men's protests and turned to Rothvar. *I'm going to find my boy. You get to shelter and take the pup with you.*

Done. Rothvar studied the sky and the advancing storm. *Not a good time to be flying.*

No. Turning away from all of them, he launched himself into the air and flew into the storm, heading for Ebon Askavi, the most likely place to find his son.

Hearing the quick knock, Daemon gave the Consort's bedroom one swift look to be sure he'd eliminated all signs that he'd been hurt. Then he opened the door.

"Geoffrey?" He smiled at the Keep's historian/librarian.

Geoffrey didn't return the smile. "You're needed."

They hurried away from the Queen's section of the Keep and continued on until they reached one of the areas reserved for guests and visitors. Spotting the boy and the Warlord Prince who stood next to him, Daemon rushed past Geoffrey.

"Daemonar! What . . . ?"

Daemon looked at Chaosti, who rested a hand on the shoulder of the defiant, bloodied, trembling boy. Still a Gray-Jeweled Warlord Prince, Chaosti had been the Warlord Prince of the Dea al Mon before he'd died in his sleep at the natural end of his life. He'd been a vigorous old man who made the transition to demon-dead with enviable ease, continuing his role as an advisor to those who now ruled his people. More important to Daemon, he had become a friend again over the past few years.

"I'm glad I beat the snot out of those wingless Jhinkas," Daemonar shouted. "I'm glad!"

Calling anyone a Jhinka—a winged race that was an old enemy of the Eyriens—was the worst kind of insult. And calling someone a wingless Jhinka was the epitome of insults if you were an Eyrien boy.

"There's a fire going in the sitting room," Chaosti said, nodding to the open door. "I've asked for a basin of warm water and cloths, but there hasn't been time to find out what sort of damage our little Brother has done to himself."

They led the boy into the sitting room and stripped him out of his drenched clothes, since he'd managed to reach one of the Keep's courtyards before the storm began pounding on the mountain, but hadn't reached shelter. Between them they washed the simple cuts —Daemon using healing Craft on a couple of deeper ones—and examined him for injured muscles and damaged bones. Bruised ribs, a split lip, and some cuts, including ripped skin on his knuckles. The worst injury was a broken bone in the boy's left arm.

After setting the bone, Daemon wrapped healing spells around the damage, then added a shield to hold the bone. And then . . .

"Hell's fire, Uncle Daemon." Daemonar stared at his arm in disgust. "What is *that*?"

"That?" Daemon looked mildly surprised by the question. "That, boyo, is a shield that will keep your forearm protected until the bone fully heals." He turned to Chaosti. "Isn't it obvious?"

Chaosti studied the arm and said solemnly, "It's quite obvious."

"It's *blue*," Daemonar protested. "It's *bright blue*. Everything and everybody will be able to see it halfway up the mountain!"

Daemon smiled at his nephew. "Only halfway? Maybe I should . . ."

Daemonar tucked the arm beneath the blanket they had wrapped around him.

Setting aside the healing supplies, Daemon remained sitting on the footstool. "It's time to tell us what this was about," he said with a quiet gentleness that wasn't any less a command made by the patriarch of the family.

Daemonar shook his head. "I can't. I *won't* tell you."

Daemon felt cold anger whisper through his blood, saw the flash of fear in Daemonar's eyes—felt Chaosti descend to the level of the Gray. Not that Gray could survive against the Black. Not that a man who was demon-dead didn't understand what it meant to challenge the High Lord of Hell.

"They said mean things about Jillian and about . . . I won't tell you. I won't."

"If you feel it isn't prudent to tell your uncle what was said, are you willing to tell me?" Chaosti asked.

Did the boy realize or remember that Chaosti had a family connection to Surreal? Probably not, since Daemonar looked relieved at the suggestion.

"All right," Daemon said. "You give Prince Chaosti a full report, including *everything* that was said. He will decide if it's best that your father and I not know the details."

"Yes, sir."

Rising, Daemon walked to the door. He looked back to see Daemonar studying the bright blue shield—and saw Chaosti's amused smile before the Dea al Mon Warlord Prince settled his lined face into a suitably grave expression before sitting on the footstool Daemon had just left.

He'd barely closed the door when he felt the presence of the Ebon-gray. Lucivar walked toward him, soaked to the skin, gold eyes hot with temper.

"Is he here?" Lucivar asked. "And when did you get back?"

Get back? He hadn't left the Keep. At least, his body hadn't left.

"He's here," Daemon replied. "He's fine. Better than you." Grabbing Lucivar's arm, he hauled his brother into another room, dragging him the last few feet until they reached the fireplace. Using witchfire, Daemon lit the logs that were stacked in the grate before turning to his brother. "Hell's fire,

Lucivar! What were you thinking, flying through a storm like that? You could have been hit by lightning."

"Almost was. Twice."

"Idiot."

"You would have done the same."

"Of course I would have, but that doesn't make *you* any less of an idiot."

Lucivar smiled and moved a little closer to the fire. "Temperature has dropped. Almost got hit with some hailstones that would fill the palm of my hand."

"Get out of those wet clothes." Daemon called in a couple of the towels from the bathroom in the Consort's suite. As soon as Lucivar stripped out of the clothes, Daemon handed him one towel and then started wiping down Lucivar's back and legs, checking for injuries. "Are your wings all right?"

Lucivar opened them. "They're fine." He didn't give Daemon time to pat the wings dry before he closed them and turned around. "The boy."

"He's bruised and a bit bloody. Has a broken bone in his left forearm. That's the worst of it. What happened? I gathered he was in a fight, but he wouldn't tell me what started it. He is giving Chaosti a full report."

"I'm surprised Chaosti isn't resting at this time of day." Lucivar wrapped a towel around his waist.

Daemon found a blanket folded over the back of one of the chairs in the room—a blanket he was certain hadn't been there a minute ago—and gave it to Lucivar.

"Five aristo Rihlander Warlords who are close to their majority if they haven't already reached it against Daemonar," Lucivar continued. "There was a sixth youngster, but he stayed out of the fight."

Daemon stared at Lucivar. "Five against one?" Of course, it was five Warlords who probably didn't know much about fighting beyond the basics against a Warlord Prince who had been learning how to fight almost from the moment he left the womb—and learning from a man who was a brilliant warrior on a killing field.

"One of them went through the glass window of a shop and is hurt fairly badly," Lucivar replied. "I'm not sure that was deliberate. The other four look like they've been in a down and dirty brawl."

Daemon shook his head. Eyrien arrogance and the natural inclination of the males to fight could never be underestimated. "What set him off? Did anyone tell you?"

"'Bitch.' 'Whore.' 'Suck cock.'"

Daemon rose to the killing edge before he made a conscious decision that violence was required. "I beg your pardon?" he said too softly.

Lucivar watched him. "I don't think Tagg knows what the words mean—except for 'bitch,' which means something different to him—but he didn't hesitate to repeat the words he'd heard before Daemonar tore into those prick-asses."

He stepped back from the killing edge, a little surprised by the effort it took to do it—and wondered if it was going to take more effort from now on. "I guess the boy was right about not wanting to tell us what was said."

"But he's telling Chaosti?" Lucivar snorted a laugh. "Well, safer, I suppose, since this isn't Chaosti's territory."

A tray appeared on a nearby table, holding a pot of coffee, a bottle of brandy, and two mugs.

"Drink?" Daemon asked.

"Sure."

He filled the mugs two-thirds of the way with coffee and topped them with brandy, giving the drinks a quick stir before bringing the mugs back to the fire.

Lucivar seemed lost in thought but roused when Daemon held out one of the mugs.

"I just contacted Marian to check on everyone. Surreal is at Nurian's eyrie, talking to Jillian," Lucivar said. "Marian and the girls are at our eyrie. The girls are teaching Morghann how to play hawks and hares, so Marian is playing with them to make sure the Sceltie learns the proper rules."

"Thank the Darkness for that," Daemon muttered. Then he studied Lucivar. "You know . . ."

"You brought three, you leave with three."

"You are so strict."

"Damn right." Lucivar studied him in turn. "You all right? You feel . . . different."

"Do I? How?" He wasn't ready to talk about being in the Misty Place with Witch.

"After the headaches started, your psychic scent felt jagged. Now it doesn't. Like something was mended and you're well again."

Not a dream. "That's accurate enough."

"Is it? Then I'm glad."

"When things are settled about the boy, I need to talk to you and Marian about my . . . recovery. About changes I need to make."

"Whenever you're ready," Lucivar replied.

They sat in companionable silence for a few minutes before Chaosti walked into the room.

"Should I ask Draca to send in some yarbarah?" Daemon asked.

Chaosti shook his head. "But I thank you for the offer." He used Craft to position another chair near the fire. They waited while he got comfortable. "What was said was sufficient cause for a Warlord Prince to defend members of his family. I believe it is in the best interest of everyone in this valley that the two of you don't seek to know the details."

"I haven't seen Daemonar yet, but . . . if I may?" Lucivar said.

Daemon felt the brush of Red power against his first inner barrier—a request to share information. Glancing at Chaosti, he realized the same request had been made of the other man.

Eyriens on one side. Riada guards on the other. A shop with its outside displays in shambles and a large window broken. And the four Warlords who were almost standing after the fight.

"Has the debt been paid?" Lucivar asked.

"It's been paid," Chaosti replied. "It's fortunate for those Warlords that your boy isn't quite old enough yet to carry a honed knife and only had the wooden practice knife I gave him." He smiled at Daemon. "As Lucivar shared Eyrien fighting techniques with some of my children and grandchildren, so I have offered instruction to Daemonar in the use of Dea al Mon fighting knives. He had a practice blade. When used with intent, they can be a formidable weapon without being a lethal one. Well, not lethal in the hands of one so young."

The door opened. Daemonar walked into the room and came to stand before his father. He wore pants he must have left at the Keep after he'd outgrown them, because the legs were high above his ankles and he'd barely managed to close enough buttons on the fly for modesty. And yet everything about him, from the way he stood to the look in his eyes, was a blend of defiance and wariness.

May the Darkness have mercy on any man who had to raise an Eyrien boy.

"I'm not sorry," Daemonar said.

"Yeah, boyo, I didn't think you were," Lucivar replied. He looked pointedly at the boy's left arm. "Nice shield."

"It's *blue*."

Lucivar snorted. "You'll be able to see the damn thing halfway up the mountain."

Daemonar turned to Daemon. "I *told* you."

"So you did," Daemon replied mildly—and then smiled. "Everything has a price. This will help you remember to consider the odds before you leap into a fight."

You think that's going to work? Lucivar asked on a Red spear thread.

Not likely. He's your son, after all. He won't consider the odds a day after the color fades.

Lucivar focused on Daemonar again. "You're going to

pay for your share of the damage to the shop out of your allowance."

"Yes, sir."

"Anything you want to tell us?"

Daemonar shook his head.

"Then make yourself comfortable, boyo. We'll head home as soon as the storm passes."

Within a minute Daemonar was sprawled on the rug in front of the hearth, sound asleep.

Daemon watched the boy for a moment, then laughed softly. "He does stop moving once in a while."

Sighing, Lucivar rested his head on the back of the chair. "Sometimes I wonder how Marian and I had time to make two more with him being the first one."

The three men talked for a few minutes more before Chaosti rose to take his leave.

"Wait for me," Daemon said quietly.

Chaosti nodded and left the room.

"Problem?" Lucivar asked.

"No, nothing like that." Daemon set his mug on the tray. "Unless you need me, I'm going back to the Hall for the night, but I'll return in the morning."

"What about . . . ?"

"Unless *you* need me."

They looked at each other, so much being understood in the silence.

"We'll be fine," Lucivar said. "See you in the morning."

Daemon left the room. Chaosti held out a note. "This came for you."

Daemon broke the seal and opened the single sheet of paper. "Lady Perzha has asked me to meet her tomorrow morning. Early." Tucking the note into his jacket pocket, he headed for the Keep's Dark Altar—that place that was a Gate between the Realms.

"Is there something you need from me, High Lord?" Chaosti asked, falling into step.

Daemon sighed. Queen's command. "I need to tell you

about some changes I have to make because of a healing that was done today—and to ask you about the sexual heat."

"A healing? Someone besides the boy?"

Daemon stopped outside the room that held the Dark Altar. "Me." He hesitated, then asked a question he had never thought he'd ask. "Do you ever hear from Witch?"

Chaosti didn't reply for a long moment. Finally, "Dreams made flesh cannot become demon-dead. You know that."

"That much power didn't disappear when the flesh died," he whispered. "Witch's Self is still in the Misty Place—and still here in the Keep."

"Why do you think that is so?"

Not a denial. Not telling him it wasn't possible.

Daemon vanished his shirt, then shrugged out of the jacket enough to reveal the gauze bandage around his biceps. "I pissed her off. This was her response."

A thoughtful silence. "You needed her particular healing skills so much that she reconnected with the living to help you? What needed healing?"

"The crystal chalice—and other things."

He saw a flash of fear in Chaosti's eyes, there and gone. Proof enough that the man knew what that meant.

"Was she successful?" Chaosti asked.

"For the most part. But everything has a price."

"Is this why you need to make some changes?"

"Yes. She said Kaeleer is going to need everything that I am. In order for me to stay sane and be who I am, I need her help. And yours."

"Then I will give what help I can. After all"—Chaosti smiled and gestured toward Daemon's arm—"*I* have no desire to rile my cousin's temper."

"I wasn't trying to rile her," Daemon muttered. "I thought I was dreaming."

"Tell me what you need. I will do what I can." Chaosti looked toward the Altar room. "You have business in Hell?"

"Not tonight. But unless there's also a storm in Hell that

makes riding the Winds dangerous, I can ride the Black Wind back to the Hall and go through the Gate there to return to Kaeleer."

"Unless you need to return to the Hall right away, why don't you tell me about these changes you need to make and what help you'd like me to give? Hopefully I will have some answers for you when you return in the morning."

Daemon told him about the headaches and the sex and the heat and the months of pain that had led to the crystal chalice cracking again and Witch's power restricting his ability to tighten the leashes beyond what she deemed safe after repairing what she could. It surprised him that Chaosti didn't express much sympathy for Surreal.

"You are nothing now that you haven't been in all the years I've known you—and in all the years Surreal has known you," Chaosti said. "I can understand how a woman can need to live away from that much power part of the time. Gabrielle needed time away from my Gray Jewels, especially after my sexual heat settled into that last phase. I do not doubt it is harder for a wife or lover to live with the Black." He paused. "Unless, of course, your wife is the living myth and outranks you to such a degree that she has to be reminded that the Black is a very dark Jewel. We all found it amusing that you had to work so hard sometimes to seduce your wife. Occasionally Gabrielle would nudge Jaenelle and point out that you would like to give your wife some husbandly attention."

"Enough," Daemon said, laughing.

Chaosti laughed with him and then sobered. "Her power was vast—is still vast, from what you've said. As her Consort and husband, you should have felt the crushing weight of being intimate with someone who wielded that much power."

"I never did."

"No, you never did. Neither did the rest of us, even before she somehow set aside all of that power to wear Twilight's Dawn. Jaenelle never feared you, any more than she feared Uncle Saetan. Maybe that's one reason why this is harder for you. You didn't expect Surreal to fear you as a husband. Now you'll have to find out how much can be mended—and if you both can accept what can't be mended."

Daemon nodded. "I'll be back to talk to Lady Perzha first thing in the morning. Then I'll return here to talk to Lucivar—and to listen to your suggestions."

Entering the Altar room, Daemon lit the candles in the four-branched candelabra, opening the Gate to Hell. Once he reached the Dark Realm, he caught the Black Wind and rode it to Dhemlan and the Gate that stood within the grounds of SaDiablo Hall.

TWENTY-NINE

———◈———

"That girl pushed her thumb into that cake on purpose, and Dillon just laughed like it was funny to ruin someone else's treat," Jillian said after telling Surreal the whole story of going to the Sweet Tooth and everything that happened afterward. "Why didn't he say something to the girl, tell her she was wrong to do that?"

"I don't know," Surreal said. "Sometimes a person makes a bad choice. Even the most honorable men make mistakes, Jillian."

"I guess." Disillusioned, Jillian watched the rain. It looked like one of those hard, fast storms that rolled down the valley and would be gone in an hour. But for that hour, everyone would be stuck where they were. There was an extra sizzle in the lightning this time, and Prince Yaslana had already sent a command that reached all the Blood in Ebon Rih that no one was to try to ride the Winds or fly until the storm passed.

A regular storm shouldn't have affected the Webs of power that the Blood used to travel through the Darkness, but that warning meant there was another kind of storm combined with a regular storm. But who was strong enough to make it unsafe to ride the Winds? Not Yaslana, since he was the one who issued the warning, but there was one other man in Ebon Rih right now whose temper might be feeding the storm.

She glanced at Surreal, who looked pale and worried but was trying to hide it. Jillian had seen plenty of adults try to hide the same kind of fear or worry when bringing a sick or injured child to Nurian's eyrie, so she recognized that look.

"Do you think Dillon has been less than honest with you?" Surreal asked.

"I don't know. Maybe." Part of her hoped he could explain it all away the next time she saw him. Part of her remembered how he dismissed her thoughts about things, making her feel her opinions had no value. If her thoughts had no value, if *she* had no value, then the only reason he wanted to spend time with her was for whatever he could persuade her to give him. That made everything he did a kind of transaction.

She didn't want to think that of him, because she *loved* him. Didn't she?

"It could have been a mistake," she said, not sure if she was talking about the cakes or about Dillon's interest in her—and her interest in him.

Surreal smiled, but her gold-green eyes were suddenly bright with tears. "Seems like the day to make them."

THIRTY

The moment the storm moved on, Surreal left Khary with Jillian and returned to Lucivar's eyrie, arriving just ahead of the man and the boy.

"Daemonar!" Marian rushed to meet them, then stopped, clearly struggling with whether to treat the boy as a boy—which was what *she* wanted—or as a warrior youth, which was what *he* clearly wanted.

Lucivar gave Daemonar a light push. "Hug your mother and apologize for being stupid."

"I'm sorry, Mother." Daemonar, as boy and son, threw his arms around Marian. "I'm not sorry I hit the prick-asses, but I'm sorry I upset you."

Surreal looked past Lucivar, expecting Daemon to walk in behind him.

Titian, Jaenelle Saetien, and Morghann rushed to the front room from wherever they had been playing.

"What happened?" Titian asked.

Daemonar carefully withdrew from his mother's embrace. "Got in a fight."

"Why?"

"Don't have to say." There was a finality in the boy's voice that sounded so much like his father, neither girl pushed for details.

But Jaenelle Saetien pointed at Daemonar's arm. "What's that?"

"It's a shield to protect his arm while the bone heals," Lucivar said.

Marian made a distressed sound.

"It's pretty," Jaenelle Saetien said, hooking her black hair behind her delicately pointed ears.

Daemonar and Titian looked at their cousin like they couldn't believe she didn't understand how terrible this was, and said in unison, "It's *blue*."

Titian reached out but didn't quite touch the shield. "Could you put another shield over it to hide the color?"

Daemonar looked disgusted. "Already tried that. It made the color *brighter*."

Surreal studied Lucivar, who was struggling to keep a straight face.

"The color doesn't matter," Lucivar drawled. "Daemonar won't be doing any hunting or weapons training until the bone fully heals."

"Papa!" Daemonar sounded horrified by that prospect.

"But you and I will be spending your training time reviewing how to properly shield before and during a fight."

"Yes, sir."

Healing requires food, Morghann said. *Daemonar should eat. We will eat with him, to keep him company.*

Lucivar turned away, coughing.

Marian stared at Morghann, who just wagged her tail and looked hopeful.

"Fine," Marian said, glancing at Surreal and Lucivar. "We'll have a snack while I start preparing dinner." She led the yappy horde into the kitchen.

As soon as they were alone, Surreal hurried over to Lucivar. "Where is Daemon? Was he at the Keep? Why didn't he come back with you?"

"He went to the Hall for the night. He'll be back in the morning."

"I have to talk to him. Can you keep Jaenelle Saetien?"

"Surreal . . . Leave him alone tonight." A warning, not a suggestion.

Shaking her head, she rushed out of the eyrie and went down to the landing web so fast she almost lost her footing on the wet stairs. Then she caught the Gray Wind and headed for SaDiablo Hall.

Daemon waited while Beale and Holt absorbed what he'd just told them about the headaches, the healing, and what needed to be done. Neither man asked how a Queen who shouldn't have existed anymore was still present in some way and still giving orders. Maybe they were so relieved to know her strength was still balancing his that they didn't want to know how it was possible, only that it was.

"There is the suite of rooms deep beneath the Hall," Beale said. "I believe your father stayed there when he needed a particular kind of solitude. However, I would recommend using the bedroom suite he used when the Queen lived here. You would have sunlight and fresh air. The other suites around that square are empty now, so you could easily put Black shields around the whole square and have access to the garden. I think that would feel less like . . ." The butler finally stumbled on the words.

"Like a cage?" Daemon said.

"Yes, Prince. There is no need to feel walled up in stone when you require solitude for your well-being and ours."

"That suite would be far enough away from the family quarters you're using now," Holt said. "The Black—or the heat—shouldn't cause problems for Lady Surreal at that distance, especially with Black shields around the rooms."

He had considered his father's private study deep beneath the Hall, but Beale had the right of it. He didn't think feeling walled in would do anything good for his continued healing or control. But if he put Black shields around the whole square of rooms that overlooked the same garden as his father's suite, he would have the isolation necessary without feeling confined. And he would have another safe way to use the Black.

"Ask Helene to get that suite ready," Daemon said. "I don't know how soon or how often I'll need it."

"If you'll permit my discussing this with Mrs. Beale in general terms, she can consider what kind of foods she can prepare that you could heat or eat as is," Beale said. "I would bring the meals to you."

"The less interaction, the better," Daemon replied. "Until we know . . ." He almost felt like himself, but he didn't have a sense of how much control he had over his power and temper—or anything else.

Beale nodded. "Until we know."

Surreal's abrupt arrival at the Hall startled Beale.

"Is he here?" she demanded. A psychic probe would have given her the answer, but she didn't want to do anything that might seem like a challenge.

"He's in his suite," Beale replied, sounding uncharacteristically flustered. "We weren't expecting you. The Prince said he would take a plate of whatever Mrs. Beale had prepared for the staff's dinner, but I can tell her that you've returned as well and—"

"Just fix two plates, if there's enough to spare." There would be plenty. No one who worked at the Hall went hungry. "We can eat in the family room." In many ways, that room was where their life together had begun, because that was where they'd been when grief over Saetan's final death turned into a physical need to give and receive comfort.

Maybe that subtle reminder would help her talk to him.

Hurrying to their suites in the family wing, she knocked on the door of Daemon's bedroom and walked in before giving him a chance to reply—or deny her entrance—and only then remembered why she shouldn't be alone in that room with him ever again.

"Surreal?" He didn't sound angry that she had followed him home, but he also didn't sound pleased to see her. "Why are you here?"

I live here. Don't I?

Instead of the tailored black trousers and jacket paired with the white silk shirt—his usual choice of attire—he wore a white cotton pullover. The casual trousers were black but loose. And he wore house slippers instead of his usual polished shoes. Nothing unusual about Daemon being dressed so casually for an evening at home. He'd learned years ago that such clothes were easier to clean after dealing with baby poop or little-girl puke. But, somehow, seeing him like this . . .

Relaxed. At least, he had been until she'd walked into the room. She braced for the feel of his sexual heat washing over her, but the heat was banked to a sensual warmth, like it had been the day of Jaenelle Saetien's Birthright Ceremony.

And the Black? Daemon's power felt like it had when she'd been pregnant, after he'd carefully drained her Gray and Green Jewels to make her comfortable and protect the baby. He'd had to use his Black power to siphon off her Gray, and when it was done, they'd often cuddled for the whole evening, content to be in each other's company.

Seeing him like this, *feeling* him like this, made her consider that maybe the overwhelming sexual heat *had* been a symptom of whatever had been causing his headaches.

"Daemon . . ." How to explain what he'd overheard that morning?

He looked away. "I've caused you significant distress over the past few months. I am sorry for that. Despite what you think, it wasn't deliberate."

"I didn't know the headaches were causing you to—"

"The headaches were a symptom, not the cause. I learned today that a Warlord Prince's sexual heat continues to gain . . . potency . . . until he's fully in his prime. I had been trying to keep it leashed to what it had been instead of accommodating this final stage. It's reached its peak now and will remain at this level."

"For how long?"

"Centuries."

Mother Night. How will I endure it?

"I've known that your visits to the family's other estates weren't about you fulfilling your duties as my second-in-command, that they were excuses to stay away from me," Daemon continued quietly. "You were unhappy being around me, so I assisted in making whatever arrangements kept us apart. The truth, Surreal? It was a relief whenever you weren't home, because I didn't have to provide sex to a woman who wanted me and hated me at the same time."

"I didn't hate you."

He gave her a bitter smile. "Yes, you did. Maybe you still do."

Surreal shook her head. Why hadn't she said something beyond demanding that he leash the heat?

"There is nothing I can do about the sexual heat that won't threaten my sanity," Daemon said. "That was another truth that was impressed on me today."

The words shocked her. Terrified her. His *sanity* had been threatened?

"But there are things that I can do to protect you and keep you from being overwhelmed by it. To that end, I am making some changes."

"What changes?" she whispered. "Are . . . Do you want me to leave?"

"No." He shook his head. "I still love you, Surreal, and I would like to remain married to you. But if you want to end the marriage, if you *need* to do that, I won't make it difficult for you."

"I don't want to do that."

He seemed relieved, and she relaxed a little.

Then he said, "It will benefit both of us to have some time alone—a few days each month. That will give us a chance to rest from the pressures produced by the heat. Even when we're both in residence, some . . . distance . . . at times will be required."

"You want to live apart?" Would she and Jaenelle Sae- tien live in Amdarh most of the time, with Daemon staying at the town house a couple of days a week to see his daugh- ter and have sex with his wife? Or would he and Jaenelle Saetien live here while she was the one who became the guest?

"Nothing so drastic, unless that is what you'd prefer. I'm taking over my father's suite and will reside there part of the time. It's far enough away from these rooms that, with the use of Black shields around the suite, the heat shouldn't cause you discomfort."

"Sadi . . ."

"My control over my temper and . . . other things . . . is not what it used to be. Will never be what it used to be. I will need solitude at times, and that's when I'll use the other suite."

She struggled to find her voice. "And the rest of the time?"

He looked around the room. "Here. Or with you when you want company."

"So I'm supposed to invite my husband to my bed every time I want him to provide me with sex?" *Fool! Don't challenge him!*

"Yes," he replied.

"No," she snapped, embracing temper and itching to call in her crossbow. "I am perfectly capable of telling you if I'm not in the mood for a ride. I can take care of myself."

"Except you didn't." His voice sharpened, grew colder. "You didn't, Surreal. You felt tormented by your response to the sexual heat and *said nothing*. You felt tortured. Wasn't that the word you used?"

She flinched.

"I can trust you to draw a line and defend Jaenelle Saetien. You've done that since the day she was born. But it's painfully clear that I can't trust you to stand up for yourself. Not against me. I thought I could—I thought you would—but you proved me wrong."

"Don't do this, Sadi," she warned.

"Do what?"

"Play games with me. Break the promise you made when we married that you would be a husband in every way."

She saw the change in his eyes, felt fear shiver through her. Remembered again where she was standing at that moment and what it meant when dealing with a Warlord Prince.

"No games, Lady," the Sadist said. "Not with you. Never again with you. At least, not for fun. But if you try to play with me . . ." He smiled that cold, cruel smile.

Then he looked away for a moment, and the feel in the room changed—and Daemon looked back at her. "Whether I remain your husband is your choice. Whether I remain your lover is your choice."

"But when you're available to be a lover is your choice?"

"Yes. It has to be that way now. But I give you my word that I will not refuse your invitation without reason."

Something had happened to him today after he left Lucivar's eyrie. He didn't quite feel like the man she'd known for the past few decades. His psychic scent was a bit . . . feral. But this wasn't the Sadist. This was the War-lord Prince of Dhemlan, in absolute control of himself, offering to provide his wife with sex out of duty to his marriage vows.

That was a knife in the belly.

Daemon studied her. "As I said, this change is nothing drastic."

And that was twisting the knife.

Nothing drastic? Maybe he believed that. But he hadn't taken one step toward her since this conversation began.

"It simply restores the distance that had previously been between us—the distance that kept you safe from dealing with the full measure of what I am," Daemon continued.

Lady? Beale said on a psychic thread. *Dinner is waiting for you.*

"Dinner is served in the family room," she said. "Unless you prefer to eat here."

Now, finally, he moved toward her, but his smile was the same one he gave other women—a warning that he would remain friendly as long as they kept their distance. "In the family room is fine." Then amusement warmed his gold eyes. "While we eat, you can tell me just how disgusted Daemonar is with having a bright blue shield around his arm."

She put on a nightgown that he always admired.

At dinner, they had talked the way they used to—the way they hadn't talked in weeks—sharing information and thoughts about family and books, and Jillian's first love, and so many other things. His presence didn't overwhelm her, and while the things he'd said worried her, she thought he would want to reestablish a feeling of physical closeness, and had made it clear that she would like his company that night.

She needed to show him that she loved him, that she desired him. That she didn't hate him.

But she waited and waited . . . and waited.

She went to the connecting door, wrapped her hand around the handle. What if he didn't let her in? How could she show him she still wanted him if he locked her out?

Relief filled her when the door opened. No lights were on in the room, but the heavier drapes didn't cover the glass door that led out to the balcony, so there was enough natural light to see that Daemon was in bed and clearly preparing to sleep in his own room, despite her invitation—and despite his assurance that he wouldn't turn down an invitation.

"Daemon?" Surreal whispered.

He turned his head. "Something wrong?"

You're here.

This was dangerous. Potentially lethal. Being in his bedroom invited him to play with her. And if he took offense and thought she was playing with him? He'd warned her—he had—but she couldn't allow herself to believe he would unleash the Sadist and really hurt her over what amounted to a marital quarrel. If she allowed herself to believe that, she'd run and never stop running.

Slipping into his bed, she leaned over to kiss him as her hand stroked down his chest and headed for the part of him hidden under the covers.

His hand caught hers a moment after she touched the fabric at his waist and realized he was wearing pajama bottoms—something he did only during the winter or at the rare times when he didn't feel well or when he slept with her during her moontime, turning a piece of clothing into a visual reassurance that he wasn't offering, or looking for, anything but her company.

"I'm tired," he said quietly.

During the whole of their marriage, he had *never* refused her when she wanted sex or lovemaking. He had *never* been too tired. Not even when she'd been relentlessly demanding, caught in the addiction his sexual heat had produced. He must have been in pain from the headaches, but he hadn't denied her his attention. Was he really going to set limits on when he was available to make love?

"Can I stay with you?" she asked, shaken.

A hesitation. "Of course."

Words politely spoken. In some ways worse than a slap, because it was duty, not desire, that said the words.

He raised his hand. Hopeful, she moved her hand once again to touch him, stroke him, invite him to take pleasure in their bodies coming together. But his hand closed over her wrist again, his touch now so cold it burned.

"No," he snarled.

All kinds of messages in the finality of that word, and none of them good.

She lay down, far enough away that she wasn't touching him, but still close enough that if he changed his mind and reached for her, she would be there to tell him without words that she did love him, that she hadn't meant the things she'd said about him torturing her with sex.

Eventually she fell asleep. When she woke in the still-dark hours of early morning, Daemon was gone. Worse, a quick look through his dresser and dressing room confirmed that he'd taken several sets of clothes with him.

Worse than that, when she found Holt and Beale already awake and working—and pretending they weren't aware of the potential collapse of her marriage—neither man knew where Daemon had gone. Neither had been given instructions about how to find him. All Daemon had said before he left was they should contact Lucivar if they needed to reach him.

A single ball of witchlight softly illuminated the stone steps that led down to the sunken garden Saetan had built long ago as a place for private meditation. A place meant to offer peace.

Carrying a large mug of coffee heavily flavored with cream and sugar, Surreal walked down the steps. She had never felt peaceful in this garden. Too much grief had been absorbed by the ground for her to feel any peace. That wasn't why she came to this spot in the Hall.

Ignoring the statue of the crouched male that was a blend of human and animal, she walked over to the fountain where a woman with an achingly familiar face rose out of the water. Then she raised the mug as if to catch someone's attention.

"I brought you coffee." Setting the mug on the grass beside the fountain, Surreal raked her fingers through her hair. "Hell's fire, Jaenelle. I made a mistake, a bad mistake, and I don't know how to fix it. But how was I to know that—"

The ball of witchlight disappeared. The cool predawn air turned viciously cold. And for just a heartbeat, maybe two, Surreal felt as if she was falling in the abyss, felt as if she was being crushed in body and mind because she was falling deeper than she could possibly survive.

Then a pale light returned and the air was chilly but no longer viciously cold.

Stone and mist. A slab of dark stone that looked like an altar. More slabs that were low enough to be seats.

"What I'm wondering," said a midnight voice, "is why you ignored the signs and let this go on for so long."

Chilled to the marrow, Surreal watched the figure shaped out of dreams walk out of the mist.

"Mother Night," she whispered. "Jaenelle?" She looked around. "Where . . . ?"

"This is the Misty Place." Witch approached the altar and stood within reach. "Why, Surreal? You've never backed down from anything. Why back down because of something that should have been simple? It's not like you haven't seen it before."

The tartness in the words scratched Surreal's temper enough for her to ignore questions about where she was and if she could get back to the Hall. Focusing on those ancient sapphire eyes allowed her to ignore the rest of Witch's shape and pretend she was dealing with the friend she remembered. "Let me tell you something, sugar. I've *never* felt like I was being swept away and drowned by a man's lust. I've *never* felt desperate to ride a cock. So you'll have to forgive me if I missed the warning signs. And when, in the name of Hell, have I seen this before?"

"You and Rainier were sharing a house when he came into his full prime and went through the same thing," Witch replied with razor-sharp sweetness. "You shrugged it off despite living with it every day."

"Rainier did not go through this," Surreal snarled.

"Of course he did. All the Warlord Princes did. But Rainier wore Opal and you wear Gray, so the increase in *his* sexual heat rolled off you, barely noticed, let alone acknowledged. Also, you and Rainier weren't lovers, so you weren't primed to be aroused by his sexual heat as you are to your lover's interest in you." Witch huffed out a sigh. "But even the Gray can't ignore the Black when the sexual heat's potency matures, so it's not surprising you felt swept away. What *is* surprising is that you and your crossbow didn't meet Daemon in the bedroom one evening so that you could tell him that something felt wrong *before* things had gone so wrong."

"But this fever of sex has opened the door for you to reclaim him, hasn't it?" Surreal snapped.

She regretted the words the moment she said them.

The air turned so cold it was hard to breathe—and the feeling of pressure being held at bay by something, or someone, reminded her that she was so deep in the abyss that she had no chance of surviving on her own. "Jaenelle . . . My apologies, Lady. Those words were unkind—and untrue."

"I didn't intend to come back," Witch said too quietly. "I didn't expect Daemon to need me beyond my being a song in the Darkness that reminded him that he wasn't alone and helped him stay connected to the living. Do you think this is easy, that I welcome this? Solitude is like ice, Surreal. When it's thick and unbroken, the world beyond it is muted, a memory that can be offered gifts that reach the living in dreams. But when that solitude is smashed, like it is now? When I know the ice will have to be smashed again and again because the survival of so many now requires it, and I will be reminded again and again that I may still be heart and mind and a great deal of power, but this"—she swept a hand down to indicate her body—"is a shadow, an illusion, not flesh that can be held. Do you really think I wanted this continual contact with the living when I had every reason to believe that you and Daemon would be happy being together?"

"I . . ." Surreal looked away, aching for both of them. All of them.

"But this is where we are now, you and I—and Daemon. Married to you, he could have survived with me being nothing more than a comforting dream, and Kaeleer could have survived *him* without me. But a vital kind of trust has been broken and will never again be strong enough to do what it could have done. What it should have done."

"He said his sanity is at risk."

"It was. It is. It will be, even beyond his last day among the living."

"All because I demanded that he leash his sexual heat."

"Not because you demanded it, but because you didn't believe him when he told you it was leashed."

"Would you have believed him?"

"Yes. And then I would have looked for another reason for the change in my reaction to the heat. The knowledge was available, but neither of you asked the right questions—or asked the right people." Witch sighed. "Some practical adjustments in your living arrangements will have to be made, and the lingering pain of the past few months will leave a coating of bitterness on your marriage that will take time to fade. You have to decide if you love him enough to give him—and yourself—that time."

"I do love him." She looked at Witch. When Jaenelle had walked among the living, she had made living with Daemon seem so easy. But living with that much power day after day after day wasn't easy. Would never be easy. "What can I do?"

"You're still his second-in-command."

She nodded, although the words were a statement, not a question.

Witch studied her. "I made a conditional bargain with Daemon. Now I'll make one with you. Continue being his second-in-command, whether you remain married to him or not. Continue being the buffer between him and women who would ignite his temper by trying to push themselves into his bed uninvited. In other words, do for him now what you did for him when he and I were married. In return, I will be the buffer between you and Daemon, giving him a place at the Keep where he can exercise all that he is without any constraints and also draining the Black enough to keep him, and everyone else, safe."

Surreal looked around. "We'll all be safe, but you'll be reminded over and over again of how alone you are in this place."

"Everything has a price," Witch said quietly.

"You love him that much?"

"Daemon is worth whatever price has to be paid. That was true when I walked among the living, and it's just as true now." A beat of silence. "It's time for you to go."

"Will I see you again?"

"There are other people in easy reach who will listen if you need to talk and who can offer advice if you ask. I don't think you'll need to come here again."

The light disappeared. The air turned viciously cold. But those feelings passed in a heartbeat and Surreal found herself standing in the sunken garden, staring at the statue of a woman with an achingly familiar face.

"Jaenelle," she whispered. "Ah, sugar. I promise I'll do my best for all of us."

THIRTY-ONE

———◆———

Daemon arrived in Little Weeble shortly after dawn. Lord Carleton greeted him effusively and beamed so much goodwill toward him he wondered if there was something wrong with Lady Perzha's Steward—until he guessed the reason for Carleton's pleasure.

"The shipment of yarbarah arrived?" Daemon asked.

"It did. A case of beef and a case of lamb," Carleton replied. "I took the liberty of sampling a bottle of the lamb and am ashamed of the inferior quality of yarbarah we had been purchasing from . . . another supplier . . . and had been serving to Lady Perzha."

"You know about supplying Perzha with fresh human blood added to the yarbarah as well as how much undiluted blood she should have each month?"

"Yes. The Queen of Ebon Askavi had provided instructions when Lady Perzha first developed her allergy to sunlight. The Lady is out on the garden terrace," Carleton continued as he led the way. "She enjoys doing a bit of gardening before she reviews paperwork and meets with me and Prince Arrick prior to retiring until evening."

Perzha smiled at Daemon when he reached the table where she sat looking over her garden and drinking yarbarah from a ravenglass goblet. "Please join me, Prince.

There were storms all along the coast yesterday. You also had storms in Ebon Rih?"

"We did. I'm sure Prince Yaslana will be flying to each of the villages in the valley to check on the people. Is there anything I should convey to him about Little Weeble?"

"Carleton and Arrick will be doing their own assessment this morning, but I don't believe we had any significant storm damage. Sit down, Prince. Please, sit. And mind the bucket."

As he pulled out a chair, Daemon eyed the bucket filled two-thirds with water. Since they weren't sitting under an awning or other kind of roof, he wondered what might be leaking.

"Carleton, have Cook prepare a plate for Prince Sadi," Perzha said. "I'm sure he didn't have time to eat this morning before coming to see me."

"Thank you." Daemon looked at Carleton. "If it's not too much trouble."

"No trouble at all, Prince." *For you.*

Carleton didn't need to say it, but Daemon heard the addendum.

He and Perzha chatted about the garden until Carleton brought the tray and set the meal in front of Daemon, along with a cup and a pot of coffee. Steak, eggs, pancakes with butter and a small jug of warm syrup, and thick slices of bread toasted to perfection.

Picking up his knife and fork, he touched the stack of pancakes, looking forward to the meal.

The top pancake suddenly bulged in the center. Suckered tentacles slid out between two pancakes and felt around until they found the edge of the plate.

Daemon shoved back from the table. "Mother Night!"

Something erupted from under the pancake and swiftly flowed across the table until . . .

Plop.

. . . it went over the edge and fell into the bucket of water.

Perzha patted her chest and looked flustered. "My apologies, Prince. Our little friend escaped from his tank this morning and we've been looking for him everywhere. Almost everywhere. Didn't think he would hide in the pancakes, but the little creatures have the ability to change color, and I suppose pancakes have a similar coloring to rocks or sand."

Carefully setting the silverware on the table, Daemon leaned over to look in the bucket. Tentacles were reaching out of the water, reaching up to the rim of the bucket.

"It looks like your beastie is trying to escape from the bucket as well," he said dryly.

"Be a dear and put a shield around the bucket."

"Over the top?"

"Oh, no. You'd have to leave openings for air, and that's a problem, you see. They're very good at squeezing through the smallest openings. I'm sure that's how he got out of the tank in the first place. You'd be surprised how far one of them can travel before needing to return to water."

At least that explained the bucket beside the table.

Daemon created a circular shield that began just below the rim of the bucket and went up a couple of hands high. He watched the beastie probe the new barrier before retreating to the bottom of the bucket to sulk—and change color to match the bucket. If he hadn't seen it change, he would have thought the bucket still contained nothing but water. "You have a tank of these as fresh seafood?"

"Oh, no. This one has become a kind of pet. Even so, we don't eat *this* kind of octopod." Perzha turned in her seat as her Steward hurried to their table. "Carleton, please bring Prince Sadi a fresh plate of food. This one had an unexpected addition. And have someone return our friend to the tank."

"Found him, did you?"

Carleton sounded as if it wasn't the least bit unusual to

find a beastie hiding under the pancakes. And it wasn't unusual, actually. But the little surprises at Perzha's dinner parties had been shadows, illusions of something real, not an actual critter hiding in the soup.

Daemon reached for his cup of coffee, then picked up a spoon and probed the liquid. When he didn't feel anything but liquid, he took a cautious sip. "That is some kind of octopus?"

"That," Perzha said with a delighted smile, "is a weeble. You are the first person outside our village to see a real one."

Daemon stared. "I beg your pardon?"

"That is a weeble." She waved a hand, setting all her bracelets jangling. "They might have another name somewhere else, but that's what we've always called them."

"They're a food?"

"Other kinds of mollusks and octopods are, but not the weebles. At least, *we* don't eat them. They're quite clever little creatures. Down the beach a ways, it's too rocky for the fishing boats to be brought to shore, but there are a lot of tidal pools. Well, generations ago, the men here put out traps for crabs and lobsters, but they noticed the catch was much better around the same time the weebles gathered to breed. As you noticed, the weebles can change color to blend in with the background. Normally it's to make them invisible to predators, but during their mating time, the males use their ability with color for another purpose. Each male stakes out a small tidal pool or a piece of a larger one and does a bit of decorating with stones and seaweed. Then, at night, when the females come to the pools, the males do a display of bright colors to attract the females. It's like watching all these little rainbows under the surface of the water. Quite lovely."

"I imagine that display also attracts all the creatures that like to eat weebles," Daemon said as Carleton set another plate of food in front of him. "Thank you."

"Best to stick a fork into everything, just in case," Carleton said cheerfully.

He did exactly that before spreading butter and warm syrup over the weeble-free pancakes.

"Yes, attracting females is always a dangerous business," Perzha agreed. "And weeble numbers were dropping because predators could devour the females as well as the males before they finished mating. Then a group of men discovered weebles in their traps eating the fish chunks that were meant to be bait for the lobsters and crabs—which were clinging to the outside of the trap, trying to get at the weeble, which, it turns out, is a preferred food. So the men built a few weeble houses as an experiment, setting in a chunk of fresh fish before closing the opening until it was too small for a lobster or crab to enter but a perfect size for a weeble. Wonderful idea. The men would go out in the morning and haul up the traps and take the crabs and lobsters that were clinging to the outside, then tuck in a new piece of food before lowering the house into the water. The weeble would leave the house when it chose, scurrying here and there in order to select its decorative bits, then return. It would do its color display to attract a mate—who discovered that the weeble males who had laid claim to the houses could provide food as well as shelter so that the business of mating could be done in relative safety. Their numbers increased, making it a beneficial arrangement for everyone."

"Except the crabs and lobsters," Daemon said, as he cut into the steak.

"Even they benefit in a way, since they can hunt the weebles who have to make do with the tidal-pool love nests."

"So that's how the village got its name?"

"Yes. Which is not something we usually share with outsiders." She smiled at him. "Although, being his brother, you may want to share that information with Prince Yaslana."

He would have loved to tell Lucivar about the origin of the village's name, if he could be sure he'd been told the truth and not one of the best damn stories he'd heard in a long time. He could picture Perzha and Jaenelle Angelline sitting around one evening, laughing themselves silly as they created this story about how the village got its name. And who here would ever contradict either Queen?

When the dishes were cleared, Perzha set her empty goblet aside and sighed. "But the next story I have to tell you is a sad one. I'm sure it's a familiar tale, but that doesn't make it any less sad."

"You have some information about Lord Dillon?" he asked.

"Pieced together from gossip and whispers." She looked at her garden. "Love betrayed leaves its own kind of scars, doesn't it?"

Even when the betrayal is unintentional, Daemon thought.

"Lord Dillon is the eldest of three sons from a minor aristo family. Regrettably, they have just enough connections to rub elbows with more influential aristo families but not enough influence themselves to be included—or given consideration when it comes to abusing a young person's heart and honor. It's a bit like standing in front of the window of a sweetshop and being offered a treat but always being on the wrong side of the glass. From what we could discover, Dillon was bright, charming, and good-looking—and was training to be an escort.

"Shortly after making the Offering to the Darkness, Dillon met a pretty girl from one of the significant Rihlander families and fell in love. The girl was a few years older and had already had several lovers since her Virgin Night. Unfortunately, she was Dillon's first love, and he believed her when she said he was different from her previous lovers and her feelings for him were real. All indications are he truly loved the girl, and she persuaded the boy to let her teach him the pleasures of sex." Perzha slanted a glance at Daemon. "Men are darling creatures, but being so easily petted and aroused does make you vulnerable when you come in contact with unscrupulous women."

"I can't disagree," he replied. "So she lured him into bed."

Perzha nodded. "There were promises of a handfast, if Dillon proved himself to be a capable lover. Believing that she truly loved him, he abandoned his training as an escort—at her request—and devoted himself to learning how to please her. After a few weeks, the girl discovered that Dillon had told his parents about her, despite her insisting that this had to be a 'discreet' liaison, and his family actually expected the girl to honor her promise of a handfast. Well, his family line wasn't good enough for *that*, so the girl broke things off and set about tarnishing Dillon's reputation, claiming that she hadn't been his first, and while he was suitable when a girl wanted a good time, he wasn't the kind of man a Lady wanted for a husband.

"Dillon's family was furious and ashamed—and blamed *him* for their family name being connected to scandal. Fearful of what that would do to the other boys' chances of making a socially valuable marriage or finding service in more than a District Queen's court, Dillon's family did create enough of a stir about the *girl's* reputation and her numerous lovers that the girl's father paid Dillon to leave the city. He left, and his family was relieved to see the back of him.

"New town, fresh start."

"Until he met a girl from another aristo family," Daemon guessed.

Perzha nodded. "No indication that he did anything that would get himself in trouble, but the rumors about him reached the girl's father. Once again, Dillon was paid to go away." She sighed. "Aristos can be such gossipmongers."

Daemon choked on a laugh, since Perzha was so good at netting the social tidbits others tossed away. Then he sobered as he considered a boy's descent from first love to an unsavory way of life where he was reduced to using a combination of spells to hold a girl's interest.

"At some point he turned rejection into a business?" he asked quietly. "Decided he would be the betrayer instead of the betrayed?"

"I don't think it's that simple. If he's the betrayer, it could be because he no longer believes he has any other choice. If you ask me, he still wants what he wanted with that first girl. He wants to be with someone who loves him—and he wants a way to repair his honor and reputation." She shook her head and *tsk*ed. "The foolish boy had no idea what he was up against when he fixed his attention on young Jillian. I doubt it even occurred to him that Eyriens do things a bit differently when it comes to suitors, especially when the Eyrien is a Warlord Prince."

Daemon snorted. "Lucivar would be more inclined to kill the problem than pay off someone who touched a girl in his family."

He refilled his coffee cup.

"I'll call for a fresh pot," Perzha said. "That must be cold by now."

It was cold and bitter, but that suited him right now. "It's fine."

They both looked at her garden, aware that there wasn't much time left before Perzha needed to retire for the day.

"He used a combination of seduction and compulsion spells on Jillian," Daemon said quietly. "It was too skillfully done to have been the first time. That's probably how he's been convincing girls that they were desperately in love with him. After that, if they were forbidden to see him, the girls themselves would cause such turmoil that the rifts created within the family might never be healed."

Surreal had been right; while under the influence of Dillon's mix of spells, Jillian would never have forgiven Lucivar if he had driven Dillon away.

Perzha nodded. "Having his own heart broken doesn't excuse his behavior since then."

"No, but it makes it more understandable." Daemon

smiled reluctantly. "We've offered Dillon the chance to become acquainted with Jillian—and us."

Perzha chuckled. "Properly chaperoned?"

"Of course." More than properly. One Sceltie would be enough. Three guaranteed a boy couldn't do more than hold a girl's hand. "If he takes advantage of the invitation, we'll give him the chance to set his past aside and show us who he is now."

"Why?" Perzha asked.

"Doesn't everyone deserve a chance to learn from past mistakes and move on to the next part of his or her life?"

"Should someone be allowed to continue doing the same harm because she got away with it?"

Everything inside him went still as he descended to the Black—the cold, glorious Black. "Do you have a name?" he asked too softly.

Perzha called in a piece of folded paper and pushed it toward him. He picked it up and vanished it before rising to the level of his Red Jewel.

"And now, Prince, I must go in and review the court's work for the day," Perzha said.

Daemon rose and pulled out her chair. "Thank you for the information—and the entertaining breakfast."

She gave him a big smile, showing her buckteeth. Then the smile softened and warmed. "This is a small village and my court is not large. But it would be a different experience for a heart that is bruised and needs time to heal. A safe place for a girl who might want to look at things beyond her own community."

"Far enough away but not too far?"

"Exactly."

He raised her hand to his lips and kissed her knuckles. She walked to the doors where Carleton hovered, waiting to coax her inside before she weakened from her allergy to sunlight. Prince Arrick, her Master of the Guard, escorted Daemon all the way to the landing web.

"If Lady Perzha needs anything that her court can't provide, you let me know," Daemon said.

Arrick tipped his head, a small bow of respect. "Thank you, Prince. We will."

Daemon stepped onto the landing web, caught the Black Wind, and returned to the Keep. Then he called Lucivar on a psychic spear thread and requested a meeting.

THIRTY-TWO

Daemon studied the listings in the two registers, which Geoffrey had fetched from the private part of the Keep's library. The listings didn't tell him much, since he wasn't familiar with the aristo families in Askavi. The registers certainly didn't provide a list of the lovers the girl had had before and after Dillon, but they did give him a good idea of the social distance between Dillon's family and the girl who had been his first, disastrous love.

There were other ways to find out about the girl's sexual conquests—and Dillon's.

"Is there something else I can help you find?" Geoffrey asked, approaching the large blackwood table.

"Not at this time, thank you," Daemon replied. When the historian/librarian didn't leave, Daemon raised an eyebrow in inquiry.

"You're asking about two Rihlander families who live in Askavi, which isn't your Territory."

A subtle reminder that rulers were not supposed to interfere in the Territory of others.

"This isn't about Territory, Geoffrey," Daemon said quietly. "This is about family."

Geoffrey gave him a long look and then smiled. "I understand."

Daemon closed the second register and set it on the table. "Let me know when Lucivar arrives. I'll be in the Consort's suite taking care of some paperwork."

"Would you like anything to eat?"

A laugh caught in his throat. "No, thank you. I've already had an interesting breakfast."

He'd been working steadily for an hour—and wondering if Holt could have stuffed one more piece of paper into the bulging satchel his secretary had handed him before he'd left the Hall that morning—when he felt a hand rest on his shoulder.

Not substance that he could touch, but he felt her warmth.

Daemon capped the pen and set it aside but kept his eyes focused on the desk. "Surreal and I made mistakes and hurt each other. Not out of malice, but that doesn't lessen the hurt. I won't hold her to the marriage if she wants to leave."

"Yes," Witch said. "Staying has to be her choice." She gave his shoulder a gentle squeeze. "I never intended to be this much of a presence in your life again. This arrangement won't be easy for her, Prince."

Or for you. "Maybe not, but you must have known this might happen. Dreams made flesh don't become demon-dead, but you found a way to stay. For me."

"Yes. For you. For as long as you need me."

"You'll be here?" Not a body he could touch, but being with her even this much settled something deep inside him and gave him peace. "I'll be able to talk to you?"

She didn't answer right away. "Mend as much as you can of your marriage, and take care of Surreal as best you can, whether she stays with you or not. Stay connected to the living. In return, when you reside in this suite, I will be with you to talk—and to help you drain enough of the reservoir of power in your Black Jewel to keep you, and everyone else, safe."

"That's our bargain?" Daemon asked.

"That's our bargain."

"Then I gratefully accept your terms, Lady."

Her hand slipped off his shoulder. He searched for something to say that would keep her with him a little while longer.

"Did you know weebles will hide in a stack of pancakes?" he asked.

Silence—but he wasn't alone.

"Oh, dear," Witch said. "You had breakfast with Perzha?"

"I did. It was educational."

"Did the weeble try to take your fork?"

Daemon twisted in the chair. Witch stood just out of reach. "Did it what?"

"Well, wouldn't you make a grab for it if someone poked you with a fork? Besides, a fork is a ready-made weapon. Very useful for discouraging lobsters and crabs, which have claws."

A fork-wielding weeble was absurd. Wasn't it?

"So towns along Askavi's coast might suddenly have—what would we call them?—pods of weebles entering houses by masquerading as appetizers in order to steal the cutlery?"

"Not all the cutlery. Just the forks." She gave him a bright smile.

Hell's fire, Mother Night, and may the Darkness be merciful. He remembered that smile. He also remembered a couple of . . . memorable . . . dinners when Perzha and Jaenelle had still been among the living.

He imagined Lucivar being called to deal with tentacled thieves—and felt laughter bubbling up. "You and Perzha already did it, didn't you?"

"That was a long time ago. No one would remember that."

"Lucivar?"

"Ah. Well. Lucivar." Witch shrugged. "They were shadow weebles, and it was a very dull party, and Perzha and I did return all the forks. Most of the forks. Turns out a couple of live weebles ended up with the shadows, and they learned a trick or two that night. Did Perzha mention they're smart little critters?"

"Yes, she did," he replied dryly.

She looked at him and her smile warmed—and he realized another part of himself that he hadn't known was hurt had begun to heal.

"Hold on to the living, Daemon. They need you."

"Your will, Lady."

She disappeared, but her psychic scent lingered in the room like a promise.

THIRTY-THREE

Are we going to the library again? I like the library. There are lots of smells. But no books for Scelties. Why aren't there books for Scelties?*

Jillian looked at Khary, who hadn't left her side except when she'd closed the bathroom door in his face. His barks and howls of protest had brought Rothvar running and almost had the Eyrien Warlord breaking down the bathroom door just when it would have been most inconvenient for her to get off the toilet. It had taken Nurian's *and* Marian's insistence that women viewed bathroom time as *private* time to get Khary to agree that, even if he was her escort for the time being, he didn't need to know *everything* she was doing when she was in her own home—or in the Yaslana eyrie.

And it had taken Rothvar pointing out that Khary wore an Opal Jewel and could have used Craft to pass right through the door to reach her for her to realize that the howls of protest had been an effort to show some restraint.

Scelties. Stubbornly certain about some things and curious about everything. And this one liked her, wanted to know her—and didn't confuse her by making her feel desirable one minute and inadequate the next.

"Scelties have books?"

*Yes. There is *Sceltie Saves the Day* and *Unicorn to the*

Rescue and *Dragon's Dangerous Deed*. Daemon is teaching me and Morghann to read and how to do the counting things. Like us. One plus one equals two.*

"Prince Sadi reads to you?"

Yes. Daemon is our teacher. Jaenelle Saetien was teaching Morghann, but Jaenelle Saetien told Morghann to do a wrong thing, so Daemon's pup is still our playmate but not our teacher.

So many things had happened in the few days since Prince Yaslana had found her kissing Dillon, and her feelings had been so confused, she hadn't appreciated that, unlike the kindred wolves who lived on Yaslana's mountain, Khary was chatty and wanted to interact with humans. Was someone she could talk to about things she didn't want to share with anyone else.

"I don't think the library here has those books, but we could look for another story that you might like. An adventure story." There were plenty of children's books at Yaslana's eyrie. Being male, Khary might not like the stories that appealed to Titian, but what about the stories that Daemonar had liked when he was little? She could borrow a couple and read them to Khary, same as she'd read them to Daemonar.

Khary growled at the same moment Dillon stepped in front of her and said, "Is that smile for me?"

Startled, Jillian almost dropped the book she was returning. She should have been delighted to see him. She *was* delighted to see him. So why was there this sudden weight in her chest? "Dillon."

"May I join you? We're in public." Dillon gave Khary a sour look. "And you have your chaperon."

Both true. "Of course."

He fell into step with her as they continued toward the library. "You finished it already?" He waved a hand to indicate the book.

"I stopped after a couple of chapters. It didn't appeal to me."

"What? How could a recounting of such a significant event not appeal to you? Especially when it's based on firsthand accounts?"

"What the author's ancestor wrote about the service fair may have been true for the aristos who had come to Kaeleer, but it wasn't true for everyone. It was dusty and dirty and there wasn't always enough water. And everyone was so scared of being sent back to Terreille."

"That might have been true for the dregs coming in, but not for the people who were an asset to the Blood in Kaeleer."

Jillian jerked to a stop and stared at Dillon.

Jillian? Khary sounded confused.

"My sister and I are not the dregs of anything, Lord Dillon," she said in a low voice that edged toward a growl. "We were desperate, yes, but we weren't drudges or dregs."

"I never said you were."

"You just did. Nurian and I came to Kaeleer during the last service fair. Prince Yaslana showed up on the last day and offered Nurian a contract. *I was there*, Dillon. I wasn't much older than Titian is now, but I remember what it looked like and felt like. It wasn't about a better opportunity; getting a contract that would allow us to stay here was about survival." She shook the book in his face. "So don't you dare dismiss what I think about this account of what you call history just because I don't agree with you."

Dillon looked stunned. "You were there? How old are you?"

Too old, Jillian thought. *And not old enough.* "Eyriens are one of the long-lived races."

"Yes, of course, but . . ."

She'd been so flattered by Dillon's attention that she hadn't seen the truth, hadn't fully appreciated what Prince Sadi had tried to tell her. She'd been caught up in her first romance, but Dillon was looking for an adult relationship.

Jillian? You are sad? Why are you sad?

Was this another lesson, that the male who expressed

concern for her feelings was the Sceltie and not the man who had said he loved her?

Had Dillon ever said he loved her?

"There's a coffee shop right over there," she said. "Why don't we get a cup of coffee and talk?"

Anger and something else she felt she should recognize filled Dillon's eyes for a moment before he donned a social mask.

"Yes, let's talk," he agreed.

When they reached the coffee shop, Jillian folded her wings and crouched so that she and Khary were closer to the same height. *Can you tell time?* she asked on a psychic thread.

A hesitation. *Daemon is teaching us, but clocks are hard.*

Jillian called in a ten-minute hourglass timer and used Craft to float it at eye level for Khary. *When all the sand runs into the bottom part, ten minutes has passed. You turn it over and let it run again. Ten plus ten equals twenty minutes. I need to talk to Dillon alone. Twenty minutes, Khary. Then you and I will go to the library.* *And then I'll go home and feel sad about the first boy I loved.*

I am your escort! I am supposed to stay with you.

We'll be in the coffee shop, a public place, in view of other people. Please, Khary.

He wasn't happy, but he said, *I will wait.*

When the last grain of sand fell a second time, he'd either be in the coffee shop with her or raise such a fuss he'd have every Warlord in Riada running to the shop, ready for battle. Yesterday that would have annoyed her. Today it gave her comfort.

Not many customers at this time of day, which was good. She didn't want to be overheard. She was headed for a table farthest from the door when Dillon grabbed her arm in a grip that hurt and pulled her through the shop and out the back door.

"I know another place to talk," he said.

"No. Let me go."

The look he gave her was close to hatred—or desperation. "I don't think so."

Before she could pull away, he launched them on the Opal Wind and she clung to him. The Webs of power the Blood used for travel stretched through the Darkness. If he shoved her off the Web, she might not find another one, might fall through the Darkness and keep falling until her body died or her mind broke.

Khary! Khary, help! The Sceltie wouldn't be able to hear her while she was riding the Winds, but maybe, because he was kindred, some whisper would reach him.

He finally had a chance to turn his life around, and she was going to ruin it.

Terrence had tried to tell him that Jillian looking old enough for a handfast didn't mean she *was* old enough to have a lover in the fullest sense. But how could she be too young and still so old she'd been at that last service fair?

She intended to end this romance. He'd seen that truth in her eyes. It was too late for him to focus his attention on another girl in the village, so he had to make this work, at least for a little while longer. Once he showed Yaslana that he wasn't a cad or disposable entertainment, he could admit that Jillian was a pleasant girl, which she was, but he now understood the significant difference in their ages and felt that stepping back was the honorable thing to do.

But he needed Jillian to remain enamored with him a little while longer.

Yas! Yas!

About to launch himself skyward to meet Daemon at the Keep, Lucivar hesitated when Khary called him on a psychic thread. The Sceltie sounded upset and angry, never a good sign. *Where are you?*

Coffee shop.

Wait there.

There was more than one coffee shop in Riada, but only one Sceltie currently down in the village. The kindred's psychic scents felt different from humans'. He wouldn't have any trouble finding Khary.

He forced himself to take a moment to consider. Then he called on a spear thread, *Rothvar! Meet me in the village. There's trouble.* Breaking the link before his second-in-command could reply, he spread his wings and flew down to Riada with reckless speed.

He didn't have to look hard to find the right place. The large ball of witchlight floating in the street near a shop was one clue. The number of Warlords converging on the shop was another.

The other men cleared a path for him as he backwinged to land near the shop.

"Lord Khary, report," he said, choking back temper and worry to avoid scaring a young male who was, essentially, an escort still learning his duties.

Jillian wanted to talk to Dillon alone, Khary said. *She told me to wait. She told me how long. But she's gone, Yas. I can't find her!*

Rothvar strode up at that moment. "Prince?"

"Jillian is missing." Lucivar ignored the murmurs of the men surrounding him and Rothvar. If that prick-ass Dillon had convinced her to ride the Winds with him, they could be anywhere. It was also possible they were just far enough away to elude a Sceltie who wasn't familiar with the village.

He looked at all the men who were ready to stand with him and said, "Check the alleyways between the shops in case Lord Dillon didn't believe I'd break his bones because of a tryst. Lord Rothvar and I will fly over the village and see if we can spot them."

As the Rihlander men scattered to search, Rothvar stepped closer and said in a low voice, "Should I call the other Eyrien Warlords?"

"Not yet. Let's see if we can find her. It's only been a few minutes since Khary sounded the alarm."

"A lot can happen to a girl in a few minutes."

He knew that too well. "I'll check the outskirts around the northern end of the village; you check south."

Rothvar flew off. Before Lucivar could head skyward, Khary said, *Yas?*

He looked at the unhappy Sceltie. "It wasn't your fault, little Brother. Any escort would have given her time in a public place like this." Not quite true. An experienced escort, human or otherwise, would have come into the shop and sat at another table to avoid hearing a civil conversation. "You stay here in case Jillian comes back."

Khary took up a position beside the door. *I will wait.*

Khary would wait. Lucivar didn't. Every minute he delayed increased the chance of his girl getting hurt.

They dropped from the Winds and landed near the old cabin on the outskirts of the village. They could have walked here faster than the time they had spent on the Winds. Did Dillon think she wouldn't recognize this place? Everyone who lived in Riada knew about this place.

The moment her feet touched the ground, Jillian tried to pull away from Dillon. He grabbed her hand and rubbed his thumb over her knuckles, but it didn't fill her with giddy warmth the way it used to.

"Hell's fire, Dillon! Are you trying to get killed?"

"I just want to talk." He gave her an odd smile. "We could go inside for a while. Nobody lives here."

"We can't go in there," she protested. "That cabin belonged to the Queen of Ebon Askavi. The *only* people who go inside are Lady Marian and Prince Sadi."

"Just on the porch, then." He rubbed his thumb over her knuckles again. "If you loved me, you would want to spend time with me."

She yanked her hand free. "Why do you keep saying that? And why is it always about me doing something to show that I love you and *never* you doing, or not doing, something because you love me?"

"How can I love you?" he snapped. "You're too young, but you led me on, let me believe you were old enough for a handfast, for the things *I* need."

"I *never* led you on," she snapped back. "I liked you, and it was flattering to have your attention because you were more sophisticated than the other boys in the village. But you were a *visitor*, Dillon. I had no reason to think this was more than a summer romance, and Prince Yaslana wouldn't have given his consent for anything more."

"Why should he care about the hired help?" Dillon sneered. "No matter what you let people believe, he's not your father."

Hearing Dillon say what she'd almost said to Lucivar because they had been arguing about this . . . *male* . . . ignited her temper.

"You bastard," she growled. "He's more of a father to me than yours is to you."

Fury filled his eyes. "You bitch!"

She realized he put a defensive shield around himself a moment before he lunged at her. She threw up her own shield—and the extra defensive shield as she'd been taught.

Dillon grabbed her, a blast of his Opal power breaking her first shield. She hadn't expected that kind of aggressive anger from Dillon, and it scared her, because he was taller and heavier and wore a darker Jewel than hers. But *she* was an Eyrien who had been trained to fight.

Jillian stopped thinking about *who* her adversary was and let training dictate her moves as she fought back.

Spotting Jillian, Lucivar folded his wings and dove for the ground. *Rothvar! Live at Witch's cabin.*

He didn't need Rothvar to deal with a Rihlander War-lord. He needed Rothvar to take Jillian away from the place before he started skinning the prick-ass alive.

He spread his wings and backwinged hard to avoid slamming into the ground. Landing a few feet behind them, he pushed aside hot fury enough to realize Jillian was on her feet and Dillon was on the ground, cupping his groin. An impressive-looking fist-sized bruise had already started to color one side of the prick-ass's face.

Dillon's eyes widened when he noticed Lucivar, and he made an effort to get to his feet.

Lucivar bared his teeth. *Stay down or the next fist you feel will be mine, and *my* fist will shatter bone.* When Dillon flopped back on the ground, Lucivar focused on the girl. "Jillian?" No answer. He took a step toward her, his heart pounding unmercifully hard. "Witchling? Are you hurt?"

She turned and looked at him, her lower lip quivering with the effort not to cry, her left hand cradling her right fist. She looked more like the young girl who had first come to Ebon Rih than the girl who was on the cusp of be-ing a woman.

"Witchling, are you hurt?" he asked again, barely able to breathe.

"I shielded like you taught me," she finally said. "I did. But . . ." She held out her hand, like Titian did when she had a boo-boo and wanted him, not Marian, to make it better.

He approached slowly, carefully.

Lucivar? Rothvar called.

I have her, he replied. Then to Jillian, "Let me see."

He took her right hand, probing gently. "Can you open your hand? That's it." More probing. Fingers. Knuck-les. "Close. Open." His chest muscles eased their grip on his lungs, allowing him to breathe. "You're all right. Nothing broken. You just need some ice on those knuck-les." He pulled her close, wrapped his arms around her—

and felt relief when her arms came around him and held on hard.

She's all right, he told Rothvar as the other man approached slowly. *She's all right.*

Rothvar studied Dillon. *He wears Opal; she wears Purple Dusk. She clobbered him hard enough through an Opal shield to leave that kind of bruise?*

Lucivar smiled. *Yeah, she did.* Then he looked at the Warlord lying on the ground. He wanted to skin him. Here. Now. But Daemon was waiting for him, and he needed to tend to his girl. *Take that piece of carrion to the communal eyrie and lock him in a room until I decide what to do with him.*

Done.

"Come on, witchling. Let's go home and find some ice for your hand." He waited until she let go of him. Then he waited a little more while she sniffled before she spread her wings and headed for his eyrie.

Bastard? he called.

Prick?

I'll be there as soon as I can. There's something I have to do first.

He'd been trembling, like he'd been afraid. She'd felt it when he put his arms around her. Lucivar Yaslana. Afraid. For her.

Jillian sat at the kitchen table at the Yaslana eyrie, watching him chop up ice and wrap it into a cloth to form a cold pad. He laid it over the knuckles of her right hand.

"I remembered what you taught me." It was the only thing she could think to say that might make him feel better.

He huffed out a laugh. "You certainly did." Then he sighed. "I have to go."

She nodded. He was the Warlord Prince of Ebon Rih. "Are you going to scold me later?"

"Should I?"

She almost wanted him to. Almost.

"I think I'll leave it to Khary to do the scolding. He's primed for it."

She looked at him, alarmed. "I wasn't *that* stupid."

She hadn't meant it to be amusing, but he laughed, kissed the top of her head, and walked out of the kitchen. A moment later, Khary rushed in and jumped into the kitchen chair beside her.

Jillian! The Sceltie's joy was real, but so was the other emotion she picked up from him.

"I'm hurt, Khary," she said quickly. "You can't scold me when I'm hurt."

Your paw is hurt, not your ears.

A quarter of an hour later, her ears—and head—did hurt as she listened to Khary's scold about wandering off without him and upsetting all the males who belonged to their family pack, but she figured listening to the Sceltie was a fair penance and price for making Lucivar Yaslana feel afraid.

THIRTY-FOUR

❖

"Sadi asked me to meet him here," Lucivar said when he finally arrived at the Keep.

"Yess," Draca said. "He iss in hiss ssuite."

"I know the way to the guest rooms." He started to walk away.

"Not thosse roomss, Prince. He iss in the Conssort'ss ssuite."

Lucivar froze, turned back to look at the Seneschal. "Why is he there?"

"He needss to be there."

Worried now, Lucivar strode through the winding corridors. He knew the way to these rooms, but he hadn't seen this part of the Keep in decades. And yet the moment he walked past the decorative gate that separated the Queen's part of the Keep from the rest of the mountain, he felt the power. Familiar, like the psychic scent that shouldn't be that strong, not after so many years. Unless . . .

He put his hand against the stone wall. *Cat?*

Was something's—someone's—attention turning toward him, focusing on him?

My thanks, Lady, for helping Marian heal. And if you're the one Daemonar comes to for advice . . . remember to give him a whack upside the head once in a while whether he needs it or not. Just to keep him honest. Lucivar smiled and blinked back tears. *You're still my Queen, so if there is anything you need from me, just ask.*

No answer. He didn't expect one. Didn't need one. Besides, he already knew what she would ask of him right now.

He gave the door of the Consort's suite one hard rap of his knuckles before walking in. Daemon rose from a desk piled with neat stacks of paperwork.

"Everything all right?" Daemon asked. "It took you a while to get here."

"Jillian had an argument with the prick-ass and clobbered him. Right now he's confined to a room at the communal eyrie and she's icing bruised knuckles."

Daemon raised one eyebrow. "Didn't he shield?"

"Yep. She didn't break his shield—couldn't, since he outranks her—but she put enough power and temper behind that punch to have him kissing dirt. Gave him an impressive bruise on his face, not to mention sore balls."

Daemon chuckled and shook his head. "At least you know she paid attention to her training."

As Lucivar studied his brother, he understood what Draca meant about Daemon needing to be here, in these rooms. Where else could a man like Daemon Sadi be accepted for everything he was? Where else could he be everything he was without being feared?

"I'd like you to do me a favor," Daemon said.

"Ask."

"I'd like you to leave Dillon's fate to me."

"Why?"

"Perzha told me some things about Lord Dillon's past, about actions that have brought him here. His actions— and the actions of others."

"You want me to forgive him," Lucivar said flatly.

"That depends on what he's done, and what others have done to him."

"Why in the name of Hell should I do that?"

"Because I'm asking."

Lucivar paced and swore. "Why are you asking, Bastard? Why should we do this? Why should *I* do this?"

"Because we've made our share of mistakes over the years. Because I'd like to believe—I *need* to believe—that a man can earn a second chance."

Hell's fire, Bastard. Yeah, they had made their share of mistakes, but . . . "He used spells on those girls."

"On Jillian, certainly. I don't know about the others. And that spell may have been used on him first."

"He's hurt girls."

"And he's been hurt by them. We've both had experience with that."

Yes, they had, and they both carried their own kinds of scars because of it.

"Prick, you have my word that if Dillon has caused any girl serious harm, he will live just long enough to regret it."

Lucivar stopped pacing. He wasn't sure who had just made that promise—Daemon, the Sadist, or the High Lord of Hell. Didn't matter. The promise had been made.

He stepped up to his brother, close enough to touch. "All right. I'll let you handle this in whatever way you think is best." He looked his fingers around the back of Daemon's neck, knowing he left himself vulnerable to nails that were, right now, sharp enough to slice clean through his ribs. "In exchange for letting you handle this, I want a promise in return."

"Ask."

"I don't know what was wrong with you. I don't need to know."

"Yes, you do. There are things we need to discuss. About me."

"Fine. We'll do that. The point is, old son, I feel the difference in you, which is why I know that whatever was wrong with you has been mended, and with you being in this suite, I can guess who did the mending. I want your word that if you start to sense that something isn't right, regardless of the reason, that you will tell me, that you'll let me help."

"And if you sense something isn't right, we'll have an agreed-upon phrase that tells me I need to retreat. That's one of the things we need to discuss."

"We'll figure it out." Lucivar squeezed Daemon's neck. "Listen to me, Bastard. If you need to fight, we'll fight. Remember when we were slaves and used to beat on each other as a way to release power and tension? We could do that again."

"Since I have a clear memory of how I felt after we did that, I'll pass, thanks."

"If you do need to scrap with someone, you come to me." Lucivar swallowed hard. Everything had a price. "And if the Sadist needs to play with someone, you come to me."

"Lucivar . . ."

"If that's what you need, you come to me. Understand?"

"Yes. I understand." Daemon rested his forehead against Lucivar's. His hands slowly rose and curled around Lucivar's wrists. "Being here helps. I can breathe here." He hesitated, then whispered, "Being here will help me stay sane."

Now Lucivar hesitated, then decided he would never bring it up again. "Surreal loves you. You know that, don't you?"

"Not all of me," Daemon whispered. "She loves what she's known, which is who I am when all the leashes are in place, but she's afraid of who, and what, I am without those leashes. And now those leashes may never be tight enough for her to be around me without feeling fear."

A hard truth. "Daemon . . ."

"It's all right, Prick. We'll work things out."

"I know you will." Lucivar eased back enough to give Daemon a soft kiss on the mouth. "You're staying here today?"

Daemon nodded. "I'll go over to the communal eyrie and have a little chat with Lord Dillon." He hesitated before adding, "I also have a couple of thoughts about Jillian."

"Let's talk about her later. You can come by the eyrie." Lucivar stepped back. "And you can loosen the leash on the sexual heat once the children are in bed."

"Lucivar, no."

"Daemon, yes. Marian was so pleased that you finally trusted her enough that you could relax completely in our home. You're not going to hurt her feelings by making her think it isn't true."

"I do feel comfortable in your home, but the heat . . . She'll feel it."

"Yes, she will. Which means you'll come back here and take a cold shower—and Marian and I won't get much sleep, but we'll have a good time."

Shock followed by a burst of laughter. "Go home. I have work to do."

As Lucivar reached the door, he said, "See you later, Bastard."

"That you will, Prick."

When he reached the gate to the Queen's part of the Keep, he brushed his fingers against the wall. "Yeah, I know. I'm a pain in the ass."

He didn't get an answer. But he thought he heard Witch's silvery, velvet-coated laugh.

THIRTY-FIVE

✦

Dillon paced the room in the communal eyrie and wondered if he'd ever see anything beyond these walls of stone. Why had he tried and tried and tried to repair a mistake if all that effort was going to end like this?

They'd brought him food and water. He'd ignored the food but drunk the water, almost hoping it was poisoned. That sounded like a more merciful end than whatever the Eyriens might be planning for him.

He didn't know what to think when a stunningly beautiful man walked into the room, moving with predatory, feline grace.

"I'm Daemon Sadi."

Mother Night. Dillon's voice cracked as he said, "Prince," and he hoped his long jacket hid his physical reaction to the sight of the man.

"My brother wants to break you into pieces," Daemon crooned, his deep, sensual voice wrapping around Dillon like silk chains. "But I'm going to give you a chance to explain yourself." He settled into a straight-backed wooden chair, crossed his legs at the knees, and steepled his fingers, resting the forefingers against his chin, drawing the eye to the luscious mouth and the long black-tinted nails. "One chance, Warlord, that will decide whether you live or die."

The words—and the sudden chill in the air—snapped Dillon out of an aroused haze. Embarrassed by his response and feeling like he had nothing left to lose, he swelled with reckless anger. "What would you know about betrayal?"

"Quite a lot, actually," Daemon replied calmly.

"A lot?" He laughed, a harsh sound, and pointed to the Black-Jeweled ring on Daemon's right hand. "Who would dare betray you?"

"I was young once, and I didn't always wear the Black. Tell me about Lady Blyte."

His painful arousal and the chill in the air faded, leaving him feeling a little sick but clearheaded. He paced, trying to gather his thoughts so he would sound reasonable, rational. But feelings that he'd had to swallow for so long rose in him and demanded a voice.

"I made a mistake," he said. "One mistake. I believed that bitch when she said she loved me. I wanted to be an escort. I wanted to serve in a court. But in order to prove I loved her, I had to walk away from the training, because she didn't want me to be around other women, didn't want me to have to meet someone else's wishes above hers. When I balked at having sex, she offered me a handfast to prove our suitability. And when she found out I had told my family about the arrangement, she denied it all, said I was the seducer, did everything she could to destroy my reputation and honor. Her family's more aristo than mine, and they backed up her story. The District Queen, who is related to her family, backed up her story. She walked away with no penalty at all, free to do it again to someone else, just like she'd done it to me.

"I wasn't the first one. Did you know that? Does anyone care about that? I wasn't the first to fall for her game, and I wasn't the last. I looked for some of those other men. They're toys for aristo bitches now. The men those girls have fun with while they wait for the men with the right family bloodlines and social standing to be husbands.

"I tried to find work, tried to stay away from the aristo girls. But they wouldn't let me. I was soiled, so I was fair game. So why shouldn't I play games with them? Why shouldn't I get something out of them? The moment one of those girls said my name and 'handfast' in the same sentence, their fathers couldn't pay me off fast enough. I figured it was a better way to earn a living than being a real whore."

Panting, sweating, Dillon faced Daemon Sadi.

"And Jillian?" Daemon asked, still sounding calm and reasonable.

He wiped sweat off his forehead with the back of his hand. "I like Jillian. I really do. I knew she was young to enter into a handfast, but I didn't think she was *too* young. I really didn't. And I didn't realize she was that old." He paused. Considered what he should say to this man. Careful words, but nothing less than the truth. "I wasn't as kind as I should have been, and I'm sorry for that. I wanted to be important. I wanted her to be impressed. She thought I was special, and it had been so long since someone had thought well of me, let alone thought I was special, and I thought . . ."

"You thought?"

"I thought a handfast with Jillian would help me restore my reputation, repair my honor. She worked for Prince Yaslana, so I figured that connection would help me find work, would give me a year when I didn't feel hunted. I thought she was old enough."

"She's not."

"No, she's not." Dillon felt wrung out, purged of emotions. "But suddenly there was an aristo family who expected me to court a girl properly, with chaperons and supervised meetings. And not just any family—the most powerful family in the valley."

"You felt protected."

"Yes." Dillon relaxed a little. Someone understood—and that someone was an aristo Warlord Prince. "If I could show the ruling families here that I wasn't a cad, I could find work, could stop moving from place to place because the aristo girls forced me out by demanding I be something I didn't want to be."

"You took Jillian away from her escort," Daemon said too softly.

"I was using a spell to make her think I was wonderful, but it stopped working." Admitting to using a spell would be enough to have him executed, but Dillon didn't care anymore. "Just when I had a chance to do things properly, Jillian was going to end things between us. I saw it in her eyes. I thought if I could make her believe in me a little while longer . . ." He smiled as he gingerly touched his face. "I thought she was malleable, but she's got a mean side to her temper."

"She's Eyrien." Daemon sighed. "Everything has a price, Warlord."

"Is Prince Yaslana going to execute me?" A day ago, he would have said that for drama. Today he believed it could happen.

Daemon uncrossed his legs and rose, a beautiful man full of power and grace. He called in several sheets of paper and a pen and placed them on the small table that also held the plate of food and the carafe of water.

"I want the names of every girl you dallied with, everyone who believed you wanted a handfast or who loaned you money because of the spell you used on them, every girl you had sex with, every girl who was a virgin before you entered her life. Every one of them, Lord Dillon. On another page, I want the names of every girl or woman who used you, who played games with you. Start with the first one. Lady Blyte. Yaslana and I are going to investigate every person on those lists, and when we're done, we'll decide what happens to you."

Dillon approached the table but stayed out of reach of the man. "Do you want the names of the other men she and her friends ruined? At least, the names of the ones I know about?"

"Yes."

Dillon's mouth twisted into a bitter smile. "One of those men killed himself after she was through with him, so I hope you know someone in Hell who can talk to him."

He couldn't interpret the odd light in Sadi's gold eyes or the meaning of the gently murderous smile.

Sadi said, "As a matter of fact, Lord Dillon, I do know someone."

Marian watched the haphazard way Surreal packed up Jaenelle Saetien's clothes and resisted taking them out of the trunks to fold them more neatly.

"We could keep Jaenelle Saetien here for a few more days, if that would help," she said.

"She doesn't have enough clothes for an extended visit," Surreal replied dully.

"Clothes can be washed. Another trunk can be packed and brought by Lord Holt or one of the other people working at the Hall."

Surreal hesitated, then shook her head. "It's best if she and I go home now. Jillian's love life is sorted out, not that I had much to do with that."

"Why do you say that? Lucivar followed your advice to let this romance run its course so that Jillian could find out for herself that Dillon wasn't as wonderful as she'd believed."

"I wasn't needed."

Annoyance flitted through Marian, but she remembered Surreal's tear-filled confession and smothered the annoyance. "Are we talking about Jillian or something else?"

"Witch has come back. Daemon saw her at the Keep." A hesitation. "I saw her in the Misty Place. We had quite a chat."

Marian sucked in a breath. "How? Jaenelle's body is gone, Surreal. If her Self has somehow managed to stay anchored to the Keep, then what he saw was just a shadow. A shadow isn't flesh to hold at night and love."

"How would you feel if she came back because you had failed somehow?" Surreal threw the clothes into the trunk. "How would *you* feel if Jaenelle was suddenly back in Lucivar's life?"

"She never left him." Marian smiled at Surreal's stunned look. "Lucivar belonged to Witch before I met him. He'll belong to her until his last breath and beyond. Lifetime contract, Surreal. She was the reason Lucivar and Daemon fought to survive everything that was done to them in Terreille. Loving her healed something inside them that made it possible for them to love someone else." She took Surreal's hands in her own. "She saved you once. Remember?"

Surreal's eyes filled with tears. "I remember."

"She saved me too. More than once. She was our friend and our sister and our Queen, and you can't blame her for being the most important love our men will know. She's their Queen, Surreal. No one comes before the Queen. Not even a wife."

"He said he needed her to stay sane," Surreal whispered.

Mother Night. "Then you need to decide if you can accept that she is the reason he can be with you."

"I—"

Marian wondered what Surreal might have said if Lucivar hadn't returned to the eyrie at that exact moment.

Lucivar felt Surreal's Gray power in his home and wondered why she had returned to Ebon Rih instead of staying at the Hall or going to the SaDiablo town house in Amdarh to get some rest and have time to think.

Then she walked into the front room, looking exhausted and resigned, and he knew why she'd returned.

"Can we talk?" she asked quietly.

"Sure." A swift probe of the eyrie told him the location of the yappy horde. He opened the glass doors that led out to the walled yard. "Let's talk out here."

As he walked to the very end of the yard, where he'd helped Marian build a decorative pool that was fed by a stream flowing down the mountain, he directed a psychic thread to his wife. *Anything I should know about Surreal?*

She says Witch has come back because she failed somehow. Is that true?

Daemon asked his Queen for help and she answered. He ended the connection so that he could focus on the woman standing beside him.

"I thought the Sadist was playing with me," Surreal said. "I made a mistake."

"Yeah, you did. A couple of them." Lucivar studied her. "I doubt it was the first mistake you've made with him, and I'm certain it won't be the last. I know I've done my share of stupid things where he's concerned, and he's done his share with me. You live around someone long enough, it will happen. If you want to stay with him, you'll work through it."

"So we'll go home and everything will be the way it was."

"No, witchling. It will never be the way it was," Lucivar said gently. "You have this between you now as part of your history together. There's been hurt on both sides. That changes things. Maybe a little, maybe a lot. Either way, things will never be the same as they were. You break or build from here."

"Are you speaking from experience?"

"Yes, I am." Lucivar looked at the valley below and the village of Riada. He could feel the Black, knew Daemon was still at the communal eyrie or at least nearby. But he couldn't feel Witch's power, which was why, despite his suspicions about who gave Daemonar advice, he hadn't known for sure that some part of her was still with them until he'd walked into the Queen's section of the Keep.

"Are you angry with me?"

He smiled. "Nah." He reached out and tucked her hair behind one delicately pointed ear. "Go home, Surreal. Get some rest. Daemon and I have a couple more things to take care of. Then I'll kick his ass back to Dhemlan."

She turned to go, then stopped. "The Gray can't survive against the Black."

"Neither can the Ebon-gray. Never could. Your head has known that for all the years you've known him. But now the truth of that has settled in your gut. He feels different when his power—and the Sadist—are leashed. Almost . . . civilized. He's never civilized under the surface, any more than I am, but it's easy to forget that. Daemon makes it easy to forget that because he yields to others in his own household, deals with them without bringing the Jewels, or anything else, into play. Saetan did the same thing for the same reason—to live in a house where he wasn't feared." When she didn't say anything, he added, "When he gets home, point a crossbow at him. It will make him feel loved."

She laughed, as he'd hoped she would. Then she walked away.

"Don't forget the Scelties," he called when she reached the glass doors.

"Take a piss in the wind, Yaslana," she replied.

The Black arrived on his doorstep. Lucivar ran to catch up with Surreal so she wouldn't face Daemon alone. They walked in from the yard just as Daemon opened the front door and entered.

No surprise at seeing Surreal. Then again, Daemon would have known the Gray was present just as he'd known.

"Surreal," Daemon said.

"Sadi." A beat of silence. "I was packing. Jaenelle Saetien and I will head home in about an hour."

Lucivar watched Daemon, whose leashes were in place. Not as firmly held as they used to be, which was something everyone would have to accommodate, but Sadi was in control of every aspect of himself, including his feelings. Especially his feelings.

"If you could postpone leaving for a day or two, we could use your help," Daemon said.

"I don't need help skinning the prick-ass, but I'm willing to share," Lucivar said.

"Skinning the . . ." Surreal looked at the two men. "What happened?"

"Jillian and Dillon had a disagreement," Lucivar said. "He got a knee to the balls and a fist in the face. She has bruised knuckles."

"If what Dillon says is true, this is more serious than one boy," Daemon said too softly.

In that softness, Lucivar heard a whisper of the Sadist slipping into a cold rage. Feeling the tension in Surreal, he knew she heard it too.

"What do we need to do?" he asked.

"Three lists." Daemon called in three sheets of paper. "The girls Dillon played, the girls who used him, and the other young men whose reputations were ruined, either directly or indirectly, by Lady Blyte, who was the bitch who was Dillon's first love." He held them out to Surreal.

She took the papers with a steady hand, as if she didn't feel the cold temper swirling in the room. "I get first pick?" She scanned the lists. "I'll talk to the girls Dillon had . . . persuaded . . . to love him. Anything in particular you want to know?"

"What harm was done—and how well the girls recovered," Daemon replied.

"I'll take the other men whose reputations were ruined," Lucivar said. He looked at Daemon and added on a spear thread, *You would have a better feel for bitches who like to play sex games, so you take that list.*

"You won't find one of the men on that list," Daemon said. "I was told to look for him in Hell." When Lucivar met his eyes, he said, "I'm sorry, Lucivar."

He'd known this day might come. "Everything has a price."

Surreal didn't ask, and for that, he was grateful. He needed to talk to Marian before anyone else.

"We head out, talk to people, and report back here each evening," Lucivar said. "No excuses, no exceptions."

Daemon raised an eyebrow.

"We're about to kick a lot of hornets' nests, Bastard. Word is going to spread fast after we start, so it's either reporting back or going in with Eyrien guards."

"Well, that will make everyone eager to talk to us," Surreal said.

They looked at her.

"I can take care of myself." She gave them a sharp smile. "I'm good with a knife, remember?"

"And a crossbow," Lucivar said. "We're not likely to forget. That doesn't change anything, witchling. My Territory, my rules."

"Your . . . ?" She stared at him, and he knew the moment she understood what was about to change and what that would mean for him and Marian and their children. Then she nodded. "Okay, sugar. Your rules."

"I'm going to contact Manny, see if she's willing to stay here a while," Lucivar said. "I'd like someone to be here with Marian while we're checking the names on those lists, and Jillian needs some time to herself."

"Sadi? If you have a moment?" Surreal asked.

Lucivar walked out of the front room.

Surreal had hit an unexpected patch of rough air that had thrown her into a free-fall spin. Could have caused serious, permanent damage, but this task would help her through it. She just had to find the courage to fly again—and she would. Even if she didn't realize it yet—or appreciate it yet—Witch would help her find her balance by helping Daemon maintain his own balance.

"You'll be all right," he said quietly. "You'll both be all right."

Surreal looked at the beautiful, lethal, terrifying man she'd married. If he thought she was a danger to the Realm or the rest of the family, he would kill her without hesitation. She knew that to the marrow of her bones. But she also knew that he loved her and would protect her in every way he could. After she had come away from the Offering to the Darkness wearing the Gray, there were very few men who were powerful enough to be a threat. Daemon was one of them.

"Are you going to stay here at the eyrie?" she asked quietly.

"No," he replied just as quietly. "I'll stay at the Keep. Until we see this done, it's not going to be safe to be around me."

She nodded. What else could she do?

He stepped close, leaned in as if to kiss her, then hesitated. Before he could withdraw, she leaned toward him and touched her lips to his. Silent permission.

His kiss was warm, gentle, giving—full of affection and empty of desire.

"Will you come back to the Hall after this is done?"

"Of course."

She didn't press him for more of an answer. He was pulling back, a Black-Jeweled predator heading out to hunt. Better for both of them if she gave him the distance he needed.

"Tell Lucivar I'll be in Hell for a while, but I'll be back in time for his curfew."

She smiled. "If you're not, I'll let him borrow my crossbow."

Daemon laughed and walked out of the eyrie.

Marian didn't know what to expect when Lucivar led her to his study, locked the door, and then put shields around the room to assure no one would interrupt them.

"We need to talk," he said.

He looked troubled. Grim.

She struggled to keep fear out of her voice. "Lucivar? What's wrong?"

Troubled. Grim. And not meeting her eyes, which wasn't like him.

"I was the Warlord Prince of Ebon Rih when you agreed to marry me," he said, his voice rough with choked-back emotions. "You knew what you were walking into, what you'd have to deal with."

"More or less," she said dryly, remembering some of the adventures she'd had with Jaenelle Angelline.

That made his lips twitch in a hint of a smile. Then even that much humor faded. "More or less. Three Blood villages and a handful of landen villages. Farms. Rustic living compared to the fancier Rihlander towns and cities in other parts of Askavi. And Queens who formed their courts knowing they were going to be living under my hand, and if anyone crossed the lines I had drawn for what I would accept in this valley, they wouldn't survive."

"We've never had serious trouble here." *At least, not since Falonar's attempt to kill you and take over Ebon Rih.*

"You're comfortable with the Queens and their courts, with the aristos living in the valley." Another momentary smile. "Maybe not comfortable, but you're used to dealing with them."

Yes, she'd gotten used to the village women stopping by the eyrie when Lucivar wasn't there in order to express a concern. She'd gotten used to Queens speaking to her in order to get a feel for how Lucivar might react to something that had come to the notice of their courts. They were always polite, even friendly at public events, but they didn't have much in common with a hearth witch.

Since he seemed to be waiting for an answer, she said, "I've gotten used to dealing with them. They're good women, and good people serve in their courts."

"We've had a good life here. Haven't we?"

Had a good life? "Lucivar . . ."

"I made a promise, Marian. I'm sorry for what it will do to you and the children, but I made a promise to my

Queen, and I can't break it." The words almost sounded like a plea.

"I would be disappointed in you if you did."

That he hadn't moved since they'd walked into the study when he'd normally pace told her how difficult this was for him—whatever it was.

"Askavi doesn't have a Territory Queen," he said. "Every Province has a Queen, and there are District Queens who rule under them."

He was right, of course. Every other Territory in Kaeleer had a Queen who ruled over the rest of the Queens. With one exception. "Is that important?"

"It wasn't. It is now."

"Why now?" She suspected the reason was locked in the communal eyrie, awaiting Lucivar's judgment, but felt the question needed to be asked.

"Because the District Queens aren't doing their jobs anymore. They're ignoring problems, and the Province Queens are letting them get away with it because they don't have to answer to anyone. Or they haven't had to answer to anyone for long enough to forget what it was like to face the Demon Prince when they failed to hold the lines of acceptable behavior and live by the Old Ways of the Blood."

She saw it then, the cliff that was crumbling beneath their lives, their marriage.

"You're going to claim all of Askavi as your Territory, aren't you? All the Queens will have to answer to you." Queens who were from powerful aristo families. Queens who wouldn't want to dine with a Purple Dusk hearth witch, no matter whom she'd married.

"I was satisfied with our life. I *am* satisfied with our life, with taking care of this valley and its people. Given a choice, I wouldn't change anything." Lucivar shook his head. "But I promised her, Marian. I gave my word that, if it became necessary, I would acknowledge the document I had signed that made me the Warlord Prince of Askavi."

"What happens if the Queens won't acknowledge your rule over them?"

He looked at her. She didn't see her husband. She didn't even see the Warlord Prince of Ebon Rih. She wondered if Andulvar Yaslana had looked the same way when he became the Demon Prince.

She closed the distance between them. The Demon Prince would be ruthless, brutal. But the man who walked off the killing fields drenched in his enemies' blood would still be Lucivar, her best friend, her husband and lover, the father of her children.

"Being the Demon Prince's wife won't be easy for you," he said quietly. "It won't be easy on the children."

She wrapped her arms around him, rested her head on his chest—and felt his arms tighten around her.

"Storms and rough winds ahead of us." She leaned back enough to look at him. "We'll help each other get through them."

"I love you," he said softly.

Smiling, she added an aural shield to the shields he already had around the room. "Show me."

"Prince Chaosti," the High Lord said with a sweetly murderous smile, "I need you and your Dea al Mon warriors to assist me in a hunt."

THIRTY-SIX

✦

Unsettled by the latest interview with one of Dillon's "conquests," Surreal passed by the dining houses in the aristo part of the Rihland town. She was hungry and wanted food, but she didn't want to be on her guard every minute.

Now, why did she think she needed to be on her guard? Was it because of the father and daughter she'd just spoken with who had heaped complaints and accusations on Dillon? Or was it because of the Warlord who had been tracking her since she'd left that aristo house?

She chose a dining house that looked clean, at least from the outside. On the inside . . . ? Definitely didn't cater to aristos. The men and women who studied her when she entered wore the clothes of shopkeepers or laborers. Maybe some farmers who had come into town for supplies and were treating themselves to a meal before heading home. But she'd wager the food here was simple and good.

She was shown to a table at the back of the room and had made her selection from the day's menu when the Warlord walked in. He didn't wait to be seated. He strode to her table, pulled out the chair opposite hers, and sat down. He wore a Sapphire Jewel, and the fire in his dark eyes said he was looking for a fight.

As the dining house's owner put a glass of wine in front

of her and a tankard of ale in front of him, she noticed how everyone else abandoned their meals and left, forming a crowd outside the dining house.

"I won't insult you by pretending I don't know who you are," he said, wrapping the fingers of his left hand around the tankard's handle—leaving the gently curled right hand free to close over the sight-shielded knife she was sure he had ready.

Couldn't blame him for that. Her right hand was gently curved around the handle of her sight-shielded stiletto.

"Just what is it you think you know, sugar?" she asked.

He looked at her right hand. "You're the wife of the Warlord Prince of Dhemlan. And you're Dea al Mon. I've heard a few whispers lately that you used to get rid of problems when you lived in Terreille."

Well, that was interesting. She looked at his right hand in the same way he'd looked at hers. "You have a problem you can't handle?"

"That depends on why you went to see *them* about Lord Dillon."

"I was asked to look into all of Lord Dillon's . . . liaisons."

"Then someone should tell you the rest of the story and not just what *they* want you to know."

"And that would be you?" She wondered how many other people in the town referred to that aristo family as *they* in a tone that held nothing but contempt.

He inclined his head. Took a long swallow of ale, his eyes never leaving hers.

She took a sip of the wine. Not a bad vintage. Better than she'd expected. "I'm listening."

"A while back, Lord Dillon came into town. He's from an aristo family, but he's not too far above ordinary folks. Pleasant enough. Crosses paths with the daughter of *that* family, and she takes a liking to him. Too much of a liking, if you follow me."

"I follow you," Surreal said.

"While Dillon is happy to be the girl's dance partner or escort her to a public gathering, she can't talk him into warming her bed on the sly. Then a letter arrives from a bosom friend in another town, and suddenly Dillon goes from being a pleasant young man who can say no to unwanted sexual invitations to being a man who is expected to provide sex to any aristo bitch who wants him, because his reputation is being trashed behind calculating smiles. I imagine you've heard this story in other towns."

"Similar stories," she agreed.

The Warlord gave Surreal a sharp smile. "The girl is a coldhearted, spoiled bitch who is serving in the District Queen's court to get some polish. If you ask me, the polish she'll get with that Queen is the kind that will get her killed."

"Will it be your hand that holds the knife?"

"Probably."

Oh, he *was* interesting. "I'm still listening."

"That whole family cares for no one and nothing but themselves—and they're a little too proud of their Terreillean bloodlines."

That was what had left her feeling unsettled—the sense of something familiar in a place where it *shouldn't* have been familiar.

"There was a woman who worked at a dressmaker's shop just down the street. Nice woman who comes from a good family, at least by the standards in this part of town. Met a Warlord at a public dance, oh, seven years ago or so. He was a persuasive and ardent suitor—until she became pregnant. Big surprise for her, since he'd sworn he was drinking a contraceptive brew."

"Hmm," she said.

"He can't marry her, of course. Too far beneath him socially for that to be a consideration. But he'll help her raise the child and he'll be there for the Birthright Ceremony."

"Did he help, at least financially?"

The Warlord snorted. "She never saw so much as a copper from him, let alone anything else. Barely ever saw him again, even though he lives in this town too. But he did show up for the Birthright Ceremony and said all the right things, and that made her hopeful. If nothing else, once paternity was officially acknowledged, her daughter wouldn't be considered a bastard."

"But . . . ?"

The Warlord focused on the tankard. "Sweet girl—and smart enough in her own way. But she's a little bit simple in the way she sees the world. Despite both parents wearing Jewels—lighter Jewels, to be sure, but still enough that you'd have expectations for the child—the girl didn't acquire a Birthright Jewel at the ceremony, and it's unlikely that she'll ever have more than basic Craft even when she's old enough to make the Offering to the Darkness.

"To say the girl's sire was viciously disappointed would be gilding him with a kindness he doesn't deserve. When the girl failed to acquire a Jewel, he refused to go through with the rest of the ceremony so that paternity could be acknowledged. He said loudly—and in front of witnesses— that he wouldn't have his name associated with a blob of flesh that might have come from the last squirt of his cock or a half dozen other men's. The woman was crushed, since he'd been her first—and only—lover. Her family is helping her as best they can, but she's been struggling, barely able to leave her home because that bastard's 'jest' was all over town by that evening and she's too ashamed to see anyone. And the girl doesn't understand why her mother is crying all the time."

"What does this have to do with Dillon?" Surreal asked. She hadn't been hired for what she was thinking. She didn't have a client.

Well, Hell's fire, she'd just hire herself—and give herself a steep discount from her usual fee. Or not.

"The Warlord who wouldn't acknowledge his daughter because she wasn't going to be anything useful to him is the uncle of the bitch who took a fancy to Dillon. I don't know how Dillon heard the story about the woman and her daughter, but when the ground was pulled out from under him and the bitch's father paid him to leave town so that he wouldn't soil the bitch's honor by association, Dillon gave the woman half the money before he left town."

The Warlord drank until he drained the tankard. He set it aside. "Maybe he's developed a skin of meanness in his dealings with the distaff gender. But that's not who he was a few months ago. I thought you should know that."

"I appreciate it." Surreal looked toward the owner, who hovered out of earshot, and wondered if she would ever see her meal. "Two things, Warlord. First, tell the woman to write up every encounter she's had with the man who sired her daughter. Make sure she records what support he provided before and after the Birthright Ceremony."

"I told you—he didn't provide anything. He has no interest in the girl. Never did."

"Exactly. And make sure what occurred at the Birthright Ceremony is part of that account, including what he said. If she won't—or can't—do that, you write it. Have that written account witnessed and give a copy to the woman's family. Another copy should be sent to the Province Queen. And the third copy should be taken to the Keep, with a request that it be included in the information for the woman's bloodline and the Warlord's."

"What's the point?"

"The point is to show that he shouldn't be granted any authority over the girl, if he starts showing interest in a year or so, since he wasn't interested before."

"Before what?"

Surreal smiled and leaned closer. "The second thing: where can I find that Warlord?"

An art exhibition. People milling around, distracted by the art—and more distracted by noticing who was noticing them attending the exhibition. The Warlord was there, showing everyone how attentive he was to the Lady he'd recently married.

Surreal strolled through the crowd, stopping to look at a painting here, a fired pot there. The spell she had crafted was ready, primed for release.

Bloodless castration. Not as much fun as the other way but useful when it needed to be done neatly. And something that might not be detected for years, since it didn't take anything away from a man except his ability to sire children.

Jaenelle Angelline had taught her that piece of Craft.

So simple, really. Looking away as if distracted when the Warlord walked toward her. Her shoulder bumping into his hard enough for anyone looking to think she'd lost her balance. Her hand brushing against his cock and balls for just a moment. Just long enough to release the spell.

"What do you think you're doing?" the Warlord said, sounding outraged. "Have you forgotten who you are?"

The question made her smile. "Actually, sugar, I finally remembered."

THIRTY-SEVEN

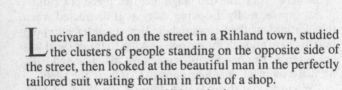

Lucivar landed on the street in a Rihland town, studied the clusters of people standing on the opposite side of the street, then looked at the beautiful man in the perfectly tailored suit waiting for him in front of a shop.

"What brings you here?" he asked.

"Followed a side trail," Daemon replied. "It led me here."

"This is the last one on my list."

"Then this is the last one." Daemon used Craft to open the shop's door. "After—"

Daemon's power broke the aural shield around the shop, revealing the voices and the struggle going on inside.

"Do it!" a female voice screamed. "If you loved me, you would do it!"

"Graham! Don't. Please don't." Another female voice, crying, pleading.

A male voice, angry and anguished. "Bekka! I can't stop. . . . I have to prove I . . . Get out of here before I hurt you!"

"Do it!" the first female screamed again. "Kill her!"

Wrapping himself in a skintight Red shield, Lucivar strode into the shop, Daemon right behind him.

One young woman trapped between a counter and a young Warlord with a knife. Three other young women—

aristos by the look of their clothes. Two of them watched with avid cruelty while the third kept screaming, "If you loved me, you would kill her!"

"Bekka!" the young Warlord cried. "I love Bekka!"

I'll take him, Daemon said. *You protect the girl he's threatening and keep those bitches in the shop.*

Lucivar formed an Ebon-gray shield around the shop, locking the building. A heartbeat later, Daemon's unleashed sexual heat hit everyone as he glided over to the Warlord. One of his hands closed over the hand holding the knife. His other hand curled around the Warlord's throat, pulling the youngster close enough to be swamped with a need that would go unfulfilled— if the youngster was lucky.

Gritting his teeth against his own response to the heat, Lucivar pulled the girl—Bekka— out of reach of the knife. Scared. Shaking. But no injuries. He put a shield around her, partly as protection and partly to keep her from doing anything that might piss him off more than he already was.

"Show me," Daemon whispered, his lips close to the Warlord's ear. "Tell me."

Graham turned his head slightly, revealing the side of his face that had been maimed by something—or someone.

The three bitches had been so focused on Graham and Bekka—and then pulled into lust by Daemon's over-whelming presence—they hadn't noticed Lucivar. Now they did.

Two tried to run and slammed into the shield across the doorway. A flick of his Ebon-gray power drained their Jewels almost to the breaking point, assuring they weren't going to do any damage to anyone at least, not with Craft. Stunned, they collapsed to the floor and began to cry because the Warlord Prince was being mean.

That left the third bitch, the one who had been scream-ing at Graham.

Lucivar tightened the leash on his temper, fighting against the fury rising in him, which wanted to wash the walls with her blood. If this was as bad as he suspected . . .

Realizing her game was spoiled, the bitch lashed out with the power of her Summer-sky Jewel. Not at him. She wasn't that stupid. No, she tried to strike Bekka.

Lucivar shaped another shield around Bekka a heart-beat before the bitch's power struck. Years ago, Saetan had shown him how to add an extra bit of Craft to a defensive shield when drama was required. The clash of the witch's power hitting the second Ebon-gray shield sounded like buildings exploding—a sure way to bring everyone who served the District Queen running to investigate.

Of course, they would be running right into him and Daemon. Wouldn't that be a kick in the balls?

Before the aristo bitch could attempt some other trouble, he stepped close to her, called in his war blade, and held it a whisper away from the side of her face. "You want to be very careful about what you say or do. If I get upset, my hand could slip, and this blade is honed for war, so it would slice right through your jaw."

"You'll answer to my father for this," she said, her haughty expression at odds with the fear in her voice. "He's an important man, not some grubby . . ." Either she couldn't think of a scathing enough insult or she'd finally noticed his Ebon-gray Jewel.

"Oh, I hope your father does show up. I have some things to say to him. None of them are good."

Sensing another male presence behind a shielded door that, most likely, led to the back of the shop, and wondering who was hiding behind that door, Lucivar broke the shield and waited. Moments later, the door opened and an older man rushed into the front room.

"What do you want?" The older man's voice trembled. "Hasn't my son been hurt enough?"

"More than enough," Lucivar agreed. "And that ends now. Lord Graham?"

"Sir?" the youngster said as Daemon released him and stepped back.

"Do you know the names of the men—or women—

who gave you those scars? Am I right in assuming that was done to your face as punishment for not accommodating these *Ladies* in some way?"

"The aristos who did it will know I told you," Graham said, "They'll hurt my parents." He glanced at the young woman wrapped in Lucivar's shields. "They'll hurt Bekka."

"They won't have time to hurt anyone," Daemon crooned. "They'll be dead by morning."

Lucivar felt fear spike through the aristo women. He felt relief flood the two men who didn't belong to that social class. That told him he'd postponed this day too long.

Everything has a price.

Prick? Daemon glided to the door and studied the crowd. *The Master of the Guard has shown up with what looks like all the Queen's guards. He seems agitated.*

Let the fool come in, Lucivar said, dropping the Ebon-gray shield around the shop.

Only the Master entered the shop. The guards must have looked at Daemon's glazed gold eyes and the cold, sweet smile and prudently decided not to provoke a Warlord Prince who was a heartbeat away from the killing edge.

Lucivar held the war blade steady against the bitch's face. He waited a moment to give the Master a chance to realize who he was. What he was. "You know this bitch?"

"My daughter. Release her," the Master blustered. "She's done nothing wrong."

"Oh, she's done plenty that's wrong any way you choose to look at it," Lucivar said as if they were discussing the weather. "She may not have held the knife, but I'm betting she's responsible for the scars on that boy's face. And she used a spell to try to force him to kill this young woman. She will pay the debt she owes for what she's done."

"This is none of your business!"

"I made it my business." Now he used Craft so that his voice thundered out of the shop and filled the street, guaranteeing someone would deliver his message to the District Queen. "If you want a war, I will give you a war. But before you gather men to stand against me on a killing field, you tell them that they're facing the Demon Prince because your daughter likes to abuse men who can't fight back. You tell them they're going to die so that she can continue to play games with any man who isn't strong enough to kill her or aristo enough to cause a scandal if she tries to trap him. You tell your Queen that she is going to forfeit her life because she looked the other way instead of calling your daughter—and you—to account.

"I'll give you a choice. You can guarantee in front of witnesses and on your life and the life of your Queen that you will keep this bitch confined until I return to collect what she owes, or I can send her to Hell right now."

Another Warlord stepped into the shop, looking grim. "Prince. I'm the Steward of the Court."

"I'm listening."

"My Queen sends her regards and her regrets. She was not aware of this misconduct. If a formal complaint had been presented to the court—"

"We appealed to the Queen," the older man said. "She did nothing, even after that bitch's friends maimed my son's face."

The Steward flinched, but he looked the man in the eyes. "The Queen did not see your complaint. Neither did I. If we had . . ." He glanced at the Master of the Guard, who was pale and sweating, then offered Lucivar a small bow. "My Queen offers her assurance that we will take this Lady with us now and confine her at the court until you're ready to collect the debt she owes."

Lucivar lifted the war blade away from the bitch's face and stepped back. "Take her."

The Steward snapped his fingers. Guards poured into the shop—frightened, angry men. They had reason to be frightened and angry. If their Queen had known about the misconduct and had done nothing, her court would fail. She would go down, and most likely they would go down with her.

Two of the guards who wore Jewels darker than Summer-sky took hold of the witch's arms and led her away, surrounded by the other men.

The Steward looked at the other two aristo women in the shop. "The Queen commands your presence tomorrow morning. She has some questions for you. Don't be late."

The two women bolted out of the shop.

The Master turned to the Steward. "You can't—"

"Don't," the Steward warned.

Lucivar had a good idea of what was silently said between the two men. If the Master was lucky, he would lose only his place in the Queen's court and his social standing in the town. If he'd been warned to curb his daughter's behavior and had ignored the warning—or had prevented complaints from reaching the Queen—he might be having a chat with the High Lord of Hell very soon.

He waited for the Master and the Steward to leave the shop before he vanished his war blade and released the shield he had wrapped around Bekka. He took the paper from the counter and vanished that too.

"Thank you, Prince," Graham said. He looked at Bekka. "Thank you for everything."

"If anyone gives you or your family trouble over this, you come to me," Lucivar said.

As soon as he walked out of the shop, the people still standing on the other side of the street scurried into shops to get out of sight.

"Are you all right?" Daemon asked quietly. He looked relaxed, standing there with his hands in his trouser pockets, but Lucivar knew better.

"I'm fine. You?" He scanned the street, then used psychic tendrils to get a taste of the emotions of the people around him. More relief than fear.

"Leave the bitch to me."

Lucivar studied his brother. "Do you know everything she's done, everything she owes?"

Daemon's smile was viciously gentle. "No, but she does."

Nothing he could imagine doing would be close to whatever savagery Daemon had in mind. "Then deal with her."

"It will be a pleasure."

He would find out soon enough. "I'm going to need your help for one more confrontation."

"I thought this was the last name on your list."

"It was. I'm going to have to attend one of those fancy dances."

"You need my help choosing your wardrobe?"

"Nah. I know what I'm wearing. I just need your help to stop me from turning a dance into a slaughter."

Now Daemon studied him. "Are you sure you want me to do that?"

"No, but it's better if you do."

"In that case, Prick, let's get back to your eyrie before Surreal rips into us for missing your curfew."

He laughed softly, then fell into step with Daemon as they headed for the town's landing web.

After dinner, all the adults had spent time with the children, playing games. Now the yappy horde was brushed and bathed, and Manny was reading them a story while Marian put the baby to bed.

Surreal settled in one of the chairs in Lucivar's study.

"Brandy?" Daemon asked, holding up the decanter.

"Please." The hunt had been invigorating, but spending the past few days listening to girls' stories about Dillon, who was dreamy or a cad or a little bit of both, had left her feeling uncomfortable, made her think too much of her own mistakes.

She was ready to go home.

Daemon poured brandy for all of them, then sat in the other chair near Lucivar's desk. He smiled at her and said, "How was your day?"

A polite, husbandly question.

"It would have been better if I could have slipped a stiletto between someone's ribs and twisted the blade, but the girl who wanted to 'squeeze his head until his eyeballs popped out' was quite entertaining." Surreal sipped her brandy. "I couldn't decide if she was talking about Dillon or her father, but I can see why Dillon ran from that one. I also talked to a woman who was about a decade older than our prick-ass. She became quite agitated when I said I didn't know where he lived. She insisted that he had invited her to stay with him, that they had an 'understanding.'" She took another sip before looking at Lucivar. "You should have a Black Widow take a look at her in order to assess her mental stability. I think she's going to cause someone serious trouble."

"Done," Lucivar said. "Anything else?"

Did she want to tell him? Damn it, she had to tell him. "And I castrated a Warlord at an art exhibition."

Lucivar and Daemon lowered their brandy snifters and looked at her. She smiled at them. A big, big smile.

"It was very neatly done with Craft, although some of the pieces of art on display would have been improved by blood and gore."

"Okay," Lucivar said. "Why?"

"Let's just say it was a debt he owed the daughter he already has but won't acknowledge. If the report doesn't show up at the Keep in a few days, I'll tell you where to find the Warlord who brought this to my attention."

"Did the Warlord understand who you are?" Daemon asked.

"He did. And I think he had a good understanding of what I would do with the information."

Lucivar rubbed his forehead and sighed. "One debt settled. More to go. What do we do about Dillon?"

Surreal set the brandy snifter on the desk. "He played some games with Jillian to make her feel uneducated and socially inferior, and I want to slap him for that. But he wasn't like that when this started—and there is still a measure of kindness in him. If Lady Blyte had done nothing more than go back on her promise of a handfast after taking him to her bed, Dillon would have been heart-bruised and his reputation would have had a smudge, but he wouldn't have been any different from plenty of other young men who went to the marriage bed before the marriage. That bitch turning him into prey for every other aristo bitch who wanted a ride and hounding him from one town to the next . . . He could have made other choices, and he's responsible for his actions, but, Hell's fire, I feel a little sorry for the fool, and I don't want to feel sorry for him." She grabbed the snifter and gulped the rest of the brandy.

"More?" Daemon asked.

"No. Thanks." The burn was kind of pleasant in a painful sort of way.

"We have a good idea of what Blyte did to Dillon, but what about what *he* did to the girls who came after her?" Lucivar said.

"He didn't have sex with any girl who was still a virgin and refused to take any girl through her Virgin Night—which the girls thought was very romantic and proved his good intentions," Surreal replied. "However, their aristo fathers, not wanting their families' social standing soiled by association, preferred to pay Dillon to sneak out of town. Paying him to leave didn't stop them from smearing his reputation further by implying—or saying outright—that he dallied with girls of good families and then left instead of going through with the handfast because he had no honor. In truth, he was driven out of some towns before he had a chance to unpack his trunk, so the actual number of girls he entangled was far fewer than you would have thought, based on what was said."

"The spell he used on Jillian?" Daemon asked.

"I'm not sure how long he'd been using that spell, because no one but you realized he'd used one." Surreal hooked her hair behind her delicately pointed ears. "I had the impression he used it more to convince the girls to lend him money than for anything more intimate. When he met

Jillian . . ." She sighed and couldn't look at either man. "I think he hoped having someone love him would give him a second chance at an honorable life."

She felt a flash of pain rising up in the abyss before it was brutally smothered. That flash was enough confirmation that Daemon's love for, and marriage to, Jaenelle Angelline had given him the same kind of second chance—and that, along with Jaenelle being the love of his life and the Queen he'd dreamed of serving, was the reason she would always be the presence he needed with him more than he needed breath or life.

She pushed out of her chair. "So that's it. Jaenelle Saetien and I will be heading out in the morning. I think Manny and Tersa are ready to go home too."

"And the Scelties," Lucivar growled.

Two of them, anyway. She was not going to be the one who said anything about the Sceltie who was currently staying in Nurian's eyrie.

"I'll be home in a couple of days," Daemon said quietly.

"We'll be there."

She walked out of Lucivar's study and wondered if Daemon really would give her a second chance.

Daemon stared at the study door a moment longer before refilling his snifter and topping up Lucivar's. He resumed his seat.

Lucivar called in a paper, then used Craft to float it across the desk. "The names of the bastards who maimed that Warlord to curry favor with the bitch."

"If you have no objection, I'll let Chaosti and his men take care of this. They would appreciate the fresh blood, and they'll take the meat back to Hell for the hounds."

"That's fine with me." Lucivar rested his head on the back of his leather chair and stared at the ceiling. "Hell's fire, Bastard. I'm tired."

He understood that kind of tired. "It's not done yet."

"I know. The spell to manipulate feelings was bad enough. Using it to compel a person to kill someone out of meanness or jealousy . . ." Lucivar sat up, stretched one side of his neck, then the other. "Whatever you want to do with Dillon, I'll back you."

"All right. I've made some inquiries already. Based on what we've discovered, I think he needs a fresh start someplace where he won't run into bad memories."

Lucivar nodded. "Coming to Kaeleer gave us that kind of fresh start."

"It did. And so much more."

Another nod. "And Jillian?"

"She needs a change of scenery too," Daemon said gently.

"She's so young."

"She's not that young, Prick. She's outgrown what she can find here in Ebon Rih. At least for right now."

He watched Lucivar struggle with the idea of letting a daughter fly beyond his protection. That was an internal battle every father faced.

"Where?" Lucivar finally said.

When Daemon told him, Lucivar groaned, "Mother Night"—and then laughed.

"My boy."

Taking a step away from the eyrie's front door, Daemon looked toward the shadows in one corner of the room.

He and Lucivar hadn't expected Tersa to accompany Manny when the older woman returned to help Marian look after the children and the eyrie, but neither of them had suggested that the broken Black Widow go home. Manny provided practical help, but the White-Jeweled witch had no fighting skills in the event that Lucivar's family was attacked during this investigation. Tersa, on the other hand, could be fiercely—and weirdly—lethal.

"Darling, it's late. Why are you still awake?"

He watched her as she approached him—his mother, with her broken mind and extraordinary knowledge.

Tersa rested one hand against the side of his face. "Not well yet, but healing."

"Yes. I'm healing."

Her hand drifted from his face, down his shoulder, stopping at the wounds on his right arm that he'd hidden from everyone. "They will scar."

"Yes. Remembrance and reminder. I will carry them with me, just as I've carried this one." He pushed up his left cuff to show her the scar she'd given him all those years ago.

Tersa smiled. "She promised that if you asked for help, she would answer."

It didn't surprise him that Tersa had been the one to ask Witch for a promise—and receive one. What surprised him was that he'd never thought to ask his mother what she knew about the song in the Darkness. Maybe she'd known all along that some part of Witch was still at the Keep. Maybe that was a gem of knowledge mislaid in the Twisted Kingdom and recently found again because it was truly needed. He doubted she could tell him, and it no longer mattered.

He took her in his arms, rested his face against her head as she rested against his chest.

"I'm not whole, Mother," he said quietly. "I might never be whole. But I will do my best to heal and stay with all of you for as long as I can."

"I know." She eased away from him. "Don't turn away from help offered with love."

"I won't."

"Don't turn away."

That sounded more like a warning that he might not recognize what was offered.

"I won't," he said again.

"The Tagg pup will live with the Mikal boy and me."

"Tagg is too young and—"

"He needs the Mikal boy."

He could hear his father telling him not to argue with his mother. Not that he'd win this argument. Clearly Tersa had already decided about boy and puppy. He'd have to see if boy and puppy agreed with her. "I'll make the arrangements."

Tersa smiled and walked away.

Daemon returned to the Keep and gave Chaosti the list of men who wouldn't see another sunrise—and wouldn't make the transition to demon-dead. After the Dea al Mon Warlord Prince and his men headed for that Rihland town, Daemon retreated to the Consort's suite.

He called in a wooden frame and his supply of spider silk and wove a tangled web for the aristo bitch who had tried to turn love into a weapon.

"Does she deserve that?" Witch asked when he sat back to consider his work.

"She does," he replied. "For everyone else, it is warning and lesson that, from now on, there will be a steep price for using the 'if you loved me' spell."

He felt her hand on his shoulder, watched her face as she leaned forward to study the tangled web. Then Witch smiled at him and said, "You need to make the teeth sharper."

If you loved me . . .

 If you loved me . . .

 If you loved me . . .

At first, she couldn't remember where she was. Not her own bedroom.

Now she remembered. She hoped Graham ended up in the bowels of Hell! If he'd done what she'd told him to do instead of fighting her control, that manthief Bekka would be dead, ripped up by Graham's own hand, and he would be so sorry that he hadn't been nicer to her, hadn't done what she'd wanted.

Something coiled around her legs, around her arms, around her waist.

If you loved me, you would tell the truth.

Before she could scream, the darkness in the room softened until she could clearly see the plant coiled around her limbs and torso.

If you loved me, you would tell them about the games you've played. All the nasty games.

Was that the plant whispering to her? But wasn't that . . . ?

As she watched, buds the size of her fist opened. Each flower had her face. Each flower whispered in her voice.

If you loved me, you would tell them about everyone you hurt.

If you loved me . . .

Dreaming. Yes. But such a delicious dream with her face blooming all around her.

"What?" she whispered. "If you loved me . . . what?"

Everything has a price, the blooms whispered in reply.

As she watched, the lips turned black and curled away from mouths filled with serrated teeth.

Tell them everything, the blooms whispered. *We feast every night until you tell them everything and the debt is paid.*

For a moment, all the flowers hung over her as if waiting for her to speak. Then the mouths opened, the teeth bit . . . and she screamed and screamed while the flowers with her face tore out chunks of her flesh.

THIRTY-EIGHT

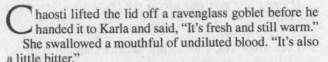

Chaosti lifted the lid off a ravenglass goblet before he handed it to Karla and said, "It's fresh and still warm."

She swallowed a mouthful of undiluted blood. "It's also a little bitter."

"Fear leaves that taste," he replied. "The blood was part of the payment for a debt owed. Drink. My men and I have had our fill. And I brought some back for Draca and Geoffrey."

She wasn't going to ask how many bodies had made up that payment. She just drank the blood and watched Chaosti watching her. "Yes?"

"Curious thing. A witch was detained in the town where we were hunting. Apparently she tried to use a spell to compel a Warlord to kill the woman he loved."

"That was naughty of her."

"In the middle of the night, she began screaming that the flowers with her face were biting her and she had to tell the Queen every bad thing she had done using the 'if you loved me' spell, because each bad thing was a bloom, and until she said it all, the flowers would come back every night and feast."

Karla shuddered. Couldn't help it. "Was there any physical confirmation of her nightmare?"

"Nothing." Chaosti considered. "Although that may

change if the blooms return on another night." He continued to watch her. "I heard the teeth were quite impressive. It occurred to me creating something like that would take a great deal of skill."

"I didn't weave that tangled web, if that's what you're asking."

"You didn't help with any details?"

Then she realized what he'd been looking to confirm. Oh, she still had the skill to create a tangled web as a form of punishment, but she wouldn't have thought to be that exquisitely cruel, and Chaosti knew that. That was when she understood what he was really asking. Who else would help the Sadist refine the details of a punishment that would not only pay a debt but be a warning to everyone who thought to play with another person's heart?

And that made her curious. "Just how impressive were those teeth?"

While Manny, Tersa, Jaenelle Saetien, and Tagg made their way to the landing web located below the eyrie and took their seats in the Coach for the journey home, Surreal and Marian searched for Morghann, who had disappeared sometime before dawn.

Morghann, Surreal called. *Come on, Morghann. It's time to go home.*

No answer.

"Maybe she went to Nurian's eyrie to stay with Khary," Marian said.

"Khary says she isn't there."

"Then she's here. Somewhere." Marian put her hands on her hips. "Daemonar and Titian swore they haven't seen her this morning. Well, you go on. She'll turn up when she gets hungry."

Surreal raked her fingers through her hair. "I brought three Scelties. I'm going back with one. Lucivar is going to bounce off the ceiling."

Marian didn't disagree but said, "You requested the Scelties as chaperons, but Daemon actually brought them to Ebon Rih."

"So this is his fault." Much better.

"I wouldn't have put it that way, but you're not wrong."

They were alone in this part of the eyrie. When would she get another chance to ask the question? "I was told Daemon's sexual heat is going to stay this potent for the centuries while he's in his prime. The same thing must be happening with Lucivar. How do you endure it?"

Marian looked uncomfortable. "If this final stage has already happened, it must have been more gradual than what Daemon experienced. And Lucivar's work takes him out of the eyrie for a good part of each day, while Daemon works at the Hall, so his sexual heat might . . . accumulate . . . despite the size of the place. A couple times each month, Lucivar stays away for a day or two, camping out on the mountain. There's a hunting eyrie not far from here. Might have been a guard post long ago. It's small, just big enough for a couple of men. His 'weather bones' don't respond well to sleeping outside in the winter, so he's fixed it up and keeps a good supply of wood for the fire. It's close enough that he can be home in a few minutes if I need him, but it's far enough away that . . ." She hesitated.

"That you don't feel the heat," Surreal finished.

"He's my husband. I've gotten used to living with his heat, but the days when he's away from home, it's like breathing in crisp air after being inside a house that's too warm. We've never talked about it, but I enjoy him more as a lover because of those absences." Marian huffed out a breath. "And if we're being honest, if Daemon is going to be spending a few days each month at the Keep in order to give you the same kind of breathing room, I hope Lucivar joins him at least part of the time."

"Why?"

"Because things are about to change for him. He's going to shoulder all the weight that Andulvar carried. I hope that won't change things for him here in the valley. I hope it won't change things for either of us here, because Ebon Rih is our home. But it's going to change who he is to the rest of the people in Askavi—to the rest of Kaeleer."

Surreal felt a shiver of alarm. "Marian? What are you talking about? What's going to change? Is this more than Lucivar becoming the Warlord Prince of Askavi?"

"He told you?"

"He said enough that I heard what wasn't said."

"I had more time to get to know Andulvar and Saetan than you did," Marian said. "I had more time to see why they needed each other. You wear the Gray, and there aren't many who do, but there are some. There are some who know what it feels like to stand where you do in the abyss. But wearing the Ebon-gray and Black, Andulvar and Saetan were alone, vessels of power so dark and deep they had no one but each other. Just like Lucivar and Daemon." She looked around. "Well. You have people waiting for you. We'll get Morghann to the Hall when we find her."

Nothing more to say right now and only one thing to do. Surreal hurried out of the eyrie and down to the landing web, where the Coach waited to take them home.

Daemon met Lucivar in one of the Keep's parlors.

"Is that your first or second breakfast?" Daemon asked as he watched Lucivar shovel in a mouthful of oatmeal.

"I wasn't expected, so I think this is part of yours." Lucivar filled the spoon with another mound of oatmeal and held it out. "Open up."

Taking the spoon, Daemon ate the oatmeal, then handed back the spoon. "Now I can say I ate my oatmeal and won't get scolded. You can have the rest and I'll have . . ." He lifted the covers off the serving dishes. "Steak, eggs, and mushrooms."

"If Daemonar picks up that 'one spoonful is sufficient' piss-ass excuse from you, you and I will have words."

"Don't be silly, Prick. A growing boy needs his oatmeal." Daemon filled his plate. "Besides, the last time Daemonar visited the Hall, I caught him sharing his bowl of oatmeal with Khary." He waited a beat. "Sharing the bowl and sharing the spoon."

Lucivar sighed. "His mother doesn't need to know that."

"Well, I'm not going to tell her. I wouldn't take any bets on your boy, though."

With a grunt that might have been suppressed laughter, Lucivar finished the oatmeal, then poured mugs of coffee for both of them.

"You sure about this?" Daemon asked. There were shadows in Lucivar's gold eyes that hadn't been there a few days ago.

"I'm sure it needs to be done."

"Tonight?"

Lucivar nodded. "I brought the papers. They just need to be witnessed."

"Then I guess we should take care of the other business today."

"Yeah, I guess we should."

Confined to the room in the communal eyrie, Dillon had plenty of time to think about the girls who had used him and the girls he, in turn, had used. He had plenty of time to consider the choices he'd made—and he wasn't proud of most of them.

He should have stopped pursuing Jillian after Yaslana choked him for nothing more than a kiss and a feel—which he shouldn't have done in the first place. At least, not in a public place, where the actions showed a lack of respect for the girl. He should have backed away from her once he realized she was too young despite being centuries old.

He should have stayed away from Blyte when she said, "If you loved me," and then broke his heart and ruined his reputation.

He should have done—and not done—a lot of things.

They clearly disliked him for using the spell on Jillian, but the Eyriens had not been unkind. Whichever one was on guard escorted him to the showers in the morning and to the toilet a few times each day. They fed him, not that he had much of an appetite, and provided him with books to read as a way to pass the time. But no one would talk to him or tell him what was going to happen to him. He was confined and awaiting judgment.

As the days dragged on, he wondered if the waiting was part of the punishment.

The door opened. Dillon turned away from the window, expecting to finally face Yaslana. But it wasn't Yaslana who walked into the room and closed the door; it was Daemon Sadi.

"Lord Dillon."

Sadi's deep voice curled around him. Tightened around him as the man glided across the room. Dillon took a step back, then another until his back was pressed against the wall and there was nowhere to go.

Sadi merely raised one eyebrow and waited a beat. "A decision has been made, Warlord," the Prince said.

Dillon pushed away from the wall and approached the small table, which was nothing more than a token barrier between them.

"There is something I'd like to say first."

"Go ahead."

Dillon let out a shaky breath. "I've made bad choices. Other people's actions may have spurred those choices, but I'm the one who made them. I've used some girls in order to get money from their families, and I let myself become just like the girls who had used me, and that's my fault and my shame. This isn't who I wanted to be."

"You wanted to be an escort and serve in a Queen's court. You wanted to be a husband someday and live an honorable life," Sadi said quietly.

"Yes. That's what I wanted." Dillon huffed out a bitter laugh. "No chance of having any of that now, is there?"

"There is a chance." Sadi called in sheets of paper and laid them on the table. "Here are the names of six District Queens—two in Dharo, two in Nharkhava, and two in Scelt. As a favor to Yaslana, and to me, these Queens are willing to give you a place in their courts—most likely as a Third Circle escort, since you haven't completed your formal training. You'll receive that training in any court listed there. You'll find information about the courts and the Territories where they're located. Think carefully about what you want before you choose."

"I can serve in a court?" District Queens meant small territories, a handful of villages at the most, in Territories far away from Askavi—places Rihlander aristo families wouldn't know. Places that, and people who, wouldn't know his past except for the Queen, her Steward, and her Master of the Guard. A fresh start. A real second chance.

"The Queen you choose will send me a report every quarter. If I'm satisfied that you are behaving honorably and being diligent in your training, I will supply you with a stipend to help with your expenses. I also want something in return—that you repay whatever unkindness you visited on the girls here in Askavi by being kind to girls who might be overlooked, whether it's as small as giving someone a compliment that brightens her day or asking a girl for a dance because you noticed no one else has asked her."

"Why are you doing this? Why isn't Prince Yaslana here to grind my bones into the floor?"

"You helped a woman and her daughter. I think that choice was a reflection of who you had been before you met Lady Blyte—and, maybe, who you still are." Then Sadi smiled. "Besides, Jillian settled things between you to everyone's satisfaction—except, perhaps, yours. As much as Yaslana dislikes you right now, your arrival in Ebon Rih made him aware of a problem that can't be allowed to continue, so he left your fate with me. As to why I'm doing this?" The smile faded. "I know how much a life can change when a man is given a second chance."

Sadi walked to the door and stopped. "You'll be escorted back to your cousin's house in Riada. When you decide which Queen you would like to serve, inform Lord Rothvar. He'll arrange for a Coach and driver to take you there."

"Thank you, Prince."

He couldn't interpret the look in Sadi's eyes when the Prince said, "Don't give us a reason to regret this decision."

Then Sadi was gone.

While he waited for the Eyrien who would escort him to his cousin's house, Dillon read over the information about the six courts. For the first time in a long time, he felt hopeful about his future.

Jillian wasn't sure what Prince Yaslana wanted her to say. She wasn't sure if *he* knew what he wanted her to say.

"You want to send me away?"

The muscles in his jaw worked, and he didn't quite meet her eyes. "Want to? No. But it has been suggested that you would benefit from experience outside of Ebon Rih."

What did that mean? "Like a visit to Dhemlan?"

Yaslana winced. "That's a bit far."

Far? She accompanied Marian and the children whenever the hearth witch wanted to visit Amdarh to shop or see a play. The SaDiablo family had a town house there, and they all usually stayed in the side of the town house kept for guests.

"This would be more than a visit," Yaslana said. "This would be a kind of apprenticeship in a court. Sadi made the inquiries and received consent. He can tell you more about it. If you're interested. Not that you have to be interested. You're young. But . . . something different for a while."

Something different. Yes. Would Dillon have seemed so attractive if she hadn't been looking for something different? But going away to somewhere that wasn't home? Living among people she didn't know? Exciting but . . .

"Could I bring a friend?" she asked.

Yaslana finally looked at her, and she had the feeling he was bracing himself because he knew what she was about to say.

"Who did you have in mind?"

When she told him, he swore softly, vigorously. Finally, he said, "It could take a few days, but I'll see if it can be arranged."

She watched him fly away and still wasn't sure what he'd wanted her to say. She'd have to talk to Marian about finding someone to help with the children, and talk to Nurian, of course. But Yaslana wouldn't have mentioned it at all if he didn't believe she was ready to fly on her own. She was sure of that much.

THIRTY-NINE

Lucivar called in the double-buckle fighting belt that Eyriens wore in battle, then sheathed a fighting knife that was bigger, heavier, and a lot meaner than the hunting knife worn as standard dress. A palm-sized knife went into the sheath between the belt buckles. Two more knives were sheathed in the boots.

Chain mail settled over the light leather vest. Metal-studded leather gauntlets closed over wrists and forearms.

Last, he created two Ebon-gray shields—one skintight, the other barely a breath above his skin.

He looked at the other man in the room and nodded. "I'm ready."

He wasn't getting ready to attend some fancy aristo dance.

Lucivar Yaslana was getting ready for war.

Lucivar scanned the crowded room filled with bright dresses and too-bright voices. Finding the enemy, he called in his war blade and moved forward a couple of steps, then braced as the unleashed sexual heat that flowed in behind him washed over the crowd of aristo Blood, making them gasp, making them want, making them think that the heat promised hot pleasure when what it really promised was frigid pain.

He had come for war. The Sadist had come to play.

It amounted to the same thing.

He took a few more steps toward his quarry. The Blood moved aside, giving him a clear path.

"Before she left the living Realms, the Queen of Ebon Askavi signed a document that put all of Askavi under my hand," Lucivar said, using Craft to make his voice thunder through the building. "She told me I wasn't required to become the Warlord Prince of Askavi, that I could allow the District Queens and the Province Queens above them independent rule, unless the time came when they permitted Terreillean practices to encroach on the Blood here. Looking the other way when reputations are ruined and honor soiled because some bitch thinks it's fun to damage other people's lives as long as she suffers no consequences? That's how the destruction of the Blood begins. Some of your ancestors fled from Terreille in order to escape those kinds of games, and those games are what I pledged to fight against when I came to Kaeleer. They are what I will always fight against, even if that means turning every Rihland city into a killing field and slaughtering every Rihland aristo in Askavi."

The stink of fear filled the room as the aristos looked at him, then looked at the Sadist, and recognized living weapons that were harnessed to a single purpose.

"As of today, I don't care if the person is male or female. I don't care how aristo their family bloodline is or who they can claim in their family line—or if they are the least powerful person in a village. I do not care. Any transaction between individuals or families that ends with a reputation at risk or honor being questioned or someone being harmed in any way will be investigated by the court of the Queen who rules that village, and monthly reports will be sent to the Province Queens for review. If I hear of any attempt to hide an impropriety, the Province Queens will answer to me, and from now on, the price for looking the other way will be steep. But tonight, as warning and lesson, I'll start with you."

Lucivar raised his war blade and pointed it at Lady Blyte, the bitch whose behavior had started Lord Dillon— and him—down this path. "All the Queens in Askavi will be given the names of the men you played by promising a handfast in exchange for them becoming your lover. You owe those men a debt because you then claimed ignorance of the promises you made and allowed your father to damage the reputation of those men to the point of them being considered prey for other women who had no honorable intentions. The Rihlander Queens will make reparation by seeing that those men are given a position in a court and sufficient income to support themselves, or they will make arrangements for those men to work at an honest trade— and they will guarantee on their Jewels that they will stop any further attempts to use the past as a hammer against those men's efforts to restore their reputations and honor. The Rihlander Queens will do this for the men who are still among the living. There was one who was so filled with despair after dealing with this *Lady* that he found death preferable to remaining among the living.

"And you, you smug bitch. Do you think I'll let you walk away from this without paying what you owe?"

That was exactly what she believed. He saw it in her eyes. He also saw a keen hatred for him because he had exposed her and made her behavior a public humiliation.

"Everything has a price," he said, letting his voice go quiet so that everyone strained to hear. "And you are the lesson of what it will cost anyone who plays Terreillean games in my Territory."

Rising out of the depths of the abyss like an Ebon-gray arrow of fury, Lucivar struck Blyte with power to shatter her Jewels, breaking her back to basic Craft. She screamed as the Jewels in her pendant and ring shattered and fell to the floor.

"You have been stripped of your power," Lucivar said. "You will always be a Blood female, but you are no longer a witch and will no longer be addressed by the title of Lady. Your debt to the men you harmed has been paid."

He turned and walked toward the doorway where his brother waited. He didn't need to see Daemon focus on something behind him. He felt the anger rushing toward him.

"You bastard!" Blyte's father cried, brandishing a decorative knife.

If it had been nothing more than the knife, which couldn't get past his shields, he might have let the man go with nothing more than a slap. But the Warlord unleashed a blast of power in a way that made Lucivar wonder if the young man who had died really had taken his own life.

Everything that made him a Warlord Prince responded to that lash of power. Lucivar pivoted, using Craft to extend the length of the war blade as he met the Warlord's eyes.

The war blade sang through muscle, humbled bone.

For a moment, nothing seemed to happen. For a moment, it looked like the blade hadn't sliced anything but the man's jacket as some of the fabric fluttered to the floor. Then blood spilled from the man's waist; his legs buckled, and the top half of the man slid off and struck the floor. Using Craft to stand on air just above the red lake rapidly forming on the ballroom floor, Lucivar looked at the stunned crowd. "Does anyone else need a lesson?"

No answer except more screams from Blyte, but he doubted her distress had anything to do with the loss of her father and more to do with finally being punished for her own actions.

Turning toward the doorway once again, Lucivar saw Chaosti walk in with two young Rihlander men.

Daemon smiled a cold, cruel smile. Not the Sadist now. This was the High Lord of Hell.

You can't leave him here to make the transition to demon-dead, the High Lord said. *He won't go to Hell on his own, as he should, not after you made his family's deceits so public. Besides, one of those men deserved a chance to see the debt paid.* He looked at the two Warlords who carried out the upper half of the girl's father.

Lucivar waited for Chaosti and Daemon to follow the demon-dead Warlords out of the room. Then he turned back one last time and looked at the Rihland aristos. "Every attempt to bring Terreille's ways into Kaeleer will be met with slaughter. Spread the word that I'll be calling on the Province Queens soon to have a little chat."

He walked away, knowing there would be more slaughter before they believed he had drawn the line—knowing some courts would be torn apart for tacitly supporting the cruelty that had destroyed the Blood in Terreille. Knowing that, after tonight, most of the Blood in Askavi would call him the Demon Prince.

Everything had a price.

FORTY

❖
─────────

Lucivar hadn't appreciated how much fury had been festering under the surface of some Rihland towns and cities until several places exploded in savage fighting, as if his breaking that one bitch had been a flame dropped on tinder, freeing that fury to blaze through Askavi. The Blood in those places didn't want his help. The Warlord Princes in those places didn't want his Eyrien warriors coming in to settle anything. They would talk to him when the fighting was done.

For two days, he stayed at the Keep with Daemon, listening to reports as Rothvar and his other men rode the Winds throughout Askavi to get a feel for what was happening in the Rihland cities. Some Provinces were untouched by fighting. Lucivar found it grimly amusing that Daemon's prediction had been right about the Queens who ruled those Provinces. They were the first to show up at the Keep to talk to him, bringing documents to prove they had been drawing the same line all along and that any smear on someone's honor or reputation was something that person had deserved.

"You're going to need help, Lucivar," Daemon said when the sun set on that second day and they were finally alone for a few minutes. "Someone besides Marian. Someone you can trust who won't be intimidated when dealing with Queens who wear darker Jewels."

"Who?" Frustrated, Lucivar raked a hand through his hair. "Every Eyrien who works for me will stand with me on a killing field, but every one of them has had his fill of dealing with Queens."

"Not to mention that most of them would rather chew off his own fingers than deal with paperwork," Daemon said dryly.

"Andulvar didn't have to deal with paperwork. If there was a problem, he went to that village and killed what couldn't be fixed."

"That might not have been how he handled things when he walked among the living," Daemon pointed out.

They both knew he wanted to ask Daemon to deal with the paperwork—and they both knew why he couldn't. Daemon already had enough under his hand.

"Rothvar is your second-in-command when it comes to defending Ebon Rih—and now all of Askavi. You need someone who can act as your second in command for the business side of ruling the Territory."

"Someone who isn't Eyrien or Rihland, someone who is willing to deal with paperwork and knows what is important and what is crap, someone who can't be intimidated by darker-Jeweled Queens. Who can do that, Bastard? Tell me who I can trust who can do that."

Lucivar looked over as the door opened, and said, "Hell's fire."

Karla gave him a bright smile and said, "Kiss kiss."

FORTY-ONE

D illon listened to the raised voices in the parlor and
winced as he looked at his cousin's pale face. "I'm
sorry, Terrence. I never meant to cause trouble for your
family. Is your father going to lose his position in the Riada Queen's court?"

"Dunno."

Seeing the misery in Terrence's eyes, Dillon suspected
that the family's social standing in the village was going to
be nonexistent because they had allowed him to stay after
his aborted romance with Jillian.

With the women's voices a shrill counterpoint to the
men's shouts, Dillon wasn't sure he'd heard someone
knock on the front door until the sound came a second
time. When none of the servants appeared to answer it,
Dillon opened the door.

Lucivar Yaslana stepped inside. "Lord Dillon."

"Prince."

Yaslana nodded to Terrence, then looked toward the
parlor. He didn't ask who was shouting or why. He just
opened the parlor door and walked in—and everyone
stopped talking.

The Warlord Prince of Askavi wagged a finger at Dillon and Terrence. "You two, in here." He waited for them,
then looked at the adults in the room before focusing on

Dillon. "The matter has been settled. The witch who destroyed your reputation and smeared your honor has been broken back to basic Craft. Reparation will be made to every man she deceived. While your actions weren't prudent where she was concerned, lots of young men go through a stage where they think with the head behind their zippers instead of the head above their shoulders."

Dillon choked. Terrence wheezed.

"And if there is a man here who didn't have sex with the woman he married before the contract was signed, let him step forward," Yaslana continued.

No one stepped forward. Women blushed. Men studied the carpet just beyond their shoes.

Now Yaslana looked at Terrence's father. "It will take a couple more days before arrangements can be made to send Lord Dillon to the court he's chosen. If you're not comfortable having him stay with you, I'll arrange to have him stay at The Tavern."

"No, no. Better for the boy to be with his family."

"I agree, but you might be criticized for that compassion, and I wouldn't want obliging me to cause problems for you." He looked around the room. "But if you do have problems, I want to know, because what happened to Lord Dillon could have happened to anyone's son, and that is something your neighbors shouldn't forget."

Dillon and Terrence walked out with him. At the front door, Yaslana paused. "You make a decision yet?"

"Almost," Dillon replied. "I decided against the two courts in Scelt. Not that I wouldn't like to visit there someday, but I can't imagine living in a place overrun by dogs who poke their noses into everyone's business."

Yaslana huffed out a laugh and muttered something that sounded like "May the Darkness have mercy on me."

As he opened the front door, Dillon gathered his courage and said, "Prince? Could I see Jillian before I leave?"

Yaslana stared at him. "That will depend on whether or not Jillian wants to see you."

Dillon and Terrence stood in the doorway and watched Lucivar Yaslana walk down the street.

"I've never been to another Territory," Terrence said. "Never considered going someplace else for part of my training. Maybe you could let me know what it's like?"

Dillon felt surprise as well as pleasure. "You want to stay in touch?"

"I do."

His parents didn't want any contact with him. Neither did his brothers. But here, where he hadn't expected anything but reluctant tolerance, he had found a friend—and family.

Terrence smiled shyly. "Maybe I could even visit after you've earned some time off."

Dillon returned the smile. "I'd like that."

FORTY-TWO

———⬦———

Jillian led Daemon Sadi to the sitting room in her sister's eyrie. "I've made coffee, if you'd like some."

"I would. Thank you." Sadi called in a box and held it out. "I brought these."

"From the Sweet Tooth?"

"No."

She waited until she was in the kitchen to open the plain white box. Fresh-baked pastries that she was pretty sure came from the bakery on Riada's main street. Nothing fancy, but the taste made up for the lack of fanciness. She filled a dish with the treats, then added it to the tray that already held two mugs of coffee and napkins. Returning to the sitting room, she set everything out on a table.

"Did Lucivar tell you about the apprenticeship in a court?" Sadi asked.

"He said you had talked to a Queen and would tell me about it. He also said you would have to decide about me bringing a friend." She handed him a mug of coffee and felt bold and a little reckless when she said, "Have you decided?"

"I had the impression that *that* decision was already made and my consent is superfluous, but you have it. As for the apprenticeship, you've been offered a six-month contract to serve in the Queen of Little Weeble's court."

Jillian blinked. "The Queen of what?"

"Little Weeble. It's a small village on the coast of Askavi. Far enough but not too far from home. No mountains there, but you'd have a chance to live in a village that focuses on fishing and spend time with Rihlanders who have a different way of looking at just about everything."

The name tickled her. But . . . "Do you think Prince Yaslana would consent to me going there?"

"He'll give his consent. He's struggling with the idea of letting you fly on your own, but if you send him a letter every few days to let him know how you're getting on, Lucivar might resist checking up on you in person every day."

"But he doesn't like to read."

Sadi smiled. "Darling, if you wrote him a letter, he would read it. And after he read it, he would tuck it in a drawer in his desk so that he could look at it every day and reassure himself that letting you go was the right thing to do."

"Then I'd like to go. I'd like to experience something beyond the villages in Ebon Rih."

"Dillon will be leaving Askavi in a few days. He asked to see you before you go."

"I—" Did she want to see him? Was there any point? "All right."

"Are you sure?"

Jillian nodded.

"Then I'll deliver the message." Sadi selected a pastry and took a bite. "I'm curious about something."

"What?" *Please don't ask me why I was attracted to Dillon in the first place. I don't want to admit that having a crush on you is the reason I liked him.*

"What did Dillon finally say that made you angry enough to hit him?"

Finally say? That meant there had been other things that should have sparked her anger. Something to think about at another time. "He said Prince Yaslana wasn't my father."

"Is he?" Sadi asked gently. "Is Lucivar your father?"

Jillian looked the Warlord Prince of Dhemlan in the eyes. "In every way that counts."

FORTY-THREE

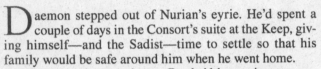

Daemon stepped out of Nurian's eyrie. He'd spent a couple of days in the Consort's suite at the Keep, giving himself—and the Sadist—time to settle so that his family would be safe around him when he went home.

He was ready to go home. But he'd been given a message to see Lucivar before leaving Ebon Rih. He caught one of the Winds and rode to the landing web below the Yaslana eyrie. As he climbed the stairs to the flagstone courtyard, he wondered why Khary hadn't been with Jillian while they had talked about the girl going to Perzha's court. He'd have thought the Sceltie would have had any number of opinions about going to an unknown village and court.

Maybe it was as simple as Jillian not wanting the Sceltie to be disappointed if he wasn't included in this apprenticeship.

Khary's absence troubled him, but not as much as the control Daemon saw on Lucivar's face when his brother opened the door and stepped aside to let him in.

Daemonar found her this morning, Lucivar said on a Red spear thread.

Found . . . ? He looked toward the corner of the room where Daemonar knelt beside a whining ball of dirty fur.

"See?" Daemonar's hand rested on the fur. "I told you he would be back."

Shock sizzled through him, struck a blow to his heart. "Morghann?" He looked at Lucivar. "What happened? Is she hurt?"

"We'll talk later," Lucivar said quietly.

The Sceltic raised her head at the sound of his voice. Dull eyes brightened with joy. She uncurled, staggered a couple of steps, then ran to him. *Daemon! My Daemon!*

Afraid she would try to leap into his arms and fall, Daemon crouched to meet her and gather her up. "Morghann. Why are you still here, little Sister? Why didn't you go home with Lady Surreal and the others?"

I couldn't find you. She licked his chin before tucking her nose under his jacket, where she could breathe in his scent. *They left us.*

Us. He had plenty of questions, but feeling the trembling dog in his arms, he focused on other priorities.

"I think we should all have a snack," Lucivar said. "Then I'll drive you and Morghann home in a Coach."

"Maybe Morghann should have a bath before you go." Daemonar wrinkled his nose. "She's stinky."

Since holding her so close to his face made his eyes sting and water, Daemon didn't disagree. But as he followed Lucivar into the kitchen, he wondered where Morghann had been and what she'd been doing to smell that bad.

Watching the boy break up a small piece of cooked venison while Lucivar prepared a snack for the three humans, he also wondered how long she'd gone without food.

"Did you finish the private work you needed to do with the Queen?" Lucivar asked.

Daemonar's head snapped up, a question in his eyes. Daemon returned the look and knew for certain the boy had known about Witch's continued existence long before he and Lucivar had made the discovery.

"For now," Daemon replied.

Private? Morghann asked.

"Yes." Looking at her, he could barely force the food

down his throat, but he kept his voice calm, conversational. "The Lady has granted me permission to stay in her part of the Keep a few days each month in order to work on some private concerns." No need to tell the Sceltie, or the boy, that the work was about maintaining his sanity.

"I told you he was doing something important for the Lady," Daemonar said, feeding Morghann another piece of venison. Whatever else he might have said was silenced by a small shake of Lucivar's head.

Taking the Sceltie to the sinks in Marian's laundry room, Daemon gave Morghann a bath, while Daemonar crowded next to him, offering unnecessary advice.

"There's still some soap there, Uncle Daemon." Daemonar pointed to a spot on Morghann's flank. "You probably didn't see it because the shield on my arm is so bright—and blue."

"And what did the Lady say when you complained about it?"

The boy gave him a sour look. "She laughed."

She was a secret Daemonar hadn't told anyone, not even his father. Still a secret kept from most of the Realm. But now it was shared by the men who still served Witch—and always would.

Daemon took the second driver's seat in the Coach and settled Morghann on his lap. He couldn't order her to stay in the passenger area of the Coach while he sat up here with Lucivar. He feared giving that order would break something inside her. Until he knew why she'd been left behind, he accepted that she needed to feel his hand on her, needed to take in his scent with every breath.

Lucivar closed the Coach and settled in the other driver's seat. After guiding the Coach to the Webs of power that flowed in the Darkness, he caught the Ebon-gray Wind and headed for the Hall in Dhemlan.

What happened? Daemon asked on a Red spear thread.

From what I pieced together from the things Marian and Daemonar told me yesterday, Morghann hid instead of going with Surreal and the others, Lucivar replied. *At first, Marian thought she wanted to stay near Khary or had some other reason for staying at the eyrie and would show up when she got hungry. No one was concerned for the first couple of days, and no one mentioned it because you and I were dealing with larger problems.*

That was one way of describing a decision that had shaken all the Blood in Askavi.

Daemonar searched for her every day, Lucivar continued. *He even enlisted Tamnar to fly over the mountain with him in case she had left the eyrie and gotten lost. He and Marian told me about Morghann when I got home yesterday. I searched the whole damn eyrie and didn't find her. Daemonar finally located her early this morning when hunger must have made her weak enough that she couldn't maintain whatever Craft she'd used to hide from us.*

Why did she hide in the first place? Did something happen with the children?

Lucivar looked at him. *No, not the children.*

They left us, Morghann had said. "Us" meaning her . . . and him.

Daemon petted the Sceltie, who dozed in his lap, not sure how to feel about such single-minded loyalty.

Best I can figure, she wasn't leaving without you, Lucivar said. *And because she couldn't find you, she kept searching the place she knew without realizing you were at the Keep.*

The three Scelties living with us hadn't been to the Keep. There was no reason to take them there.

From what Daemonar could get out of her after he found her, she had decided that she must have done a wrong thing and that was why you had abandoned her.

I didn't—

No, you didn't.

Daemon closed his eyes. *She's an insecure baby. I should have asked Khary to stay with her and Tagg, but he thought Jillian needed him more.*

Wouldn't have made any difference if Khary had been staying in my home instead of with Jillian. This was about you, old son. You're Morghann's special friend in the same way that Jaenelle Angelline was Ladvarian's special friend.

Daemon opened his eyes and studied Lucivar. *What bothers you about this? Besides the obvious.*

Your insecure baby, who wears a Purple Dusk Jewel, managed to hide from me in my own home. From me, Daemon. That shouldn't have been possible.

Now Daemon studied the Sceltie. *How did she do it?*

You had an Arcerian cat staying with you for a while.

*And a unicorn. They went back to their home Territories soon after Jaenelle Saetien's Birthright Ceremony. She liked them, and they seemed to like her, but . . . *

She wasn't their dream, Lucivar finished. *The Arcerians haven't maintained ties to any of the human Blood, but they're still connected to the Scelties.*

Daemon nodded. *Yes, they are.*

Well, I think your Arcerian visitor taught your furry baby how to sight shield the way the cats do. Unless you know what that particular bit of Craft feels like when they use it, you don't know one of those cats is there until he kills you. I played enough games of stalk and pounce with Kaelas to identify the feel of that specific shield. If I'd known she'd learned from an Arcerian, I might have found her sooner—or not, since it wouldn't feel quite the same with a Sceltie shaping that bit of Craft.

You're worried about this?

An Arcerian uses the sight shield to hunt undetected, but they're in their own Territory and have little contact with humans. Scelties live in the same villages as humans and are aware of a lot more than we want to believe. Luci-var paused. *Let's just say I'm relieved that Morghann chose you to be her teacher and special friend, because a Sceltie who is that skillful at hiding is not a witch I would want learning to do wrong things.*

Point taken. More than one point when added to Ter-sa's warning to accept help offered with love. Uncondi-tional love. Love without fear. Love that would do anything that was needed—including doing what everyone else had thought impossible. Ladvarian had felt that kind of love for Witch. Was Morghann offering the same kind of love to him?

They stopped at one of the family's estates to give Morghann a little more food and water. While Lucivar kept an eye on the dog, Daemon talked to the estate's man-ager and confirmed what he'd suspected: news that the De-mon Prince once more walked the living Realms had already spread beyond Askavi.

Lucivar didn't say anything for a while after they re-sumed their journey. Finally, he said, *They know?*

They know, Daemon replied, still keeping their con-versation private. *Although the surprise seems to be that you're just now laying claim to the whole of Askavi. The estate manager and housekeeper thought you'd done it years ago but hadn't made a fuss about it.*

Lucivar snorted a laugh. Then his amusement faded. *Things will change because of the choice I made, and not just for me.*

Not everything will change, Prick, Daemon replied softly. *And we won't make the mistakes our father made or Andulvar made.*

You sure about that?

He nodded. *They served the idea of Witch, held a line they believed the living myth would want them to hold. But I imagine, in the loneliest hours of the night, they must have wondered if they were holding on to hollow beliefs.*

Hollow or not, they passed those beliefs on to us, taught us both where to draw the line.

And having lived under the corruption spawned by Dorothea, Hekatah, and Prythian, we'll recognize that foulness before it sinks its roots too deep in Kaeleer. The biggest difference between us and our father and uncle is that we have someone holding the leash. She may not be flesh anymore, but Witch is still present, and our lives are still shaped by her will.

The Queen's weapons.

Always.

A few minutes passed in companionable silence before Lucivar said, *If Perzha's court complains about that damn Sceltie trying to rearrange the village to suit himself, you and I are going to have words.*

Well, if the Rihland courts start whining about being under your hand, offer them a choice: you or a Sceltie Warlord Prince. There are a couple at the school in Scelt who are looking for a challenge. After a week or so of being nipped and herded by one of them, the Rihlanders will be pathetically grateful to have you take over.

"May the Darkness be merciful," Lucivar muttered. Then he laughed, long and loud.

After escorting Dillon to Nurian's eyrie, Rothvar remained in the kitchen while Jillian led Dillon to the sitting room. Khary abandoned the bone he'd been gnawing, faced the other Opal-Jeweled Warlord, and growled.

He's a guest, Khary, she said on a psychic thread. *No biting.*

No touching, Khary replied.

She couldn't argue with that, but she thought it was better for everyone if she didn't agree with the Sceltie, since Khary had a strict interpretation of "touching."

"Would you like to sit down?" Jillian said, waving a hand at the furniture.

"No. Thank you." Dillon tucked his hands in his pockets. "I'm sorry I used that spell on you. I'm not sorry I used it on the other girls. They would have done the same to me without a second thought. But I'm sorry I used it on you."

"Why?"

"Because I liked you. I wanted you to be impressed so that you would love me, at least for a little while, so I used that stupid spell instead of courting you properly."

"Prince Yaslana wouldn't have allowed a courtship," Jillian said.

"Maybe not, but he might have allowed us to be friends." Dillon sighed. "I wanted to stay in a place without feeling hunted. I wanted to repair my honor. I think I said things that hurt you, things that might have made you feel small so that I could feel important. I wasn't like that before I met Blyte. You have no reason to believe me, but I wasn't like that."

She did believe him. Dillon looked . . . younger, less sophisticated. Maybe she was seeing him without any posturing for the first time. She wasn't sure she would have seen him as a romantic figure, but she thought she could have been friends with this boy.

Jillian looked at the fading bruise on Dillon's face. "I'm sorry I hit you." She wasn't in the least bit sorry, but it seemed like the polite thing to say.

He smiled. "Don't be. I deserved it." He shifted his weight from one foot to the other. "That's all I came to say." He turned toward the door, then hesitated. "Jillian? One more thing."

"What?" she asked when he didn't say anything.

"Just that Prince Yaslana is more of a father to you than my own father ever was to me. I think, in a way, I was a little bit jealous."

Jillian remained in the sitting room for a while after Dillon left. Khary returned to the rug by her chair and gave his attention to the bone.

Mixed feelings and a bruised heart. Maybe that was what a first love was in the end. Maybe her memory of Dillon and that first love would fade over the years, but that other love—that fierce father's love—would stay with her forever.

Karla walked into the Queen's sitting room and waited.

"There's no point in you pretending you don't know I'm here. There's no point in me pretending that I don't know some part of you still exists here at the Keep. And there's no point in either of us pretending that you can maintain the solitude that has kept loneliness at bay when it's constantly being shattered by what the boyos need from you. Especially Sadi."

So what is the point?

Words rising from deep in the abyss. Rising.

"The point is you asked me to stay if I could. I did, and here I am, helping Lucivar now that everyone in Askavi knows that he's scary."

He was always scary.

Rising. "Yes, but now they all know it, and it's going to scare a few Queens pissless to realize his administrative second-in-command is a demon-dead Black Widow Queen who wears Gray Jewels."

Which you'll find entertaining.

That was beside the point. "I should receive compensation for this."

Silence. Then a whisper of midnight in the voice rising out of the abyss. *Such as?*

"Having someone sensible to talk to. Meaning someone who doesn't have a wiggle-waggle."

A different kind of silence. *Please tell me you didn't use that term around Lucivar.*

"Of course not," Karla replied primly. "I said it to Sadi."

Jaenelle's silvery, velvet-coated laugh filled the sitting

room. And then she was there. Witch. Myth and dreams and the extraordinary friendship that had changed the lives of a generation of Queens.

Witch gave Karla a wickedly gleeful smile and said, "Kiss kiss."

FORTY-FOUR

Surreal felt Black power roll softly through the Hall and knew Daemon had returned.

She'd had a few days without his presence clouding her mind and swamping her with lust for his body. She'd had a few days to think about everything that had happened between them.

She still loved him. She still wanted to be married to him, still wanted him to be her husband in every way. She figured the best way to show him that *she* was willing to do that was to treat him as if the past few months hadn't happened.

She paced and waited and waited and paced, listening for any movement in his bedroom. Then she walked over to the section of the Hall that held the suite Saetan had occupied until he withdrew from the living Realms to make room for Daemon to take his place as the Warlord Prince of Dhemlan. But the only person she found in the suite was Helene. The housekeeper gave the sitting room one more critical look before nodding to Surreal.

"Is he staying here?" Surreal asked. No point pretending with the senior staff, since they'd probably know where Daemon was sleeping on any given night before she did.

"I don't know," Helene replied. "He handed off his trunk to Jazen so that the clothes could be sorted and cleaned, but I don't think he's gotten farther than his study since he returned." She waited a moment before adding, "The bedroom adjoining yours is also clean and ready for his return. Is there anything special you would like me to add to that room?"

Was that Helene's way of offering assistance in coaxing the Warlord Prince of Dhemlan to stay close to his wife?

"If I think of anything, I'll let you know," Surreal said. "Thank you, Helene."

"It's my pleasure, Lady Surreal."

Wanting to send the right message to the rest of the staff, Surreal moved briskly through the corridors of the Hall, heading for the rooms where visitors were met, which included Daemon's study.

"Holt?" she called when she spotted Sadi's secretary walking toward the door that led to the senior staff's work area and his office.

Holt reversed direction, passing the open study door as he approached her. He offered Surreal an amused smile and tipped his head toward the door. "Important affairs to discuss."

"Oh? Whose?" She nodded when Holt's smile widened. "Of course. I should have known she'd pounce on him the moment he walked through the door."

"Actually, I got to pounce first and point out the stacks of paperwork that Lord Marcus and I agreed most urgently required the Prince's attention. The young Lady had to run down from the playroom in order to see him."

"Since you've both had a chance at him, now it's my turn."

Holt bowed and, once again, headed for his office.

Surreal approached the study door. Since no one else was in the front hall at that moment, she wrapped herself in a sight shield. It wouldn't prevent Daemon from knowing she was there, but she wanted a moment to see him with Jaenelle Saetien without the girl spotting her.

"I did them the way you asked," Jaenelle Saetien said.

Surreal stepped into the doorway far enough to see

them—Daemon sitting in his chair behind the desk, one arm around the girl, who leaned against him.

"You did an excellent job preparing these requests. You've included all the information I need to make an informed decision, which is the kind of decision a father wants to make." Releasing his daughter, Daemon reached for a pen.

"You should sign them properly, like you do the papers for Holt," Jaenelle Saetien said.

"Quite right." He signed three papers on his desk. "Should I add my personal seal as well?"

Jaenelle Saetien grinned. "Yes!"

Surreal watched man and girl as they worked together to melt a stick of red wax and apply the seal Sadi used for his personal correspondence. She was about to drop the sight shield and step into the study when Jaenelle Saetien said, "Papa? Are you angry with Mama and me?"

Daemon set aside the seal and the remainder of the wax stick and put his arms around his daughter. "No, I'm not angry with either of you."

"You didn't come home with us."

"Your uncle Lucivar needed my help." Daemon gently brushed the hair away from Jaenelle Saetien's face. "And there was another reason I didn't come home with you. I thought it was a small thing, but it wasn't. It isn't." He hesitated. "I haven't been well, witch-child."

"You're sick?"

Surreal felt her daughter's alarm like a knife between the ribs.

"Not sick the way you mean, but I haven't been well. It's going to take a while before I'm well again. That means a couple of times a month I'll have to spend some time at the Keep. That's where a special kind of healing can be done."

"Can I come with you?"

Daemon shook his head. "This kind of healing needs to be private."

"Are you better?"

"I am."

"Does Mama know?"

Surreal dropped the sight shield and stepped into the study. "I know enough, but your father and I have some things to discuss."

Daemon met her eyes, then turned his attention back to the child. "Witch-child, could you and Morghann take a short walk?"

"Yes, Papa." Jaenelle Saetien looked around. "Where is she?"

"Morghann," Daemon said quietly. "Kindly oblige me."

The Sceltic walked around the desk, gave Jaenelle Saetien a small tail wag, and followed the girl out of the room.

Surreal closed the door and approached the desk, noting that Daemon remained seated—and watchful.

"You are better," she said. "I can feel the difference— just like I felt the difference when you began the decline into . . . this. I wish I'd said something."

"I understand why you didn't."

"Do you?" *What do you think you understand?* "We have things to discuss, but your attention is required elsewhere for the next few hours."

Daemon looked at the stacks of papers on his desk and smiled wryly. "I noticed."

She felt like she was walking across a frozen lake, with the ice cracking beneath her feet with every step and the shore a long ways away. One wrong move and she would break through and go under—and never find her way back to safe ground.

"Jaenelle Saetien has been joining me for dinner these past few days, but if you prefer not to listen to chatter, I could have her eat in her room tonight."

"I'd like her to join us. Besides, after listening to the yappy horde, listening to one child should be easy enough."

"Don't count on it. She's been waiting to tell you *everything* she did during her stay with her cousins."

His laugh sounded genuine, so she asked the question she really wanted to ask. "Will you stay with me tonight?"

A heartbeat of hesitation before he said, "It will be my pleasure."

"Then I'll let you deal with some of this, and we'll see you at dinner."

Leaving the study, Surreal met up with Jaenelle Saetien and Morghann as the two returned from their walk. Morghann headed straight for the study door. When it didn't open, she lay down in front of it and sighed.

"Come on." Surreal put an arm around her daughter's shoulders. "We'll see your papa at dinner."

As they went up to the family room, Surreal felt Sadi's words gather weight and settle around her heart. *It will be my pleasure.* A Consort said that to a Queen. Sometimes he meant it. Other times it was an acknowledgment of duty.

Genuine pleasure or simply duty? She wasn't sure which way Sadi had meant the words.

Daemon stood under the shower, letting the hot water pound some of the tension out of his neck and shoulders. He'd been glad to have Jaenelle Saetien as a chatty buffer at dinner. While he'd been dealing with avalanches of emotion—his own and others'—his girl had had a good time with her cousins. Unfortunately, in the middle of describing one of her adventures, she lobbed a question at him he would have preferred to ignore.

"Papa, why did you ask Tarl to pile up all those rocks at the end of the garden?"

"Those are for your mother."

"Why does Mama need rocks?"

For reasons he wasn't about to explain to a child.

After drying off and styling his hair, he slipped into a pair of black silk pants and the matching robe. He wasn't sure what Surreal expected from him—or wanted from him tonight. He wasn't sure what he wanted to offer—and he couldn't say with any honesty that he was looking forward to spending the night in his wife's bed.

When he walked out of the bathroom, he found Jazen waiting for him. His valet looked pointedly at the room's other occupant.

He'd asked Beale to bring Morghann's cushioned bed up to his room. With Tagg now living with Mikal and Tersa, and Khary still in Ebon Rih, he felt concerned that Morghann would feel abandoned, especially after making the choice to hide and starve when she couldn't find him.

It wasn't the bed or the Sceltie herself that was the reason for Jazen's annoyance. It was . . .

That's my shirt? he asked, seeing a white cuff between the Sceltie's front paws. The rest of the material was under her, making him think of a broody hen sitting on a silk egg—a thought he kept to himself, since he didn't think dog or valet would appreciate the comparison.

Yes, that's the shirt you removed a few minutes ago—the one I was going to take down to the laundry room, Jazen replied. *She growled at me when I tried to take it back.*

Daemon looked at Morghann, who gave him a tail tip wag.

Sighing, he looked at Jazen. *Let her have the shirt.*

You will explain that she can only have one shirt at a time. She can't hoard them.

He stared at Jazen, but his valet didn't back down, leaving him in the middle of a farce where Sceltie and valet would play a continual game of hoard and retrieve with his clothes.

I'll talk to her, he said, fighting the urge to laugh.

Very well.

There's no need to get huffy.

I'll remind you of that when you complain about not having any clean shirts in the closet.

Hell's fire, man, just order more shirts and go away tonight.

Judging by the look on Jazen's face before the man made a quick exit, Daemon realized he'd been herded into agreeing to exactly what his valet wanted.

"Damned impertinent," he muttered. But there was something to be said for impertinence. A man couldn't be completely terrifying if his valet was willing to argue with him about shirts.

Going over to the cushioned bed, he crouched in front of Morghann. It would crush her if he said she had done a wrong thing. Instead, he tugged the other sleeve out from under her and laid it over her like an arm casually draped around her.

"I'm going to be in the other room with Lady Surreal tonight," he said quietly. "You need to stay in this room. Do you understand?"

I will wait here for you.

"Yes. You sleep here, and I will see you in the morning."

He gave her one caress before he rose, walked over to the door that separated the bedrooms, and knocked.

Their lovemaking often began in what Surreal thought of as the social area of her room—the mix of tables, chairs, and love seat where she could read in solitude or talk privately with a close friend or her daughter. Or cuddle with her husband while they talked about their respective days or shared observations made during that evening's dinner or social gathering.

She had a feeling that Sadi wouldn't join her on the love seat tonight and might deliberately misinterpret her invitation to discuss things as strictly verbal communication. So she waited for him in bed, propped up with pillows, a book open in her lap.

"Come in," she said in response to a knock on the adjoining room's door. Her smile froze when he saw her and hesitated, which meant his saying, "It will be my pleasure," when they had talked earlier had been an acknowledgment of his duty as a husband.

Hell's fire! She'd been a whore for decades. She'd been the *most expensive whore* for decades. Tonight she would need all of that skill to show him he was still wanted, still loved.

She flipped the covers back on his side of the bed. She closed her book but didn't put it on the bedside table, a subtle way of telling him she didn't expect him to perform immediately.

He stretched out beside her, propped up on one elbow. Not touching her.

"It's confirmed now?" she asked. "Lucivar has taken over rule of all of Askavi?"

"He signed the document that gives him the whole Territory," Daemon replied. "Draca and I witnessed it, so it's official."

"How does Marian feel about that?"

"She seemed to take it in stride after being assured that she wouldn't have to be the buffer between Lucivar and all the Queens in Askavi beyond the ones whose territories are in Ebon Rih."

"Someone has to arrange for audiences and prioritize meetings."

Daemon looked amused. "It's been sorted out. Marian will help Lucivar in his capacity as the Warlord Prince of Ebon Rih, same as she's done since she married him. Rothvar will be his second-in-command for the whole Territory when it comes to defending the Territory or any of its people from an outside invader or from each other. The Blood in Askavi will have a choice of living by the Old Ways or leaving. If they want to follow Terreillean ways, they can go back to Terreille—or face the Demon Prince on a killing field."

"Mother Night."

"There have been some savage fights in some of the Provinces, and several courts have broken. I imagine there will be quite a few people who want to talk to him in the next few days."

"Who's going to represent him when he's not available to talk to the Queens and meet with the First Circles of newly formed courts?"

"Karla."

Surreal blinked. "Karla?"

"Yeah." Daemon laughed. "Lady Karla, the former Queen of Glacia, in all her Gray-Jeweled terrifying glory. She is Lucivar's second-in-command when it comes to the Warlord Prince of Askavi's administrative duties. With Draca's permission, she set up an office in the Keep and will command from there."

"Will she have helpers?"

"I expect so."

"Will any of them be among the living?"

"I didn't ask. I played least in sight and let Lucivar deal with her."

"Well, he did choose her."

"Not exactly."

She laughed and set her book aside. Before she could turn to him, he placed a hand over hers, and his mood sobered.

"The rocks at the back of the garden," he said.

"If you want a rock garden, Sadi, you and Tarl can build it." The sass in her voice should have made him smile. It didn't.

"They aren't there to grow anything. They're there . . ." He sighed. "It's dangerous to thin the shields around that chamber beneath the Hall. I must insist that you stop doing that."

"What's in the chamber?"

"Nothing that concerns you—and not something we'll discuss."

She studied his face, tried to read the warning. "Something Saetan left in your care?"

"Yes."

She nodded her acceptance, since there was nothing else she could do.

"The rock pile is a place where you can drain your Gray Jewel whenever you need to," Daemon said. "I've laced Black shields around them and filled pockets between the rocks with Black power. You can strike the shields without worrying about damage or danger."

Meaning she wouldn't have to engage with him directly for help draining the Gray or the Green. Since she'd avoided asking for his help for months, why did his creating this solution make her sad?

"Well," he said.

She touched his face, kissed his mouth. "Stay. I need you, Daemon. Stay."

She could barely feel the sexual heat that had been such a torment and wondered what he had done to quiet it so much that it was barely a sensual warmth tonight.

He didn't reject her kisses or withdraw from her touch, but it took a while before he began to respond with some excitement, before he began kissing her back with some enthusiasm. Then she pulled the robe off his shoulders and ran her hand down his right arm—and found the scars.

She jerked back and stared at the white, thin ridges. "Hell's fire, Sadi. What happened?"

He said nothing.

"Why didn't Nurian heal these wounds so they wouldn't leave scars?"

"They were meant to scar," he said quietly. "Just as the one on my left wrist was meant to scar."

"Why?"

"A reminder."

Of what? she almost asked him. Then she remembered what he'd told Jaenelle Saetien about a private kind of healing at the Keep and knew who had given him those scars.

He kissed her, a lover intent on pleasuring his woman—or at least pleasuring the one he could touch. He took his time and loved her in all the ways she liked best. And when he finally sheathed his cock inside her, she knew he enjoyed it, knew he wanted her.

And yet . . .

Surreal invited Daemon to her bed each night, and they made love until they were both spent. The sexual heat became more noticeable with each passing day, and she knew Daemon watched her, always assessing whether the pleasure he gave her, and his presence, was still enjoyable or had slipped into torment. On the fourth night, instead of joining her in her bed, he kissed her good night and retreated to the suite that now served as his sanctuary.

He never stayed with her more than three nights in a row. Sometimes he retreated to the suite that had been his father's. Sometimes he went to the Keep after Jaenelle Saetien fell asleep, and stayed for a day or two. When he returned, the sexual heat was drained to the point that it was just enough to add a fillip of arousal to everyday desire.

The edgy play that had been the merest whisper of the Sadist and had been an exciting part of being in bed with him was missing altogether, even when the heat became uncomfortably intense, and she regretted the loss.

She couldn't breach the barrier between them—and admitted to herself that maybe she didn't want to. She felt comfortable being around him again, felt they had reestablished the partnership they'd had for decades. This arrangement gave her breathing room so that she didn't have to look at the full truth about the man she had married.

The truth had terrified her, but, Hell's fire, it had been exciting too. The problem was, if she managed to break that barrier, could she survive the man now contained behind it?

Her feelings were conflicted. Daemon's feelings were not. In bed and out, he maintained that careful distance between them in order to keep her safe, and he did it out of courtesy, out of respect, out of kindness.

Out of love.

FORTY-FIVE

❖

They stood in front of the gate of a sprawling patch-work house.

Jillian had never seen the ocean, was already fascinated by the fishing boats that were heading out. Would any of those fish find their way to Riada? Would she have the opportunity to learn how to catch one?

Her first apprenticeship in a real court. What would her duties be? What . . . ?

Lucivar sighed.

She looked up at him. "You're going to have to do this three more times."

"Don't remind me."

He sounded unhappy. He sounded like a father who wanted to keep his girl close to his own wings but knew he had to let her soar on her own. Had the other steps he'd let her take been as hard for him, or was this a bigger leap?

Nurian and Marian had both given her spending money as a farewell gift, after learning that she'd given all her savings to Dillon. The first thing she would look for once she got settled in was some nice stationery that might reflect the sea or this village so that Lucivar would know she had bought it in order to write to him.

She saw the homely woman walking toward them, talk-ing to two men who were escorting her away from the

Queen's home. She wore skirts and shawls and so many jangly bracelets, she could be heard down the street.

"It's kind of the Queen to grant an audience to the village rag lady," she said, trying to sound grown-up.

Lucivar choked on a laugh. "That's not a rag lady, witchling. That's Perzha, the Queen of Little Weeble."

Her jaw dropped as the woman smiled at them and waved.

"Another thing," Lucivar said. "Perzha has an allergy to sunlight and rests during the day. Some members of my family had a similar allergy."

Jillian blinked. "You mean she—"

"Has an allergy to sunlight and has to drink a special tonic." His gold eyes held two parts warning and one part amusement.

"Right. Allergy to sunlight. Special tonic."

"Come in, come in." Perzha waved her hand. "Don't just stand at the gate."

The other member of their little party didn't require a further invitation. He trotted over to the gate and wagged his tail.

I am Khary. I am a Sceltie. I am Jillian's special friend.

"Oh, my." Perzha patted her chest. "How delightful. Welcome, Lord Khary."

"Should have warned her," Lucivar muttered.

"It's been a long time since one of your people came to our village, but I remember when Lord Ladvarian used to accompany the Queen when she came for a visit. You know he was the Lady's special friend."

Khary seemed stunned into momentary silence.

"Last thing, witchling," Lucivar said quietly. "Perzha wears a Red Jewel and comes from one of the oldest aristo Rihlander families in Askavi. And she and the Queen of Ebon Askavi were good friends."

The rag lady Queen wore a Red Jewel? Was aristo? Had been a friend of Witch?

Baffled and dazzled, Jillian followed the adults to a table on a terrace overlooking a garden.

"Do you know anything about plants?" Perzha asked. "I so enjoy spending a little time in my garden, but I'm afraid I never get to all the weeding." She held out a hand and smiled. "I'm Perzha, in case Prince Yaslana forgot to tell you. And you must be Jillian. Such a pretty girl. Do you like fish? We have a lot of fish here."

Do I like fish? Khary asked Jillian. *Do fish like Scelties?*

"I've heard that you should stick a fork in the pancakes and not eat any that sprout tentacles and run away," Lucivar said dryly.

Perzha laughed. "Did Prince Sadi tell you the rest?"

"There's more?"

Instead of replying, Perzha looked at Jillian. "Little Weeble is a small village and everyone looks out for one another, but I'd still like you to have an escort at least for the first few days." She looked at Khary. "An additional escort."

"Yes, Lady."

"Did anyone mention that I have an allergy to sunlight?"

Jillian didn't dare look at Lucivar. "Yes, Lady."

"And you know what that means?"

"I think so, Lady."

"Good." Perzha studied Lucivar. "Are you staying for breakfast?"

"No."

She shook her head. "I wouldn't have thought you and your brother would be so squeamish."

"We're not squeamish. We just don't like having our food run away after it's on the plate."

"Well, Prince Sadi certainly wasn't going to eat the little creature, so what difference did it make as long as it got out of the way?" Perzha patted her chest. "Besides, Carleton brought him a fresh plate of food after the incident."

None of the Rihlanders Jillian knew would have spoken to Yaslana or Sadi that way.

You sure about this, witchling? Lucivar asked on a psychic thread.

Oh, yes.

He grunted. "If either of you has a problem, let me know. Otherwise . . ."

"Go," Perzha said. It was gently said, but there was no doubt that it was a dismissal. "They'll both be fine."

Lucivar slanted a glance at Khary, then at Perzha. "Will you?"

Perzha smiled at him—and Lucivar Yaslana walked away.

"This is one of the hardest things he's ever done," Perzha said. "You know that, don't you?"

Jillian blinked away sentimental tears. "I know."

"Good. Then let's get you both settled in your room so that you can begin."

Far enough away from home, but not too far. She and Khary would learn new things and have adventures—and she would remember every day that Lucivar had given her the chance to have those things, just as he'd been giving her chances to learn and grow since the day he brought her and Nurian to Ebon Rih.

"Yes," Jillian said, smiling. "We're ready to begin." She looked at her special friend. *Are you ready?*

Yes, Khary replied. *There are many interesting smells here, and many humans we can help.*

Swallowing a laugh, Jillian followed Perzha into the house.

ACKNOWLEDGMENTS

My thanks to Blair Boone for continuing to be my first reader and for providing encouragement and feedback in the story's roughest stage; to Debra Dixon for being second reader; to Doranna Durgin for maintaining the website; to Adrienne Roehrich for running the official fan page on Facebook; to Jennifer Crow for being a sounding board during our dinner-and-book-binge evenings; to Anne Sowards and Jennifer Jackson for the feedback that helps me write a better story; to Alexis Nixon and all the other publicity and marketing folks at PRH who help get the book into readers' hands; and to Pat Feidner for always being supportive and encouraging.

NEW YORK TIMES BESTSELLING AUTHOR

ANNE BISHOP

"The Queen of Fantasy...Bishop's literary skills
continue to astound and enchant."

—Heroes and Heartbreakers